Once Upon a Time II

More Timeless Tales for Young Hearts

Curated by Christopher Ball

Chanthology

No part of this publication may be copied, recorded, transmitted or reproduced in any way without the publisher's express written permission.

Published by: Chanthology Limited

www.chanthology.com

Paperback Edition: ISBN 978-1-915449-75-7
Kindle Edition: ISBN 978-1-915449-76-4
Hardback Edition: ISBN 978-1-915449-77-1

Contents

Introduction

Embark on a new journey with "Once Upon A Time 2". Building on the cherished tradition that "Once Upon A Time" began, we present the second volume in the series, a collection that opens new doors to wonder, adventure, and timeless wisdom. This book, curated from my personal journey of nightly storytelling, is a testament to the moments of connection and joy that stories can bring to our lives. It serves as a reminder of the powerful stories to bond us, inspire growth, and ignite imagination in both children and adults alike.

In this volume, we venture further into the realm of magic and discovery with tales that have captured the hearts and stimulated the minds across generations. From the enduring charm of "The Velveteen Rabbit" by Margery Williams Bianco to the timeless lessons of "The Emperor's New Clothes" by Hans Christian Andersen, each story has been selected for its unique ability to enchant and educate. We explore the haunting beauty of "Briar Rose" by The Brothers Grimm, the tiny but mighty spirit of "Thumbelina," the cunning adventures of "Puss in Boots" by Charles Perrault, the whimsical wisdom of "The Magic Fishbone" by Charles Dickens, the sunny tales of "Under The Sun" by Juliana Horatia Ewing, the magical voyage of "The Enchanted Boat" by Abbie Phillips Walker and many more. These stories, each with their own lesson of courage, resilience, and the magic of believing, are more than just entertainment. They are bridges to understanding the world around us, illustrating that challenges are opportunities for growth, and that true strength is born of kindness and imagination. They underscore the virtues that help us navigate life's journey with grace and courage.

"Once Upon A Time 2" is more than a sequel; it's an expansion of a beloved universe where families are invited to come together and explore new worlds. It's a collection that promises to deepen the bonds of family storytelling, encouraging young readers to dream big, think broader, and laugh louder.

As you turn these pages with your children, let the adventures within inspire you to create your own stories of joy, discovery, and connection. May this book be a lantern lighting the way for your family's journey through the vast landscape of imagination, laying down memories that will last a lifetime. Here's to the stories that move us, the adventures that await, and the endless possibilities that storytelling brings into our lives.

CHRIS BALL

The Animal Children: the Friends of the Forest and the Plain

by Edith Brown Kirkwood

Sometimes I am so sorry that my papa is a king.

It's really most annoying and hurts like everything

To have the little girls and boys all want to run away,

For if I am a Lion prince, I'm a baby, anyway!

Some jungle boys, by mischief, made quite bold,

Once took the baby Tiger, so we're told,

And in broad stripes, they smeared his coat so fine,

And 'round his neck they hung a "Fresh Paint" sign.

This monkey thought the Leopard's spots

Were pasted on for polka-dots.

He asked her how much it would cost

New ones to buy if those were lost.

In her red and white gown, Miss Weasel's so pert.

We are very afraid she's a gay little flirt;

She is fearful of no one—the beast, reptile or man.

Just winks and cries gaily: "Catch me, if you can."

This dapper young chappy is Dude Ocelot,

With coat trimmed in many a dash and a spot;

He's graceful and elegant, sly, too, as well,

Just what he'll do next; no one ever can tell.

The cheetah is a great big cat,

But very quickly, for all that,

She's cunning, but she's gentle, too,

And if you're good, she's good to you.

The little Bobcat and Canadian Lynx

Just must be related (so everyone thinks).

Except for their ears, they're alike as two pins

And look every whit as if they were twins.

A dainty, fastidious man is Lord Otter,

Who can live just as well on land as in water,

He'll eat but the flakiest part of a fish,

And this he considers his favourite dish.

"It really is a bother to be sought by everyone",

The vain young Ermine boasted. "Why, it keeps me on
the run

To get away from kings and queens and peers and
ladies great—

It truly gets me all fussed up and in a dreadful state."

Young ferret, the detective, said: "I'll show you where

To track the bold rabbit right into his lair."

Then he never saw bunny right under his eyes,

But went swaggering off looking wondrously wise.

"Now, Johnnie, my child," said wise Mamma Sable,

"When you see a trap run as fast as you're able,

Or else, ere you know it, your skin will be gone

As a beautiful fur for some lady to don."

Mother opossum says she'd like to ask

Just why other mothers should find it a task

To care for one baby. Here she has four,

And there's plenty of room on her tail for some more!

Mr and Mrs Mongoose are popular as can be,

The reason being very plain, as you will all agree,

They are cunning and affectionate and clean and very
nice.

They kill all snakes and insects and naughty rats and
mice.

It must be very easy for the busy Beaver mother

To feed the Beaver sister and her little Beaver brother,

For when they beg: "We're hungry, give us something to
eat, please!"

She sends them off to nibble at the bark of the big trees.

The puma is a bandit who'll not meet you face to face

But waits to spring upon you from some well-hidden
place.

He'll strike you when your back is turned, but away
he's sure to fly

If you should turn to look him right squarely in the eye.

Lemur stays in bed all day

And waits until the night to play;

That's why his soft feet make no sound

And why his eyes are big and round.

The bowery boy of the woods is young Mink.

His coat is so lovely one never would think

That'd he do naughty things, but we've often been told

He is tricky and wicked and saucy and bold.

"I'm not so very big around and not great as to length,

But one thing Peccaries have learned—in numbers,
there is strength.

Now, if you do not bother me, I will not bother you,

But all my friends and family will help me if you do."

who is this boy in clothes so neat?

Young Spring-bok, Africa's athlete.

He lives up in the mountains tall,

And as a jumper, beats them all.

The Long-Eared Bat and the Flying Fox and the Flying
Squirrel, too,

Decided to give an aero-meet just to show what they
could do.

So they formed a club and went around and invited
everyone.

Then up, they flew and did their stunts and had a lot of
fun.

She is dainty as snowdrops that fall from the skies.

Is this dear little Kitten with bright, shiny eyes

And velvety ears and pretty pink nose

And a lovely white suit of soft, furry clothes?

Baby raccoon takes all his food and goes straight to the
pool.

He eats not one small bite of it until it's wet and cool.

Now, although you may think this strange and stop to
wonder why,

He, no doubt, thinks it just as queer for you to like
yours dry.

The greatest of travellers that one can meet

Is the little Deer-mouse with the pretty white feet;

North, south, east or west, she will go at her will,

And never, no never, is known to keep still.

The baby zebra ne'er should roam

So very far away from home,

Lest someone, thinking her striped gown

Was candy-stick, might eat her down.

"I'm stopping for a moment just to say 'How-do-you-
do?'

I've just been decorated with this ribbon of deep blue

Because of all the gracefulness with which I trot and
prance—

No wonder that you give Sir Horse your most admiring
glance!"

This tale is not so very new,

And, no doubt, has been told to you,

But Donkey went to school to play,

And now he sits dressed up this way.

Here is the only baby who never makes a noise

(Which must be very puzzling to little girls and boys).

Yet the Giraffe is happy 'though he cannot shout or
sing,

For with that great long neck of his, he can reach
anything.

The tapir feeds on leaves and fruit

He's very, very hard to suit,

For boys who don't like bread and meat

Have to find other things to eat.

He has climbed to the top of a rocky throne

To look down on a land once so proudly his own,

His people are scattered, he has no place to go,

He is weary and sad, poor King Buffalo.

"Lemonade, lemonade," the bold monkey cried,

"It's only five cents, and it's cooling beside."

Miss Camel just sniffed and tossed high her head—

"I drink only every nine days, sir," she said.

Milk or meat or leather for shoes,—

Almost anything that we choose,—

We'll find the good Cow gives with joy

To every nice little girl and boy.

I wonder where the names come from (I'm sure that
you do, too).

For instance, there's the animal that has been called the
Gnu.

His race is just as strange, too, for no one seems to
know

Just what he is—an antelope, horse, bull or buffalo.

Big moose came boldly from behind the tall trees,

And said in loud voice: "Who called, if you please?

I'm ready to meet anyone who says 'Fight,'

But we'll come in the open and do the thing right."

I am not sure I'd care to meet

This Big Horn Goat upon the street.

Not when his eyes and smile and air

Just seem to shout: "Come, if you dare!'

Brave soldier ibex stalks before the mountain fortress
high

And watches eagerly to note a stranger passing by.

"Who's there?" he calls, and to his friends, he whistles
the alarm,

And off they go to mountain tops where they are safe
from harm.

The chamois live in the mountains high.

He's ever and ever and ever so spry;

He leaps, and he plays with never a fall—

I'm sure that you never could do that at all.

Billy Goat and Nanny Goat went out one day to tea.

They promised Mother Goat they'd be good as they
could be,

But on the way, they passed some goats who cried: "Oh,
see the dude!"

And then they had to go back home for Billy got really
rude.

Her coat is soft as velvet, of a lovely yellow-brown,

With a bit of fawn for trimming and a lining white as
down.

Her eyes are large and kind, and she is gentle, too, as
well.

You would love a little playmate as sweet as Miss
Gazelle.

A sturdy young American is Rocky Mountain Goat

With big, strong horns upon his head and a shaggy,
furry coat;

He loves to scramble over rocks or leap a mountain
brook,

And should you chase him, he will fly into his hidden
nook.

"We reindeer come straight from your own Santa Claus,

In our gallop of joy, we never will pause;

We eat from the mountain-tops, drink from the dells,

And use for our skipping-ropes merry sleigh-bells."

A large and handsome personage is the Noblest Yak.

His mantle is a fringe of hair that drapes his sides and
back;

He's very, very grand, indeed, when he stands up, you
see—

In fact, he's just as noble as a noble ought to be.

When young Mrs Kangaroo goes for a hop,

To call or to market or, perhaps, out to shop,

She has no nice carriage where the baby can ride,

So he creeps in a pocket that hangs at her side.

He does not care when the sleet comes down or the
chilly wind blows strong,

For he wears a hat that is made of horn and a fur coat,

warm and long.

He never gets frostbitten toes 'though in snow and ice
he plays;

Now, being a Muskox can't be bad on the long, cold
winter days!

"The very best I have, sir, fine and a whole yard wide.

It wears and has no bother of a right and wrong side;

I'm sure she'd like a dress of it—it will not spot or pull."

Then Miss Alpaca added: "I know—it's my own wool."

This dear little Sheep has lost Bo-Peep,

She wandered away as he lay asleep,

He has found her bonnet and shepherd's crook,

But for little Bo-Peep, in vain does he look.

Young Miss Rhinoceros gave a beach party;

She greeted her friends with a welcome most hearty.

They laughed and they joked and they swam in the sea,

And the party was gay, as a party should be.

She comes from Spain, and this proud, proud Dame,

Mistress Merino, is her name.

Her wool weaves into dress goods rare.

Her skin makes gloves the ladies wear.

Merry guinea pigs one day
Went out in the fields to play.
Daisy smiled and wished that they
Would never, never go away.

Here is a Sister Piggy and a Brother Piggy, too.
The story they are telling here would not apply to you,
For selfish little sisters who make their brothers cry.
Do not belong in houses but with piggies in the sty.

Now here's a little lady who seems a wee bit shy,
Or is it that a teardrop is trembling in her eye?
Well, I am sure that you or I would make an awful fuss
If we should have to have her name—"Miss
Hippopotamus."

In animal land, as everywhere, there lives a Mr Boar
Who never is contented unless he holds the floor;
His fellows all may frown at him, but he cannot refrain
From pushing into everything—he's so selfish and so
vain.

Once Upon a Time II

Mother and father and little Miss Bear

Went out for a walk and a bit of fresh air,

Not through the dark woods (the old tale to repeat).

But in their best clothes, right down the front street.

When little Miss Polar Bear goes out to skate,

She never is bothered by having to wait

Until her mother wraps her all snugly in fur,

For those are the clothes that she carries with her!

Just look about and see if you

Can find a friend who's quite as true

As this old Doggie that you see

A-smiling here at you and me.

I'm just a little Puppy and good as good can be,

And why they call me naughty, I'm sure I cannot see.

I've only carried off one shoe and torn the baby's hat

And chased the ducks and spilled the milk—there's
nothing bad in that!

The mandrill looks so very queer.

I'm glad he lives way off from here;

He's purple, blue, red, black and brown.

I'm sure he is the jungle clown.

The baby gorilla of the family, called Ape,

Is very like you in size and in shape,

But he lives in the jungle with black hair for clothes,

And he gets very naughty the older he grows.

This cute little brother and sister you see

Seated cosily high on the limb of a tree

Are the Marmoset twins, whose appealing round eyes

Look from flower-like faces in wondering surprise.

"I've climbed up here to smile at you and, oh, what do
you think?

I've scattered master's papers and upset all of his ink,

But then if little Monkeys always were so very good

They'd not be little monkeys who just can't act as they
should."

He is so very lazy that he is even loath

To walk on his own feet—this funny boy named Sloth.

He swings upon the branches from morning until night

And eats the leaves about him with the laziest delight.

He works on tunnels night and day.

This Marmot boy is from far away.

When winter comes then in he creeps,

And there until the spring, he sleeps.

The woodchuck resides in a hole in the ground,

He is surly and crosses, and he never is found

Out in the bright sunlight unless it's to see

If he can't make more winter for you and for me.

This naughty boy just eats and eats until he is a sight.

He eats until he cannot hold another tiny bite.

Of course, he's just an animal—they call him Wolverine

—

But does he make you think of boys that you have
never seen?

Old Mr Walrus climbs out of the deep

For a breath of air and an hour of sleep.

You will note that he isn't much on looks,

But his skin we make into pocket-books.

He sits on the top of a gay wooden stand,

He stands on his head, or he shakes your hand,

He dances a jig, or he trumps a chant—

This jolly old circus Elephant.

Naughty, naughty Squirrel baby, just as a mother has you dressed

In your ribbons and your laces and your go-to-meeting best,

Then run and grab an apple and get yourself all mussed!

Are you not afraid that your mother will be very, very fussed?

To market, to market, with baskets of eggs,

Jack Rabbit goes hurrying on his long legs;

He'll buy him some colors—red, green, yellow, blue,

And when Easter comes 'round you know what he'll do.

Chipmunk is a jolly lad,

Always friendly—never sad,

and Shares with friends his wheat grains yellow.

He's a genuinely good fellow.

The coney lives in Palestine

But he is very seldom seen.

You see he is so small and shy

He hides when folks are passing by.

They call this boy the Coati,

His name is strange, and so is he.

He laps to drink, and digs with his snout.

On the ground or trees, he runs about.

The cute little dogs that live on the prairie

Were having a party and making quite merry.

When Big Dog, on watch, heard a noise and called,
"Hush!"

And into their holes went the guests in a rush!

What do you suppose is in Gray Wolf's pack?

He carries so stealthily over his back.

Some chickens, a lamb and an old mother hen

He has stolen to hide away in his den.

His manners are so charming and his eyes so very
bright,

I do believe that we might call young Fox a gallant
knight;

But then when he is cunning and just a little pert,

I'm not so sure, but we should call this same young fox
a flirt.

We just want to ask if you have ever seen a

Much dirtier boy than this little Hyena.

He has played in the street making mud pies

Till nothing is clean save the whites of his eyes.

Beau coyote sings a nightly tune

To his lady fair in the big, round moon.

She smiles and throws moonbeams to him,

And he serenades till her light is dim.

Tommie and Tillie Badger went out to the field to play.

Said Tommie: "Here, I'll teach you—put down your
head this way,

Then toss your heels into the air and give a little twirl—

You can't help turning somersaults although you are a
girl."

Miss Leopard Spermophilus, with her high-sounding
name,

Says just to be called "Gopher" is really a shame,

And she's right here to tell you—if this knowledge you
should lack—

She's the only one who wears the stars and stripes upon
her back.

Doggy barked and said: "What fun

To make that Porcupine girl run;

Girls for boys to tease were meant."—

But girls with pins are different.

Sir Knight Armadillo, from tail tip to nose,

In armour that's sure to bring terror to foes,

Goes forth with his weapons to his battleground,

And looks like a pineapple walking around.

Away in Australia, the Echidna stays.

He is noted because of his strange little ways;

His claws are so sharp that in a manner quite tragic,

When frightened, he sinks into the ground as by magic.

Miss Ant Eater's mouth is so dreadfully small

It scarce seems it could be a real mouth at all,

And her long, furry tail is her blanket at night.

It covers and tucks her in, all snug and tight.

This queer little Mole has a star for a nose,

Just the shade of the pink in a dew-wet rose.

He lives down in the ground where 'tis always like
night,

So perhaps his star nose is to twinkle for light.

Here we have Mr Duckbill of no little fame;

His mouth, you will see, is what gives him his name.

He can walk, swim or burrow and (so we have heard)

His wife, Mrs Duckbill, lays eggs like a bird.

Such a dainty little person in her coat of pale, clear grey,

Is this maiden, Miss Chinchilla, and the hunter-folks all
say

She is so clean she's exquisite and never dreams of
harm

When they go to take her silken fur which helps to keep
her warm.

The circus fat lady is big Mrs Whale

With her very large head and her very long tail,

And her ears and her eyes almost covered from sight

In the folds of thick skin that wrap her up tight.

The Cruise of the Little Dipper

by Susanne K. Langer

Once upon a time, there was a very poor boy, who had no cap on his head, no shoes on his feet, and never a penny in his pocket. He was so poor that he did not even have a name. His father had gone to sea many years ago in a ship called The Big Dipper, and as he had never returned, people said surely he must be dead. So the boy had gone to live in a small, dark house beside the sea with his great-aunt, who was very old and cross and strict. She did not let him have any sugar on his cereal or butter on his bread, and every day after school, she spanked him soundly for all the mistakes he had made that day, and if he had not made any, she spanked him just the same for all those he would probably make tomorrow, or the next day, or the next. When he asked for a bit of soap to blow bright soap bubbles, she cried:

"Soap-bubbles, indeed! Soap is made only to wash one's face with. You may have all you want for that, but for bubbles, no, no! Bless my boots, what will you ask for next?"

When the other children played on the beach, building castles in the sand or picking up pretty shells, this poor boy had to gather driftwood for his great-aunt's kitchen fire.

But for all his hard luck, he was always whistling blithely at his work. He would whistle all the tunes in the hymn book, all the sailor's songs, and the nursery songs, and then some more that he made up as he ran along the beach picking up driftwood. Of course, his great-aunt had forbidden his whistling about the house, but other people liked to hear him, and since he had no name, they called him "Birdling." His great-aunt called him "You!"

One day, after he had come home from school, washed his hands, eaten his dry bread and drunk his tea without sugar or cream, he went as usual to the beach to gather wood; but this day, all the boys from school were down by the sea-side making sail-boats. Their mothers and aunts and grandmas had given them odd bits of muslin from the rag bag for sails, and their fathers and uncles and grandpas had given them little pots of paint, and the old boat-builder who lived on the beach had supplied the nails and boards and no end of good advice. They were building a splendid fleet, and when Birdling whistled along the sands, they all hailed him and shouted:

"Birdling, Birdling, come and build a boat! We have nails to spare, and surely you have some nice boards in your load of driftwood! Come, come and build a boat!"

So Birdling, forgetting all about his duties and his great-aunt, sat down in the warm yellow sand and built a boat of driftwood; and while he worked, he whistled.

The boys were all so glad to hear him and be able to play with him that they gave him all the paint and nails that they could spare, as well as a string for his rigging and a lead sinker for his anchor. Of course, he had many kinds of paint and not enough of any one colour to paint his whole boat, so her hull was black, the trimming golden-yellow, the deck bright blue and the mast green. She was a funny boat indeed, but Birdling liked her nonetheless and wanted to name her after his father's ship, the Big Dipper.

"But she isn't big!" said the other boys. "She's the smallest boat of all!"

So he called her the Little Dipper.

"What will you do for a sail?" the others asked. "We'd love to give you some muslin, but we haven't a bit to spare."

Here was a dilemma, indeed. Then Birdling remembered that he had a patch on the seat of his trousers that he did not need at all, for his great-aunt always patched them before they went into holes ("If I didn't," she would say, "why bless my boots, he'd sit them through in two minutes!"); and now he did a dreadful thing, he took off the patch and used it for a sail!

They had such a good time with the boats, loading them with cargoes of sea shells and digging harbours and chasing away the crabs who came to watch, that they did not notice how the sun had dipped down behind the sand dunes and the light-house brightened far out at sea. Suddenly they heard the curfew ring.

"Why, it's past supper-time!" they cried, and all the boys snatched up their boats and ran home. In a moment, the beach was as deserted as the sea, and Birdling sat alone on the sands, his boat between his knees, while the shadows of night crept down to the water. At the furthest end of the beach gleamed a dull square of light—that was his great-aunt's window, brightened by the oil lamp behind it:

Oh, how she was going to scold him now! For this time, he had really been naughty. He had gathered no driftwood, he was late to supper, and he had ripped the patch off the seat of his trousers!

"I don't dare take you home, Little Dipper," he said as he placed his boat in the safest harbour, as far as possible from the incoming tide. "My great-aunt would burn you in the kitchen stove. Goodby, Little Dipper!"

His great-aunt met him at the door as he came home. She was so angry that her cap had slid over one ear, her eyes were like tiny hot coals, and her very apron strings curled with wrath. She boxed Birdling's ears, smack, smack, smack!—until they were as pink as seashells.

"You, you, you," she cried, "You shall have no supper, sir, but a very good whipping! Go up on the hill behind the house and cut a switch, a strong one, a long one, for a long strong whipping, sir!"

Obediently Birdling went up to the hill where the witch-hazel bushes held out their long, strong boughs to be cut for switches. But somehow, he could not find just the switch he wanted; one was not long enough, and another was too long, or one would not be strong enough and the next too strong. He looked them all over very carefully.

The witch-hazel bushes were in blossom. There were fuzzy little yellow stars on their boughs; Birdling saw a bumblebee (who should have been in bed an hour ago) darting from bush to bush and tasting the little flowers. Then the boy remembered that he was to have no supper tonight, and as he felt dreadfully hungry, he touched one of the yellow blossoms and licked his finger that was covered with fine golden pollen just to see what it tasted like.

Behold what happened to Birdling! He did not know that the witch-hazel flowers were full of Fairy Bread! Suddenly he grew smaller and smaller, like a candle on a birthday cake, till he thought he must go out altogether—but just before it was time to go out he stopped shrinking and saw, to his great relief, that he was still a good inch taller than the bumble bee.

He sat down with surprise, hands on the ground and feet apart, and the short grasses closed above his head. All around him, the daisies, who always enjoy a joke, were tittering and looking at him through the grass. Somewhere behind a huge fuzzy mullen plant was a great noise, like the motor of an aeroplane—it was the bumble bee coming to see what was going on.

"What's happened?" he boomed in his rolling bass voice.

"That's what I'd like to know," replied the boy, picking himself up. "I never felt so small in my life, not even when I tore my Sunday shirt and my great-aunt scolded me before everybody! Why, I'm no bigger than a sea-horse!"

The daisies were still laughing, and now they could no longer contain themselves.

"He ate fairy-bread," they giggled, "and he grew as little as a balloon when the air goes out, ho, ho, ho, ho! Tee, tee, tee, tee!"

"Ate fairy-bread!" exclaimed Birdling, "do you mean to say I am a fairy now?"

The Bumblebee put his head on one side and deliberated.

"No," he said slowly, "You're not a fairy. You're only fairyish. What's your name?"

"I haven't any. But people call me Birdling."

"Well, that's not so bad. What can you do?"

"Nothing. Oh, yes—I can whistle!"

"Where will you live? You are too small to live with your great-aunt. She would surely step on you."

Birdling looked around; there was a groundsparrow's nest under the witch-hazel bushes, very near the fairy-bread flowers.

"Here," he said, "If nobody minds, I'll live here."

So that is where he lived all summer. Everybody on the hill grew fond of him, and in the mornings, when the robin sang to the sun, Birdling too would be up and whistling.

But one day, the Bumblebee came to call. His face was serious, and his voice unusually rumbly. It was a cool day, so Birdling was all wrapped in a mullen leaf.

"It's Autumn!" said Bumble. "What will you do when Winter comes?"

"I don't know. What do the birds do?"

"They go to the Fairy Islands."

"Mayn't I go?"

"You aren't a bird or a fairy," objected the visitor.

"But I'm fairyish, you know."

"Then you may, I suppose."

Birdling got up, ready to start at once.

"How do the birds get there, Bumble?"

"They fly."

"But I can't fly!"

"Then you can't go."

"But you said I could if I was fairyish!"

"No, I said you might. You may, but you can't. See?"

Birdling shook his head.

"Where are the Fairy Islands?" he asked.

"Beyond the Deep Sea."

"Could one go in a boat?"

"Possibly."

Then Birdling remembered the Little Dipper, lying forlorn on the sands beyond the reaches of the tide. Perhaps some boy had picked her up, or perhaps the waves had taken her—or perhaps she was still in her harbour!

Neatly he folded some mullen leaves, for sailors need warm clothes and blankets, and with these over his arm, he began the long journey from the hilltop to the harbour. It was ten fairy miles of rather rough walking. The Bumblebee went with him, and when they had come as far as his great-aunt's house, which was just halfway between the hill and the beach, he flew up on her roof where you could get a splendid view of the country.

"Oh, can you see the Little Dipper?" cried Birdling from below.

"I see a boat on the sand," reported Bumble, "a very queer boat—her hull is black, her trimmings golden-yellow, her decks bright-blue and the mast and sails are green."

"That's the Little Dipper!" shouted Birdling, and he began to run as fast as he could. He quite forgot that his great-aunt sat by the window, knitting wristlets and watching everything outside the house. She saw the tiny creature running along the beach, and as she was very old and could not see very clearly through her spectacles, she opened the window and leaned far out.

"It must be a mouse," she decided, and hobbling across the room, she called her cat and opened the door for him.

"Mousie outside, Puss!" she said. "Go catch the Mousie, catch the Mousie!"

The big black cat never had much to eat, so he was

very glad to go and catch a mouse. Poor Birdling dropped his mullen leaves and ran faster and faster but could not run fast enough. The Cat came nearer and nearer.

"Oh, I can't run any more!" panted Birdling at last. In another moment, the Cat would have pounced upon him and devoured him—but just then, the Bumblebee came booming through the air and stung the Cat on his big, black, S-shaped tail. The cat gave a terrible cry, turned around and ran home three times as fast as he had come.

Birdling had to sit down and rest for a while after the Cat had gone. Then he and the Bumblebee went on, hoping to reach the Little Dipper before noon. But they had not gone one-half a fairy mile further when a cross, scratchy voice shouted at them: "Get off the beach!"

"I can't," said Birdling timidly. "There's a board fence on one side and water on the other, and I can't go back the way I came, because there's a cat."

He could not even see who was speaking. There was only a big brown hill in front of him.

"I'm not on the beach," replied Bumblebee. "I'm in the air. Who are you, anyway?"

"Who am I! Well, I like that—who am I? Why, I'm ME!"

The big brown hill lifted itself up a bit, and they saw that it was the back of a Horse-Shoe Crab.

"Get off the beach, you civilians, this is a parade-ground! I'm drilling the new regiment from the Deep Sea."

Then they noticed a long line of little pink Crabs emerging from the foamy water and slowly ascending the sands.

"Backward—march!" shouted the Horse-Shoe Crab.

There was nothing for Birdling to do but sit down on an empty oyster shell and wait until the parade was over. They marched backwards, and marked time with two feet, three feet, four feet, till they had learned to keep all six of them going, and they did squads right and left and exercised their jaws and joints and pincers. There was nothing they did not do.

At last, the Horse-Shoe Crab shouted: "Dismiss!" and all the little Crabs tumbled back into the sea, pinching each other and betting who would be first down the beach. Then the old commander turned his attention to Birdling and Bumble.

"Who are you?"

"Nobody."

"Where are you going?"

"I'm not going at all," replied Bumble.

"You want to cross the parade-ground?"

"Yes."

"What for?"

"To get to my ship."

"Show your passport."

"Here!" and Bumble unsheathed his shiny long bayonet.

"That will do," said the Horse-Shoe Crab quickly, backing away a few steps and pulling in his tail. "You may pass."

It was the night before they reached the Little Dipper. She looked very forlorn, lying a bit sideways, sails furled and decks covered with sand. Worst of all, a whole brotherhood of Shrimps had set up housekeeping in her hold, and not even at the point of Bumble's bayonet would they move out. They wore little coats of mail that made them quite indifferent to a mere bumblebee's sting.

"But you must move out," pleaded Birdling, standing on the deck and shouting down into the hold. "I want to go to the Fairy Islands, and I simply must have my ship."

"Going to the Fairy Islands?" echoed the Shrimps. "That's a long trip, without food or water aboard and without a crew!"

"Oh, we'll lay in food and water soon enough," said Bumble, who sat in the rigging. "As for a crew—"

"Let us be the crew," cried the Shrimps. "We're not

clever, but we're really very obedient and faithful. We don't want to spoil your trip, Birdling, but we don't want to move, either; there are very few houses along the beach, and none as nice as this. Let us be your crew!"

"But then I'll have to pay you," said Birdling, "and I have no money. Shall I pay you with music? I'll whistle one tune for every Shrimp once a week."

"It's a bargain," replied the crew.

All night long, Bumble flew to-and-fro between the witch-hazel bushes on the hill and the boat upon the beach, carrying fairy bread and honeydew for the voyage. The crew packed all these provisions into big barnacles that made splendid kegs and barrels. Birdling was brave enough to go back along the beach by moonlight and pick up the mullen-leaf blankets he had dropped when he fled from the Cat, and at the crack of dawn, the Little Dipper was ready to put to sea. They cleared the harbour and, with the outgoing tide, floated out upon the ocean. Bumble flew above the mast and accompanied them for several miles; two fiddler crabs came to the edge of the beach and fiddled until the good ship was out of sight, and Birdling stood at the bow with the great green sail blowing behind him. At last, everybody shouted: "Goodby, goodby, goodluck, thank you, thank-you!," then the Little Dipper sailed out of sight.

For three days they journeyed, always pointing their course Eastward, but they did not know just where to look for the Fairy Islands. Sometimes a flock of birds would fly above them, also going Eastward, but they flew so fast that it was never possible to follow and learn their path.

On the fourth day, just as the pink dawn spread over the sky, Birdling saw a whole fleet of tiny sails. They were no bigger than his own, but they were pearly white and shimmered with lovely colours, so he knew they must be Nautilus ships.

"Heigh-ho!" he shouted, catching up to them. "Heigh-ho, heigh-ho!"

The Nautilus ships have deep, deep holds with many little cabins in them. When he shouted, a whole troop of fairy sailors came popping out to see who had called to them.

"Heigh-ho!" they replied.

"Where are you going?" asked Birdling.

"To the Fairy Islands."

"Take me along?"

"With pleasure," said the fairies. "Who are you?"

"I'm Birdling, and the Shrimps are my crew."

The Little Dipper was surrounded by the ships of pearl, and as the sea was quiet and the wind very low, they could talk from deck to deck. The oldest one of the fairy captains was a Brownie named Trick. He was seven hundred years old and knew about everything from the North Pole to the great Antarctic.

"We are going to the Fairy Islands with a cargo of ants'-eggs," he told Birdling, "Our King likes to eat them poached, or fried, or scrambled, on his breakfast toast. We would do anything to cheer up the King."

"Why does the King need cheering up?" Birdling inquired sympathetically. "I thought Kings were always happy."

"Oh no, no, no, our Fairy King is very unhappy. His little son has been kidnapped by Shag."

"Who is Shag?"

Trick shook his head and rolled his eyes at Birdling's ignorance.

"What! You have sailed the Sea for fully half a week, and don't know who Shag is? Ask your crew!"

But the Shrimps did not know about Shag, either. They were not very clever, you know, and had not gone to school.

"Won't you please tell us?" said Birdling, a bit ruffled at the Brownie's airs.

"Shag is the King of the Deep Sea!" shouted all the Fairies together so loudly that the Nautilus ships rocked with the noise.

"He has kidnapped our little Fairy Prince," Trick

explained, "and nobody knows whether he is ill, or imprisoned, or dead. Our King is so sad that he will not wear his crown, he has locked it in a closet and hidden the key. As for the queen, the poor lady has turned into a weeping willow!"

"That's awful," said Birdling, and the Shrimps were moved to tears. "Where does Shag live?"

"Under the rock where the Sea Lion sleeps."

"Can't somebody sneak into his house and take a peep to see what has become of the little Prince?"

"You make us shiver to think of it," replied the fairies, pulling their caps down over their ears and their sailor collars up. "The Sea-Lion wakes at the slightest noise and catches anyone who comes near. And if you did get by, Shag would be sure to see you and eat you at a gulp!"

But Birdling went on asking questions.

"Where is the Rock?"

"We are just passing it," said a Shrimp from the top of the mast. "I see it, far to leeward."

Birdling turned his rudder, and waved his hand as his boat swung away from the Nautilus fleet.

"Goodby," he shouted. "Tell your King that Birdling has gone to take a peep into Shag's palace, to see whether the young Prince be ill, or imprisoned, or dead! You shall not see me again till I bring word of your prince."

The fairies set up a great cry of amazement, but already the Little Dipper was far too leeward, steering toward the terrible Rock. So they continued on their way to the Fairy Islands, and all the way home, they could talk of nothing but the adventurous captain of the many-coloured sailboat and his crew.

Birdling sailed straight up to the Rock. It was black and high, and the waves ran up on it in great white ruffles. Then he noticed that the top of the Rock was not of stone at all—it was the outstretched form of the Sea Lion, sound asleep.

When the Shrimps saw the monster, their courage failed them. They fell upon their knees and begged the Skipper to turn back, for they were dreadfully afraid of being eaten, and when Birdling would not turn back, they mutinied and said they would not mind the sails and would not go one inch nearer the terrible Rock! Then Birdling grew angry at their cowardice and locked them all into the hold, where their cries could not be heard, for he was afraid they would wake the Sea Lion. He then took the ropes and the rudder in his own hand and steered his craft into a cove so near the Sea Lion that he could hear the great creature breathing.

In the cove and under the rock ran a deep cave that he guessed at once to be the entrance to Shag's palace, where you could go down into the sea without drowning, as the Mermen and Mermaids do. Very quietly, he fastened his boat to the rock, then climbed onto the gunwale and dived like a dolphin into the deep, dark, ripply water.

Yes, this was the entrance to the Palace of King Shag! At the bottom of the cave was a winding stairway, like the inside of a huge shell. Strange, fantastic fish swam up and down and churned up the water so that it was very hard for Birdling to keep his balance. But fortunately, they did not see him, so he crept on slowly down the steps.

Suddenly he saw a gleam of light, and he felt sure it must be from Shag's palace. Faster and faster, he ran down the wet, mossy stairs till a current of water caught him and took him all the way down just as a fly goes down the hole in a washbowl. When he landed at the foot of the stairs, he was sitting on golden sand, and the bright lights blinded his eyes.

"Why, what's this?" said a thundering voice in his ear, and a huge fin picked him up. He looked up and saw Shag himself, a huge silvery fish with long whiskers and pop-eyes and a golden crown on his head. He was very hideous, and Birdling was terribly frightened, but he looked all around, hoping to see the Prince.

"I don't know who you are," said Shag, "but you look as if you'd make a nice little morsel."

"I will let you have one chance for your life. Before I eat you, you shall come and see the wonderful treasures I have collected, and if you are able to pick out the most precious jewel in my vault, I will let you go. You shall have the jewel for a prize, and I will give you one day's grace before pursuing you with my soldiers.

So Birdling was led down some more long stairs to the cellar of the palace, where shining jellyfish lights hung from the ceiling. In their dim radiance, he saw a heap of treasure such as no one had ever seen in all the world—diamonds that shone like stars, rubies and sapphires and emeralds, brooches and necklaces, pearl-set combs, wonderful pins and lockets and vessels of hammered gold!

Then Birdling noticed a queer locket lying close to his foot; it seemed to be made of two big oyster shells closed with a band of tin. There was nothing very precious about it.

"But it must be precious, or it wouldn't be here," he thought quickly.

So, while Shag waved his whiskers in a bored and superior way, and his soldiers craned their necks to see Birdling, the boy suddenly stooped and picked up the locket.

"I choose this," he said and held it up with both hands.

Shag uttered a howl of rage.

"He has guessed, he has guessed!" The bodyguard drew back in terror as their King beat the water with his fins till a cloud of mud came up from the floor of the cave, and his crown slipped over one eye. Now he would really have liked to eat up Birdling, but of course, the soldiers had all heard the rules of the game, so he had to abide by his word. Birdling was escorted back to the hall and allowed to go up the winding stairs, back to the Little Dipper, the heavy oyster shell under his arm. It seemed to him about as big as a suitcase but harder to carry because it had no handle. No one knows how he could ever have carried it to the top of the stairs had he not met a Sea-Horse who gave him a ride.

"Heigh-ho!" he cried when he stood once more aboard the Little Dipper, "are you asleep or awake down there in the hold?"

"Awake!" cried one voice.

"Asleep!" murmured all the others.

"Then wake up, for we must flee! We have one day of grace and then Shag will pursue us: Heave the anchors and hoist the sails!"

So he raised the trap door of the hold, and the Shrimps climbed out, looking very shamefaced and small, as well they might, and in a few minutes, the Little Dipper was under sail.

When the Rock was well out of sight and the Little Dipper making good speed, Birdling gave the wheel to the first mate and decided to open the oyster-locket. It took three Shrimps and the captain himself to move the heavy band of tin that held the two half-shells together.

But at last, they fell apart—and what do you suppose was inside?

A perfect little bedroom, all wrought of finest gold, with a canopy-bed of rosy silk and a tiny chair and table and even a dresser—and in the bed, on pillows of down, lay the young Fairy Prince! When the locket opened, and the light shone into his room, he rubbed his eyes and said: "What time is it?"

"Time to go home," replied Birdling. "Don't be afraid, for we are taking you there."

They gave him some witch-hazel bread and a drink of honeydew, and one of the Shrimps was appointed to tell him stories to pass the time. The young Prince was cheerful and well-behaved, and everyone who saw him loved him at once. He had yellow curls and bright, laughing eyes and clothes made of flower petals that made Birdling feel very plain in his rough coat of mullen leaves.

Everybody aboard the Little Dipper was perfectly happy, so they quite forgot that tomorrow morning, Shag would pursue them with his soldiers. Imagine their terror when they woke up at sunrise in a raging storm that made the waves dash over the very mast of their boat! They could hear Shag howling at the bottom of the Deep Sea, and as he whisked his tail, he made more and more bubbles and white caps come up. The white-caps pursued the Little Dipper like ranks of horsemen.

The young prince, hidden under Birdling's mullen coat, began to tremble and cry, for he was dreadfully afraid of Shag.

"Don't be afraid," said Birdling. "I'm sure we will reach the Fairy Islands very soon now, and then we will be safe."

"But where are the Fairy Islands? Where are they?" queried the young prince, scanning the sea with his bright eyes. "I don't see them, and I am so frightened!"

Birdling had just been hit on the head by a hailstone, but he pretended it did not hurt.

"You mustn't be frightened," he said cheerfully. "I'll whistle you a tune if you'll stop crying." And he began to whistle as though he did not mind the storm at all.

As he whistled, the sea became calm and began to shimmer with a thousand lovely colours—and out of the rippling waters rose three snow-capped mountains surrounded on every side by sunny green plains. He had found the Fairy Islands!

Birdling ran his boat into the harbour, where he saw the Nautilus fleet lying at anchor, and he called out joyfully, "Yo, ho, yo, ho, heigh-ho! Where is Trick?"

A crowd of fairies came running to the harbour's edge and cried, "Hush, hush! No one is allowed to shout or whistle or sing on this island. Even the birds do not sing. The King and Queen have commanded silence to prevail, until they have some news of their son."

"Here's news for you, then," replied Birdling. "Go and tell your King and Queen that the young prince has returned!" So saying, he picked up the fairy child and stood him on the gunwale of the ship for everyone to see, and the well-behaved child doffed his little diadem and bowed.

So great was the joy of the fairy people that they stumbled over each other in their haste to go and tell the King that the good ship Little Dipper had brought back his son. The queen, who had turned into a weeping willow, came back to life and wept now with delight; the king hunted all over the palace for the key to his closet, for he could hardly wait to put on his crown once more and hold a great banquet in honour of Birdling, who had restored the heir to the throne. The birds burst into song and the bluebells chimed and even the butterflies, who are usually silent, began to trill and chirp until the whole island rang with joyous sounds. As soon as the cook could get the banquet ready, they all sat down and feasted, from the fairy King, with Birdling by his side, to the meekest under-earthworm, and the shy Shrimps had a table by themselves because they did not possess very fairyish manners. There was cake for everybody, and ice cream, and chocolate with whipped cream, and candy and favours. The best thing about the party was that all the goodies were fairy food which couldn't make you sick however much you ate, and they all drank Birdling's health in pink lemonade.

Three days later, when the feasting was over and the

hundreds of golden dishes had been washed and dried, Birdling was playing on the beach with the fairies, and he saw a ship out at Sea.

"Look," he said to his friend Trick, "there is a ship just like mine, only a hundred times bigger! That isn't a fairy ship. How do you suppose she came into these waters?"

"Oh, that is a ship which came here long ago," said Trick. "Shag caught it and tied it to the light-house rock. It has been there for years and years. I suppose the storm which Shag made when he was angry at you, must have torn the rope and set the poor vessel free. Do you suppose the people on board are still alive?"

"I'll go and see," said Birdling. "Of course I'm very small, but I might be able to help them." So he took the Little Dipper and sailed out to the schooner.

"Heigh-ho!" he cried, standing up and putting his hands to his mouth. "Heigh-ho!"

Somebody certainly was alive on the ship; a tall captain dressed in oil skins stood up in the bow and shouted back:

"We are the Big Dipper! Who are you?"

"The Little Dipper! And you must be my father," cried Birdling, dancing for joy.

At first, the Captain could not believe his eyes and ears, but when Birdling stood on his right hand (he had the good ship Little Dipper in the left one), he looked at him very closely and saw that it really was his son

"Oh Father, now we can go home together," exclaimed the boy, hugging his father's thumb. "But will you wait till I go and say goodby to my fairy friends?"

"Yes, I will wait," said the Captain, "for you should never leave your friends without saying goodby and thank you."

The fairies were sorry to see Birdling go. They let him take along all the treasures he wanted from the King's storeroom and helped him carry them down to the harbour and put them in his hold. He took a bag of gold for his father and a little one for himself, besides the oyster-locket with the golden chamber inside, which he had won from Shag, and a little pearly crown for his friend the Bumblebee at home. He even took a gold thimble for his great-aunt and a little silver bell for the Cat to show that he bore no malice.

"And here is some fairy wine you must drink when you are safely aboard your father's ship," said the King, handing Birdling a tiny vial just as he said goodbye. "It will make you grow up again and be as big as other boys. We will miss you, Birdling. Farewell!"

So Birdling, a life-sized boy once more, went home with his father whistling happy songs. As his whistle died away in the distance, the Fairy Islands sank down into the water, the waves closed over them, and you could not even guess where the three snowy peaks and the green plains and sunny harbours had been.

And no one has ever seen them since.

In the Moonlight

by Mrs W.K. Clifford

He picked a buttercup and held it up to her chin. "Do you like butter?" he asked. "Butter!" she exclaimed. "They are not made into butter. They are made into crowns for the Queen; she has a new one every morning."

"I'll make you a crown," he said. "You shall wear it tonight."

"But where will my throne be?" she asked.

"It shall be on the middle step of the stile by the cornfield."

So when the moon rose, I went out to see.

He wore a red jacket and a cap with a feather in it. Round her head, there was a wreath of buttercups; it was not much like a crown. On one side of the wreath, there were some daisies, and on the other was a little bunch of blackberry blossoms.

"Come and dance in the moonlight," he said, so she climbed up and over the stile and stood in the cornfield holding out her two hands to him. He took them in his, and then they danced round and round all down the pathway while the wheat nodded wisely on either side, and the poppies awoke and wondered. On they went, on and on through the cornfield towards the broad green meadows stretching far into the distance. On and on, he shouted for joy, and she laughed out so merrily that the sound travelled to the edge of the wood, and the thrushes heard and dreamed of Spring. On they went, on and on, and round and round, he in his red jacket, and she with the wildflowers dropping one by one from her wreath, on and on in the moonlight, on and on till they had danced all down the cornfield, till they had crossed the green meadows, till they were hidden in the mist beyond.

That is all I know, but I think that in the far, far off somewhere, where the moon is shining, he and she still dance along a cornfield, he in his red jacket, and she with the wildflowers dropping from her hair.

Goody Two Shoes

by John Newbery

Farmer Meanwell was at one time a very rich man. He owned large fields and had fine flocks of sheep and plenty of money. But all at once, his good fortune seemed to desert him. Year after year, his crops failed, his sheep died off, and he was obliged to borrow money to pay his rent and the wages of those who worked on the farm.

At last, he had to sell his farm, but even this did not bring him enough money to pay his debts, and he was worse off than ever.

Among those who had lent money to Farmer Meanwell were Sir Thomas Gripe and a Farmer named Graspall.

Sir Thomas was a very rich man indeed, and Farmer Graspall had more money than he could possibly use. But they were both very greedy and covetous and particularly hard on those who owed them anything. Farmer Graspall abused Farmer Meanwell and called him all sorts of dreadful names, but the rich Sir Thomas Gripe was crueller still and wanted the poor debtor to shut up in jail.

So poor Farmer Meanwell had to hasten from the place where he had lived for so many years in order to get out of the way of these greedy men.

He went to the next village, taking his wife and his two little children with him. But though he was free from Gripe and Graspall, he was not free from trouble and care.

He soon fell ill, and when he found himself unable to get food and clothes for his family, he grew worse and worse and soon died.

His wife could not bear the loss of her husband, whom she loved so dearly, and in a few days, she was dead.

The two orphan children seemed to be left entirely alone in the world, with no one to look after them or care for them but their Heavenly Father.

They trotted around hand in hand, and the poorer they became, the more they clung to each other. Poor, ragged, and hungry enough they were!

Tommy had two shoes, but Margery went barefoot. They had nothing to eat but the berries that grew in the woods and the scraps they could get from the poor people in the village, and at night they slept in barns or under haystacks.

Their rich relations were too proud to notice them. But Mr Smith, the clergyman of the village where the children were born, was not that sort of a man. A rich relation came to visit him—a kind-hearted gentleman— and the clergyman told him all about Tommy and Margery. The kind gentleman pitied them and ordered Margery a pair of shoes and gave Mr Smith money to buy her some clothes, which she needed sadly. As for Tommy, he said he would take him off to sea with him and make him a sailor. After a few days, the gentleman said he must go to London and would take Tommy with him, and sad was the parting between the two children.

Poor Margery was very lonely indeed, without her brother, and might have cried herself sick but for the new shoes that were brought home to her.

They turned her thoughts from her grief, and as soon as she had put them on, she ran into Mrs Smith and cried out: "Two shoes, ma'am, two shoes!" These words she repeated to everyone she met, and thus it was she got the name Goody Two Shoes.

Little Margery had seen how good and wise Mr Smith was and thought it was because of his great learning, and she wanted, above all things, to learn to read. At last, she made up her mind to ask Mr Smith to teach her when he had a moment to spare. He readily agreed to do this, and Margery read to him for an hour every day and spent much time with her books.

Then she laid out a plan for teaching others more ignorant than herself. She cut out of thin pieces of wood ten sets of large and small letters of the alphabet and carried these with her when she went from house to house. When she came to Billy Wilson's, she threw down the letters all in a heap, and Billy picked them out and sorted them in lines, thus:

A   B   C   D   E   F   G   H
I J   K,

a   b   c   d   e   f   g   h
i j   k,

and so on until all the letters were in their right places.

From there, Goody Two Shoes trotted off to another cottage, and there were several children waiting for her. As soon as the little girl came in, they all crowded around her and were eager to begin their lessons at once.

Then she threw the letters down and said to the boy next to her, "What did you have for dinner today?" "Bread," answered the little boy. "Well, put down the first letter," said Goody Two Shoes. Then he put down B, and the next child R, and the next E, and the next A, and the next D, and there was the whole word— BREAD.

"What did you have for dinner, Polly Driggs?"

"Apple-pie," said Polly, upon which she laid down the first letter, A, and the next put down a P, and the next another P, and so on until the words, Apple and Pie were united and stood thus: APPLE PIE.

Now it happened one evening that Goody Two Shoes was going home rather late. She had made a longer round than usual, and everybody had kept her waiting, so that night came on before her day's work was done. Right glad was she to set out for her own home, and she walked along contentedly through the fields, lanes, and roads, enjoying the quiet evening. The evening was not cool, however, but close and sultry and betokened a storm. Presently a drop fell on Goody's face. What should she do? If she did not make haste she would soon be wet to the skin.

Fortunately, there was an old barn down the road, in which she could find shelter, and Goody Two Shoes gathered her skirts about her and took to her heels, and ran as if somebody was after her. The owner of the barn had died lately, and the property was to be sold, and there was a lot of loose hay on the floor which had not yet been taken away.

Goody Two Shoes cuddled down in the soft hay,

glad of a chance to rest her weary limbs and quite out of breath with her long run; and just then, down rattled the rain, the thunder roared, the lightning flashed, and the old barn trembled, and so did Goody Two Shoes.

She had not been there long before she heard footsteps, and three men came into the barn for shelter. The hay was piled up between her and them so that they could not see her, and, thinking they were alone, they spoke quite loudly.

They were plotting to rob Squire Trueman, who lived in the great house in Margery's village and were to break in and steal all they could see that very night. This was quite enough for Goody Two Shoes. She waited for nothing but dashed out of the barn and ran through rain and mud till she came to the Squire's house.

He was at dinner with some friends, and anyone else but Goody would have found it difficult to gain admission to him. But she was well known to the servants and was so kind and obliging that even the big fat butler could not refuse to do her bidding and went and told the squire that Goody Two Shoes wished very much to see him.

So the squire asked his friends to excuse him for a moment and came out and said, "Well, Goody Two Shoes, my good girl, what is it?" "Oh, sir," she replied, "if you do not take care you will be robbed and murdered this very night!"

Then she told all she had heard the men say while she was in the barn.

The squire saw there was not a moment to lose, so he went back and told his friends the news he had heard. They all said they would stay and help him take the thieves. So the lights were put out to make it appear as if all the people in the house were in bed, and servants and all kept a close watch both inside and outside.

Sure enough, at about one o'clock in the morning, the three men came creeping, creeping up to the house with a dark lantern and the tools to break in with. Before they were aware, six men sprang out on them and held them fast. The thieves struggled in vain to get away. They were locked in an outhouse until daylight when a cart came and took them off to jail.

They were afterwards sent out of the country, where they had to work in chains on the roads, and it is said that one of them behaved so well that he was pardoned and went to live in Australia, where he became a rich man.

The other two went from bad to worse, and it is likely that they came to some dreadful end. For sin never goes unpunished.

But to return to Goody Two Shoes. One day as she was walking through the village, she saw some wicked boys with a raven, at which they were going to throw stones. To stop this cruel sport, she gave the boys a penny for the raven and brought the bird home with her. She gave him the name "Ralph," and he proved to be a very clever creature indeed. She taught him to spell and to read, and he was so fond of playing with the large letters that the children called them "Ralph's Alphabet."

Some days after Goody had met with the raven, she was passing through a field when she saw some naughty boys who had taken a pigeon and tied a string to its legs in order to let it fly and draw it back again when they pleased.

Goody could not bear to see anything tortured like that, so she bought the pigeon from the boys and taught him how to spell and read. But he could not talk. And as Ralph, the raven, took the large letters, Peter, the pigeon, took care of the small ones.

Mrs Williams, who lived in Margery's village, kept school and taught little ones their A B C's. She was now old and feeble and wanted to give up this important trust.

This being known to Sir William Dove, he asked Mrs Williams to examine Goody Two Shoes and see if she was not clever enough for the office. This was done, and Mrs Williams reported that little Margery was the best scholar and had the best heart of anyone she had ever examined. All the country had a great opinion of Mrs Williams, and this report made them think highly of Miss MARGERY, as we must now call her.

So Margery Meanwell was now a schoolmistress and

a capital one she made. The children all loved her, for she was never weary of making plans for their happiness.

The room in which she taught was large and lofty, and there was plenty of fresh air in it; and as she knew that children liked to move about, she placed her sets of letters all around the school so that everyone was obliged to get up to find a letter, or spell a word when it came to their turn.

This exercise not only kept the children in good health but fixed the letters firmly in their minds.

The neighbours were very good to her, and one of them made her a present of a little skylark, whose early morning song told the lazy boys and girls that it was time they were out of bed.

Sometime after this, a poor lamb lost its dam, and the farmer being about to kill it, she bought it from him and brought it home to play with the children.

Soon after this, a present was made to Miss Margery of a dog, and as he was always in good humour and always jumping about, the children gave him the name of Jumper. It was his duty to guard the door, and no one could go out or come in without leave from his mistress.

Margery was so wise and good that some foolish people accused her of being a witch, and she was taken to court and tried before the judge. She soon proved that she was a most sensible woman, and Sir Charles

Jones was so pleased with her that he offered her a large sum of money to take care of his family and educate his daughter. At first, she refused but afterwards went and behaved so well and was so kind and tender that Sir Charles would not permit her to leave the house and soon after made her an offer of marriage.

The neighbours came in crowds to the wedding, and all were glad that one who had been such a good girl, and had grown up such a good woman, was to become a grand lady.

Just as the clergyman had opened his book, a gentleman, richly dressed, ran into the church and cried, "Stop! stop!"

Great alarm was felt, especially by the bride and groom, with whom he said he wished to speak privately.

Sir Charles stood motionless with surprise, and the bride fainted away in the stranger's arms. This richly-dressed gentleman turned out to be little Tommy Meanwell, who had just come from the sea, where he had made a large fortune.

Sir Charles and Lady Jones lived very happily together, and the great lady did not forget the children but was just as good to them as she had always been. She was also kind and good to the poor and the sick and a friend to all who were in distress. Her life was a great blessing, and her death was the greatest calamity that ever took place in the neighbourhood where she lived, and she was known as goody two shoes.

Punky Dunk and the Goldfish

by Charlotte B. Herr

Punky Dunk, so fat, was a black and white cat

Of exceedingly tender years.

He had black on his nose and the tips of his toes,

On the end of his tail and his ears.

He cast his lot in a very soft spot

For his bed was a box full of straw,

And he slept all night with his eyes shut tight

And his little black nose on his paw.

Punky Dunk would peep, though he seemed asleep,

At the bird in its cage of brass,

And his tail he swayed when the goldfish played

In their little clear bowl of glass.

"Though my coat's like silk from my drinking milk,"

He would say, "I often wish

I might change my food——as I think I should——

To a meal on a nice plump fish."

So he winked his eye, and he heaved a sigh,

And he said: "I really think

That it would be grand to jump on that stand

And see how the fishes drink."

The fish globe round he reached with a bound

And stood with his paws on the rim,

Looking in with an air that was certain to scare

The fish as they looked at him.

His cunning head bent, and his little nose went

Right down, while his tongue flashed red——

When, O, what a sight! The fish, in their fright,

Splashed water all over his head.

His cunning head bent, and his little nose went

Right down, while his tongue flashed red——

When, O, what a sight! The fish, in their fright,

Splashed water all over his head.

In the big glass bowl, when the waves ceased to roll,

All the little goldfish were so glad

That each wiggled his fins as he said through his grins:

"That's the most fun we ever have had."

Now Punky Dunk lies on the floor, and he sighs:

"It is best for a cat to be good,

For I cannot forget how I got my coat wet

When I didn't do just as I should."

The Violets

by Mrs W.K. Clifford

The sun came out and shone down on the leafless trees that cast hardly any shadows on the pathway through the woods. "Surely the Spring is coming," the birds said; "it must be time to wake the flowers."

The thrush, the lark, and the linnet sang sweetly. A robin flew up from the snow, and perched upon a branch; a little ragged boy at the end of the wood stopped and listened.

"Surely the Spring is coming," he too said, "and mother will get well."

The flowers that all through the Winter had been sleeping in the ground heard the birds, but they were drowsy and longed to sleep on. At last, the snowdrops came up and looked shiveringly about; and a primrose leaf peeped through the ground and died of cold. Then some violets opened their blue eyes and, hidden beneath the tangle of the wood, listened to the twittering of the birds. The ragged little boy came by; he saw the tender flowers and, stooping down, gathered them one by one, and put them into a wicker basket that hung upon his arm.

"Dear flowers," he said, with a sigh, as if loth to pick them, "you will buy poor mother some breakfast," and, tying them up into little bunches, he carried them to the town. All morning he stood by the roadside, offering his flowers to the passers-by, but no one took any notice of him, and his face grew sad and troubled. "Poor mother!" he said longingly, and the flowers heard him and sighed.

"Those violets are very sweet," a lady said as she passed; the boy ran after her.

"Only a penny," he said, "just one penny, for mother is at home." Then the lady bought them and carried them to the beautiful house in which she lived and gave them some water, touching them so softly that the poor violets forgot to long for the woods and looked gratefully up into her face.

"Mother," said the boy, "see, I have brought some bread for your breakfast. The violets sent it to you," and he put the little loaf down before her.

The birds knew nothing of all this and went on singing till the ground was covered with flowers, till the leaves had hidden the brown branches of the trees, and the pathway through the woods was all shade, save for the sunshine that flecked it with light.

The Jungle Baby

by G.E. Farrow

There was once a little white baby boy called Bab-ba, he had bright blue eyes and golden curls, and he had a black Ayah for his nurse. She had been with Bab-ba ever since he was quite a tiny baby in long robes, and she was very fond of him. Her name was Jeejee-walla, but they just called her Ayah.

Bab-ba's Father was an English Officer in India, and they lived in a beautiful white house on the Simla Hills, with a big verandah running all around it. Round about the verandah was a garden, and outside the garden, the jungle stretched for miles and miles, and in the jungle were all sorts of beasts and birds.

Little Bab-ba used to play on the verandah with his pets, Mioux-Mioux, the cat, and Wooff-Wooff, the dog, and they both loved him very dearly. Mioux-Mioux never scratched him when he accidentally pulled her tail, although she felt very much like doing so, and Wooff-Wooff used to stand on his hind legs and perform all sorts of funny tricks to make Bab-ba laugh.

Every morning after breakfast, Bab-ba threw bread crumbs out to the little birds on the lawn, and they used to sit in the trees and watch for him and sing about him till he came out of the house. "Good little Bab-ba, who gives us our food," one would sing, and "We all love little Bab-ba," several of the others would reply from another part of the garden.

Mioux-Mioux used to watch them out of the corner of her eyes, but she never attempted to catch them because she knew that Bab-ba loved them, and Wooff-Wooff used to sit with his head on one side and wonder however they managed with only two legs and not four like his.

But one day, when Bab-ba was feeding the birdies, the big snake Hoodo, who lived in the garden, came creeping under the verandah and tried to catch some of the birds while they were eating, but Bab-ba saw him and called out!—

"Go away, bad Hoodo, go away!"

and his Ayah heard him and came running out to see what was the matter.

When she saw Hoodo, the big snake, she caught Bab-ba up in her arms and ran with him into the house, and two of the men-servants came out with big sticks and beat Hoodo over the head and body till he could hardly crawl away again into his hole under a big tree in the garden.

Now Hoodo was a very wicked snake and was very angry about all this, and he thought and thought about it and wondered how he could be revenged on little Bab-ba, for he put all that had occurred down to him, and so one day after he had got better he went out into the jungle to see an old friend of his, Tig, the Tiger, and talk the matter over with him.

Hoodo thought that Tig the Tiger was as greedy and cruel as he was himself, and so he asked him how he would like a little white fat baby boy for his dinner, and Tig licked his lips and said, "H'M! we shall see."

Then Hoodo went further into the jungle and met Prowl, the Wolf.

"How would you like a little fat white baby to eat?" asked Hoodo, and Prowl, the Wolf, licked his lips and said, "Ha!" and nothing else.

A little further on, Hoodo met Bluf, the big brown Bear, and he asked him what he would do if he met a little fat white baby in the jungle.

And Bluf stood up on his hind legs, hugged himself and said, "Ough! Very nice, very nice indeed!"

And then Poon-dah, the big wild Elephant, came crashing through the jungle, and Hoodo had to scurry out of his way so that he didn't get trampled upon.

"How would you like a little white ——" he screamed out, but Poon-dah made a loud noise with his trunk and went on, for he didn't converse with snakes.

Nevertheless, Hoodo was satisfied, for he said, "If Poon-dah would trample on me in passing, so he would on a little white baby if he were here;" and his wicked black beady eyes were bright and he laughed maliciously.

After this, Hoodo went home to his hole under the tree in Bab-ba's Father's garden and watched and waited till Bab-ba should be quite by himself; and one day, when Wooff-Wooff had gone off after a wild rabbit, and Mioux-Mioux was fast asleep in the sun, the Ayah went into the house to fetch Bab-ba's Noah's ark, and he was left alone on the verandah.

Then Hoodo came sliding out of his hole very quickly and stood before the verandah, waving his head backwards and forwards and shooting out his little tongue while the sun showed all the colours of the rainbow on his smooth, shiny skin.

"Oh, pretty Hoodo!" said Bab-ba, "but you're

naughty. Go away!"

"No," said Hoodo sweetly, "I'm not naughty, dear Bab-ba, and I know where some such beautiful flowers grow. Come with me and I'll show you!"

"No," said Bab-ba, shaking his head, but Hoodo continued to look at him steadily, and presently Bab-ba slid down from the verandah and came towards him.

Then Hoodo laughed and drew back quickly into the thick part of the garden, with Bab-ba running after him.

When the Ayah returned to the verandah with Bab-ba's Noah's Ark, and she saw his little empty chair and Mioux-Mioux asleep in the sun, she grew alarmed and ran about calling Bab-ba's name, and wringing her hands, and Bab-ba's Mother came out, and his Father and they and all the servants hunted about in the garden for a very long while, but could not find any trace of him, and Mioux-Mioux woke up and wondered what all the commotion was about, and Wooff-Wooff came back without the rabbit and wondered too.

Wooff-Wooff went over to where Mioux-Mioux was sitting and talked the matter over with her. While they were talking, some little birds overhead called out to them to attract their attention.

"Bab-ba," they said, "Bab-ba has followed Hoodo, the Snake, into the jungle, and he will be lost and eaten by the wild beasts unless he is brought back. Quick! Quick! Go after him! Haste!"

And so Wooff-Wooff ran to Bab-ba's Father and Mother and tried to tell them.

He ran backwards and forwards towards the jungle and barked and tried to make them follow, but they wouldn't understand, and so, at last, he had to set out himself to try and find him.

Now, after Bab-ba had followed Hoodo a little way through the garden, the snake turned to a little path which led to a hole broken in the wall.

"You must crawl through here," said Hoodo, "the pretty flowers are on the other side."

So Bab-ba crawled through and found himself in the jungle.

"Further on! further on!" cried Hoodo every time Bab-ba stopped to gather any, "there are prettier ones further on." And so Bab-ba went on and on till he came to where Tig the Tiger lay asleep in the long grass.

"Now's your time," whispered Hoodo in his ear, "here's the little white baby for your dinner." And Tig sprang up with a roar.

But Bab-ba wasn't a bit frightened, and he only laughed and said, "what a big, big Mioux-Mioux!" And he put his arms around Tig's neck and nestled his head in his soft fur till Tig forgot all about his dinner, and purred with delight just like Mioux-Mioux did when she was pleased.

Hoodo was very angry at this, and finding that Tig

was making friends with Bab-ba instead of eating him up, he called Bab-ba to him and said, "Come, let us be going, or we shall be late home." And Bab-ba kissed Tig, the Tiger, and followed Hoodo further into the jungle till they met Prowl, the Wolf. "Here's the little white baby," whispered Hoodo. And Prowl said, "Ha!" and was going to spring upon him and eat him up. But Bab-ba only laughed and said, "What a big Wooff-Wooff!" and patted him on the head and looked into his eyes so that Prowl forgot all about eating him and licked his hands and frisked about him just as Wooff-Wooff would have done.

"This is silly," said Hoodo angrily. "Come away, it is near to sunset, and we must be getting home," and he led the way to where Bluf, the big brown Bear, lived. "I've brought the little white baby for you," said Hoodo. And Bluf said, "Ough! very nice, very nice indeed!" And caught Bab-ba up in his arms and hugged him.

"Just like my Ayah does!" laughed Bab-ba, and he patted Bluf's cheeks and kissed him so that Bluf didn't want to eat him at all, but only to hug him and keep him warm.

Just then, there was a loud trumpeting heard, and Bluf put Bab-ba down to the ground, and Hoodo slid off into the grass, hissing. "Now Poon-dah is coming and you will be trampled to death. Good-bye, little Bab-ba, I hate you!"

But when Poon-dah came and saw the little white

baby, he remembered that he had not always been a wild elephant but had once himself belonged to a white man, and so he picked little Bab-ba up with his trunk and placed him gently on his back.

And that's the position in which Bab-ba's Father found him when at last he had understood Wooff-Wooff's barking and had followed him into the jungle, accompanied by some native servants armed with guns and sticks. Wooff-Wooff traced the little boy by his scent till they came upon him riding on Poon-dah's back.

And now a funny thing happened, for amongst the servants was one who had once been Poon-dah's keeper, and Poon-dah remembered him and allowed himself to be led by him to Bab-ba's home. And so they returned in triumph with Bab-ba and his Father on Poon-dah's back and good Wooff-Wooff barking and frisking by his side.

The wicked Hoodo was justly punished, for just as he was going into his hole under the tree, he met an old enemy of his, Tiv, the Mongoose, and the two fought and fought for a long while, till at last, Hoodo was exhausted and stretched himself out and died, while little Tiv sat up and rubbed his paws together to clean them, and then skipped off to his new little home under Bab-ba's verandah, where he still lives to keep away any other wicked snakes from harming him.

The Velveteen Rabbit

by Margery Bianco

There was once a velveteen rabbit, and in the beginning, he was really splendid. He was fat and bunchy, as a rabbit should be; his coat was spotted brown and white, he had real thread whiskers, and his ears were lined with pink sateen. On Christmas morning, when he sat wedged in the top of the Boy's stocking, with a sprig of holly between his paws, the effect was charming.

There were other things in the stocking, nuts and

oranges and a toy engine, and chocolate almonds and a clockwork mouse, but the Rabbit was quite the best of all. For at least two hours, the Boy loved him, and then Aunts and Uncles came to dinner, and there was a great rustling of tissue paper and unwrapping of parcels, and in the excitement of looking at all the new presents, the Velveteen Rabbit was forgotten.

For a long time, he lived in the toy cupboard or on the nursery floor, and no one thought very much about him. He was naturally shy and being only made of velveteen, some of the more expensive toys quite snubbed him. The mechanical toys were very superior and looked down upon everyone else; they were full of modern ideas and pretended they were real. The model boat, who had lived through two seasons and lost most of his paint, caught the tone from them and never missed an opportunity of referring to his rigging in technical terms. The Rabbit could not claim to be a model of anything, for he didn't know that real rabbits existed; he thought they were all stuffed with sawdust like himself, and he understood that sawdust was quite out-of-date and should never be mentioned in modern circles. Even Timothy, the jointed wooden lion, who was made by the disabled soldiers, and should have had broader views, put on airs and pretended he was connected with Government. Between them, all the poor little Rabbit was made to feel very insignificant and commonplace, and the only person who was kind to him at all was the Skin Horse.

The Skin Horse had lived longer in the nursery than

any of the others. He was so old that his brown coat was bald in patches and showed the seams underneath, and most of the hairs in his tail had been pulled out to string bead necklaces. He was wise, for he had seen a long succession of mechanical toys arrive to boast and swagger, and by-and-by break their mainsprings and pass away, and he knew that they were only toys and would never turn into anything else. For the nursery, magic is very strange and wonderful, and only those playthings that are old and wise and experienced, like the Skin Horse, understand all about it.

"What is REAL?" asked the Rabbit one day when they were lying side by side near the nursery fender before Nana came to tidy the room. "Does it mean having things that buzz inside you and a stick-out handle?"

"Real isn't how you are made," said the Skin Horse. "It's a thing that happens to you. When a child loves you for a long, long time, not just to play with, but REALLY loves you, then you become Real."

"Does it hurt?" asked the Rabbit.

"Sometimes," said the Skin Horse, for he was always truthful. "When you are Real you don't mind being hurt."

"Does it happen all at once, like being wound up," he asked, "or bit by bit?"

"It doesn't happen all at once," said the Skin Horse. "You become. It takes a long time. That's why it doesn't happen often to people who break easily, or have sharp edges, or who have to be carefully kept. Generally, by the time you are Real, most of your hair has been loved off, and your eyes drop out and you get loose in the joints and very shabby. But these things don't matter at all, because once you are Real you can't be ugly, except to people who don't understand."

"I suppose you are real?" said the Rabbit. And then he wished he had not said it, for he thought the Skin Horse might be sensitive. But the Skin Horse only smiled.

"The Boy's Uncle made me Real," he said. "That was a great many years ago; but once you are Real you can't become unreal again. It lasts for always."

The Rabbit sighed. He thought it would be a long time before this magic called Real happened to him. He longed to become Real, to know what it felt like, and yet the idea of growing shabby and losing his eyes and whiskers was rather sad. He wished that he could become it without these uncomfortable things happening to him.

There was a person called Nana who ruled the nursery. Sometimes she took no notice of the playthings lying about, and sometimes, for no reason whatever, she went swooping about like a great wind and hustled them away in cupboards. She called this "tidying up," and the playthings all hated it, especially the tin ones. The Rabbit didn't mind it so much, for wherever he was thrown, he came down soft.

One evening, when the Boy was going to bed, he couldn't find the china dog that always slept with him. Nana was in a hurry, and it was too much trouble to hunt for china dogs at bedtime, so she simply looked about her, and seeing that the toy cupboard door stood open, she made a swoop.

"Here," she said, "take your old Bunny! He'll do to sleep with you!" And she dragged the Rabbit out by one ear and put him into the Boy's arms.

That night, and for many nights after, the Velveteen Rabbit slept in the Boy's bed. At first, he found it rather uncomfortable, for the Boy hugged him very tight, and sometimes he rolled over on him, and sometimes he pushed him so far under the pillow that the Rabbit could scarcely breathe. And he missed, too, those long moonlight hours in the nursery, when all the house was silent, and his talks with the Skin Horse. But very soon, he grew to like it, for the Boy used to talk to him and made nice tunnels for him under the bedclothes that he said were like the burrows the real rabbits lived in. And they had splendid games together, in whispers when Nana had gone away to her supper and left the night-light burning on the mantelpiece. And when the Boy dropped off to sleep, the Rabbit would snuggle down close under his little warm chin and dream with the Boy's hands clasped close around him all night long.

And so time went on, and the little Rabbit was very happy–so happy that he never noticed how his beautiful velveteen fur was getting shabbier and shabbier, and his tail becoming unsewn, and all the pink rubbed off his nose where the Boy had kissed him.

Spring came, and they had long days in the garden, for wherever the Boy went, the Rabbit went too. He had rides in the wheelbarrow, picnics on the grass, and lovely fairy huts built for him under the raspberry canes behind the flower border. And once, when the Boy was called away suddenly to go out to tea, the Rabbit was left out on the lawn until long after dusk, and Nana had to come and look for him with the candle because the Boy couldn't go to sleep unless he was there. He was wet through with the dew and quite earthy from diving into the burrows the Boy had made for him in the flower bed, and Nana grumbled as she rubbed him off with a corner of her apron.

"You must have your old Bunny!" she said. "Fancy all that fuss for a toy!"

The Boy sat up in bed and stretched out his hands.

"Give me my Bunny!" he said. "You mustn't say that. He isn't a toy. He's REAL!"

When the little Rabbit heard that, he was happy, for he knew that what the Skin Horse had said was true at last. The nursery magic had happened to him, and he was a toy no longer. He was Real. The Boy himself had said it.

That night he was almost too happy to sleep, and so much love stirred in his little sawdust heart that it almost burst. And into his boot-button eyes, that had long ago lost their polish, there came a look of wisdom and beauty, so that even Nana noticed it the next morning when she picked him up and said, "I declare if that old Bunny hasn't got quite a knowing expression!"

That was a wonderful Summer!

Near the house where they lived, there was a wood, and in the long June evenings, the Boy liked to go there after tea to play. He took the Velveteen Rabbit with him, and before he wandered off to pick flowers, or play at brigands among the trees, he always made the Rabbit a little nest somewhere among the bracken, where he would be quite cosy, for he was a kind-hearted little boy and he liked Bunny to be comfortable. One evening, while the Rabbit was lying there alone, watching the ants that ran to and fro between his velvet paws in the grass, he saw two strange beings creep out of the tall bracken near him.

They were rabbits like himself but quite furry and brand-new. They must have been very well made, for their seams didn't show at all, and they changed shape in a queer way when they moved; one minute, they were long and thin, and the next minute, fat and bunchy, instead of always staying the same like he did. Their feet padded softly on the ground, and they crept quite close to him, twitching their noses, while the Rabbit stared hard to see which side the clockwork stuck out, for he knew that people who jump generally have something to wind them up. But he couldn't see it. They were evidently a new kind of rabbit altogether.

They stared at him, and the little Rabbit stared back.

And all the time, their noses twitched.

"Why don't you get up and play with us?" one of them asked.

"I don't feel like it," said the Rabbit, for he didn't want to explain that he had no clockwork.

"Ho!" said the furry rabbit. "It's as easy as anything," And he gave a big hop sideways and stood on his hind legs.

"I don't believe you can!" he said.

"I can!" said the little Rabbit. "I can jump higher than anything!" He meant when the Boy threw him, but of course, he didn't want to say so.

"Can you hop on your hind legs?" asked the furry rabbit.

That was a dreadful question, for the Velveteen Rabbit had no hind legs at all! The back of him was made all in one piece, like a pincushion. He sat still in the bracken and hoped that the other rabbits wouldn't notice.

"I don't want to!" he said again.

But wild rabbits have very sharp eyes. And this one stretched out his neck and looked.

"He hasn't got any hind legs!" he called out. "Fancy a rabbit without any hind legs!" And he began to laugh.

"I have!" cried the little Rabbit. "I have got hind legs!

I am sitting on them!"

"Then stretch them out and show me, like this!" said the wild rabbit. And he began to whirl round and dance till the little Rabbit got quite dizzy.

"I don't like dancing," he said. "I'd rather sit still!"

But all the while, he was longing to dance, for a funny new tickly feeling ran through him, and he felt he would give anything in the world to be able to jump about as these rabbits did.

The strange rabbit stopped dancing and came quite close. He came so close this time that his long whiskers brushed the Velveteen Rabbit's ear, and then he wrinkled his nose suddenly and flattened his ears and jumped backwards.

"He doesn't smell right!" he exclaimed. "He isn't a rabbit at all! He isn't real!"

"I am Real!" said the little Rabbit. "I am Real! The Boy said so!" And he nearly began to cry.

Just then, there was a sound of footsteps, and the Boy ran past them, and with a stamp of feet and a flash of white tails, the two strange rabbits disappeared.

"Come back and play with me!" called the little Rabbit. "Oh, do come back! I know I am Real!"

But there was no answer, only the little ants ran to and fro, and the bracken swayed gently where the two strangers had passed. The Velveteen Rabbit was all alone.

"Oh, dear!" he thought. "Why did they run away like that? Why couldn't they stop and talk to me?"

For a long time, he lay very still, watching the bracken and hoping that they would come back. But they never returned, and presently the sun sank lower and the little white moths fluttered out, and the Boy came and carried him home.

Weeks passed, and the little Rabbit grew very old and shabby, but the Boy loved him just as much. He loved him so hard that he loved all his whiskers off, and the pink lining to his ears turned grey, and his brown spots faded. He even began to lose his shape, and he scarcely looked like a rabbit anymore except to the Boy. To him, he was always beautiful, and that was all that the little Rabbit cared about. He didn't mind how he looked to other people because the nursery magic had made him Real, and when you are Real, shabbiness doesn't matter.

And then, one day, the Boy was ill.

His face grew very flushed, and he talked in his sleep, and his little body was so hot that it burned the Rabbit when he held him close. Strange people came and went in the nursery, and a light burned all night, and through it all, the little Velveteen Rabbit lay there, hidden from sight under the bedclothes, and he never stirred, for he was afraid that if they found him someone might take him away, and he knew that the

Boy needed him.

It was a long weary time, for the Boy was too ill to play, and the little Rabbit found it rather dull with nothing to do all day long. But he snuggled down patiently and looked forward to the time when the Boy should be well again, and they would go out in the garden amongst the flowers and the butterflies and play splendid games in the raspberry thicket like they used to. All sorts of delightful things he planned, and while the Boy lay half asleep, he crept up close to the pillow and whispered them in his ear. And presently, the fever turned, and the Boy got better. He was able to sit up in bed and look at picture books while the little Rabbit cuddled close at his side. And one day, they let him get up and dress.

It was a bright, sunny morning, and the windows stood wide open. They had carried the Boy out onto the balcony, wrapped in a shawl, and the little Rabbit lay tangled up among the bedclothes, thinking.

The Boy was going to the seaside tomorrow. Everything was arranged, and now it only remained to carry out the doctor's orders. They talked about it all while the little Rabbit lay under the bedclothes, with just his head peeping out, and listened. The room was to be disinfected, and all the books and toys that the Boy had played with in bed must be burnt.

"Hurrah!" thought the little Rabbit. "Tomorrow we shall go to the seaside!" For the boy had often talked of the seaside, and he wanted very much to see the big waves coming in, and the tiny crabs, and the sand castles.

Just then, Nana caught sight of him.

"How about his old Bunny?" she asked.

"That?" said the doctor. "Why, it's a mass of scarlet fever germs!–Burn it at once. What? Nonsense! Get him a new one. He mustn't have that any more!"

And so the little Rabbit was put into a sack with the old picture books and a lot of rubbish and carried out to the end of the garden behind the fowl-house. That was a fine place to make a bonfire. Only the gardener was too busy just then to attend to it. He had the potatoes to dig and the green peas to gather, but the next morning he promised to come quite early and burn the whole lot.

That night the Boy slept in a different bedroom, and he had a new bunny to sleep with him. It was a splendid bunny, all white plush with real glass eyes, but the Boy was too excited to care very much about it. For tomorrow, he was going to the seaside, and that in itself was such a wonderful thing that he could think of nothing else.

And while the Boy was asleep, dreaming of the seaside, the little Rabbit lay among the old picture books in the corner behind the fowl house, and he felt very lonely. The sack had been left untied, and so by wriggling a bit, he was able to get his head through the opening and look out. He was shivering a little, for he had always been used to sleeping in a proper bed, and by this time, his coat had worn so thin and threadbare from hugging that it was no longer any protection to him. Nearby, he could see the thicket of raspberry canes, growing tall and close like a tropical jungle, in whose shadow he had played with the Boy on bygone mornings. He thought of those long sunlit hours in the garden–how happy they were–and a great sadness came over him. He seemed to see them all pass before him, each more beautiful than the other, the fairy huts in the flower bed, the quiet evenings in the wood when he lay in the bracken and the little ants ran over his paws; the wonderful day when he first knew that he was Real. He thought of the Skin Horse, so wise and gentle, and all that he had told him. Of what use was it to be loved and lose one's beauty and become Real if it all ended like this? And a tear, a real tear, trickled down his little shabby velvet nose and fell to the ground.

And then a strange thing happened. For where the tear had fallen, a flower grew out of the ground, a mysterious flower, not at all like any that grew in the garden. It had slender green leaves the colour of emeralds and in the centre of the leaves, blossom like a golden cup. It was so beautiful that the little Rabbit forgot to cry and just lay there watching it. And presently, the blossom opened, and out of it there stepped a fairy.

She was quite the loveliest fairy in the whole world. Her dress was of pearl and dew drops, and there were flowers around her neck and in her hair, and her face was like the most perfect flower of all. And she came close to the little Rabbit and gathered him up in her arms and kissed him on his velveteen nose that was all damp from crying.

"Little Rabbit," she said, "don't you know who I am?"

The Rabbit looked up at her, and it seemed to him that he had seen her face before, but he couldn't think where.

"I am the nursery magic Fairy," she said. "I take care of all the playthings that the children have loved. When they are old and worn out and the children don't need them any more, then I come and take them away with me and turn them into Real."

"Wasn't I Real before?" asked the little Rabbit.

"You were Real to the Boy," the Fairy said, "because he loved you. Now you shall be Real to every one."

And she held the little Rabbit close in her arms and flew with him into the wood.

It was light now, for the moon had risen. All the forest was beautiful, and the fronds of the bracken shone like frosted silver. In the open glade between the tree trunks, the wild rabbits danced with their shadows on the velvet grass, but when they saw the Fairy, they all stopped dancing and stood round in a ring to stare at her.

"I've brought you a new playfellow," the Fairy said. "You must be very kind to him and teach him all he needs to know in Rabbit-land, for he is going to live with you for ever and ever!"

And she kissed the little Rabbit again and put him down on the grass.

"Run and play, little Rabbit!" she said.

But the little Rabbit sat quite still for a moment and never moved. When he saw all the wild rabbits dancing around him, he suddenly remembered about his hind legs, and he didn't want them to see that he was made all in one piece. He did not know that when the Fairy kissed him that last time, she had changed him altogether. And he might have sat there a long time, too shy to move if just then something hadn't tickled his nose, and before he thought what he was doing, he lifted his hind toe to scratch it.

And he found that he actually had hind legs! Instead of dingy velveteen, he had brown fur, soft and shiny, his ears twitched by themselves, and his whiskers were so long that they brushed the grass. He gave one leap, and the joy of using those hind legs was so great that he went springing about the turf on them, jumping sideways and whirling round as the others did, and he grew so excited that when at last he did stop to look for the Fairy she had gone.

He was a Real Rabbit at last, at home with the other rabbits.

Autumn passed and Winter, and in the Spring, when the days grew warm and sunny, the Boy went out to play in the wood behind the house. And while he was playing, two rabbits crept out from the bracken and peeped at him. One of them was brown all over, but the other had strange markings under his fur, as though long ago he had been spotted, and the spots still showed through. And about his little soft nose and his round black eyes, there was something familiar so that the Boy thought to himself:

"Why, he looks just like my old Bunny that was lost when I had scarlet fever!"

But he never knew that it really was his own Bunny, coming back to look at the child who had first helped him to be Real.

The Emperor's New Clothes

by Hans Christian Andersen

Many years ago, there lived an Emperor who was so monstrously fond of fine new clothes that he spent all his money on being really smart. He didn't care about his army. He didn't care for going to the play or driving out in the park unless it was to show his new clothes. He had a coat for every hour of the day, and just as people say about a king, that "he's holding a council", so in this country, they always said, "The Emperor is in his dressing room". In the great city where he lived, life was very pleasant, lots of strangers came there every day, and one day there, arrived two swindlers. They gave out that they were weavers and said they knew how to make the loveliest stuff that could possibly be imagined. Not only were the colours and patterns extraordinarily pretty, but the clothes that were made of the stuff had this marvellous property: that they were invisible to anyone who was either unfit for his situation or else was intolerably stupid. "Very excellent clothes those must be," thought the Emperor; "if I wore them I could tell which are the men in my realm who aren't fit for the posts they hold. I could tell clever people from stupid ones: to be sure that stuff must be made for me directly." Accordingly he gave the two swindlers a large sum in advance so that they might begin their work. They set up two looms and pretended to be working, but they hadn't a vestige of anything on the looms. In hot haste, they demanded the finest of silk and the best of gold, which they stuffed into their own pockets, and they worked away at the bare looms till any hour of the night.

"I should like to know how they are getting on with the stuff," thought the Emperor. But to tell the truth, he had a little misgiving when he reflected that anyone who was stupid or unsuited to his post couldn't see the stuff. Of course, he was confident that he needn't be afraid for himself: all the same, he decided to send someone else first to see how things were. Everybody in the whole city knew what a marvellous power was in the stuff, and everybody was agog to see how incompetent and how stupid his neighbour was.

"I'll send my good old minister down to the weavers," thought the Emperor; "he can quite well see how the stuff is shaping: he's an intelligent man, and no one is better fitted for his post than he."

So the worthy old minister went into the hall where the two swindlers were sitting, working at the bare loom. "Heaven help us," thought the old minister, staring with all his eyes; "I can't see a thing",; but he didn't say so.

Both the swindlers begged him to be pleased to step nearer and asked if there was not a pretty pattern and beautiful colours, and they pointed to the bare looms, and the poor old minister kept staring at it, but he couldn't see anything because there was nothing to be seen. "Gracious goodness!" thought he; "can I be stupid? I never thought so, and nobody must get to know it. Can I be unfit for my office? No, no! It won't do for me to say I can't see the stuff." "Well, have you nothing to say about it?" said the one who was weaving.

"Oh, it's charming! Most delightful!" said the old minister, looking through his spectacles. "The pattern! The colour! Yes, indeed, I must tell the Emperor I am infinitely pleased with it."

"We are glad indeed to hear it," said both the weavers and proceeded to describe the colours, naming them and the uncommon pattern. The old minister listened carefully so as to be able to repeat it when he went back to the Emperor, and so he did. The swindlers now demanded more money and more silk and gold to be used in the weaving. They pocketed it all; not a thread was put up, but they went on, as before, weaving at the bare loom.

Very soon, the Emperor sent another honest official over to see how the weaving progressed and whether the stuff would be ready soon. He fared just like the minister. He looked and looked, but as there was nothing there but the empty loom, nothing could be seen.

"Well, isn't that a fine piece of stuff?" said both the swindlers, exhibiting and explaining the lovely patterns that weren't there at all. "Stupid, I am not," thought the man; "it must be my nice post that I'm not fit for? That would be a good joke! But I mustn't let people notice anything." Whereupon he praised the stuff which he couldn't see and assured them of his pleasure in the pretty colours and the exquisite pattern. "Yes, it is positively sweet," he told the Emperor. Everybody in the city was talking of the splendid stuff.

At last, the Emperor decided to see it while it was still on the loom, with a large suite of select people— among them the two worthy officials who had been there before. He went over to the two clever swindlers, who were now weaving with all their might; only without a vestige of a thread.

"Now, is not that magnificent?" said both the worthy

officials. "Will Your Majesty deign to note the beauty of the pattern and the colours"; and they pointed to the bare loom, for they supposed that all the rest could certainly see the stuff. "What's the meaning of this?" thought the Emperor. "I can't see a thing! This is terrible! Am I stupid? Am I not fit to be Emperor? That would be the most frightful thing that could befall me. Oh, it's very pretty, it has my all-highest approval!" said he, nodding complacently and gazing on the empty loom: of course, he wouldn't say he could see nothing. The whole of the suite he had with him looked and looked but got no more out of that than the rest. However, they said, as the Emperor had said: "Oh, it's very pretty!" And they advised him to put on this splendid new stuff for the first time on the occasion of a great procession which was to take place shortly. "Magnificent! Exquisite! Excellent!" went from mouth to mouth; the whole company was in the highest state of gratification. The Emperor gave each of the swindlers a knight's cross to hang in his buttonhole and the title of "Gentleman in Weaving".

The whole night, previous to the morning on which the procession was to take place, the swindlers sat up and had upwards of sixteen candles lit; people could see they were hard put to it to get the Emperor's new clothes finished. They pretended to be taking the stuff off the loom; they clipped with scissors in the air, they sewed with a needle without thread—and finally, they said: "Look now! The clothes are finished." The Emperor with the noblest of his personal attendants came thither himself. Each of the swindlers raised an arm in the air as if holding something up and said: "See, here are the hose, this is the coat, this is the mantle, and so on. It is as light as a spider's web, you would think you had nothing whatever on; but that is, of course, the beauty of it." "Yes," said all the attendants; but they couldn't see anything, for there was nothing to be seen.

"Will Your Imperial Majesty be graciously pleased to take off your clothes?" said the swindlers. "We can then put the new ones upon you here, before the large mirror." The Emperor took off all his clothes, and the swindlers behaved as if they were handing him each piece of the new suit which was supposed to have been made, and they put their hands about his waist and pretended to tie something securely. It was the train. The Emperor turned and twisted himself in front of the glass.

"Heaven! How well it fits? How beautifully it sets," said everyone. "The pattern! The colours! It is indeed a noble costume!"

"They are waiting, outside, with the canopy which is to be borne over Your Majesty in the procession," said the chief master of the ceremonies. "Very well, I am ready," said the Emperor; "doesn't it set well?" Once more, he turned about in front of the glass so that it might seem as if he was really examining his finery. The lords in waiting, who were to carry the train, fumbled with their hands in the direction of the floor as if they were picking the train up. They walked on, holding the air—they didn't want to let it be noticed that they could see nothing at all.

So the Emperor walked in the procession under the beautiful canopy, and everybody in the streets and at the windows said: "Lord! How splendid the Emperor's new clothes are. What a lovely train he has to his coat! What a beautiful fit it is!" Nobody wanted to be detected seeing nothing: that would mean that he was no good at his job, or that he was very stupid. None of the Emperor's costumes had ever been such a success.

"But he hasn't got anything on!" said a little child. "Lor! Just hark at the innocent," said its father. And one whispered to the other what the child had said: "That little child there says he hasn't got anything on."

"Why, he hasn't got anything on!" the whole crowd was shouting at last, and the Emperor's flesh crept, for it seemed to him they were right. "But all the same," he thought to himself, "I must go through with the procession." So he held himself more proudly than before, and the lords in waiting walked on bearing the train—the train that wasn't there at all.

The Town Mouse and the Country Mouse

by Aesop

A Town Mouse once visited a relative who lived in the country. For lunch, the Country Mouse served wheat stalks, roots, and acorns, with a dash of cold water for drink. The Town Mouse ate very sparingly, nibbling a little of this and a little of that, and by her manner, making it very plain that she ate the simple food only to be polite.

After the meal, the friends had a long talk, or rather

the Town Mouse talked about her life in the city while the Country Mouse listened. They then went to bed in a cozy nest in the hedgerow and slept in quiet and comfort until morning. In her sleep, the Country Mouse dreamed she was a Town Mouse with all the luxuries and delights of city life that her friend had described for her. So the next day, when the Town Mouse asked the Country Mouse to go home with her to the city, she gladly said yes.

When they reached the mansion in which the Town Mouse lived, they found on the table in the dining room the leavings of a very fine banquet. There were sweetmeats and jellies, pastries, delicious cheeses, indeed, the most tempting foods that a Mouse can imagine. But just as the Country Mouse was about to nibble a dainty bit of pastry, she heard a Cat mew loudly and scratched at the door. In great fear, the Mice scurried to a hiding place, where they lay quite still for a long time, hardly daring to breathe. When at last they ventured back to the feast, the door opened suddenly and in came the servants to clear the table, followed by the House Dog.

The Country Mouse stopped in the Town Mouse's den only long enough to pick up her carpet bag and umbrella.

"You may have luxuries and dainties that I have not," she said as she hurried away, "but I prefer my plain food and simple life in the country with the peace and security that go with it."

Teeny Tiny

by Paul Galdone

Once upon a time, there was a teeny-tiny woman who lived in a teeny-tiny house in a teeny-tiny village. Now, one day this teeny-tiny woman put on her teeny-tiny bonnet and went out of her teeny-tiny house to take a teeny-tiny walk. And when this teeny-tiny woman had gone a teeny-tiny way, she came to a teeny-tiny gate, so the teeny-tiny woman opened the teeny-tiny gate and went into a teeny-tiny churchyard. And when this teeny-tiny woman had got into the teeny-tiny churchyard, she saw a teeny-tiny bone on a teeny-tiny grave, and the teeny-tiny woman said to her teeny-tiny self, "This teeny-tiny bone will make me some teeny-tiny soup for my teeny-tiny supper." So the teeny-tiny woman put the teeny-tiny bone into her teeny-tiny pocket and went home to her teeny-tiny house.

Now when the teeny-tiny woman got home to her teeny-tiny house, she was a teeny-tiny bit tired, so she went up her teeny-tiny stairs to her teeny-tiny bed and put the teeny-tiny bone into a teeny-tiny cupboard. And when this teeny-tiny woman had been to sleep a teeny-tiny time, she was awakened by a teeny-tiny voice from the teeny-tiny cupboard, which said:

"Give me my bone!"

And this teeny-tiny woman was a teeny-tiny frightened, so she hid her teeny-tiny head under the teeny-tiny clothes and went to sleep again. And when she had been to sleep again a teeny-tiny time, the teeny-tiny voice again cried out from the teeny-tiny cupboard a teeny-tiny louder, "Give me my bone!"

This made the teeny-tiny woman a teeny-tiny more frightened, so she hid her teeny-tiny head a teeny-tiny further under the teeny-tiny clothes. And when the teeny-tiny woman had been to sleep again a teeny-tiny time, the teeny-tiny voice from the teeny-tiny cupboard said again a teeny-tiny louder,

"Give me my bone!"

And this teeny-tiny woman was a teeny-tiny bit more frightened, but she put her teeny-tiny head out of the teeny-tiny clothes and said in her loudest teeny-tiny voice, "TAKE IT!"

Hans, Who Made the Princess Laugh

by Peter Christen Asbjörnsen

Once upon a time, there was a king, who had a daughter, and she was so lovely that the reports of her beauty went far and wide; but she was so melancholy that she never laughed, and besides she was so grand and proud that she said "No" to all who came to woo her—she would not have any of them, were they ever so fine, whether they were princes or noblemen.

The king was tired of this whim of hers long ago and thought she ought to get married like other people;

there was nothing she need wait for—she was old enough, and she would not be any richer either, for she was to have half the kingdom, which she inherited after her mother.

So he made known every Sunday after the service, from the steps outside the church, that he that could make his daughter laugh should have both her and half the kingdom. But if there were anyone who tried and could not make her laugh, he would have three red stripes cut out of his back and salt rubbed into them— and, sad to relate, there were many sore backs in that kingdom. Lovers from the south and from the north, from the east and from the west, came to try their luck —they thought it was an easy thing to make a princess laugh. They were a queer lot altogether, but for all their cleverness and for all the tricks and pranks they played, the princess was just as serious and immovable as ever.

But close to the palace lived a man who had three sons, and they had also heard that the king had made known that he who could make the princess laugh should have her and half the kingdom.

The eldest of the brothers wanted to try first, and away he went; and when he came to the palace, he told the king he wouldn't mind trying to make the princess laugh.

"Yes, yes! that's all very well," said the king, "but I am afraid it's of very little use, my man. There have been many here to try their luck, but my daughter is just as sad, and I am afraid it is no good trying. I do not like to see any more suffer on that account."

But the lad thought he would try anyhow. It couldn't be such a difficult thing to make a princess laugh at him, for had not everybody, both grand and simple, laughed so many a time at him when he served as a soldier and went through his drill under Sergeant Nils?

So he went out on the terrace outside the princess's windows and began drilling just as if Sergeant Nils himself were there. But all in vain! The princess sat just as serious and immovable as before, and so they took him and cut three broad, red stripes out of his back and sent him home.

He had no sooner arrived home than his second brother wanted to set out and try his luck. He was a schoolmaster, and a funny figure he was altogether. He had one leg shorter than the other and limped terribly when he walked. One moment he was no bigger than a boy, but the next moment when he raised himself up on his long leg, he was as big and tall as a giant—and besides, he was great at preaching.

When he came to the palace and said that he wanted to make the princess laugh, the king thought that it was not so unlikely that he might; "but I pity you, if you don't succeed," said the king, "for we cut the stripes broader and broader for every one that tries."

So the schoolmaster went out on the terrace and took his place outside the princess's window, where he began preaching and chanting, imitating seven of the parsons, and reading and singing just like seven of the clerks whom they had had in the parish.

The king laughed at the schoolmaster till he was obliged to hold on to the door-post, and the princess was just on the point of smiling, but suddenly she was as sad and immovable as ever, and so it fared no better with Paul the schoolmaster than with Peter, the soldier —for Peter and Paul were their names, you must know!

So they took Paul and cut three red stripes out of his back, put salt into them, and sent him home again.

Well, the youngest brother thought he would have a try next. His name was Hans. But the brothers laughed and made fun of him and showed him their sore backs. Besides, the father would not give him leave to go, for he said it was no use his trying, who had so little sense; all he could do was to sit in a corner on the hearth, like a cat, rooting about in the ashes and cutting chips. But Hans would not give in—he begged and prayed so long till they got tired of his whimpering, and so he got leave to go to the king's palace and try his luck.

When he arrived at the palace, he did not say he had come to try to make the princess laugh but asked if he could get a situation there. No, they had no situation for him; but Hans was not so easily put off—they might want one to carry wood and water for the kitchenmaid in such a big place as that, he said. Yes, the king thought so too, and to get rid of the lad, he gave him leave to remain there and carry wood and water for the kitchenmaid.

One day, when he was going to fetch water from the brook, he saw a big fish in the water just under an old root of a fir tree, which the current had carried all the soil away from. He put his bucket quietly under the fish and caught it. As he was going home to the palace, he met an old woman leading a golden goose.

"Good day, grandmother!" said Hans. "That's a fine bird you have got there; and such splendid feathers too! he shines a long way off. If one had such feathers, one needn't be chopping firewood."

The woman thought just as much of the fish which Hans had in the bucket and said if Hans would give her the fish, he should have the golden goose; and this goose was such that if anyone touched it, he would be sticking fast to it if he only said: "If you'll come along, then hang on."

Yes, Hans would willingly exchange on those terms. "A bird is as good as a fish any day," he said to himself. "If it is as you say, I might use it instead of a fish-hook," he said to the woman and felt greatly pleased with the possession of the goose.

He had not gone far before he met another old woman. When she saw the splendid golden goose, she must go and stroke it. She made herself so friendly and spoke so nicely to Hans and asked him to let her stroke that lovely golden goose of his.

"Oh, yes!" said Hans, "but you mustn't pluck off any of its feathers!"

Just as she stroked the bird, Hans said: "If you'll come along, then hang on!"

The woman pulled and tore, but she had to hang on, whether she would or not, and Hans walked on as if he only had the goose with him.

When he had gone some distance, he met a man who had spite against the woman for a trick she had played upon him. When he saw that she fought so hard to get free and seemed to hang on so fast, he thought he might safely venture to pay her off for the grudge he owed her, and so he gave her a kick.

"If you'll come along, then hang on!" said Hans, and the man had to hang on and limp along on one leg, whether he would or not, and when he tried to tear himself loose, he made it still worse for himself, for he was very nearly falling on his back whenever he struggled to get free.

So on they went till they came into the neighborhood of the palace. There they met the king's smith; he was on his way to the smithy and had a large pair of tongs in his hand. This smith was a merry fellow and was always full of mad pranks and tricks, and when he saw this procession coming jumping and limping along, he began laughing till he was bent in two, but suddenly he said:

"This must be a new flock of geese for the princess: but who can tell which is goose and which is gander? I suppose it must be the gander toddling on in front.

Goosey, goosey!" he called, and pretended to be strewing corn out of his hands as when feeding geese.

But they did not stop. The woman and the man only looked in great rage at the smith for making a game of them. So said the smith: "It would be great fun to see if I could stop the whole flock, many as they are!"—He was a strong man and seized the old man with his tongs from behind in his trousers, and the man shouted and struggled hard, but Hans said:

"If you'll come along, then hang on!"

And so the smith had to hang on too. He bent his back and stuck his heels in the ground when they went up a hill and tried to get away, but it was of no use; he stuck on to the other as if he had been screwed fast in the great vice in the smithy, and whether he liked it or not, he had to dance along with the others.

When they came near the palace, the farm dog ran against them and barked at them as if they were a gang of tramps, and when the princess came to look out of her window to see what was the matter and saw this procession she burst out laughing. But Hans was not satisfied with that. "Just wait a bit, and she will laugh still louder very soon," he said and made a tour around the palace with his followers.

When they came past the kitchen, the door was open, and the cook was just boiling porridge, but when she saw Hans and his train after him, she rushed out of the door with the porridge stick in one hand and a big ladle full of boiling porridge in the other, and she laughed till her sides shook; but when she saw the smith there as well, she thought she would have burst with laughter. When she had had a regular good laugh, she looked at the golden goose again and thought it was so lovely that she must stroke it.

"Hans, Hans!" she cried and ran after him with the ladle in her hand; "just let me stroke that lovely bird of yours."

"Rather let her stroke me!" said the smith.

"Very well," said Hans.

But when the cook heard this, she got very angry. "What is it you say!" she cried and gave the smith a smack with the ladle.

"If you'll come along, then hang on!" said Hans, and so she stuck fast to the others too, and for all her scolding and all her tearing and pulling, she had to limp along with them.

And when they came past the princess's window again, she was still there waiting for them, but when she saw that they had got hold of the cook too, with the ladle and porridge stick, she laughed till the king had to hold her up. So Hans got the princess and half the kingdom, and they had a wedding which was heard of far and wide.

Mercury and the Woodman

by Aesop

Apoor Woodman was cutting down a tree near the edge of a deep pool in the forest. It was late in the day, and the Woodman was tired. He had been working since sunrise, and his strokes were not so sure as they had been early that morning. Thus it happened that the axe slipped and flew out of his hands into the pool.

The Woodman was in despair. The axe was all he possessed with which to make a living, and he had not enough money to buy a new one. As he stood wringing his hands and weeping, the god Mercury suddenly appeared and asked what the trouble was. The Woodman told what had happened, and straightway the kind Mercury dived into the pool. When he came up again, he held a wonderful golden axe.

"Is this your axe?" Mercury asked the Woodman.

"No," answered the honest Woodman, "that is not my axe."

Mercury laid the golden axe on the bank and sprang back into the pool. This time he brought up an axe of silver, but the Woodman declared again that his axe was just an ordinary one with a wooden handle.

Mercury dived down for the third time, and when he came up again, he had the very axe that had been lost.

The poor Woodman was very glad that his axe had been found and could not thank the kind god enough. Mercury was greatly pleased with the Woodman's honesty.

"I admire your honesty," he said, "and as a reward you may have all three axes, the gold and the silver as well as your own."

The happy Woodman returned to his home with his treasures, and soon the story of his good fortune was known to everybody in the village. Now there were several Woodmen in the village who believed that they could easily win the same good fortune. They hurried out into the woods, one here, one there, and hiding their axes in the bushes, pretended they had lost them. Then they wept and wailed and called on Mercury to help them.

And indeed, Mercury did appear, first to this one, then to that. To each one he showed an axe of gold, and each one eagerly claimed it to be the one he had lost. But Mercury did not give them the golden axe. Oh no! Instead, he gave them each a hard whack over the head with it and sent them home. And when they returned the next day to look for their own axes, they were nowhere to be found.

missing, and usually, it was a little baby chick that was gone. The worst of it was that no one else knew any more about it than she did. To be sure, little Bantam Rooster had said it was the hawk. But then Bantam always thought he knew everything and was almost always wrong so nobody ever believed anything he said.

Besides, if it had been, the big white cock would have known it, for the big white cock knew everything. He was the king of the barnyard and took care of them all. He had a bright red comb and beautiful, long, green tail feathers, and Mamma Goose thought him the most wonderful being in the whole world.

But something seemed to be wrong with him, too. He did not crow half so often as he used to, and his beautiful red comb did not stand stiff and straight anymore. It drooped to one side, and he looked very tired and very unhappy, as if he, too, had been trying to think. But if he did not know what it was that came night after night, then nobody knew.

Everything had been very different when old Fido lived in his little house by the barnyard gate. Nothing had ever happened to trouble them then. But old Fido was gone now, and nobody knew about that either. One morning after breakfast, he had trotted off behind the wagon, and nobody had seen him since. Everyone liked old Fido, and they all missed him, but he had never come back, and his little house stood empty all night long.

So she waddled down to the brook to get them. Some thought that he had gone to take care of the sheep who lived in the big field on the other side of the hill. But it was only little Bantam Rooster who said so. Nobody knew. Things had been better, though, before Fido went away, for he had always stayed awake all night and watched to see that no harm came to any of them.

Then suddenly, Mamma Goose had a thought and a very bright idea it was, too. She would stay awake all night herself and watch and see with her own eyes what it was that carried away the little chicks. As soon as she had made this plan, she stopped thinking, for it was such hard work, and the sun was getting very hot on her poor head. Besides, the goslings had been in the water long enough. They never did know when to come out!

So she waddled down to the brook to get them. Then they all went for a walk in the meadow where the red clover-tops nod in the wind, and Mamma Goose did no more thinking that day.

But when night came, she did not forget her plan. As soon as the sun had gone down behind the hill, the chickens all perched themselves along the roost with the big white cock at the end of the row, and soon they were all fast asleep. Little Red Hen gathered her chicks under her wing to keep them cosy and warm, and then she, too, went to sleep.

Mamma Goose tucked her babies in also and spread

her wings wide over them all, but she did not go to sleep.

Instead, she kept both eyes wide open and stared straight at the big white cock, so that she might not go to sleep without knowing it. It was very hard to sit so long in the dark and keep awake. First, one eye and then the other would close tight, but Mamma Goose would stretch them wide open again and stare harder than ever at the big cock, and then she saw that the cock was watching, too, and that made it much easier.

Then it happened after a long time when the moon had climbed high above the trees, and everything was very quiet, that a long, slim fox stole softly beneath the fence and came creeping--creeping across the barnyard. Mamma Goose was so frightened that she almost said, "Quack! quack!" out loud, but still, she kept her eyes on the big white cock, and that was a great help.

The fox was creeping softly toward the roost where the chickens slept in a row,—but not straight toward it. He was keeping as far away from old Fido's house as he possibly could. Although she was so frightened, Mamma Goose wondered why. She had always heard that the fox was afraid of old Fido, but didn't he know that Fido was far away? Didn't he know that his little house was empty? It did not take the fox long, however, to creep softly past it, and in the morning, another little chick was gone!

No one would listen! But a new thought had come to Mamma Goose. If the fox would not go near old Fido's house, then he could not find the goslings if they hid inside. It seemed to Mamma Goose the only thing to do and a very sensible plan indeed. She would ask all the chickens to come in, too, and then they would all be safe!

But when she went the next day to her best friends and told them about her plan, most of them only made fun of her, and all of them turned their backs on her. No one would listen!

But Mamma Goose was not to be talked out of it. If the others wished to sit still and let the fox carry them away one at a time, that was one thing, but for her to do nothing to keep her little goslings safe—that was quite another.

So that very evening, when the sun had gone down behind the hill, and the chickens had perched themselves on the roost with the big cock at the end, Mamma Goose led all the little goslings into Fido's house. Everyone laughed when she went in, but Mamma Goose had made up her mind, and she kept straight on as if she had not heard them! But the big white cock--he did not laugh at her!

So every night, Mamma Goose led her babies into Fido's house and every morning brought them out again safe and whole. But always, a little chick was missing!

Then one night, when the sun was sinking low, the big white cock flew up to the top of the fence and crowed. All the chickens listened then while he told them that they were everyone to go into old Fido's house that night with Mamma Goose; for that was the only way to keep the fox from carrying them all away.

The big white cock flew up to the top of the fence and crowed. Now when the big cock said that they were to do anything, it was always done, and no words about it! So that night, all the chickens went into Fido's house. It was all they could do to get in, for the house was not large, and some of them were not polite and pushed against the others to make more room. But the big cock did all he could to keep them in order, and at last, all the little chicks went to sleep.

But the next morning, when the farmer's boy came to scatter the corn for breakfast, he looked at the empty roost and did not know what to think!

By and by, however, he found them, and at first, he only laughed, but after he had seen that no little chick was missing, he looked as if he were thinking, too. And that evening, when the sun had gone down behind the hill, the farmer's boy came back, and who do you think was with him?--old Fido, wagging his tail and looking as if he were very glad to get back!

The big white cock and all the chickens were just as glad as he was. For now, they knew that the fox would never come anymore. Mamma Goose, too, was just as glad as the rest. For now, she knew that she would never need to bother herself to think about the goslings again.

But she didn't dream that anything more could happen, and she was too much surprised to think about anything at all when old Fido came trotting straight up to her, wagged his tail just for her alone, and told her how glad he was that she had been wise enough to use his house, and had taken such good care of the chickens while he was gone, and what a sensible little goose he thought she was! You might almost have knocked Mamma Goose over with one of her own feathers! She couldn't imagine who had told him.

But perhaps it was the big white cock.

Thumbelina

by Hans Christian Andersen

Once upon a time, there was a woman who very much wanted to have a little tiny child but didn't know where she could get one from, so she went to an old witch and said to her: "I do so want to have a little child; will you kindly tell me where I can get one?"

"Oh, we can manage that," said the witch, "there's a barleycorn for you! it isn't the kind that grows in the farmers' fields or that the chickens have to eat; just put it in a flower-pot, and you shall see what you shall see."

"Much obliged," said the woman, and gave the witch twelve pence, and went home and planted the barleycorn; and very soon a fine large flower came up which looked just like a tulip, but the petals were closed up tight as if it were still a bud.

"That's a charming flower," said the woman and gave it a kiss on its pretty red and yellow petals. But just as she kissed it, the flower gave a loud crack and opened. You could see it was a real tulip, only right in the middle of it, on the green stool that is there sat a tiny little girl, as delicate and pretty as could be. She was only a thumb joint long, so she was called Thumbelina. She was given a splendid lacquered walnut shell for a cradle, blue-violet leaves for mattresses, and a rose leaf for a counterpane. There she slept at night, but in the daytime, she played about on the table, where the woman had put a plate, around which she put a whole wreath of flowers with their stalks in the water; and on the water floated a large tulip leaf on which Thumbelina could sit and sail from one side of the plate to the other. She had two white horse hairs to row with. It was really beautiful to see her; she could sing too—oh, so delicately and prettily as no one had ever heard.

One night, as she lay in her pretty bed, a horrid Toad came hopping in at the window, which had a broken pane. The Toad was ugly and big and wet and hopped right down onto the table where Thumbelina lay asleep under her rose leaf.

"That would make a lovely wife for my son," said the Toad, so she took hold of the walnut shell where Thumbelina slept and hopped off with her through the window and down into the garden. Through it flowed a big broad stream, but just at the edge, it was marshy and muddy, and there the Toad lived with her son. Ugh! he was ugly and horrid, too, just like his mother. "Koäx, koäx, brekke-ke-kex," was all he could say when he saw the pretty little girl in the walnut shell. "Don't talk so loud, you'll wake her," said the old Toad, "and she might run away from us now, for she's as light as a swansdown feather. We'll put her out in the river on one of the broad water-lily leaves. It'll be like an island for her, she's so little and light. She can run about there while we get the drawing-room under the mud ready for you two to make your home in."

There were a great many water lilies growing out in the stream, with broad green leaves that looked as if they were floating on the water, and the leaf that was furthest out was also the biggest of all. To this leaf, the old Toad swam out and put the walnut shell with Thumbelina on it. The poor little wretch woke up very early in the morning, and when she saw where she was, she began to cry—oh, so bitterly!—for there was water all around the big leaf, and she couldn't possibly get to land.

The old Toad stayed down in the mud and set about decorating her room with rushes and yellow water-lily buds so as to make it nice and neat for her new daughter-in-law, and then she swam out with her ugly son to the leaf where Thumbelina stood; they were going to fetch her pretty bed and put it up in the bridal chamber before she came there herself. The old Toad curtsied low in the water before her and said: "I present my son to you. He is going to be your husband, and you will have a delightful life with him down in the mud."

"Koäx, koäx, brekke-ke-kex," was all the son could say.

So they took the beautiful little bed and swam off with it while Thumbelina sat all alone on the green leaf crying, for she didn't want to live with the horrid Toad or have her ugly son for a husband. The little fishes, swimming beneath in the water, had seen the Toad and heard what she said, so they put their heads up; they wanted to see the little girl. But as soon as they saw her, they thought her so pretty that it grieved them very much to think that she had to go down to the ugly Toad. No, that could never be. So they swarmed together down in the water, all round the green stalk that held the leaf she was on, and gnawed it through with their teeth; so the leaf went floating down the stream, and bore Thumbelina far, far away, where the Toad could not go. Thumbelina sailed past many places, and the little birds in the bushes saw her and sang, "What a pretty little maid!" The leaf floated further and further away with her, and thus it was that Thumbelina went on her travels.

A beautiful little white butterfly kept flying around her and at last settled on the leaf, for it took a fancy to

Thumbelina, and she was very happy, for now, the Toad could not get at her, and everything was beautiful where she was sailing: the sun shone on the water and made it glitter like gold. She took her sash and tied one end of it to the butterfly, and the other end she fastened to the leaf, and it went along much faster with her, for, of course, she was standing on the leaf. Just then, a large Cockchafer came flying by and caught sight of her, and in an instant, he had grasped her slender body in his claws and flew up into a tree with her. But the green leaf went floating downstream and the butterfly with it, for he was tied to the leaf and could not get loose.

Goodness! how frightened poor Thumbelina was when the Cockchafer flew up into the tree with her. But she was most of all grieved for the pretty white butterfly which she had tied to the leaf, for unless it got loose, it would be starved to death. However, the Cockchafer cared nothing about that. He alighted with her on the largest green leaf on the tree, gave her honey out of the flowers to eat, and told her she was very pretty, though she wasn't in the least like a Cockchafer. Later on, all the other Cockchafers that lived in the tree came and paid calls. They looked at Thumbelina, and the young lady Cockchafers brushed their feelers and said: "Why, she's only got two legs! a wretched sight!" "She's got no feelers," they said. "She's quite thin in the waist. Dreadful! She looks just like a human being! How ugly she is!" said all the lady Cockchafers, yet Thumbelina was as pretty as could be, and so thought the Cockchafer who had carried her off; but when all the rest said she was horrid, he came to think so too at last, and wouldn't have anything to do with her, she could go wherever she chose. They flew down from the tree with her and put her on a daisy, and there she sat and cried because she was so ugly that the Cockchafers wouldn't keep her—and yet she was the prettiest thing you could imagine, and delicate and bright like the loveliest rose-leaf. All the summer through, poor Thumbelina lived quite alone in the big wood. She plaited herself a bed of green stalks and hung it up under a large dock leaf so as to be out of the rain. She picked the honey out of the flowers and ate it, and she drank the dew which lay every morning on the leaves. There she spent the summer and the autumn, but then came winter, the long cold winter. All the birds that had sung so prettily to her flew their way; the trees and flowers withered, and the big dock leaf under which she had lived rolled up and turned to nothing but a dry yellow stalk, and she was terribly cold, for her clothes were in rags, and she herself was so little and delicate. Poor Thumbelina! She was like to be frozen to death! Then it began to snow, and every snowflake that fell on her was just as when anybody throws a whole shovelful on any of us—for we are big, and Thumbelina was only an inch high. So she wrapped herself up in a dead leaf, but there was no warmth in it, and she shivered with the cold.

Just outside the wood where she was now laying a large cornfield, but the corn had long been off it, and only the bare, dry stubble stuck out of the frozen ground. This was like a whole forest for her to get through, and oh! how she did shiver with the cold! At last, she came to a Fieldmouse's door, which was a little hole down among the stubble. There the Fieldmouse lived snug and happy, with a whole room full of corn, a lovely kitchen and a dining room. Poor Thumbelina went up to the door just like any little beggar girl and asked for a little bit of barleycorn, for she hadn't had anything whatever to eat for two days. "Poor little thing," said the Fieldmouse, who was at heart a kind old fieldmouse, "you come into my warm room and have dinner with me." And as she had taken a liking to Thumbelina, she said: "You can stay the winter with me and welcome, only you'll have to keep my room nice and clean and tell me stories, for I'm very fond of them." And Thumbelina did as the kind old Fieldmouse asked and had a very pleasant time of it.

"We shall soon be having a visitor," said the Fieldmouse. "My neighbour calls on me every weekday; he's even better housed than I am; his rooms are big, and he goes about in such a beautiful black velvet coat! Ah, if only you could get him for a husband! You would be well set up. But he can't see. Mind and tell him the very prettiest stories you know!" But Thumbelina didn't care much about this—she didn't want to marry the neighbour, for he was a Mole. He came and paid a call in his black velvet coat. He was very well off and very learned, the Fieldmouse said: "His mansion was more than twenty times the size of hers, and he was very well informed"; but he didn't like the sun and the pretty flowers, and abused them, for he had never seen them. Thumbelina had to sing, and she sang both

"Cockchafer, Cockchafer fly away home" and also "The monk walked in the meadow", and the Mole fell in love with her for her pretty voice, but said nothing about it, for he was a very cautious man.

He had recently dug a big passage through the earth from his house to theirs and gave the Fieldmouse and Thumbelina leave to walk there whenever they liked, but he begged them not to be frightened at the dead bird that lay in the passage—a whole bird with beak and feathers which had certainly been dead only a little time, at the beginning of the winter and was now buried just where he had made his passage.

The Mole took a bit of touchwood in his mouth (for that shines like fire in the dark) and went in front and lighted them along through the long dark passage, and when they got to where the dead bird lay, the Mole pushed his broad back against the ceiling and lifted the earth so that there was a big hole which let in the light: in the middle of this floor lay a dead swallow with its pretty wings close against its sides and its legs and head down in among its feathers: the poor bird had certainly died of cold. Thumbelina was very sorry for it; she was fond of all the little birds that had sung and twittered so prettily to her all the summer long, but the Mole kicked it with his short leg and said: "He won't be squeaking any more! It must be wretched to be born a little bird! Thank God, none of my children will be like that. A bird has nothing but its twit, twit, and is bound to starve to death in winter."

"Yes, you may well say so as a reasonable man," said

the Fieldmouse; "what has the bird to show for all its twit, twit, when winter comes? Why, it has to starve and freeze, and yet they're so proud about it!"

Thumbelina said nothing, but when the others turned their backs on the bird, she stooped down and parted the feathers that covered its head and kissed its dead eyes. "Perhaps this was the one that sang to me so prettily in the summer," she thought; "what a lot of pleasure it gave me, the dear little bird."

The Mole now stopped up the hole through which the daylight shone in and saw the ladies' home. But that night, Thumbelina couldn't sleep at all, so she got out of bed and plaited a nice large coverlet of hay, and carried it down and spread it about the dead bird, and then she laid some soft cotton wool she had found in the Fieldmouse's room, on the bird's sides, so that it might lie warmly on the cold ground. "Farewell, you pretty little bird," said she; "farewell, and thank you for your lovely singing in the summer when all the trees were green and the sun shone so hot on us." She laid her head against the bird's heart and got quite a fright all at once, for it seemed as if something was knocking inside! It was the bird's heart. The bird was not dead; it was only in a swoon, and now that it was warmed, it came to life again.

In autumn, you know, all the swallows fly away to the warm countries, but if there is one that lags behind, it gets frozen so that it tumbles down quite dead and lies where it fell, and the cold snow covers it over.

Thumbelina really shivered, so frightened was she: for the bird was enormously big compared with her, who was only an inch high: but she took courage and laid the cotton wool closer about the poor swallow, and folded a peppermint leaf, that she had for her own counterpane, and put it over the bird's head. Next night she stole down to it again, and this time it was quite alive but so weak that it could only open its eyes for a second and look at Thumbelina, who stood there with a bit of touchwood in her hand; for other light, she had none.

"Thank you, you pretty little child," the sick swallow said to her, "I've been beautifully warmed. Soon I shall get back my strength and be able to fly about again in the warm sun outside."

"Oh," said Thumbelina, "but it's dreadfully cold outside, snowing and freezing! You must stay in your warm bed. I'll nurse you, be sure!" Then she brought the swallow some water in the leaf of a plant, and it drank and told her how it had hurt its wing on a thorn bush and so couldn't fly as well as the other swallows when they set out to fly, far, far away to the warm countries. At last, it had fallen to the ground, but it couldn't remember anymore and didn't know in the least how it had gotten to where it was.

All the winter it stayed down there, and Thumbelina was very kind to it and got very fond of it, but neither the Mole nor the Fieldmouse heard anything whatever about it; they disliked the poor wretched swallow.

As soon as spring came and the sun's warmth got into the ground, the swallow said goodbye to Thumbelina, who opened the hole which the Mole had made above. The sun shone in delightfully, and the swallow asked if Thumbelina would not come with it: she could sit on its back, and they would fly away into the greenwood. But Thumbelina knew that it would grieve the old Fieldmouse if she left her like that. "No, I can't," said Thumbelina. "Good-bye, good-bye, you kind pretty maid," said the swallow and flew out into the sunshine. Thumbelina stood looking after it, and the water stood in her eyes, for she was very fond of the poor swallow.

"Twit, twit," sang the bird and flew off into the greenwood.

Thumbelina was very unhappy; she got no chance to go out into the warm sunshine because the corn that had been sown in the field over the Fieldmouse's house was grown tall and made a thick forest for the poor little maid, no more than an inch high.

"This summer, you must make your trousseau," the Fieldmouse told her; for their neighbour, the tiresome Mole in the black velvet coat, had proposed to her. "You shall have both woollen and linen—something to sit in and to lie on when you are the Mole's wife." So Thumbelina had to spin on the distaff, and the Fieldmouse hired four spiders to spin and weave day and night. Every evening the Mole called in, and they always talked about how when summer was over, the sun wouldn't be near as hot: just now, it was scorching the ground as hard as a stone: ah yes, when the summer was over, Thumbelina should be married. But she wasn't at all pleased; she didn't like the tiresome Mole one bit. Every morning when the sun rose and every evening when it set, she stole out to the doorway, and there when the wind parted the heads of corn so that she could see the blue sky, she thought how bright and pretty it was outside and longed to get another sight of the dear swallow: but he never came, he must certainly be flying far away in the beautiful greenwood. By the time autumn came, Thumbelina had all her trousseau ready.

"In four weeks' time you shall be married," the Fieldmouse told her, but Thumbelina cried and said she wouldn't marry the tiresome Mole. "Rubbish," said the Fieldmouse, "don't be pigheaded or I'll bite you with my white teeth. It's a splendid husband you're getting. The queen herself hasn't the like of his black velvet coat, and a full kitchen and cellar he has, too! Just you thank your Maker for him."

So the wedding was to be; already the Mole had come to fetch Thumbelina, and with him, she must go deep down underground and never come out into the warm sun, for he couldn't stand it. The poor child was bitterly grieved, for now, she must bid farewell to the beautiful sunshine that she had at least had the chance of seeing from the Fieldmouse's door.

"Farewell! Farewell! bright sun," she said, stretching her arms upwards and stepping a little way outside the Fieldmouse's house. For now, the corn was reaped, and only the dry stubble was left. "Farewell! Farewell!" she said again and threw her arms about a little red flower that grew there. "Give my love to the dear swallow for me if ever you see him."

Twit! Twit! sounded at that moment above her head. She looked up, and there was the swallow just flying by. He was overjoyed when he caught sight of Thumbelina, and she told him how she hated to have the ugly Mole for a husband and how she must live right down underground where the sun never shone. She couldn't help crying.

"Cold winter is coming," said the swallow. "I am going to fly far away to the warm countries, will you come with me? You can sit on my back, only tie yourself tight with your sash, and we'll fly far away from the ugly Mole and his dark home, far over the mountains to the warm countries where the sun shines fairer than here, and there is always summer and lovely flowers. Do fly away with me, you sweet little Thumbelina, who saved my life when I lay frozen in that dark cellar underground."

"Yes, I will come with you," said Thumbelina. So she got up on the bird's back, put her feet upon his outspread wings, tied her belt fast to one of his strongest feathers, and off flew the swallow high in the air over forest and lake, high above the great mountains where the snow always lies, and where Thumbelina might have frozen in the cold air but that she crept in among the bird's warm feathers, and only put her little head out to see all the beauty beneath her.

At last, they got to the warm countries. There the sun shone far brighter than here, the sky seemed twice as high, and on hedges and ditches grew the loveliest clusters of grapes, green and purple. In the woods grew oranges and lemons, there was a scent of myrtle and mint, and in the roads, pretty children ran about and played with great gay butterflies. But the swallow flew still further, and the country grew more and more delightful. Under splendid trees, beside a blue lake, stood a shining palace of white marble, built in ancient days, with creepers twining about its tall pillars. At its top were a number of swallows' nests, one of which was the home of the swallow who was carrying Thumbelina.

"Here is my house," said the swallow, "but won't you look out for yourself one of the finest of the flowers that grow down below? and I'll put you there, and you shall find everything as happy as your heart can wish."

"That will be lovely," said she and clapped her little hands.

A great white marble column lay there, which had fallen down and broken into three pieces: between them grew large beautiful white flowers. The swallow flew down with Thumbelina and set her on one of the broad leaves. But what a surprise for her! A little man was sitting in the middle of the flower, as white and transparent as if he were made of glass, with the prettiest gold crown on his head and the loveliest bright wings on his shoulders, and he was no bigger than Thumbelina. He was the angel of the flower. In each of them, there lived such another little man or woman, but this one was the king of them all.

"Goodness, how beautiful he is," Thumbelina whispered to the swallow. The little prince was quite alarmed by the swallow, which was a giant bird to him, tiny and delicate as he was, but when he saw Thumbelina, he was delighted, for she was by far the prettiest girl he had ever seen. He took his gold crown off his head and laid it upon hers, asked what her name was and whether she would be his wife, for then she would become queen of all the flowers. Here indeed, was a husband—very different from the Toad's son or the Mole with his black velvet coat. So she said "Yes" to the handsome prince, and out of every flower, there came a lady or a lord, so pretty that it was a pleasure to see them. Everyone brought Thumbelina a present, but the best of all was a pair of beautiful wings taken from a big white fly. They were fastened to Thumbelina's back, and then she could fly from flower to flower. There were great rejoicings, and the swallow sat on his nest up there and sang to them as well as ever he could; but at heart, he was sad, for he was very fond of Thumbelina and would have liked never to be parted from her. "You shan't be called Thumbelina," the angel of the flower said to her; "it's an ugly name, and you are very pretty; we will call you Maia."

"Good-bye, good-bye," said the swallow when he flew back, away from the warm countries far, far, back to Denmark. There he had a little nest above the window, where the man who can tell stories lives, and to him, he sang, "Twit, twit", and that's the way we came by the whole story.

The Adventures of Puss In Boots

by Charles Perrault
Published by J.L. Marks

There once lived a young man who was very poor.

For all that he had was a Cat;

His food was gone, he could get no more,

And so he resolv'd to kill that.

Now Puss from the cupboard came out and thus spoke,

"Grieve not my good master, I pray,

Provide me with boots, and a bag—'tis no joke—

Your fortune I'll make then straightway."

Puss baited his bag with parsley and bread,

And away to a warren he hied,

Where he laid himself down as if he was dead,

Until some young rabbits he spied.

One entered the bag, and puss pulled at the string.

The rabbit was killed in a trice.

Puss said this fine game. I'll take to the king.

I'm sure he will say it is nice.

Next day to a wheat-field Grimalkin repair'd,

And there two fine partridges caught.

These he took to the king who kindly enquired,

From whence the fine present was brought.

"From the Marquis Carabas, great Monarch," said he,

"These birds and the rabbit I bring,"

They both were accepted and puss in high glee.

Received a reward from the king.

This king took a journey, his kingdom to view,

With his daughter so fine and so gay,

What happened then, I will now tell unto you,

To my tale, therefore, listen I pray.

Puss ran to a cornfield, to the reapers, he said,

"When the king comes to these words you repeat,

'To the Marquis Carabas these fields all belong,

Or I'll chop you as small as minced meat.'"

To an Ogre's grand castle grimalkin now went,

Which was opened by servants so gay,

'Is his highness the Ogre at home, sir,' said he,

'For my business is urgent today.'

The Ogre received him with kindness, and now,

Puss entered the castle so gay.

When making a low and reverend bow,

He marched to the parlour straightway.

'Tis thought mighty Ogre by all in the nation,

That miraculous power you possess,

The power, when you please, of complete
transformation,

This a miracle is and no less.

To convince you 'tis true, the Ogre replied,

I will change myself now in your sight:

He did so—a lion he now roars by his side,

Which put the poor cat in a fright.

"Mighty sir," said the Cat, "such a change I must say,

I never expected to view:

Yet I venture to doubt—your pardon I pray,

If a mouse you could change yourself to."

Doubt not, told the Ogre, my power to do so.

When a mouse he directly became,

On his victim, Grimalkin immediately flew,

And sealed in an instant his doom.

The king and princess now arrived at the place,

But Puss, who had travelled much faster,

Came out and invited them in with much grace,

In the name of the Marquis, his master.

In a spacious saloon, they sat themselves down,

Where a banquet was already spread,

And that day, "PUSS IN BOOTS" gained greater renown,

For the marquis and princess were wed.

Where the Sparks Go

by Abbie Phillips Walker

One night, when the wind was blowing, and it was clear and cold out of doors, a cat and a dog, who were very good friends, sat dozing before a fireplace. The wood was snapping and crackling, making the sparks fly. Some flew up the chimney, others settled into coals in the bed of the fireplace, while others flew out on the hearth and slowly closed their eyes and went to sleep.

One spark ventured farther out upon the hearth and fell very near Pussy. This made her jump, which awakened the dog.

"That almost scorched your fur coat, Miss Pussy," said the dog.

"No, indeed," answered the cat. "I am far too quick to be caught by those silly sparks."

"Why do you call them silly?" asked the dog. "I think them very good to look at, and they help to keep us warm."

"Yes, that is all true," said the cat, "but those that fly up the chimney on a night like this certainly are silly, when they could be warm and comfortable inside; for my part, I cannot see why they fly up the chimney."

The spark that flew so near Pussy was still winking, and she blazed up a little when she heard the remark the cat made.

"If you knew our reason you would not call us silly," she said. "You cannot see what we do, but if you were to look up the chimney and see what happens if we are fortunate enough to get out at the top, you would not call us silly."

The dog and cat were very curious to know what happened, but the spark told them to look and see for themselves. Pussy was very cautious and told the dog to look first, so he stepped boldly up to the fireplace and thrust his head in. He quickly withdrew it, for his hair was singed, which made him cry and run to the other side of the room.

Miss Pussy smoothed her soft coat and was very

glad she had been so wise; she walked over to the dog and urged him to come nearer the fire, but he realized why a burnt child dreads the fire and remained at a safe distance.

Pussy walked back to the spark and continued to question it. "We cannot go into the fire," she said. "Now, pretty, bright spark, do tell us what becomes of you when you fly up the chimney. I am sure you only become soot and that cannot make you long to get to the top."

"Oh, you are very wrong," said the spark. "We are far from being black when we fly up the chimney, for once we reach the top, we live forever sparkling in the sky. You can see, if you look up the chimney, all of our brothers and sisters, who have been lucky and reached the top, winking at us almost every night. Sometimes the wind blows them away, I suppose, for there are nights when we cannot see the sparks shine."

"Who told you all that?" said the cat. "Did any of the sparks ever come back and tell you they could live forever?"

"Oh no!" said the spark, "but we can see them, can we not? And, of course, we all want to shine forever."

"I said you were silly," said the cat, "and now I know it; those are not sparks you see; they are stars in the sky."

"You can call them anything you like," replied the spark, "but we make the bright light you see."

"Well, if you take my advice," said the cat, "you will stay right in the fireplace, for once you reach the top of the chimney out of sight you go. The stars you see twinkling are far above the chimney, and you never could reach them." But the spark would not be convinced. Just then, someone opened a door, and the draught blew the spark back into the fireplace. In a few minutes, it was flying with the others toward the top of the chimney.

Pussy watched the fire for a minute and then looked at the dog.

"The spark may be right, after all," said the dog. "Let us go out and see if we can see it."

Pussy stretched herself and blinked. "Perhaps it is true," she replied; "anyway, I will go with you and look."

The Frog Who Would a-Wooing Go

by Randolph Caldecott

A Frog he would a-wooing go,

Heigho, says Rowley!

Whether his Mother would let him or not

With a rowley-powley, gammon and spinach,

Heigho says, Anthony Rowley!

So off he set with his opera hat,

Heigho, says Rowley!

And on his way, he met with a Rat.

With a rowley-powley, gammon and spinach,

Heigho says, Anthony Rowley!

So off he set with his opera hat,

Heigho, says Rowley!

And on his way, he met with a Rat.

With a rowley-powley, gammon and spinach,

Heigho says, Anthony Rowley!

Now they soon arrived at Mousey's Hall,

Heigho, says Rowley!

And gave a loud knock, and gave a loud call.

With a rowley-powley, gammon and spinach,

Heigho, says Anthony Rowley!

"Pray, Miss MOUSEY, are you within?"

Heigho, says Rowley!

"Oh, yes, kind Sirs, I'm sitting to spin."

With a rowley-powley, gammon and spinach,

Heigho says, Anthony Rowley!

"Pray, Miss MOUSE, will you give us some beer?"

Heigho, says Rowley!

"For Froggy and I are fond of good cheer."

With a rowley-powley, gammon and spinach,

Heigho says, Anthony Rowley!

"Pray, Mr FROG, will you give us a song?

Heigho, says Rowley!

"But let it be something that's not very long."

With a rowley-powley, gammon and spinach,

Heigho says, Anthony Rowley!

"Indeed, Miss MOUSE," replied Mr FROG

Heigho says, Rowley!

"A cold has made me as hoarse as a Hog."

With a rowley-powley, gammon and spinach,

Heigho says, Anthony Rowley!

"Since you have caught a cold," Miss MOUSEY said.

Heigho, says Rowley!

"I'll sing you a song that I have just made."

With a rowley-powley, gammon and spinach,

Heigho says, Anthony Rowley!

But while they were all thus a merry-making,

Heigho, says Rowley!

A Cat and her Kittens came tumbling in.

With a rowley-powley, gammon and spinach,

Heigho says, Anthony Rowley!

The Cat she seized the Rat by the crown;

Heigho, says Rowley!

The Kittens they pulled the little Mouse down.

With a rowley-powley, gammon and spinach,

Heigho says, Anthony Rowley!

This put Mr FROG in a terrible fright;

Heigho, says Rowley!

He took up his hat, and he wished them good night.

With a rowley-powley, gammon and spinach,

Heigho says, Anthony Rowley!

But as Froggy was crossing a silvery brook,

Heigho, says Rowley!

A lily-white Duck came and gobbled him up.

With a rowley-powley, gammon and spinach,

Heigho says, Anthony Rowley!

So there was an end of one, two, and three,

Heigho, says Rowley!

The Rat, the Mouse, and the little Frog-gee!

With a rowley-powley, gammon and spinach,

Heigho says, Anthony Rowley!

"Where away?" cried Captain Boldheart, starting up.

"On the larboard bow, sir," replied the fellow at the masthead, touching his hat. For such was the height of discipline on board of the Beauty that even at that height, he was obliged to mind it or be shot through the head.

"This adventure belongs to me," said Boldheart. "Boy, my harpoon. Let no man follow;" leaping alone into his boat, the captain rowed with admirable dexterity in the direction of the monster.

All was now excitement.

"He nears him!" said an elderly seaman, following the captain through his spy-glass.

"He strikes him!" said another seaman, a mere stripling but also with a spy-glass.

"He tows him towards us!" said another seaman, a man in the full vigour of life but also with a spy-glass.

In fact, the captain was seen approaching, with the huge bulk following. We will not dwell on the deafening cries of "Boldheart! Boldheart!" with which he was received when, carelessly leaping on the quarter-deck, he presented his prize to his men. They afterwards made two thousand four hundred and seventeen pounds ten and sixpence by it.

Ordering the sails to be braced up, the captain now stood W.N.W. The Beauty flew rather than floated over the dark blue waters. Nothing particular occurred for a fortnight except taking, with considerable slaughter, four Spanish galleons and a Snow from South America, all richly laden. Inaction began to tell upon the spirits of the men. Captain Boldheart called all hands aft and said:

"My lads, I hear there are discontented ones among ye. Let any such stand forth."

After some murmuring, in which the expression, "Aye, aye, sir!" "Union Jack!" "Avast," "Starboard," "Port," "Bowsprit," and similar indications of a mutinous undercurrent, though subdued, were audible. Bill Boozey, captain of the foretop, came out from the rest. His form was that of a giant, but he quailed under the captain's eye.

"What are your wrongs?" said the captain.

"Why, d'ye see, Captain Boldheart," replied the towering mariner, "I've sailed man and boy for many a year, but I never yet know'd the milk served out for the ship's company's teas to be so sour as 'tis aboard this craft."

At this moment the thrilling cry, "Man overboard!" announced to the astonished crew that Boozey, in stepping back, as the captain (in mere thoughtfulness) laid his hand upon the faithful pocket-pistol which he wore in his belt, had lost his balance, and was struggling with the foaming tide.

All was now stupefaction.

But, with Captain Boldheart, to throw off his uniform coat regardless of the various rich orders with which it was decorated, and to plunge into the sea after the drowning giant, was the work of a moment. Maddening was the excitement when boats were lowered; intense the joy when the captain was seen holding up the drowning man with his teeth; deafening the cheering when both were restored to the main deck of the Beauty. And from the instant of his changing his wet clothes for dry ones, Captain Boldheart had no such devoted though humble friend as William Boozey.

Boldheart now pointed to the horizon and called the attention of his crew to the taper spars of a ship lying snug in harbour under the guns of a fort.

"She shall be ours at sunrise," said he. "Serve out a double allowance of grog, and prepare for action."

All was now preparation.

When morning dawned after a sleepless night, it was seen that the stranger was crowding on all sail to come out of the harbour and offer battle. As the two ships came nearer to each other, the stranger fired a gun and hoisted Roman colours. Boldheart then perceived her to be the Latin Grammar Master's bark. Such indeed she was and had been talking about the world in unavailing pursuit from the time of his first taking to a roving life.

Boldheart now addressed his men, promising to blow them up if he should feel convinced that their reputation required it and giving orders that the Latin Grammar Master should be taken alive. He then dismissed them to their quarters, and the fight began with a broadside from The Beauty. She then veered around and poured in another. The Scorpion (so was the bark of the Latin Grammar Master appropriately called) was not slow to return her fire, and a terrific cannonading ensued, in which the guns of The Beauty did tremendous execution.

The Latin Grammar Master was seen upon the poop in the midst of the smoke and fire, encouraging his men. To do him justice, he was no Craven, though his white hat, his short grey trousers, and his long snuff-coloured surtout reaching to his heels—the self-same coat in which he had spat Boldheart—contrasted most unfavourably with the brilliant uniform of the latter. At this moment, Boldheart, seizing a pike and putting himself at the head of his men, gave the word to the board.

A desperate conflict ensued in the hammock nettings —or somewhere in about that direction—until the Latin Grammar Master, having all his masts gone, his hull and rigging shot through and through, and seeing Boldheart slashing a path towards him, hauled down his flag himself, gave up his sword to Boldheart, and asked for quarter. Scarce had he been put into the captain's boat, 'ere The Scorpion went down with all on board.

On Captain Boldheart's now assembling his men, a circumstance occurred. He found it necessary with one blow of his cutlass to kill the Cook, who, having lost his brother in the late action, was making at the Latin Grammar Master in an infuriated state, intent on his destruction with a carving knife.

Captain Boldheart then turned to the Latin Grammar Master, severely reproaching him for his perfidy, and put it to his crew what they considered that a master who spat a boy deserved.

They answered with one voice, "Death."

"It may be so," said the Captain, "but it shall never be said that Boldheart stained his hour of triumph with the blood of his enemy. Prepare the cutter."

The cutter was immediately prepared.

"Without taking your life," said the Captain, "I must yet forever deprive you of the power of spiting other boys. I shall turn you adrift in this boat. You will find in her two oars, a compass, a bottle of rum, a small cask of water, a piece of pork, a bag of biscuits, and my Latin grammar. Go! and spite the natives if you can find any."

Deeply conscious of this bitter sarcasm, the unhappy wretch was put into the cutter and was soon left far behind. He made no effort to row but was seen lying on his back with his legs up when last made out by the ship's telescopes.

A stiff breeze now beginning to blow, Captain Boldheart gave orders to keep her S.S.W., easing her a little during the night by falling off a point or two W. by

W., or even by W.S., if she complained much. He then retired for the night, having in truth, much need of repose. In addition to the fatigues he had undergone, this brave officer had received sixteen wounds in the engagement but had not mentioned it.

In the morning, a white squall came on and was succeeded by other squalls of various colours. It thundered and lightened heavily for six weeks. Hurricanes then set in for two months. Waterspouts and tornadoes followed. The oldest sailor on board—and he was a very old one—had never seen such weather. The Beauty lost all idea where she was, and the carpenter reported six feet two of water in the hold. Everybody fell senseless at the pumps every day.

Provisions now ran very low. Our hero put the crew on a short allowance and put himself on a shorter allowance than any man on the ship. But his spirit kept him fat. In this extremity, the gratitude of Boozey, the captain of the foretop whom our readers may remember, was truly affecting. The loving though lowly William repeatedly requested to be killed and preserved for the captain's table.

We now approach a change in affairs.

One day during a gleam of sunshine and when the weather had moderated, the man at the masthead—too weak now to touch his hat, besides its having been blown away—called out,

"Savages!"

All was now an expectation.

Presently fifteen hundred canoes, each paddled by twenty savages, were seen advancing in excellent order. They were a light green colour (the Savages were) and sang, with great energy, the following strain:

Choo a choo a choo tooth.

Muntch, muntch. Nycey!

Choo a choo a choo tooth.

Muntch, muntch. Nyce!

As the shades of night were by this time closing in, these expressions were supposed to embody these simple people's views of the Evening Hymn. But it too soon appeared that the song was a translation of "For what we are going to receive," &c.

The chief, imposingly decorated with feathers of lively colours, and having the majestic appearance of a fighting Parrot, no sooner understood (he understood English perfectly) that the ship was The Beauty, Captain Boldheart than he fell upon his face on the deck and could not be persuaded to rise until the captain had lifted him up, & told him he wouldn't hurt him. All the rest of the savages also fell on their faces with marks of terror and also had to be lifted up one by one. Thus the fame of the great Boldheart had gone before him, even among these children of Nature.

Turtles and oysters were now produced in astonishing numbers, and on these and yams, the people made a hearty meal. After dinner, the Chief told Captain Boldheart that there was better feeding up at the village and that he would be glad to take him and his officers there. Apprehensive of treachery, Boldheart ordered his boat's crew to attend to him completely armed. And well, was it for other commanders if their precautions—but let us not anticipate.

When the canoes arrived at the beach, the darkness of the night was illumined by the light of an immense fire. Ordering his boat's crew (with the intrepid though illiterate William at their head) to keep close and be upon their guard, Boldheart bravely went on, arm-in-arm with the Chief.

But how to depict the captain's surprise when he found a ring of Savages singing in the chorus that barbarous translation of "For what we are going to receive, &c.," which has been given above, and dancing hand-in-hand round the Latin-Grammar-Master, in a hamper with his head shaved, while two savages floured him, before putting him to the fire to be cooked!

Boldheart now took counsel with his officers on the course to be adopted. In the meantime, the miserable captive never ceased begging for pardon and imploring to be delivered. On the generous Boldheart's proposal, it was at length resolved that he should not be cooked but should be allowed to remain raw on two conditions. Namely,

1. That he should never under any circumstances presume to teach any boy anything anymore.

2. That, if taken back to England, he should pass his life in travelling to find out boys who wanted their exercises done, and should do their exercises for those boys for nothing, and never say a word about it.

Drawing his sword from its sheath, Boldheart swore him to these conditions on its shining blade. The prisoner wept bitterly and appeared acutely to feel the errors of his past career.

The captain then ordered his boat's crew to make ready for a volley and after firing, to re-load quickly. "And expect a score or two on ye to go head over heels," murmured William Boozey, "for I'm a looking at ye." With those words, the derisive though deadly William took good aim.

"Fire!"

The ringing voice of Boldheart was lost in the report of the guns and the screeching of the savages. Volley after volley awakened the numerous echoes. Hundreds of savages were killed, hundreds wounded, and thousands ran howling into the woods. The Latin Grammar Master had a spare nightcap lent him and a longtail coat which he wore hind side before. He presented a ludicrous though pitiable appearance and served him right.

We now find Captain Boldheart, with this rescued wretch on board, standing off for other islands. At one of these, not a cannibal island, but a pork and vegetable one, he married (only in fun on his part) the King's daughter. Here he rested some time, receiving from the natives' great quantities of precious stones, gold dust, elephants' teeth, and sandalwood, and getting very rich. This, too, though he almost every day made presents of enormous value to his men.

The ship being at length as full as she could hold of all sorts of valuable things, Boldheart gave orders to weigh the anchor and turn the Beauty's head towards England. These orders were obeyed with three cheers, and ere the sun went down full many a hornpipe had been danced on deck by the uncouth though agile William.

We next find Captain Boldheart about three leagues off Madeira, surveying through his spy-glass a stranger of suspicious appearance making sail towards him. On his firing a gun ahead of her to bring her to, she ran up a flag, which he instantly recognized as the flag from the mast in the back garden at home.

Inferring from this, that his father had put to sea to seek his long-lost son, the captain sent his own boat on board the stranger to inquire if this was so and if so, whether his father's intentions were strictly honourable. The boat came back with a present of greens and fresh meat and reported that the stranger was The Family of twelve hundred tons and had not only the captain's father on board but also his mother, with the majority of his aunts and uncles and all his cousins. It was further reported to Boldheart that the whole of these relations had expressed themselves in a becoming manner and was anxious to embrace him and thank him for the glorious credit he had done them. Boldheart at once invited them to breakfast the next morning on board the Beauty and gave orders for a brilliant ball that should last all day.

It was in the course of the night that the captain discovered the hopelessness of reclaiming the Latin-Grammar-Master. That thankless traitor was found out as the two ships lay near each other, communicating with The Family by signals and offering to give up Boldheart. He has hanged at the yard arm the first thing in the morning after having it impressively pointed out to him by Boldheart that this was what spiters came to.

The meeting between the captain and his parents was attended with tears. His uncles and aunts would have attended their meeting with tears too, but he wasn't going to stand that. His cousins were very much astonished by the size of his ship and the discipline of his men and were greatly overcome by the splendour of his uniform. He kindly conducted them around the vessel and pointed out everything worthy of notice. He also fired his hundred guns and found it amusing to witness their alarm.

The entertainment surpassed everything ever seen on board the ship and lasted from ten in the morning until seven the next morning. Only one disagreeable incident occurred. Captain Boldheart found himself obliged to put his cousin Tom in the irons for being disrespectful. On the boy's promising amendment, however, he was humanely released after a few hours of close confinement.

Boldheart now took his mother down into the great cabin and asked after the young lady with whom, it was well known to the world, he was in love. His mother replied that the object of his affections was then at school at Margate, for the benefit of sea-bathing (it was the month of September), but that she feared the young lady's friends were still opposed to the union. Boldheart at once resolved, if necessary, to bombard the town.

Taking the command of his ship with this intention and putting all but fighting men on board The Family, with orders to that vessel to keep in company, Boldheart soon anchored in Margate Roads. Here he went ashore well-armed and attended by his boat's crew (at their head the faithful though ferocious William) and demanded to see the Mayor, who came out of his office.

"Dost know the name of yon ship, Mayor?" asked Boldheart fiercely.

"No," said the Mayor, rubbing his eyes, which he could scarce believe when he saw the goodly vessel riding at anchor.

"She is named the Beauty," said the captain.

"Hah!" exclaimed the Mayor with a start. "And you, then, are Captain Boldheart?"

"The same."

A pause ensued. The Mayor trembled.

"Now, Mayor," said the captain, "choose. Help me to my Bride, or be bombarded."

The Mayor begged for two hours' grace in which to make inquiries respecting the young lady. Boldheart accorded him but one and, during that one, placed William Boozey sentry over him, with a drawn sword and instructions to accompany him wherever he went and to run him through the body if he showed a sign of playing false.

At the end of the hour, the Mayor re-appeared more dead than alive, closely waited on by Boozey more alive than dead.

"Captain," said the Mayor, "I have ascertained that the young lady is going to bathe. Even now she waits her turn for a machine. The tide is low, though rising. I, in one of our town-boats, shall not be suspected. When she comes forth in her bathing-dress into the shallow water from behind the hood of the machine, my boat shall intercept her and prevent her return. Do you the rest."

"Mayor," returned Capt. Boldheart, "thou hast saved thy town."

The captain then signalled his boat to take him off and, steering her himself, ordered her crew to row towards the bathing ground and there to rest upon their oars. All happened as had been arranged. His lovely bride came forth. The Mayor glided in behind her. She became confused and had floated out of her depth when, with one skilful touch of the rudder and one quivering stroke from the boat's crew, her adoring Boldheart held her in his strong arms. There her shrieks of terror were changed to cries of joy.

Before the Beauty could get underweight, the hoisting of all the flags in the town and harbour, and the ringing of all the bells, announced to the brave Boldheart that he had nothing to fear. He, therefore, determined to be married on the spot and signalled for a clergyman and clerk, who came off promptly in a sailing boat named the Skylark. Another great entertainment was then given on board the Beauty, in the midst of which the Mayor was called out by a messenger. He returned with the news that the Government had sent down to know whether Captain Boldheart, in acknowledgement of the great services he had done his country by being a Pirate, would consent to be made a Lieutenant-Colonel. For himself, he would have spurned the worthless boon, but his Bride wished it, and he consented.

Only one thing further happened before the good ship Family was dismissed, with rich presents to all on board. It is painful to record (but such is human nature in some cousins) that Captain Boldheart's unmannerly cousin Tom was actually tied up to receive three dozen with a rope's end "for cheekyness and making games," when Captain Boldheart's lady begged for him, and he was spared. The Beauty then refitted, and the Captain and his Bride departed for the Indian Ocean to enjoy themselves forevermore.

A Snow Image: a Childish Miracle

by Nathaniel Hawthorne

One afternoon on a cold winter's day, when the sun shone forth with chilly brightness, after a long storm, two children asked leave of their mother to run out and play in the new-fallen snow. The elder child was a girl, whom, because she was of a tender and modest disposition, and was thought to be very beautiful, her parents, and other people who were familiar with her, used to call Violet. But her brother was known by the style and title of Peony on account of the ruddiness of his broad and round little phiz, which made everybody think of sunshine and great scarlet flowers. The father of these two children, a certain Mr Lindsey, it is important to say, was an excellent but exceedingly matter-of-fact sort of man, a dealer in hardware, and was sturdily accustomed to take what is called the common-sense view of all matters that came under his consideration. With a heart about as tender as other people's, he had a head as hard and impenetrable and, therefore, perhaps, as empty as one of the iron pots which it was a part of his business to sell. The mother's character, on the other hand, had a strain of poetry in it, a trait of unworldly beauty—a delicate and dewy flower, as it were, that had survived out of her imaginative youth and still kept itself alive amid the dusty realities of matrimony and motherhood.

So, Violet and Peony, as I began with saying, besought their mother to let them run out and play in the new snow; for, though it had looked so dreary and dismal, drifting downward out of the gray sky, it had a very cheerful aspect, now that the sun was shining on it. The children dwelt in a city and had no wider play-place than a little garden before the house, divided by a white fence from the street, with a pear tree and two or three plum trees overshadowing it and some rose bushes just in front of the parlour-windows. The trees and shrubs, however, were now leafless, and their twigs were enveloped in the light snow, which thus made a kind of wintry foliage, with here and there a pendent icicle for the fruit.

"Yes, Violet—yes, my little Peony," said their kind mother; "you may go out and play in the new snow."

Accordingly, the good lady bundled up her darlings in woollen jackets and wadded sacks put comforters around their necks, and a pair of striped gaiters on each little pair of legs, and worsted mittens on their hands, and gave them a kiss apiece, by way of a spell to keep away Jack Frost. Forth sallied the two children with a hop-skip-and-jump that carried them at once into the very heart of a huge snow drift, whence Violet emerged like a snow-bunting while little Peony floundered out with his round face in full bloom. Then what a merry time had they! To look at them, frolicking in the wintry garden, you would have thought that the dark and pitiless storm had been sent for no other purpose but to provide a new plaything for Violet and Peony; and that they themselves had been created, as the snowbirds were, to take delight only in the tempest, and in the white mantle which it spread over the earth.

At last, when they had frosted one another all over with handfuls of snow, Violet, after laughing heartily at little Peony's figure, was struck with a new idea.

"You look exactly like a snow-image, Peony," said she, "if your cheeks were not so red. And that puts me in mind! Let us make an image out of snow—an image of a little girl—and it shall be our sister, and shall run about and play with us all winter long. Won't it be nice?"

"O, yes!" cried Peony, as plainly as he could speak, for he was but a little boy. "That will be nice! And mamma shall see it!"

"Yes," answered Violet; "mamma shall see the new little girl. But she must not make her come into the warm parlour; for, you know, our little snow-sister will not love the warmth."

And forthwith, the children began this great business of making a snow image that should run about while their mother, who was sitting at the window and overheard some of their talks, could not help smiling at the gravity with which they set about it. They really seemed to imagine that there would be no difficulty whatever in creating a live little girl out of the snow. And, to say the truth, if miracles are ever to be wrought, it will be by putting our hands to the work in precisely such a simple and undoubting frame of mind as that in which Violet and Peony now undertook to perform one, without so much as knowing that it was a miracle. So thought the mother, and thought, likewise, that the new snow, just fallen from heaven, would be excellent material to make new beings of if it were not so very cold. She gazed at the children a moment longer, delighting in watching their little figures—the girl, tall for her age, graceful and agile, and so delicately coloured that she looked like a cheerful thought, more than a physical reality, while Peony expanded in breadth rather than height, and rolled along on his short and sturdy legs as substantial as an elephant, though not quite so big. Then the mother resumed her work. What it was, I forget; but she was either trimming a silken bonnet for Violet or darning a pair of stockings for little Peony's short legs. Again, however, and again, and yet other again, she could not help turning her head to the window to see how the children got on with their snow image.

Indeed, it was an exceedingly pleasant sight, those bright little souls at their task! Moreover, it was really wonderful to observe how knowingly and skilfully they managed the matter. Violet assumed the chief direction and told Peony what to do while, with her own delicate fingers, she shaped out all the nicer parts of the snow figure. It seemed, in fact, not so much to be made by the children as to grow up under their hands while they were playing and prattling about it. Their mother was quite surprised at this, and the longer she looked, the more and more surprised she grew.

"What remarkable children mine are!" thought she, smiling with a mother's pride and smiling at herself, too, for being so proud of them. "What other children could have made anything so like a little girl's figure out of snow at the first trial? Well, but now I must finish Peony's new frock, for his grandfather is coming tomorrow, and I want the little fellow to look handsome."

So she took up the frock and was soon as busily at work again with her needle as the two children with their snow image. But still, as the needle travelled hither and thither through the seams of the dress, the mother made her toil light and happy by listening to the airy voices of Violet and Peony. They kept talking to one another all the time, their tongues being quite as active as their feet and hands. Except at intervals, she could not distinctly hear what was said but had merely a sweet impression that they were in a most loving mood and were enjoying themselves highly and that the business of making the snow image went prosperously on. Now and then, however, when Violet and Peony happened to raise their voices, the words were as audible as if they had been spoken in the very parlour where the mother sat. O, how delightfully those words echoed in her heart, even though they meant nothing so very wise or wonderful, after all!

But you must know a mother listens with her heart, much more than with her ears, and thus she is often delighted with the trills of celestial music when other people can hear nothing of the kind.

"Peony, Peony!" cried Violet to her brother, who had gone to another part of the garden, "bring me some of that fresh snow, Peony, from the very farthest corner, where we have not been trampling. I want it to shape our little snow sister's bosom. You know that part must be quite pure, just as it came out of the sky!"

"Here it is, Violet!" answered Peony, in his bluff tone—but a very sweet tone, too—as he came floundering through the half-trodden drifts. "Here is the snow for her little bosom. O Violet, how beautiful she begins to look!"

"Yes," said Violet, thoughtfully and quietly, "our snow-sister does look very lovely. I did not quite know, Peony, that we could make such a sweet little girl as this."

The mother, as she listened, thought how fit and delightful an incident it would be if fairies, or, still better, if angel children were to come from paradise, and play invisibly with her own darlings, and help them to make their snow image, giving it the features of celestial babyhood! Violet and Peony would not be aware of their immortal playmates—only they could see that the image grew very beautiful while they worked at it and would think that they themselves had done it all.

"My little girl and boy deserve such playmates if mortal children ever did!" said the mother to herself, and then she smiled again at her own motherly pride.

Nevertheless, the ideas seized upon her imagination, and ever and anon, she took a glimpse out of the window, half dreaming that she might see the golden-haired children of paradise sporting her own golden-haired Violet and bright-cheeked Peony.

Now, for a few moments, there was a busy and earnest but indistinct hum of the two children's voices as Violet and Peony wrought together with one happy consent. Violet still seemed to be the guiding spirit, while Peony acted rather as a labourer and brought her the snow from far and near. And yet the little urchin evidently had a proper understanding of the matter, too!

"Peony, Peony!" cried Violet; for the brother was again at the other side of the garden. "Bring me those light wreaths of snow that have rested on the lower branches of the pear tree. You can clamber on the snow-drift, Peony, and reach them easily. I must have them to make some ringlets for our snow sister's head!"

"Here they are, Violet!" answered the little boy. "Take care you do not break them. Well done! Well done! How pretty!"

"Does she not look sweet?" said Violet, with a very satisfied tone, "and now we must have some little shining bits of ice, to make the brightness of her eyes. She is not finished yet. Mamma will see how very beautiful she is; but papa will say, 'Tush! nonsense!—come in out of the cold!'"

"Let us call mamma to look out," said Peony, and then he shouted lustily, "Mamma! Mamma!! Mamma!!! Look out, and see what a nice little girl we are making."

The mother put down her work for an instant and looked out of the window. But it so happened that the sun—for this was one of the shortest days of the whole year—had sunken so nearly to the edge of the world that his setting shine came obliquely into the lady's eyes. So she was dazzled, you must understand, and could not very distinctly observe what was in the garden. Still, however, through all that bright, blinding dazzle of the sun and the new snow, she beheld a small white figure in the garden that seemed to have a wonderful deal of human likeness about it. And she saw Violet and Peony—indeed, she looked more at them than at the image—she saw the two children still at work; Peony bringing fresh snow, and Violet applying it to the figure as scientifically as a sculptor adds clay to his model. Indistinctly as she discerned the snow child, the mother thought to herself that never before was there a snow figure so cunningly made, nor ever such a dear little girl and boy to make it.

"They do everything better than other children," said she, very complacently. "No wonder they make better snow images!"

She sat down again to her work and made as much haste with it as possible; because twilight would soon come, Peony's frock was not yet finished, and grandfather was expected, by railroad, pretty early in the morning. Faster and faster, therefore, went her flying fingers. The children, likewise, kept busily at work in the garden, and still the mother listened whenever she could catch a word. She was amused to observe how their little imaginations had got mixed up with what they were doing and were carried away by it. They seemed positive to think that the snow child would run about and play with them.

"What a nice playmate she will be for us all winter long!" said Violet. "I hope papa will not be afraid of her giving us a cold! Sha'n't you love her dearly, Peony?"

"O yes!" cried Peony. "And I will hug her and she shall sit down close by me, and drink some of my warm milk!"

"O no, Peony!" answered Violet, with grave wisdom. "That will not do at all. Warm milk will not be wholesome for our little snow-sister. Little snow-people, like her, eat nothing but icicles. No, no, Peony; we must not give her anything warm to drink!"

There was a minute or two of silence; for Peony, whose short legs were never weary, had gone on a pilgrimage again to the other side of the garden. All of a sudden, Violet cried out loudly and joyfully—

"Look here, Peony! Come quickly! A light has been shining on her cheek out of that rose-coloured cloud! and the colour does not go away! Is not that beautiful!"

"Yes; it is beau-ti-ful," answered Peony, pronouncing the three syllables with deliberate accuracy. "O Violet, only look at her hair! It is all like gold!"

"O, certainly," said Violet, with tranquillity, as if it were very much a matter of course. "That colour, you know, comes from the golden clouds, that we see up there in the sky. She is almost finished now. But her lips must be made very red—redder than her cheeks. Perhaps, Peony, it will make them red if we both kiss them!"

Accordingly, the mother heard two smart little smacks, as if both her children were kissing the snow image on its frozen mouth. But, as this did not seem to make the lips quite red enough, Violet next proposed that the snow child should be invited to kiss Peony's scarlet cheek.

"Come, 'ittle snow-sister, kiss me!" cried Peony.

"There! she has kissed you," added Violet, "and her lips are very red. And she blushed a little, too!"

"O, what a cold kiss!" cried Peony.

Just then, there came a breeze of the pure west wind, sweeping through the garden and rattling the parlour windows. It sounded so wintry cold that the mother was about to tap on the window pane with her thimbled finger to summon the two children in when they both cried out to her in one voice. The tone was not a tone of surprise, although they were evidently a good deal excited; it appeared rather as if they very much rejoiced at some event that had now happened but which they had been looking for and had reckoned upon all along.

"Mamma! mamma! We have finished our little snow sister, and she is running about the garden with us!"

"What imaginative little beings my children are!" thought the mother, putting the last few stitches into Peony's frock. "And it is strange, too, that they make me almost as much a child as they themselves are! I can hardly help believing, now, that the snow image has really come to life!"

"Dear mamma!" cried Violet, "pray to look out and see what a sweet playmate we have!"

The mother, being thus entreated, could no longer delay looking forth from the window. The sun was now gone out from the sky, leaving, however, a rich inheritance of his brightness among those purple and golden clouds which make the sunsets of winter so magnificent. But there was not the slightest gleam or dazzle, either on the window or on the snow, so that the good lady could look all over the garden and see everything and everybody in it. And what do you think she saw there? Violet and Peony, of course, her own two darling children. Ah, but whom or what did she see besides? Why, if you will, believe me, there was a small figure of a girl, dressed all in white, with rose-tinged cheeks and ringlets of golden hue, playing about the garden with the two children! A stranger though she was, the child seemed to be on as familiar terms with Violet and Peony, and they with her, as if all the three had been playmates during the whole of their little lives. The mother thought to herself that it must certainly be the daughter of one of the neighbours and that, seeing Violet and Peony in the garden, the child had run across the street to play with them. So this kind lady went to the door, intending to invite the little runaway into her comfortable parlour; for, now that the sunshine was withdrawn, the atmosphere, out of doors, was already growing very cold.

But, after opening the house door, she stood an instant on the threshold, hesitating whether she ought to ask the child to come in or whether she should even speak to her. Indeed, she almost doubted whether it was a real child, after all, or only a light wreath of the new-fallen snow, blown hither and thither about the garden by the intensely cold west wind. There was certainly something very singular in the aspect of the little stranger. Among all the children of the neighbourhood, the lady could remember no such face, with its pure white and delicate rose colour, and the golden ringlets tossing about the forehead and cheeks. And as for her dress, which was entirely of white, and fluttering in the breeze, it was such as no reasonable woman would put upon a little girl when sending her out to play in the depth of winter. It made this kind and careful mother shiver only to look at those small feet with nothing in the world on them except a very thin pair of white slippers. Nevertheless, airily as she was clad, the child seemed to feel not the slightest inconvenience from the cold but danced so lightly over the snow that the tips of her toes left hardly a print on its surface; while Violet could but just keep pace with her, and Peony's short legs compelled him to lag behind.

Once, in the course of their play, the strange child placed herself between Violet and Peony and, taking a hand of each, skipped merrily forward, and they along with her. Almost immediately, however, Peony pulled away his little fist and began to rub it as if the fingers were tingling with cold, while Violet also released herself, though with less abruptness, gravely remarking that it was better not to take hold of hands. The white-robed damsel said not a word but danced about just as merrily as before. If Violet and Peony did not choose to play with her, she could make just as good a playmate for the brisk and cold west wind, which kept blowing her all about the garden, and took such liberties with her, that they seemed to have been friends for a long time. All this while, the mother stood on the threshold, wondering how a little girl could look so much like a flying snow drift or how a snow-drift could look so very like a little girl.

She called Violet and whispered to her.

"Violet, my darling, what is this child's name?" asked she. "Does she live near us?"

"Why, dearest mamma," answered Violet, laughing to think that her mother did not comprehend so very plain an affair, "this is our little snow-sister, whom we have just been making!"

"Yes, dear mamma," cried Peony, running to his mother and looking up simply into her face, "This is our snow image! Is it not a nice little child?"

At this instant, a flock of snowbirds came flitting through the air. As was very natural, they avoided Violet and Peony. But—and this looked strange—they flew at once to the white-robed child, fluttered eagerly about her head, alighted on her shoulders, and seemed to claim her as an old acquaintance. She, on her part, was evidently as glad to see these little birds, old Winter's grandchildren, as they were to see her and welcomed them by holding out both her hands. Hereupon, they each and all tried to alight on her two palms and ten small fingers and thumbs, crowding one another off with an immense fluttering of their tiny wings. One dear little bird nestled tenderly in her bosom; another put its bill to her lips. They were as joyous, all the while, and seemed as much in their element as you may have seen them when sporting with a snowstorm.

Violet and Peony stood laughing at this pretty sight: for they enjoyed the merry time that their new playmate was having with their small-winged visitants almost as much as if they themselves took part in it.

"Violet," said her mother, greatly perplexed, "tell me the truth without any jest. Who is this little girl?"

"My darling mamma," answered Violet, looking seriously into her mother's face and apparently surprised that she should need any further explanation, "I have told you truly who she is. It is our little snow-image, which Peony and I have been making. Peony will tell you so, as well as I."

"Yes, mamma," asseverated Peony, with much gravity in his crimson little phiz, "this is 'ittle snow-child. Is not she a nice one? But, mamma, her hand, is oh, so very cold!"

While mamma still hesitated what to think and what to do, the street gate was thrown open, and the father of Violet and Peony appeared, wrapped in a pilot-cloth sack, with a fur cap drawn down over his ears and the thickest of gloves upon his hands. Mr Lindsey was a middle-aged man with a weary and yet happy look on his wind-flushed and frost-pinched face as if he had been busy all day long and was glad to get back to his quiet home. His eyes brightened at the sight of his wife and children, although he could not help uttering a word or two of surprise at finding the whole family in the open air on so bleak a day and after sunset too. He soon perceived the little white stranger, sporting to and fro in the garden, like a dancing snow wreath, and the flock of snow birds fluttering about her head.

"Pray, what little girl may that be?" inquired this very sensible man. "Surely her mother must be crazy to let her go out in such bitter weather as it has been today, with only that flimsy white gown and those thin slippers!"

"My dear husband," said his wife, "I know no more about the little thing than you do. Some neighbour's child, I suppose. Our Violet and Peony," she added, laughing at herself for repeating so absurd a story, "insist that she is nothing but a snow-image, which they have been busy about in the garden, almost all the afternoon."

As she said this, the mother glanced her eyes toward the spot where the children's snow image had been made. What was her surprise on perceiving that there was not the slightest trace of so much labour?—no image at all—no piled up a heap of snow—nothing whatever, save the prints of little footsteps around a vacant space!

"This is very strange!" said she.

"What is strange, dear mother?" asked Violet. "Dear

father, do not you see how it is? This is our snow image, which Peony and I made because we wanted another playmate. Did not we, Peony?"

"Yes, papa," said crimson Peony. "This be our little snow-sister. Is she not beautiful? But she gave me such a cold kiss!"

"Pooh, nonsense, children!" cried their good, honest father, who, as we have already intimated, had an exceedingly common-sensible way of looking at matters. "Do not tell me of making live figures out of snow. Come, wife; this little stranger must not stay out in the bleak air a moment longer. We will bring her into the parlour; and you shall give her a supper of warm bread and milk, and make her as comfortable as you can. Meanwhile, I will inquire among the neighbours; or, if necessary, send the city-crier about the streets, to give notice of a lost child."

So saying, this honest and very kind-hearted man was going toward the little white damsel with the best intentions in the world. But Violet and Peony, each seizing their father by the hand, earnestly besought him not to make her come in.

"Dear father," cried Violet, putting herself before him, "it is true what I have been telling you! This is our little snow-girl, and she cannot live any longer than while she breathes the cold west-wind. Do not make her come into the hot room!"

"Yes, father," shouted Peony, stamping his little foot,

so mightily was he in earnest, "this be nothing but our 'ittle snow-child! She will not love the hot fire!"

"Nonsense, children, nonsense, nonsense!" cried the father, half vexed, half laughing at what he considered their foolish obstinacy. "Run into the house, this moment! It is too late to play any longer now. I must take care of this little girl immediately, or she will catch her death a-cold!"

"Husband! Dear husband!" said his wife, in a low voice—for she had been looking narrowly at the snow child and was more perplexed than ever—there is something very singular in all this. "You will think me foolish—but—but—may it not be that some invisible angel has been attracted by the simplicity and good faith with which our children set about their undertaking? May he not have spent an hour of his immortality playing with those dear little souls? And so the result is what we call a miracle. No, no! Do not laugh at me; I see what a foolish thought it is!"

"My dear wife," replied the husband, laughing heartily, "you are as much a child as Violet and Peony."

And in one sense so she was, for all through life she had kept her heart full of childlike simplicity and faith, which was as pure and clear as crystal; and, looking at all matters through this transparent medium, she sometimes saw truths so profound, that other person laughed at them as nonsense and absurdity.

But now kind Mr Lindsey had entered the garden,

breaking away from his two children, who still sent their shrill voices after him, beseeching him to let the snow child stay and enjoy herself in the cold west wind. As he approached, the snowbirds took to flight. The little white damsel also fled backwards, shaking her head as if to say, "Pray, do not touch me!" and roguishly, as it appeared, leading him through the deepest of the snow. Once, the good man stumbled and floundered down upon his face so that, gathering himself up again, with the snow sticking to his rough pilot-cloth sack, he looked as white and wintry as a snow image of the largest size. Some of the neighbours, meanwhile, seeing him from their windows, wondered what could possess poor Mr Lindsey to be running about his garden in pursuit of a snow drift, which the west wind was driving hither and thither! At length, after a vast deal of trouble, he chased the little stranger into a corner where she could not possibly escape him. His wife had been looking on, and, it being nearly twilight, was wonderstruck to observe how the snow-child gleamed and sparkled, and how she seemed to shed a glow all around about her; and when driven into the corner, she positively glistened like a star! It was a frosty kind of brightness, too, like that of an icicle in the moonlight. The wife thought it strange that good Mr Lindsey should see nothing remarkable in the snow child's appearance.

"Come, you odd little thing!" cried the honest man, seizing her by the hand, "I have caught you at last and will make you comfortable in spite of yourself. We will put a nice warm pair of worsted stockings on your frozen little feet, and you shall have a good thick shawl to wrap yourself in. Your poor white nose, I am afraid, is actually frost-bitten. But we will make it all right. Come along in."

And so, with a most benevolent smile on his sagacious visage, all purple as it was with the cold, this very well-meaning gentleman took the snow child by the hand and led her towards the house. She followed him, droopingly and reluctant; for all the glow and sparkle was gone out of her figure; and whereas just before she had resembled a bright frosty, star-gemmed evening, with a crimson gleam on the cold horizon, she now looked as dull and languid as a thaw. As kind Mr Lindsey led her up the steps of the door, Violet and Peony looked into his face—their eyes full of tears, which froze before they could run down their cheeks— and again entreated him not to bring their snow image into the house.

"Not bring her in!" exclaimed the kind-hearted man. "Why you are crazy, my little Violet!—quite crazy, my small Peony! She is so cold already that her hand has almost frozen mine in spite of my thick gloves. Would you have her freeze to death?"

His wife, as he came up the steps, had been taking another long, earnest, almost awe-stricken gaze at the little white stranger. She hardly knew whether it was a dream or not, but she could not help fancying that she saw the delicate print of Violet's fingers on the child's neck. It looked just as if, while Violet was shaping out the image, she had given it a gentle pat with her hand

and had neglected to smooth the impression quite away.

"After all, husband," said the mother, recurring to her idea that the angels would be as much delighted to play with Violet and Peony as she herself was—"after all, she does look strangely like a snow image! I do believe she is made of snow!"

A puff of the west wind blew against the snow child, and again she sparkled like a star.

"Snow!" repeated good Mr Lindsey, drawing the reluctant guest over this hospitable threshold. "No wonder she looks like snow. She is half frozen, poor little thing! But a good fire will put everything to rights."

Without further talk and always with the same best intentions, this highly benevolent and common-sensible individual led the little white damsel—drooping, drooping, drooping, more and more—out of the frosty air and into his comfortable parlour. A Heidenberg stove, filled to the brim with intensely burning anthracite, was sending a bright gleam through the isinglass of its iron door and causing the vase of water on its top to fume and bubble with excitement. A warm, sultry smell was diffused throughout the room. A thermometer on the wall farthest from the stove stood at eighty degrees. The parlour was hung with red curtains and covered with a red carpet and looked just as warm as it felt. The difference betwixt the atmosphere here and the cold, wintry twilight out of doors was like stepping at once from Nova Zembla to the hottest part of India or from the North Pole into an oven. O, this was a fine place for the little white stranger!

The common-sensible man placed the snow child on the hearth rug right in front of the hissing and fuming stove.

"Now she will be comfortable!" cried Mr Lindsey, rubbing his hands and looking about him with the pleasantest smile you ever saw. "Make yourself at home, my child."

Sad, sad and drooping looked the little white maiden as she stood on the hearth-rug, with the hot blast of the stove striking through her like a pestilence. Once, she threw a glance wistfully toward the windows and caught a glimpse, through its red curtains, of the snow-covered roofs, the stars glimmering frostily, and all the delicious intensity of the cold night. The bleak wind rattled the window-panes as if it were summoning her to come forth. But there stood the snow child, drooping, before the hot stove!

But the common-sensible man saw nothing amiss.

"Come, wife," said he, "let her have a pair of thick stockings and a woollen shawl or blanket directly and tell Dora to give her some warm supper as soon as the milk boils. You, Violet and Peony, amuse your little friend. She is out of spirits, you see, at finding herself in a strange place. For my part, I will go around among the neighbours, and find out where she belongs."

The mother, meanwhile, had gone in search of the shawl and stockings; for her own view of the matter, however subtle and delicate, had given way, as it always did, to the stubborn materialism of her husband. Without heeding the remonstrances of his two children, who still kept murmuring that their little snow-sister did not love the warmth, good Mr Lindsey took his departure, shutting the parlour door carefully behind him. Turning up the collar of his sack over his ears, he emerged from the house and had barely reached the street gate when he was recalled by the screams of Violet and Peony and the rapping of a thimbled finger against the parlour window.

"Husband! husband!" cried his wife, showing her horror-stricken face through the window panes. "There is no need of going for the child's parents!"

"We told you so, father!" screamed Violet and Peony as he re-entered the parlour. "You would bring her in; and now our poor—dear—beautiful little snow-sister is thawed!"

And their own sweet little faces were already dissolved in tears; so that their father, seeing what strange things occasionally happen in this everyday world, felt not a little anxious lest his children might be going to thaw too! In the utmost perplexity, he demanded an explanation from his wife. She could only reply that being summoned to the parlour by the cries of Violet and Peony, she found no trace of the little white maiden unless it were the remains of a heap of snow, which, while she was gazing at it, melted quite away upon the hearth-rug.

"And there you see all that is left of it!" added she, pointing to a pool of water, in front of the stove.

"Yes, father," said Violet, looking reproachfully at him through her tears, "there is all that is left of our dear little snow-sister!"

"Naughty father!" cried Peony, stamping his foot and —I shudder to say—shaking his little fist at the common-sensible man. "We told you how it would be! What for did you bring her in?"

And the Heidenberg stove, through the isinglass of its door, seemed to glare at good Mr Lindsey, like a red-eyed demon, triumphing in the mischief which it had done!

This, you will observe, was one of those rare cases, which yet will occasionally happen, where common sense finds itself at fault. The remarkable story of the snow image, though to that sagacious class of people to whom good Mr Lindsey belongs it may seem but a childish affair, is, nevertheless, capable of being moralised in various methods, greatly for their edification. One of its lessons, for instance, might be that it behoves men, and especially men of benevolence, to consider well what they are about and, before acting on their philanthropic purposes, to be quite sure that they comprehend the nature and all the relations of the business in hand. What has been established as an element of good to one being may prove absolute mischief to another; even as the warmth of the parlour was proper enough for children of flesh and blood, like Violet and Peony—though by no means very wholesome, even for them—involved nothing short of annihilation to the unfortunate snow-image.

But, after all, there is no teaching anything to wise men of good Mr Lindsey's stamp. They know everything—O, to be sure!—everything that has been, and everything that is, and everything that, by any future possibility, can be. And should some phenomenon of nature or providence transcend their system, they will not recognise it, even if it comes to pass under their very noses.

"Wife," said Mr Lindsey, after a fit of silence, "see what a quantity of snow the children have brought in on their feet! It has made quite a puddle here before the stove. Pray tell Dora to bring some towels and sop it up!"

New History of the Life and Adventures of Tom Thumb

by Sidney Babcock

Illustrated by Alexander Anderson

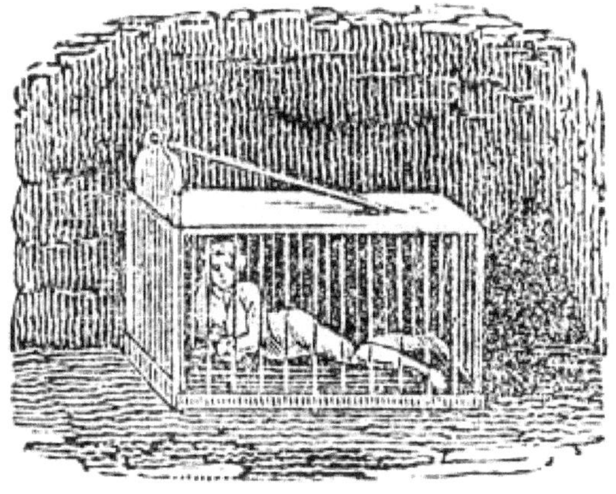

When I was a little boy, children's books were not quite as plentiful, as cheap, or as good as they are now. In those days, children did not often have a present of a pretty book with beautiful pictures; but when they did get one, it was highly prized.

We had Cock Robin, Jack the Giant Killer, Blue Beard, The Forty Thieves, and many other amusing but not very instructive tales. Tom Thumb was one of the numbers and was a favorite book of mine, although I knew the story was not true and that there were no such beings as magicians and fairies. Perhaps my little readers would like to know what kind of stories we old folks read when we were such little bodies as you are now. I think I remember enough of Tom Thumb to be able to tell you the story.

Once upon a time, Merlin, a famous magician, was traveling, and being weary, he stopped at a plowman's cottage to ask for some refreshment. The plowman's wife kindly brought him a bowl of milk, and a wooden plate of good brown bread, which she urged him to partake of.

Merlin could not help seeing that the honest couple looked quite sad and sorrowful; so he asked the cause and learned that they had no children; the wife was declaring, with tears in her eyes, that she should be happy if she had a son, even if he were no bigger than his father's thumb!

Merlin was much amused with the idea of a boy, no bigger than a man's thumb, and sending for the queen of the fairies, he told her of the desire of the plowman's wife. The queen was no less pleased than Merlin, and she said the wish should be granted. Accordingly, the plowman's wife had a son who was just the size of his father's thumb and was named the queen Tom Thumb.

One day his mother was making a pudding, and that he might see how it was made, Tom climbed on the top of the bowl; but his foot happened to slip, and he fell over head and ears into it, and his mother, not seeing him, she stirred him into the batter, and then popped the whole into the pot.

The hot water made Tom kick and struggle, and his mother, seeing the pudding jump up and down in the pot, thought it was bewitched. A pedlar going by at that moment, she gave him the pudding, which he put in his pack and then walked on. As soon as Tom could get the batter out of his mouth, he began to cry out. This so frightened the peddler that he flung the pudding over a fence and took to his heels. The pudding was broken by the fall, and poor Tom crawled out and ran home.

Tom never was any bigger, but as he grew older, he grew cunning and sly. When he played with boys for cherry stones and had lost his own, he used to creep into his playmates' bags, fill his pockets, and come out to play again. One day, as he was doing this, the owner chanced to see him. "Ah, ha, my little Tom," said he, "I have caught you at last; now I will punish you for stealing." So he drew the bag-string tight about his neck and then shaking the bag, Tom's legs and thighs were so badly bruised that he was thrown into a raging fever.

Just at this time, the queen of the fairies came in a coach drawn by six flying mice and, placing Tom by her side, drove through the air to her palace in fairyland, where she kept him till he was restored to health. Then, taking advantage of a fair wind, she blew him straight to the court of king Arthur. But just as Tom was about to land in the palace yard, the king's cook happened to pass with a huge bowl of soup, into which Tom fell plump and splashed the hot soup all in the cook's face and eyes.

"Oh, dear! Oh, dear!" cried Tom, half scalded and half-drowned in his hot bath; "murder! murder! murder!" bellowed the cook, who was a cross, red-faced old fellow and supposed Tom had done all this mischief on purpose. Determined to be revenged on the little fellow for the imaginary insult, he urged his brother, who was a miller, and as cross and cruel as himself, to take little Tom home with him and put him where he could do no more mischief.

Accordingly, the miller pocketed Tom and, carrying him to his mill, dropped him from a window into the river. But Tom was not born to be drowned. A large salmon swimming by at that moment caught him in its mouth and swallowed him without any trouble.

The salmon was soon caught, and, being a fine large fish, it was presented to the king, who ordered it to be dressed immediately. When it was cut open, everybody was delighted to see little Tom Thumb step out. He soon became the favorite of the king, who knighted him and gave him a little golden palace to live in, and also a tiny coach, which was drawn by six white mice.

King Arthur one day questioned Tom about his parents, and Tom informed his majesty that they were worthy people but very poor. Then the king led him into his treasury and, showing him the piles of gold and silver, told him he might pay his parents a visit, and take with him as much money as he could carry! Accordingly, Tom procured a little purse and, putting a sixpence into it, he with much labor and difficulty, got the purse upon his back and started for home.

His mother met him at the door, where he arrived almost tired to death, having traveled nearly half a mile with a huge sixpence on his back. His parents were delighted to see him, especially as he brought such an amazing sum of money.

Tom remained at home for some time, but at last, getting weary of his humble life, he watched for an opportunity to reach king Arthur's court again. One day he sauntered out into the fields, and seeing a butterfly seated on the ground, he ventured to get astride of him. The butterfly soon took wing and, mounting into the air with Tom on his back, flew from field to field till, at last, he reached the king's court.

The king, queen, and nobles, all tried to catch the butterfly but could not. At last poor Tom, having no saddle or bridle, slipped off and tumbled into a watering pot, where he was nearly drowned before he could be taken out. But he soon recovered from this mishap and once more became the pride and ornament of king Arthur's court.

At last, a huge spider one day attacked him, and though he drew his sword and fought well, the spider's poisonous breath, at last, overcame him.

King Arthur and his whole court went into mourning for little Tom Thumb. They buried him under a rose bush and raised a white marble monument over his grave, with this epitaph on it, in letters of gold:

Here lies Tom Thumb, a gallant knight,

Who died by a cruel spider's bite.

He was well known in king Arthur's court,

Where he afforded pleasant sport;

He rode at tilt and tournament,

And on a mouse hunting went.

Alive, he filled the court with mirth;

His death to general grief gave birth.

Good people, tears of sorrow shed,

And cry, Alas! Sir Tom is dead!

The Magic Mirror

by Edith Howes

There was once a wise old king in a far-off land who said to himself, "I have a daughter as well as a son; why should she not have a kingdom too? I will see to it at once." He called the chief map-maker to him and said: "Make a map of my kingdom and divide it by a line so evenly that each part shall be exactly half. There must not be one hair's breadth more on the east of the line than on the west."

The chief map-maker worked hard and soon had the map ready, and it was divided so evenly that there was not a hair's breadth more on the east of the line than on the west. Then the king made a law that when he died, the Prince should rule over all the country on one side of the line, and the Princess should rule over all the country on the other side. The Prince's land he called Eastroyal, and the Princess's land he called Westroyal, and from that day to this, there have always been kings over Eastroyal and queens over Westroyal.

But it was soon noticed that in Eastroyal, the people became discontented and quarrelsome and poor and were always finding fault with the government, whereas in the western country over the border, they were so happy and kind that they praised each queen from the beginning of her reign to the end. Nobody knew why there should be so great a difference, but a great difference there was. Things grew worse and worse in Eastroyal until at last, the people rose and turned the reigning king off his throne and set his little son in his place. "Perhaps we shall be better satisfied now!" they said.

The new king's mother walked alone, deep in thought, and she was very troubled. "How can I teach my little son to please his people better than his father did?" she wondered. "It would break my heart if he too angered them and lost his crown, yet already he is showing a haughty temper in his treatment of his lords, and I know not what to do."

"I know! I know!" said a voice.

The Queen's mother was much startled; though she had not spoken aloud, the words seemed an answer to her thought. She looked over the low wall of the garden into the road. There, an old woman hobbled, leaning on a stick and muttering to herself. She was poor and ragged and bent with age. "I know, I know!" she said again.

"What do you know?" asked the Queen-mother gently.

The old woman looked up at her. "Go to Westroyal," she said; and she hobbled away.

"Ah, a witch!" thought the Queen's mother, "and she is right. The Queens of the West have undoubtedly some secret means of making their people love them. I will find out what it is."

She prepared for a visit to Westroyal and arrived a few days later at the palace of the reigning queen. Here she was welcomed and feasted and treated right lovingly, but though she kept her eyes and her ears as wide open as it was possible for eyes and ears to be, she could not discover the secret. She grew sad with disappointment.

The young queen saw that she was sorrowful. "You are not happy here. What is the matter?" she asked. "What can I do to make you glad?"

The Queen's mother held out her hands imploringly. "Only give me your secret," she begged. "Tell me how you gain the love of your people and keep it through all the years. Tell me so that I may teach my young son how to hold his throne?"

"Is that all?" exclaimed the Queen. "Come, I will show you."

She led the way to her own lovely sleeping chamber, hung with rose silk and panelled with polished silver and amethyst, and she pointed to a great mirror set strongly into the wall. "Look within!" she said.

Wonderingly, the Queen-mother obeyed. On the surface of the mirror, the faces and forms of herself and the young queen were reflected; but after a few moments, as she gazed, these faded away, and in their places came a picture of a mine, with blackened toilers filling tracks with coal. That, too, faded, and a golden cornfield showed upon the polished glass; under the hot summer sun, the busy reapers moved, wiping the sweat from their brows when they stopped a moment to rest. A third picture was of weavers making cloth. A cottage home came next, and a lordly mansion of the rich and a homeless child seeking shelter under a city bridge. So the scene followed scene, beautiful, sad, or sordid, sometimes wild and violent, and sometimes gay and peaceful, showing in the main a people happy and content.

"What is it?" asked the amazed Queen-mother at last. "How come these pictures here?"

"They are the life of my state reflected on this magic mirror for my help," replied the Queen. "Long ago, when the first queen came to rule the new kingdom of Westroyal, the fairies brought this mirror and set it in the wall as here you see it. Faithfully ever since it has reflected the daily happenings through-out the land, the people's toil and pleasures, their dangers and their comforts and rewards. So each queen has known her country. Your son, looking in his mirror, sees but himself; I see the sufferings of my people and know what things they need, and so plainly are these pictures set before me that I cannot rest till I have used my power to give relief."

"Oh!" cried the Queen-mother, "now I see why you are loved. How can I get such a mirror for my son?"

"That I know not," replied the Queen.

Then the Queen's mother returned sadly at heart to the kingdom of her son, pondering on what she had seen.

Once again, she walked in her garden alone. "How shall I get such a mirror?" she wondered. "What should I do?"

As once before, a voice replied, "I know! I know!"

The Queen's mother looked over the garden wall. Hobbling along the road was the old woman who had bade her go to Westroyal. "You who helped me before, help me again!" cried the Queen's mother. "I have obeyed you. How now shall I get a magic mirror for my son?"

The old woman looked up at her. "Go to the Deeps," she said, and she hobbled off.

Now, this was a dreadful command to the Queen's

mother, for the Deeps was a horrible black pool in the roughest and most dangerous part of the country. It was said to be formed of the country's tears and to be also bottomless, and to be haunted by beings of strange shapes. There were stories of their mysterious power and evil ways. Yet go she must, if going meant the gaining of a magic mirror for her son. And she must go alone, for only so could any seeker find the pathway to the pool, so it was said.

"I will go at once before my courage fails," she said, and she left her sheltered garden and set off across the land.

She had many weary miles to travel past villages and towns and fields, and she was footsore and faint when at last, she reached the winding track that led between the darkening hills. Yet on she went, following the murmur of a tiny stream that dropped through thick-set bushes into a shadowed valley. On she went still, and now the darkness came, and she had lost her way. She stumbled over fallen logs, pushed with bleeding hands and torn clothes through bramble wildernesses, and found at last her way again to the narrow track beside the little stream that murmured in the dark.

On she went and down. The stream suddenly widened into a round blackness open to the sky but walled in by jagged rocks. It was the pool. Utterly spent through weariness and fear, she sank down among the rocks to rest and waited there for what might come to her.

Strange rustlings sounded around the rocks, strange forms loomed close beside her, and strange voices asked her: "What are you? Why come you to our haunts?" Though her heart was sick with dread, she answered boldly in a firm, clear voice. "Give me a magic mirror for my son, that he may learn to rule."

There was a flash, and the pool and all the rocks were lit by a light brighter and softer than that of the moon or stars. All around her stood the beings who had loomed so strangely in the darkness. They were fairies, exquisite in shape and fineness, robed in flowing gossamer of many colours. They smiled at her and touched her with their gentle hands, and immediately she was well. "Your love has brought you nobly through much fear and hurt," they said. "You shall have your due reward. Look into the Deeps."

One took her hand and led her to the edge, and the Queen-mother, fearless and smiling now, looked down into the fathomless water of the pool. As she gazed, ripples came upon its surface. They broke away into shining cascades of diamonds and pearls, and between them appeared the face and shoulders of the old woman of the road. "I have your magic mirror," she cried. "It is formed of the lowest teardrops of the Deeps."

She sprang out and trod the water to the shore, and as she went, her rags fell from her, and she rose into the air a shining queen of fairies, more beautiful than any other there, holding in her hand a tiny gleaming mirror. "Come," she said, "let us set it in its place."

She touched the Queen-mother's hand, and in a flash, they were all at the palace, within the young king's sleeping chamber of turquoise and gold. There as he lay asleep, the fairies set the mirror in its place with magic words, and as it touched the wall, it lengthened out and widened till it stood as large as that of the young queen across the borderline. Over the polished glass began to float the pictures of the country's life. "How can I show my gratitude?" the Queen's mother asked, but the fairies were gone.

The next morning when the little king awoke, he ran to see the fine new mirror in his room. He gazed and gazed upon the strange, entrancing pictures that came on it, and every day he spent long hours in the mirror. And as he learned to recognise the hardships and the sufferings of his people his heart grew hot to give relief, and he was no more haughty but used his power to ease their woes. So in Eastroyal as in Westroyal, there was content, and the people loved their king and praised him through all his days until the end. And all the kings who followed after him ruled wisely and were loved.

Willie Mouse

by Alta Tabor

Willie Mouse had often heard his Ma and Pa say that the moon was made of green cheese, and one evening he thought he would see if he could find it. He packed up a piece of cheese and a crust of bread and, taking his lantern, set out on his travels.

He had not gone far when he met his friend, Mr Woodmouse, who asked him where he was going.

"Oh!" said Willie, "I'm going to find the moon; it's made of green cheese, you know."

"I don't believe it's made of green cheese at all," said Mr Woodmouse, but Willie wouldn't listen to him and went on his way.

Coming round by Clover Green, whom should he meet but Miss Jenny Wren, looking very gay in her yellow bonnet.

"Where are you off to?" she asked.

"I'm on my way to find the moon."

"The moon!" cried Miss Wren, "you'll never reach it."

"I flew ever so high one evening and I didn't seem to get any nearer."

"Well," said Willie, "why should it be made of green cheese if you can't reach it?" And on he went.

Presently he came up to a block of wood and looked up. He saw Mr Squirrel jumping from branch to branch.

"Good afternoon," he said.

"You do seem high up. Surely you can tell me the way to the moon. It's made of green cheese, you know."

"I don't think it's made of green cheese; why shouldn't it be made of nuts?"

"How ignorant everybody is," said Willie Mouse to himself.

So on he went once more until he came to a little hole

in the ground, and being very curious, he peeped inside. There sat Mrs Mole, who came out when she saw him.

"Do you live down there?" asked Willie politely.

"Yes," replied Mrs Mole.

"Then I'm afraid you can't tell me how to get to the moon. It's made of green cheese, you know; Ma says so."

"Nonsense, my child. Don't waste your time looking for the moon; keep your eyes open for worms."

Willie said "Good-bye" to Mrs Mole. Then he sat down and opened his parcel because it was getting late and he thought he had better have some dinner.

"I may not reach the moon yet awhile," he thought, "so I had better save a little piece of cheese for supper."

After dinner, he fell asleep, and on waking, he found that it was quite dark. He looked up, and there was the moon right high up in the sky.

"Oh, Mr. Moon!" he cried, "You do seem a long way away. I think it would be much easier for you to come down here than for me to get up there." But Mr Moon stayed where he was.

Looking up, Willie Mouse saw two big eyes gleaming in the dark. They belonged to Mrs Owl, and as Willie was only a little mouse, he didn't know that Mrs Owl had a special liking for little mice.

"Please, Mrs Owl," said he, "how can I get to the moon?"

Down flew Mrs Owl. "This is the way to the moon," she said, and she caught him up in her beak and carried him back to the owl house where she lived.

When Willie Mouse saw all the owlets with their beaks gaping open, he began to be frightened, for he feared that Mrs Owl was going to eat him all up. But he didn't know that a good green elf, who lived in the trunk of the tree, was near at hand, and just as Mrs Owl opened her beak, the leaves rustled and there stood Mr Elf, who jumped to the ground with Willie on his back.

When the good green elf had shown him the way home, he thought he would ask him if the moon were really made of green cheese, but all of a sudden, Mr Elf disappeared, and Willie Mouse still thinks that one day he will find the moon and have enough cheese to last him all his life.

But he will wait until he is a little older and bigger before he tries to jump to the moon. And perhaps by that time, he may be wiser, too.

The Magic Fishbone

by Charles Dickens

He saw the Fish-bone on her Plate

There was once a King, and he had a Queen, and he was the manliest of his sex, and she was the loveliest of hers. The King was, in his private profession, Under Government. The Queen's father had been a medical man out of town.

They had nineteen children and were always having more. Seventeen of these children took care of the baby, and Alicia, the eldest, took care of them all. Their ages varied from seven years to seven months.

Let us now resume our story.

One day the King was going to the office when he stopped at the fishmonger's to buy a pound and a half of salmon not too near the tail, which the Queen (a careful housekeeper) had requested him to send home. Mr Pickles, the fishmonger, said, "Certainly, sir, is there any other article, Good-morning."

The King went on towards the office in a melancholy mood, for the quarter day was such a long way off, and several dear children were growing out of their clothes. He had not proceeded far when Mr Pickles's errand boy came running after him and said, "Sir, you didn't notice the old lady in our shop."

"What old lady?" enquired the King. "I saw none."

Now, the King had not seen any old lady because this old lady had been invisible to him, though visible to Mr Pickles's boy. Probably because he messed and splashed the water about to that degree and flopped the pairs of soles down in that violent manner, that, if she had not been visible to him, he would have spoilt her clothes.

Just then, the old lady came trotting up. She was dressed in shot-silk of the richest quality, smelling of dried lavender.

"King Watkins the First, I believe?" said the old lady.

"Watkins," replied the King, "is my name."

"Papa, if I am not mistaken, of the beautiful Princess

Alicia?" said the old lady.

"And of eighteen other darlings," replied the King.

"Listen. You are going to the office," said the old lady.

It instantly flashed upon the King that she must be a Fairy, or how could she know that?

"You are right," said the old lady, answering his thoughts, "I am the Good Fairy Grandmarina. Attend. When you return home to dinner, politely invite the Princess Alicia to have some of the salmon you bought just now."

"It may disagree with her," said the King.

The old lady became so very angry at this absurd idea that the King was quite alarmed and humbly begged her pardon.

"We hear a great deal too much about this thing disagreeing, and that thing disagreeing," said the old lady, with the greatest contempt it was possible to express. "Don't be greedy. I think you want it all yourself."

The King hung his head under this reproof and said he wouldn't talk about things disagreeing anymore.

"Be good, then," said the Fairy Grandmarina, "and don't! When the beautiful Princess Alicia consents to partake of the salmon—as I think she will—you will find she will leave a fish-bone on her plate. Tell her to dry it, and to rub it, and to polish it till it shines like mother-of-pearl, and to take care of it as a present from me."

"Is that all?" asked the King.

"Don't be impatient, sir," returned the Fairy Grandmarina, scolding him severely. "Don't catch people short, before they have done speaking. Just the way with you grown-up persons. You are always doing it."

The King again hung his head and said he wouldn't do so anymore.

"Be good then," said the Fairy Grandmarina, "and don't! Tell the Princess Alicia, with my love, that the fish-bone is a magic present which can only be used once; but that it will bring her, that once, whatever she wishes for, provided she wishes for it at the right time. That is the message. Take care of it."

The King was beginning, "Might I ask the reason—?" when the Fairy became absolutely furious.

"Will you be good, sir?" she exclaimed, stamping her foot on the ground. "The reason for this, and the reason for that, indeed! You are always wanting the reason. No reason. There! Hoity toity me! I am sick of your grown-up reasons."

The King was extremely frightened by the old lady's flying into such a passion and said he was very sorry to have offended her, and he wouldn't ask for reasons any more.

"Be good then," said the old lady, "and don't!"

With those words, Grandmarina vanished, and the King went on and on and on till he came to the office. There he wrote and wrote and wrote till it was time to go home again. Then he politely invited Princess Alicia, as the Fairy had directed him, to partake of the salmon. And when she had enjoyed it very much, he saw the fishbone on her plate, as the Fairy had told him he would, and he delivered the Fairy's message, and Princess Alicia took care to dry the bone and to rub it and to polish it till it shone like mother-of-pearl.

And so when the Queen was going to get up in the morning, she said, "O, dear me, dear me; my head, my head!" and then she fainted away.

Princess Alicia, who happened to be looking in at the chamber door, asking about breakfast, was very much alarmed when she saw her Royal Mamma in this state, and she rang the bell for Peggy, which was the name of the Lord Chamberlain. But remembering where the smelling bottle was, she climbed on a chair and got it, and after that, she climbed onto another chair by the bedside and held the smelling bottle to the Queen's nose, and after that, she jumped down and got some water, and after that, she jumped up again and wetted the Queen's forehead, and, in short, when the Lord Chamberlain came in, that dear old woman said to the little Princess, "What a Trot you are! I couldn't have done it better myself!"

But that was not the worst of the good Queen's illness. Oh, no! She was very ill indeed for a long time. Princess Alicia kept the seventeen young Princes and Princesses quiet, dressed and undressed and danced the baby, made the kettle boil, heated the soup, swept the hearth, poured out the medicine, nursed the Queen, and did all that ever she could, and was as busy busy busy, as busy could be. For there were not many servants at that Palace for three reasons; because the King was short of money, because a rise in his office never seemed to come, and because the quarter day was so far off that it looked almost as far off and as little as one of the stars.

But on the morning when the Queen fainted away, where was the magic fishbone? Why, there it was in Princess Alicia's pocket. She had almost taken it out to bring the Queen to life again when she put it back and looked for the smelling bottle.

After the Queen had come out of her swoon that morning and was dozing, Princess Alicia hurried upstairs to tell a most particular secret to a most particularly confidential friend of hers, who was a Duchess. People did suppose her to be a Doll, but she was really a Duchess, though nobody knew it except the Princess.

This most particular secret was a secret about the magic fishbone, the history of which was well known to the Duchess because the Princess told her everything. The Princess kneeled by the bed on which the Duchess was lying, full-dressed and wide awake, and whispered the secret to her. The Duchess smiled and nodded. People might have supposed that she never smiled and nodded, but she often did, though nobody knew it except the Princess.

Then Princess Alicia hurried downstairs again to keep watch in the Queen's room. She often kept watch by herself in the Queen's room, but every evening, while the illness lasted, she sat there watching with the King. And every evening, the King sat looking at her with a cross look, wondering why she never brought out the magic fishbone. As often as she noticed this, she ran upstairs, whispered the secret to the Duchess over again, and said to the Duchess besides, "They think we children never have a reason or a meaning!" And the Duchess, though the most fashionable Duchess that ever was heard of, winked her eye.

"Alicia," said the King one evening when she wished him Good Night.

"Yes, Papa."

"What is become of the magic fishbone?"

"In my pocket, Papa."

"I thought you had lost it?"

"O, no, Papa."

"Or forgotten it?"

"No, indeed, Papa."

And so another time, the dreadful little snapping pug-dog next door made a rush at one of the young Princes as he stood on the steps coming home from school and terrified him out of his wits, and he put his hand through a pane of glass and bled bled bled. When the seventeen other young Princes and Princesses saw him bleed bleed bleed, they were terrified out of their wits too and screamed themselves black in their seventeen faces all at once. But Princess Alicia put her hands over all their seventeen mouths, one after another, and persuaded them to be quiet because of the sick Queen. And then she put the wounded Prince's hand in a basin of fresh cold water, while they stared with their twice seventeen are thirty-four put down four and carry three eyes, and then she looked in hand for bits of glass, and there were, fortunately, no bits of glass there. And then she said to two chubby-legged Princes who were sturdy though small, "Bring me in the Royal rag-bag; I must snip and stitch and cut and contrive." So those two young Princes tugged at the Royal rag bag and lugged it in. Princess Alicia sat down on the floor with a large pair of scissors and a needle and thread, and snipped and stitched and cut and contrived, and made a bandage and put it on, and it fitted beautifully, and so when it was all done she saw the King her Papa looking on by the door.

"Alicia."

"Yes, Papa."

"What have you been doing?"

"Snipping stitching cutting and contriving, Papa."

"Where is the magic fish-bone?"

"In my pocket, Papa."

"I thought you had lost it?"

"O, no, Papa."

"Or forgotten it?"

"No, indeed, Papa."

After that, she ran upstairs to the Duchess and told her what had passed and told her the secret over again, and the Duchess shook her flaxen curls and laughed with her rosy lips.

Well! and so another time the baby fell under the grate. The seventeen young Princes and Princesses were used to it, for they were almost always falling under the grate or down the stairs, but the baby was not used to it yet, and it gave him a swelled face and a black eye. The way the poor little darling came to tumble was that he slid out of Princess Alicia's lap just as she was sitting in a great coarse apron that quite smothered her in front of the kitchen fire, beginning to peel the turnips for the broth for dinner. The way she came to be doing that was that the King's cook had run away that morning with her own true love, who was a very tall but very tipsy soldier. Then, the seventeen young Princes and Princesses, who cried at everything that happened, cried and roared. But Princess Alicia (who couldn't help crying a little herself) quietly called to them to be still, on account of not throwing back the Queen upstairs, who was fast getting well, and said, "Hold your tongues, you wicked little monkeys, every one of you, while I examine baby!" Then she examined the baby and found that he hadn't broken anything, and she held cold iron to his poor dear eye and smoothed his poor dear face, and he presently fell asleep in her arms. Then, she said to the seventeen Princes and Princesses, "I am afraid to lay him down yet, lest he should wake and feel pain, be good, and you shall all be cooks." They jumped for joy when they heard that and began making themselves cooks' caps out of old newspapers. So to one she gave the saltbox, and to one she gave the barley, and to one she gave the herbs, and to one she gave the turnips, and to one she gave the carrots, and to one she gave the onions, and to one she gave the spice-box, till they were all cooks, and all were running about at work, she sitting in the middle smothered in the great coarse apron, nursing baby. By and by, the broth was done, and the baby woke up smiling like an angel and was trusted to the most sedate Princess to hold, while the other Princes and Princesses were squeezed into a far-off corner to look at Princess Alicia, turning out the saucepan-full of broth, for fear (as they were always getting into trouble) they should get splashed and scalded. When the broth came tumbling out, steaming beautifully and smelling like a nosegay good to eat, they clapped their hands. That made the baby clap his hands, and that, and his looking as if he had a comic toothache, made all the Princes and Princesses laugh. So Princess Alicia said, "Laugh and be good, and after dinner we will make him a nest on the floor in a corner, and he shall sit in his nest and see a dance of eighteen cooks." That delighted the young Princes and Princesses, and they ate up all the broth, washed up all the plates and dishes, cleared away, and pushed the table into a corner, and then they, in their cooks' caps. Princess Alicia in the smothering coarse apron that belonged to the cook that had run away with her true love that was the very tall but very tipsy soldier, danced a dance of eighteen cooks before the angelic baby, who forgot his swelled face and his black eye and crowed with joy.

And so then, once more, Princess Alicia saw King Watkins the First, her father, standing in the doorway looking on, and he said: "What have you been doing, Alicia?"

"Cooking and contriving, Papa."

"What else have you been doing, Alicia?"

"Keeping the children light-hearted, Papa."

"Where is the magic fishbone, Alicia?"

"In my pocket, Papa."

"I thought you had lost it?"

"O, no, Papa."

"Or forgotten it?"

"No, indeed, Papa."

The King then sighed so heavily, seemed so low-spirited, and sat down so miserably, leaning his head upon his hand and his elbow upon the kitchen table pushed away in the corner, that the seventeen Princes and Princesses crept softly out of the kitchen and left him alone with Princess Alicia and the angelic baby.

"What is the matter, Papa?"

"I am dreadfully poor, my child."

"Have you no money at all, Papa?"

"None my child."

"Is there no way left of getting any, Papa?"

"No way," said the King. "I have tried very hard, and I have tried all ways."

When she heard those last words, Princess Alicia began to put her hand into the pocket where she kept the magic fishbone.

"Papa," said she, "when we have tried very hard, and tried all ways, we must have done our very very best?"

"No doubt, Alicia."

"When we have done our very very best, Papa, and that is not enough, then I think the right time must have come for asking help of others." This was the very secret connected with the magic fishbone, which she had found out for herself from the good fairy

Grandmarina's words, and which she had so often whispered to her beautiful and fashionable friend Duchess.

So she took out of her pocket the magic fishbone that had been dried and rubbed and polished till it shone like mother-of-pearl, and she gave it one little kiss and wished it was the quarter day. And immediately, it was quarter-day; and the King's quarter's salary came rattling down the chimney and bounced into the middle of the floor.

But this was not half of what happened, no not a quarter, for immediately afterwards, the good fairy Grandmarina came riding in, in a carriage and four (Peacocks), with Mr Pickles's boy up behind, dressed in silver and gold, with a cocked hat, powdered hair, pink silk stockings, a jewelled cane, and a nosegay. Down jumped Mr Pickles's boy with his cocked hat in his hand and wonderfully polite (being entirely changed by enchantment), and handed Grandmarina out, and there she stood in her rich shot silk smelling of dried lavender, fanning herself with a sparkling fan.

"Alicia, my dear," said this charming old Fairy, "how do you do, I hope I see you pretty well, give me a kiss."

Princess Alicia embraced her, and then Grandmarina turned to the King and said rather sharply:—"Are you good?"

The King said he hoped so.

"I suppose you know the reason, now, why my god-

Daughter here," kissing the Princess again, "did not apply to the fishbone sooner?" said the Fairy.

The King made her a shy bow.

"Ah! but you didn't then!" said the Fairy.

The King made her a shyer bow.

"Any more reasons to ask for?" said the Fairy.

The King said no, and he was very sorry.

"Be good then," said the Fairy, "and live happy ever afterwards."

Then, Grandmarina waved her fan, and the Queen came in most splendidly dressed, and the seventeen young Princes and Princesses, no longer grown out of their clothes, came in newly fitted out from top to toe, with tucks in everything to admit of its being let out. After that, the Fairy tapped Princess Alicia with her fan, and the smothering coarse apron flew away, and she appeared exquisitely dressed, like a little Bride, with a wreath of orange flowers and a silver veil. After that, the kitchen dresser changed itself into a wardrobe made of beautiful wood and gold and looking glass, which was full of dresses of all sorts, all for her and all exactly fitting her. After that, the angelic baby came in, running alone, with his face and eye not a bit the worse but much, the better. Then, Grandmarina begged to be introduced to the Duchess, and when the Duchess was brought down, many compliments passed between them.

A little whispering took place between the Fairy and the Duchess, and then the Fairy said out loud, "Yes. I thought she would have told you." Grandmarina then turned to the King and Queen and said, "We are going in search of Prince Certainpersonio. The pleasure of your company is requested at church in half an hour precisely." So she and Princess Alicia got into the carriage, and Mr Pickles's boy handed in the Duchess, who sat by herself on the opposite seat, and then Mr Pickles's boy put up the steps and got up behind, and the Peacocks flew away with their tails spread.

Prince Certainpersonio was sitting by himself, eating barley sugar and waiting to be ninety. When he saw the Peacocks followed by the carriage, coming in at the window, it immediately occurred to him that something uncommon was going to happen.

"Prince," said Grandmarina, "I bring you your Bride."

The moment the Fairy said those words, Prince Certainpersonio's face left off being sticky, and his jacket and corduroys changed to peach-bloom velvet, and his hair curled, and a cap and feather flew in like a bird and settled on his head. He got into the carriage at the Fairy's invitation, and he renewed his acquaintance with the Duchess, whom he had seen before.

In the church were the Prince's relations and friends, Princess Alicia's relations and friends, the seventeen Princes and Princesses, the baby, and a crowd of neighbours. The marriage was beautiful beyond expression. The Duchess was a bridesmaid and beheld the ceremony from the pulpit, where she was supported by the cushion of the desk.

Grandmarina gave a magnificent wedding feast afterwards, in which there was everything and more to eat and everything and more to drink. The wedding cake was delicately ornamented with white satin ribbons, frosted silver and white lilies, and was forty-two yards round.

When Grandmarina had drunk her love to the young couple, Prince Certainpersonio made a speech, and everybody cried, Hip hip, hip hurrah! Grandmarina announced to the King and Queen that in future, there would be eight quarter days in every year, except in leap year, when there would be ten. She then turned to Certainpersonio and Alicia and said, "My dears, you will have thirty-five children, and they will all be good and beautiful. Seventeen of your children will be boys, and eighteen will be girls. The hair of the whole of your children will curl naturally. They will never have the measles and will have recovered from the whooping cough before being born."

On hearing such good news, everybody cried out, "Hip hip hip, hurrah!" again.

"It only remains," said Grandmarina in conclusion, "to make an end of the fishbone."

So she took it from the hand of Princess Alicia, and it instantly flew down the throat of the dreadful little

snapping pug-dog next door and choked him, and he
expired in convulsions.

245

The Wonderful Sheep

by Andrew Lang

Once upon a time—in the days when the fairies lived—there was a king who had three daughters, who were all young, clever, and beautiful, but the youngest of the three, who was called Miranda, was the prettiest and the most beloved.

The King, her father, gave her more dresses and jewels in a month than he gave the others in a year; but she was so generous that she shared everything with her sisters, and they were all as happy and as fond of one another as they could be.

Now, the King had some quarrelsome neighbors who, tired of leaving him in peace, began to make war upon him so fiercely that he feared he would be altogether beaten if he did not make an effort to defend himself. So he collected a great army and set off to fight them, leaving the Princesses with their governess in a castle where news of the war was brought every day—sometimes that the King had taken a town or won a battle, and, at last, that he had altogether overcome his enemies and chased them out of his kingdom, and was coming back to the castle as quickly as possible, to see his dear little Miranda whom he loved so much.

The three Princesses put on dresses of satin, which they had made on purpose for this great occasion, one green, one blue, and the third white; their jewels were the same colors. The eldest wore emeralds, the second turquoise, and the youngest diamonds, and thus adorned, they went to meet the King, singing verses which they had composed about his victories.

When he saw them all so beautiful and so gay, he embraced them tenderly but gave Miranda more kisses than either of the others.

Presently a splendid banquet was served, and the King and his daughters sat down to it, and as he always thought that there was some special meaning in everything, he said to the eldest:

"Tell me why you have chosen a green dress."

"Sire," she answered, "having heard of your victories, I thought that green would signify my joy and the hope of your speedy return."

"That is a very good answer," said the King, "and

you, my daughter," he continued, "why did you take a blue dress?"

"Sire," said the Princess, "to show that we constantly hoped for your success and that the sight of you is as welcome to me as the sky with its most beautiful stars."

"Why," said the King, "your wise answers astonish me and you, Miranda. What made you dress yourself all in white?

"Because, sire," she answered, "white suits me better than anything else."

"What!" said the King angrily, "was that all you thought of, vain child?"

"I thought you would be pleased with me," said the Princess; "that was all."

The King, who loved her, was satisfied with this and even pretended to be pleased that she had not told him all her reasons at first.

"And now," said he, "as I have supped well, and it is not time yet to go to bed, tell me what you dreamed last night."

The eldest said she had dreamed that he brought her a dress, and the precious stones and gold embroidery on it were brighter than the sun.

The dream of the second was that the King had brought her a spinning wheel and a distaff, that she might spin him some shirts.

But the youngest said: "I dreamed that my second sister was to be married, and on her wedding day, you, father, held a golden ewer and said: 'Come, Miranda, and I will hold the water that you may dip your hands in it.'"

The King was very angry indeed when he heard this dream and frowned horribly; indeed, he made such an ugly face that everyone knew how angry he was, and he got up and went off to bed in a great hurry, but he could not forget his daughter's dream.

"Does the proud girl wish to make me her slave?" he said to himself. "I am not surprised at her choosing to dress herself in white satin without a thought of me. She does not think me worthy of her consideration! But I will soon put an end to her pretensions!"

He rose in a fury, and although it was not yet daylight, he sent for the Captain of his Bodyguard and said to him:

"You have heard the Princess Miranda's dream? I consider that it means strange things against me, therefore I order you to take her away into the forest and kill her, and, that I may be sure it is done, you must bring me her heart and her tongue. If you attempt to deceive me you shall be put to death!"

The Captain of the Guard was very much astonished when he heard this barbarous order, but he did not dare to contradict the King for fear of making him still more angry or causing him to send someone else, so he answered that he would fetch the Princess and do as the King had said. When he went to her room, they would hardly let him in, it was so early, but he said that the King had sent for Miranda, and she got up quickly and came out; a little black girl called Patypata held up her train, and her pet monkey and her little dog ran after her. The monkey was called Grabugeon, and the little dog was Tintin.

The Captain of the Guard begged Miranda to come down into the garden where the King was enjoying the fresh air. When they got there, he pretended to search for him, but as he was not to be found, he said:

"No doubt his Majesty has strolled into the forest," and he opened the little door that led to it, and they went through.

By this time, the daylight had begun to appear, and the Princess, looking at her conductor, saw that he had tears in his eyes and seemed too sad to speak.

"What is the matter?" she said in the kindest way. "You seem very sorrowful."

"Alas! Princess," he answered, "who would not be sorrowful who was ordered to do such a terrible thing as I am? The King has commanded me to kill you here, and carry your heart and your tongue to him, and if I disobey I shall lose my life."

The poor Princess was terrified. She grew very pale and began to cry softly.

Looking up at the Captain of the Guard with her beautiful eyes, she said gently:

"Will you really have the heart to kill me? I have never done you any harm, and have always spoken well of you to the King. If I had deserved my father's anger I would suffer without a murmur, but, alas! he is unjust to complain of me, when I have always treated him with love and respect."

"Fear nothing, Princess," said the Captain of the Guard. "I would far rather die myself than hurt you; but even if I am killed you will not be safe: we must find some way of making the King believe that you are dead."

"What can we do?" said Miranda; "unless you take him my heart and my tongue he will never believe you."

The Princess and the Captain of the Guard were talking so earnestly that they did not think of Patypata, but she had overheard all they said and now came and threw herself at Miranda's feet.

"Madam," she said, "I offer you my life; let me be killed, I shall be only too happy to die for such a kind mistress."

"Why, Patypata," cried the Princess, kissing her, "that would never do; your life is as precious to me as my own, especially after such a proof of your affection as you have just given me."

"You are right, Princess," said Grabugeon, coming forward, "to love such a faithful slave as Patypata; she is of more use to you than I am, I offer you my tongue and my heart most willingly, especially as I wish to make a great name for myself in Goblin Land."

"No, no, my little Grabugeon," replied Miranda, "I cannot bear the thought of taking your life."

"Such a good little dog as I am," cried Tintin, "could not think of letting either of you die for his mistress. If anyone is to die for her it must be me."

And then began a great dispute between Patypata, Grabugeon, and Tintin, and they came to high words until at last Grabugeon, who was quicker than the others, ran up to the very top of the nearest tree, and let herself fall, head first, to the ground, and there she lay —quite dead!

The Princess was very sorry, but as Grabugeon was really dead, she allowed the Captain of the Guard to take her tongue; but, alas! It was such a little one—not bigger than the Princess's thumb—that they decided sorrowfully that it was of no use at all: the King would not have been taken in by it for a moment!

"Alas! my little monkey," cried the Princess, "I have lost you, and yet I am no better off than I was before."

"The honor of saving your life is to be mine," interrupted Patypata, and before they could prevent her, she had picked up a knife and cut her head off in an instant.

But when the Captain of the Guard would have taken her tongue, it turned out to be quite black, so that would not have deceived the King either.

"Am I not unlucky?" cried the poor Princess; "I lose everything I love, and am none the better for it."

"If you had accepted my offer," said Tintin, "you would only have had me to regret, and I should have had all your gratitude."

Miranda kissed her little dog, crying so bitterly that, at last, she could bear it no longer and turned away into the forest. When she looked back, the Captain of the Guard was gone, and she was alone, except for Patypata, Grabugeon, and Tintin, who lay upon the ground. She could not leave the place until she had buried them in a pretty little mossy grave at the foot of a tree, and she wrote their names upon the bark of the tree and how they had all died to save her life. And then she began to think where she could go for safety—for this forest was so close to her father's castle that she might be seen and recognized by the first passer-by, and, besides that, it was full of lions and wolves, who would have snapped up a princess just as soon as a stray chicken. So she began to walk as fast as she could, but the forest was so large, and the sun was so hot that she nearly died of heat and terror and fatigue; look which way she would there seem to be no end to the forest, and she was so frightened that she fancied every minute that she heard the King running after her to kill her. You may imagine how miserable she was and how she cried as she went on, not knowing which path to follow, with the thorny bushes scratching her dreadfully and tearing her pretty frock to pieces.

At last, she heard the bleating of a sheep and said to herself:

"No doubt there are shepherds here with their flocks; they will show me the way to some village where I can live disguised as a peasant girl. Alas! it is not always kings and princes who are the happiest people in the world. Who could have believed that I should ever be obliged to run away and hide because the King, for no reason at all, wishes to kill me?"

So saying, she advanced toward the place where she heard the bleating, but what was her surprise when, in a lovely little glade quite surrounded by trees, she saw a large sheep; its wool was as white as snow, and its horns shone like gold; it had a garland of flowers round its neck, and strings of great pearls about its legs, and a collar of diamonds; it lay upon a bank of orange-flowers, under a canopy of cloth of gold which protected it from the heat of the sun. Nearly a hundred other sheep were scattered about, not eating the grass, but some drinking coffee, lemonade, or sherbet, others eating ices, strawberries and cream, or sweetmeats, while others, again, were playing games. Many of them wore golden collars with jewels, flowers, and ribbons.

Miranda stopped short in amazement at this unexpected sight and was looking in all directions for the shepherd of this surprising flock when the beautiful sheep came bounding toward her.

"Approach, lovely Princess," he cried; "have no fear of such gentle and peaceable animals as we are."

"What a marvel!" cried the Princess, starting back a little. "Here is a sheep that can talk."

"Your monkey and your dog could talk, madam," said he; "are you more astonished at us than at them?"

"A fairy gave them the power to speak," replied Miranda. "So I was used to them."

"Perhaps the same thing has happened to us," he said, smiling sheepishly. "But, Princess, what can have led you here?"

"A thousand misfortunes, Sir Sheep," she answered.

"I am the unhappiest princess in the world, and I am seeking a shelter against my father's anger."

"Come with me, madam," said the Sheep; "I offer you a hiding-place which you only will know of, and where you will be mistress of everything you see."

"I really cannot follow you," said Miranda, "for I am too tired to walk another step."

The Sheep with the golden horns ordered that his chariot should be fetched, and a moment after appeared six goats, harnessed to a pumpkin, which was so big that two people could quite well sit in it and was all lined with cushions of velvet and down. The Princess stepped into it, much amused at such a new kind of carriage. The King of the Sheep took his place beside her, and the goats ran away with them at full speed and only stopped when they reached a cavern, the entrance to which was blocked by a great stone. This the King touched with his foot, and immediately it fell down, and he invited the Princess to enter without fear. Now, if she had not been so alarmed by everything that had happened, nothing could have induced her to go into this frightful cave, but she was so afraid of what might be behind her that she would have thrown herself even down a well at this moment. So, without hesitation, she followed the Sheep, who went before her, down, down, down, until she thought they must come out at the other side of the world—indeed, she was not sure that he wasn't leading her into Fairyland. At last, she saw before her a great plain, quite covered with all sorts of flowers, the scent of which seemed to her nicer than anything she had ever smelled before; a broad river of orange-flower water flowed around it, and fountains of wine of every kind ran in all directions and made the prettiest little cascades and brooks. The plain was covered with the strangest trees. There were whole avenues where partridges, ready roasted, hung from every branch, or if you preferred pheasants, quails, turkeys, or rabbits, you had only to turn to the right hand or to the left, and you were sure to find them. In places, the air was darkened by showers of lobster patties, white puddings, sausages, tarts, and all sorts of sweetmeats or with pieces of gold and silver, diamonds and pearls. This unusual kind of rain, and the pleasantness of the whole place, would, no doubt, have attracted numbers of people to it if the King of the

Sheep had been of a more sociable disposition, but from all accounts, it is evident that he was as grave as a judge.

As it was quite the nicest time of the year when Miranda arrived in this delightful land, the only palace she saw was a long row of orange trees, jasmines, honeysuckles, and musk roses, and their interlacing branches made the prettiest rooms possible, which were hung with gold and silver gauze, and had great mirrors and candlesticks, and most beautiful pictures. The Wonderful Sheep begged that the Princess would consider herself queen over all that she saw and assured her that, though for some years he had been very sad and in great trouble, she had it in her power to make him forget all his grief.

"You are so kind and generous, noble Sheep," said the Princess, "that I cannot thank you enough, but I must confess that all I see here seems to me so extraordinary that I don't know what to think of it."

As she spoke, a band of lovely fairies came up and offered her amber baskets full of fruit, but when she held out her hands to them, they glided away, and she could feel nothing when she tried to touch them.

"Oh!" she cried, "what can they be? Whom am I with?" and she began to cry.

At this instant, the King of the Sheep came back to her and was so distracted to find her in tears that he could have torn his wool.

"What is the matter, lovely Princess?" he cried. "Has anyone failed to treat you with due respect?"

"Oh! No," said Miranda, "only I am not used to living with sprites and with sheep that talk, and everything here frightens me. It was very kind of you to bring me to this place, but I shall be even more grateful to you if you will take me up into the world again."

"Do not be afraid," said the Wonderful Sheep; "I entreat you to have patience and listen to the story of my misfortunes. I was once a king, and my kingdom was the most splendid in the world. My subjects loved me, and my neighbors envied and feared me. I was respected by everyone, and it was said that no king ever deserved it more.

"I was very fond of hunting, and one day, while chasing a stag, I left my attendants far behind; suddenly, I saw the animal leap into a pool of water, and I rashly urged my horse to follow it, but before we had gone many steps I felt an extraordinary heat, instead of the coolness of the water; the pond dried up, a great gulf opened before me, out of which flames of fire shot up, and I fell helplessly to the bottom of a precipice.

"I gave myself up for lost, but presently a voice said: 'Ungrateful Prince, even this fire is hardly enough to warm your cold heart!'

"'Who complains of my coldness in this dismal place?' I cried.

"'An unhappy being who loves you hopelessly,' replied the voice, and at the same moment, the flames began to flicker and cease to burn, and I saw a fairy, whom I had known as long as I could remember, and whose ugliness had always horrified me. She was leaning upon the arm of a most beautiful young girl, who wore chains of gold on her wrists and was evidently her slave.

"'Why, Ragotte,' I said, for that was the fairy's name, 'what is the meaning of all this? Is it by your orders that I am here?'

"'And whose fault is it,' she answered, 'that you have never understood me until now? Must a powerful fairy like myself condescend to explain her doings to you, who are no better than an ant by comparison, though you think yourself a great king?'

"'Call me what you like,' I said impatiently, 'but what is it that you want—my crown, or my cities, or my treasures?'

"'Treasures!' said the fairy, disdainfully. 'If I chose I could make any one of my scullions richer and more powerful than you. I do not want your treasures, but,' she added softly, 'if you will give me your heart—if you will marry me—I will add twenty kingdoms to the one you have already; you shall have a hundred castles full of gold and five hundred full of silver, and, in short, anything you like to ask me for.'

"'Madam Ragotte,' said I, 'when one is at the bottom

of a pit where one has fully expected to be roasted alive, it is impossible to think of asking such a charming person as you are to marry one! I beg that you will set me at liberty, and then I shall hope to answer you fittingly.'

"'Ah!' said she, 'if you really loved me you would not care where you were—a cave, a wood, a fox-hole, a desert, would please you equally well. Do not think that you can deceive me; you fancy you are going to escape, but I assure you that you are going to stay here and the first thing I shall give you to do will be to keep my sheep—they are very good company and speak quite as well as you do.

"As she spoke, she advanced and led me to this plain where we now stand and showed me her flock, but I paid little attention to it or to her.

"To tell the truth, I was so lost in admiration of her beautiful slave that I forgot everything else, and the cruel Ragotte, perceiving this, turned upon her so furious and terrible a look that she fell lifeless to the ground.

"At this dreadful sight, I drew my sword and rushed at Ragotte, and should certainly have cut off her head had she not by her magic arts chained me to the spot on which I stood; all my efforts to move were useless, and at last, when I threw myself down on the ground in despair, she said to me, with a scornful smile:

"'I intend to make you feel my power. It seems that

you are a lion at present. I mean you to be a sheep.'

"So saying, she touched me with her wand, and I became what you see. I did not lose the power of speech or of feeling the misery of my present state.

"'For five years,' she said, 'you shall be a sheep, and lord of this pleasant land, while I, no longer able to see your face, which I loved so much, shall be better able to hate you as you deserve to be hated.'

"She disappeared as she finished speaking, and if I had not been too unhappy to care about anything, I should have been glad that she was gone.

"The talking sheep received me as their king and told me that they, too, were unfortunate princes who had, in different ways, offended the revengeful fairy and had been added to her flock for a certain number of years; some more, some less. From time to time, indeed, one regains his own proper form and goes back again to his place in the upper world; but the other beings whom you saw are the rivals or the enemies of Ragotte, whom she has imprisoned for a hundred years or so; though even they will go back at last. The young slave of whom I told you about is one of these; I have seen her often, and it has been a great pleasure to me. She never speaks to me, and if I were nearer to her, I know, I should find her only a shadow, which would be very annoying. However, I noticed that one of my companions in misfortune was also very attentive to this little sprite, and I found out that he had been her lover, whom the cruel Ragotte had taken away from her long before; since then I have cared for and thought of, nothing but how I might regain my freedom. I have often been in the forest; that is where I have seen you, lovely Princess, sometimes driving your chariot, which you did with all the grace and skill in the world sometimes riding to the chase on so spirited a horse that it seemed as if no one but yourself could have managed it, and sometimes running races on the plain with the Princesses of your Court—running so lightly that it was you always who won the prize. Oh! Princess, I have loved you so long, and yet how dare I tell you of my love! what hope can there be for an unhappy sheep like myself?"

Miranda was so surprised and confused by all that she had heard that she hardly knew what answer to give to the King of the Sheep, but she managed to make some kind of little speech, which certainly did not forbid him to hope, and said that she should not be afraid of the shadows now she knew that they would someday come to life again. "Alas!" she continued, "if my poor Patypata, my dear Grabugeon, and pretty little Tintin, who all died for my sake, were equally well off, I should have nothing left to wish for here!"

Prisoner though he was, the King of the Sheep still had some powers and privileges.

"Go," said he to his Master of the Horse, "go and seek the shadows of the little black girl, the monkey, and the dog: they will amuse our Princess."

And an instant afterwards, Miranda saw them

coming toward her, and their presence gave her the greatest pleasure, though they did not come near enough for her to touch them.

The King of the Sheep was so kind and amusing and loved Miranda so dearly that, at last, she began to love him too. Such a handsome sheep, who was so polite and considerate, could hardly fail to please, especially if one knew that he was really a king and that his strange imprisonment would soon come to an end. So the Princess's days passed very gaily while she waited for the happy time to come. The King of the Sheep, with the help of all the flock, got up balls, concerts, and hunting parties, and even the shadows joined in all the fun and came, making believe to be their own real selves.

One evening, when the couriers arrived (for the King sent most carefully for news—and they always brought the very best kinds), it was announced that the sister of Princess Miranda was going to be married to a great Prince and that nothing could be more splendid than all the preparations for the wedding.

"Ah!" cried the young Princess, "how unlucky I am to miss the sight of so many pretty things! Here am I imprisoned under the earth, with no company but sheep and shadows, while my sister is to be adorned like a queen and surrounded by all who love and admire her, and everyone but myself can go to wish her joy!"

"Why do you complain, Princess?" said the King of

the Sheep. "Did I say that you were not to go to the wedding? Set out as soon as you please; only promise me that you will come back, for I love you too much to be able to live without you."

Miranda was very grateful to him and promised faithfully that nothing in the world should keep her from coming back. The King caused an escort suitable to her rank to be got ready for her, and she dressed splendidly, not forgetting anything that could make her more beautiful. Her chariot was of mother-of-pearl, drawn by six dun-coloured griffins just brought from the other side of the world, and she was attended by a number of guards in splendid uniforms, who were all at least eight feet high and had come from far and near to ride in the Princess's train.

Miranda reached her father's palace just as the wedding ceremony began, and everyone, as soon as she came in, was struck with surprise at her beauty and the splendor of her jewels. She heard exclamations of admiration on all sides; and the King, her father, looked at her so attentively that she was afraid he must recognize her; but he was so sure that she was dead that the idea never occurred to him.

However, the fear of not getting away made her leave before the marriage was over. She went out hastily, leaving behind her a little coral casket set with emeralds. On it was written in diamond letters: "Jewels for the Bride," and when they opened it, which they did as soon as it was found, there seemed to be no end to the pretty things it contained. The King, who had hoped to join the unknown Princess and find out who she was, was dreadfully disappointed when she disappeared so suddenly and gave orders that if she ever came again, the doors were to be shut so that she might not get away so easily. Short as Miranda's absence had been, it had seemed like a hundred years to the King of the Sheep. He was waiting for her by a fountain in the thickest part of the forest, and the ground was strewn with splendid presents that he had prepared for her to show his joy and gratitude at her coming back.

As soon as she was in sight, he rushed to meet her, leaping and bounding like a real sheep. He caressed her tenderly, throwing himself at her feet and kissing her hands, and told her how uneasy he had been in her absence and how impatient for her return, with an eloquence which charmed her.

After some time came, the news that the King's second daughter was going to be married. When Miranda heard it, she begged the King of the Sheep to allow her to go and see the wedding as before. This request made him feel very sad as if some misfortune must surely come of it, but with his love for the Princess being stronger than anything else, he did not like to refuse her.

"You wish to leave me, Princess," said he; "it is my unhappy fate—you are not to blame. I consent to your going, but, believe me, I can give you no stronger proof of my love than by so doing."

The Princess assured him that she would only stay a very short time, as she had done before, and begged him not to be uneasy, as she would be quite as much grieved if anything detained her as he could possibly be.

So, with the same escort, she set out and reached the palace as the marriage ceremony began. Everybody was delighted to see her; she was so pretty that they thought she must be some fairy princess, and the Princes who were there could not take their eyes off her.

The King was more glad than anyone else that she had come again and gave orders that the doors should all be shut and bolted that very minute. When the wedding was all but over, the Princess got up quickly, hoping to slip away unnoticed among the crowd, but, to her great dismay, she found every door fastened.

She felt more at ease when the King came up to her and, with the greatest respect, begged her not to run away so soon but at least to honor him by staying for the splendid feast which was prepared for the Princes and Princesses. He led her into a magnificent hall, where all the Court was assembled, and himself taking up the golden bowl full of water, he offered it to her that she might dip her pretty fingers into it.

At this, the Princess could no longer contain herself; throwing herself at the King's feet, she cried out:

"My dream has come true after all—you have offered me water to wash my hands on my sister's wedding day, and it has not vexed you to do it."

The King recognized her at once—indeed, he had already thought several times how much like his poor little Miranda she was.

"Oh! my dear daughter," he cried, kissing her, "can you ever forget my cruelty? I ordered you to be put to death because I thought your dream portended the loss of my crown. And so it did," he added, "for now your sisters are both married and have kingdoms of their own—and mine shall be for you." So saying, he put his crown on the Princess's head and cried:

"Long live Queen Miranda!"

All the Court cried: "Long live Queen Miranda!" after him, and the young Queen's two sisters came running up, threw their arms around her neck, and kissed her a thousand times, and then there was such a laughing and crying, talking and kissing, all at once, and Miranda thanked her father and began to ask after everyone—, particularly the Captain of the Guard, to whom she owed so much; but, to her great sorrow, she heard that he was dead. Presently they sat down to the banquet, and the King asked Miranda to tell them all that had happened to her since the terrible morning when he had sent the Captain of the Guard to fetch her. This she did with so much spirit that all the guests listened with breathless interest. But while she was thus enjoying herself with the King and her sisters, the King of the Sheep was waiting impatiently for the time of her return, and when it came and went, and no Princess appeared, his anxiety became so great that he could bear it no longer.

"She is not coming back any more," he cried. "My miserable sheep's face displeases her, and without Miranda what is left to me, wretched creature that I am! Oh! cruel Ragotte; my punishment is complete."

For a long time, he bewailed his sad fate like this, and then, seeing that it was growing dark and that there was still no sign of the Princess, he set out as fast as he could in the direction of the town. When he reached the palace, he asked for Miranda, but by this time, everyone had heard the story of her adventures and did not want her to go back again to the King of the Sheep, so they refused sternly to let him see her. In vai,n he begged and prayed them to let him in; though his entreaties might have melted hearts of stone, they did not move the guards of the palace, and at last, quite broken-hearted, he fell dead at their feet.

In the meantime, the King, who had not the least idea of the sad thing that was happening outside the gate of his palace, proposed to Miranda that she should be driven in her chariot all around the town, which was to be illuminated with thousands and thousands of torches, placed in windows and balconies, and in all the grand squares. But what a sight met her eyes at the very entrance of the palace! There lay her dear, kind sheep, silent and motionless, upon the pavement!

She threw herself out of the chariot and ran to him, crying bitterly, for she realized that her broken promise had cost him his life, and for a long, long time, she was so unhappy that they thought she would have died too.

So you see that even a princess is not always happy —especially if she forgets to keep her word, and the greatest misfortunes often happen to people just as they think they have obtained their heart's desires! (1)

(1) Madame d'Aulnoy.

The Brownies

by Juliana Horatia Ewing

A little girl sat sewing and crying on a garden seat. She had fair floating hair, which the breeze blew into her eyes, and between the cloud of hair, and the mist of tears, she could not see her work very clearly. She neither tied up her locks nor dried her eyes, however; for when one is miserable, one may as well be completely so.

"What is the matter?" said the Doctor, who was a friend of the Rector's and came into the garden whenever he pleased.

The Doctor was a tall, stout man with hair as black as crow's feathers on the top and grey underneath and a bushy beard. When young, he had been slim and handsome, with wonderful eyes, which were wonderful still; but that was many years past. He had a great love for children, and this one was a particular friend of his.

"What is the matter?" said he.

"I'm in a row," murmured the young lady through her veil, and the needle went in damp and came out with a jerk, which is apt to result in what ladies called "puckering."

"You are like London in a yellow fog," said the Doctor, throwing himself onto the grass, "and it is very depressing to my feelings. What is the row about, and how come you get into it?"

"We're all in it," was the reply; and apparently, the fog was thickening, for the voice grew less and less distinct—"the boys and everybody. It's all about forgetting, and not putting away, and leaving about, and borrowing, and breaking, and that sort of thing. I've had Father's new pocket handkerchiefs to hem, and I've been out climbing with the boys and kept forgetting and forgetting, and Mother says I always forget; and I can't help it. I forget to tidy his newspapers for him, and I forget to feed Puss, and I forgot these; besides, they're a great bore, and Mother gave them to Nurse to do, and this one was lost, and we found it this morning tossing about in the toy cupboard."

"It looks as if it had been taking violent exercise," said the Doctor. "But what have the boys to do with it?"

"Why, then there was a regular turn out of the toys," she explained, "and they're all in a regular mess. You know, we always go on till the last minute, and then things get crammed in anyhow. Mary and I did tidy them once or twice; but the boys never put anything away, you know, so what's the good?"

"What, indeed!" said the Doctor. "And so you have complained of them?"

"Oh! no!" answered she. "We don't get them into rows, unless they are very provoking; but some of the things were theirs, so everybody was sent for, and I was sent out to finish this, and they are all tidying. I don't know when it will be done, for I have all this side to hem; and the soldiers' box is broken, and Noah is lost out of the Noah's Ark, and so is one of the elephants and a guinea pig, and so is the rocking-horse's nose; and nobody knows what has become of Rutlandshire and Wash, but they're so small, I don't wonder; only North America and Europe are gone too."

The Doctor started up in affected horror. "Europe has gone, did you say? Bless me! what will become of us!"

"Don't!" said the young lady, kicking petulantly with her dangling feet and trying not to laugh. "You know I mean the puzzles, and if they were yours, you wouldn't like them."

"I don't half like it as it is," said the Doctor. "I am

seriously alarmed. An earthquake is one thing; you have a good shaking and settle down again. But Europe has gone—lost—Why here comes Deordie, I declare, looking much more cheerful than we do; let us humbly hope that Europe has been found. At present I feel like Aladdin when his palace had been transported by the magician; I don't know where I am."

"You're here, Doctor; aren't you?" asked the slow curly-wigged brother, squatting himself on the grass.

"Is Europe found?" said the Doctor tragically.

"Yes," laughed Deordie. "I found it."

"You will be a great man," said the Doctor. "And—it is only common charity to ask—how about North America?"

"Found too," said Deordie. "But the Wash is completely lost."

"And my six shirts in it!" said the Doctor. "I sent them last Saturday as ever was. What a world we live in! Any more news? Poor Tiny here has been crying her eyes out."

"I'm so sorry, Tiny," said the brother. "But don't bother about it. It's all square now, and we're going to have a new shelf put up."

"Have you found everything?" asked Tiny.

"Well, not the Wash, you know. And the elephant and the guinea pig are gone for good, so the other elephant and the other guinea pig must walk together as a pair now. Noah was among the soldiers, and we put the cavalry into a night-light box. Europe and North America were behind the bookcase, and would you believe it? the rocking horse's nose has turned up in the nursery oven."

"I can't believe it," said the Doctor. "The rocking horse's nose couldn't turn up, it was the purest Grecian, modelled from the Elgin marbles. Perhaps it was the heat that did it, though. However, you seem to have got through your troubles very well, Master Deordie. I wish poor Tiny were at the end of her task."

"So do I," said Deordie ruefully. "But I tell you what I've been thinking, Doctor Nurse is always nagging at us, and we're always in rows of one sort or another for doing this, and not doing that, and leaving our things about. But, you know, it's a horrid shame, for there are plenty of servants, and I don't see why we should be always bothering to do little things, and—"

"Oh! come to the point, please," said the Doctor; "you do go round the square so, in telling your stories, Deordie. What have you been thinking of?"

"Well," said Deordie, who was as good-tempered as he was slow, "the other day Nurse shut me up in the back nursery for borrowing her scissors and losing them; but I'd got 'Grimm' inside one of my knickerbockers, so when she locked the door, I sat down to read. And I read the story of the Shoemaker and the little Elves who came and did his work for him before he got up; and I thought it would be so jolly if we had some little Elves to do things instead of us."

"That's what Tommy Trout said," observed the Doctor.

"Who's Tommy Trout?" asked Deordie.

"Don't you know, Deor?" said Tiny. "It's the good boy who pulled the cat out of the what's-his-name.

'Who pulled her out?

Little Tommy Trout.'

Is it the same Tommy Trout, Doctor? I never heard anything else about him except his pulling the cat out; and I can't think how he did that."

"Let down the bucket for her, of course," said the Doctor. "But listen to me. If you will get that handkerchief done, and take it to your mother with a kiss, and not keep me waiting, I'll have you all to tea, and tell you the story of Tommy Trout."

"This very night?" shouted Deordie.

"This very night."

"Every one of us?" inquired the young gentleman with rapturous incredulity.

"Every one of you.—Now, Tiny, how about that work?"

"It's just done," said Tiny.—"Oh! Deordie, climb up

behind and hold back my hair. There's a darling while I fasten off. Oh! Deor, you're pulling my hair out. Don't."

"I want to make a pigtail," said Deor.

"You can't," said Tiny, with feminine contempt. "You can't plait. What's the good of asking boys to do anything? There! it's done at last. Now go and ask Mother if we may go.—Will you let me come, Doctor," she inquired, "if I do as you said?"

"To be sure I will," he answered. "Let me look at you. Your eyes are swollen with crying. How can you be such a silly little goose?"

"Did you never cry?" asked Tiny.

"When I was your age? Well, perhaps so."

"You've never cried since, surely," said Tiny.

The Doctor absolutely blushed.

"What do you think?" said he.

"Oh, of course not," she answered. "You've nothing to cry about. You're grown up, and you live all alone in a beautiful house, and you do as you like, and never get into rows, or have anybody but yourself to think about, and no nasty pocket-handkerchiefs to hem."

"Very nice, eh, Deordie?" said the Doctor.

"Awfully jolly," said Deordie.

"Nothing else to wish for, eh?"

"I should keep harriers and not a poodle, if I were a man," said Deordie, "but I suppose you could, if you wanted to."

"Nothing to cry about, at any rate?"

"I should think not!" said Deordie.—"There's Mother, though; let's go and ask her about the tea;" and off they ran.

The Doctor stretched his six feet of length upon the sward, dropped his grey head on a little heap of newly-mown grass, and looked up into the sky.

"Awfully jolly—no nasty pocket-handkerchiefs to hem," said he, laughing to himself. "Nothing else to wish for; nothing to cry about."

Nevertheless, he lay still, staring at the sky, till the smile died away, and tears came into his eyes. Fortunately, no one was there to see.

What could this "awfully jolly" Doctor be thinking of to make him cry? He was thinking of a gravestone in the churchyard close by and of a story connected with this gravestone which was known to everybody in the place which was old enough to remember it. This story has nothing to do with the present story, so it ought not to be told.

And yet it has to do with the Doctor and is very short, so it shall be put in, after all.

The Land of the Lost Toys

by Juliana Horatia Ewing

An Earthquake in the Nursery

It was certainly an aggravated offence. It is generally understood in families that "boys will be boys," but there is a limit to the forbearance implied in the extenuating axiom. Master Sam was condemned to the back nursery for the rest of the day.

He always had the knack of breaking his own toys—he not infrequently broke other people's, but accidents will happen, and his twin sister and factotum, Dot, was long-suffering.

Dot was fat, resolute, hasty, and devotedly unselfish. When Sam scalped her new doll and fastened the glossy black curls to a wigwam improvised with the curtains of the four-post bed in the best bedroom, Dot was sorely tired. As her eyes passed from the crownless doll on the floor to the floss-silk ringlets hanging from the bed furniture, her round rosy face grew rounder and rosier, and tears burst from her eyes. But in a moment more, she clenched her little fists, forced back the tears, and gave vent to her favorite saying, "I don't care."

That sentence was Dot's bane and antidote; it was her vice and her virtue. It was her standing consolation, and it brought her into all her scrapes. It was her one panacea for all the ups and downs of her life (and in the nursery where Sam developed his organ of destructiveness, there were ups and downs, not a few), and it was the form her naughtiness took when she was naughty.

"Don't care fell into a goose-pond, Miss Dot," said nurse, on one occasion of the kind.

"I don't care if he did," said Miss Dot, and as nurse knew no further feature of the goose-pond adventure which met this view of it, she closed the subject by putting Dot into the corner.

In the strength of Don't care and her love for Sam,

Dot bore much and long. Her dolls perished by ingenious but untimely deaths. Her toys were put to purposes for which they were never intended and suffered accordingly. But Sam was penitent, and Dot was heroic. Fiorinda's scalp was mended with a hot knitting needle and a perpetual bonnet, and Dot rescued her paint-brushes from the glue pot and smelt her india rubber as it boiled down in Sam's waterproof manufactory with long-suffering forbearance.

There are, however, as we have said, limits to everything. An earthquake celebrated with the whole contents of the toy cupboard is not to be borne.

The matter was this. Early one morning, Sam announced that he had a glorious project on hand. He was going to give a grand show and entertainment, far surpassing all the nursery imitations of circuses, conjurors, lectures on chemistry, and so forth, with which they had ever amused themselves. He refused to confide his plans to the faithful Dot, but he begged her to lend him all the toys she possessed in return for which she was to be the sole spectator of the fun. He let out that the idea had suggested itself to him after the sight of a Diorama to which they had been taken, but he would not allow that it was anything of the same kind, in proof of which she was at liberty to keep back her paint-box. Dot tried hard to penetrate the secret and to reserve some of her things from the general conscription. But Sam was obstinate. He would tell nothing, and he wanted everything. The dolls, the bricks (especially the bricks), the tea things, the German farm, the Swiss cottages, the animals, and all the dolls' furniture. Dot gave them with a doubtful mind and consoled herself as she watched Sam carrying pieces of board and a green table cover into the back nursery, with the prospect of a show. At last, Sam threw open the door and ushered her into the nursery rocking chair.

The boy had certainly some constructive as well as destructive talent. Upon a sort of impromptu table covered with green cloth, he had arranged all the toys in rough imitation of a town with its streets and buildings. The relative proportion of the parts was certainly not good, but it was not Sam's fault that the doll's house and the German farm, his own brick buildings, and the Swiss cottages were all on totally different scales of size. He had ingeniously put the larger things in the foreground, keeping the small farm buildings from the German box at the far end of the streets, yet after all, the perspective was extreme. The effect of three large horses from the toy stables in front, with the cows from the small Noah's Ark in the distance, was admirable; but the big dolls seated in an unroofed building, made with wooden bricks on no architectural principle but that of a pound, and taking tea out of the new china tea things, looked simply ridiculous.

Dot's eyes, however, saw no defects, and she clapped vehemently.

"Here, ladies and gentlemen," said Sam, waving his hand politely towards the rocking chair, "you see the great city of Lisbon, the capital of Portugal——"

At this display of geographical accuracy Dot fairly cheered, and rocked herself to and fro in unmitigated enjoyment.

"—as it appeared," continued the showman, "on the morning of November 1st, 1755."

Never having had occasion to apply Mangnall's Questions to the exigencies of everyday life, this date in no way disturbed Dot's comfort.

"In this house," Sam proceeded, "a party of Portuguese ladies of rank may be seen taking tea together."

"Breakfast, you mean," said Dot; "you said it was in the morning, you know."

"Well, they took tea to their breakfast," said Sam. "Don't interrupt me, Dot. You are the audience, and you mustn't speak. Here you see the horses of the English ambassador out airing with his groom. There you see two peasants—no! they are not Noah and his wife, Dot, and if you go on talking I shall shut up. I say they are peasants peacefully driving cattle. At this moment a rumbling sound startles every one in the city"—here Sam rolled some croquet balls up and down in a box, but the dolls sat as quiet as before, and Dot alone was startled;—"this was succeeded by a slight shock"—here he shook the table, which upset some of the buildings belonging to the German farm.—"Some houses fell."—Dot began to look anxious.—"This shock was followed by several others.—" "Take care," she begged—"of increasing magnitude—" "Oh, Sam!" Dot shrieked, jumping up, "you're breaking the china!—" "The largest buildings shook to their foundations,—" "Sam! Sam! the doll's house is falling," Dot cried, making wild efforts to save it: but Sam held her back with one arm, whilst with the other, he began to pull at the boards which formed his table—"Suddenly the ground split and opened with a fearful yawn"—Dot's shrieks shamed the impassive dolls, as Sam jerked out the boards by a dexterous movement, and doll's house, brick buildings, the farm, the Swiss cottages, and the whole toy-stock of the nursery, sank together in ruins. Quite unabashed by the evident damage, Sam continued—"and in a moment the whole magnificent city of Lisbon was swallowed up. Dot! Dot! don't be a muff! What's the matter? It's splendid fun. Things must be broken sometime, and I'm sure it was exactly like the real thing. Dot! why don't you speak? Dot! my dear Dot! You don't care, do you? I didn't think you'd mind it so. It was such a splendid earthquake. Oh! try not to go on like that!"

But Dot's feelings were far beyond her own control, much more that of Master Sam at this moment. She was gasping and choking, and when at last she found breath, it was only to throw herself on her face upon the floor with bitter and uncontrollable sobbing.

It was certainly a mild punishment that condemned Master Sam to the back nursery for the rest of the day. It had, however, this additional severity that during the afternoon, Aunt Penelope was expected to arrive.

Aunt Penelope

Aunt Penelope was one of those dear, good souls who, single themselves, have, as real or adopted relatives, the interests of a dozen families, instead of one, at heart. There are few people whose youth has not owned the influence of at least one such friend. It may be a good habit, the first interest in some life-loved pursuit or favorite author, some pretty feminine art, or delicate womanly counsel enforced by those narratives of real life that are more interesting than any fiction: it may be only the periodical return of gifts and kindness, and the store of family histories that no one else can tell; but we all owe something to such an aunt or uncle—the fairy godmothers of real life.

The benefits which Sam and Dot reaped from Aunt Penelope's visits, may be summed up under the heads of presents and stories, with a general leaning to indulgence in the matters of punishment, lessons, and going to bed, which perhaps is natural to aunts and uncles who have no positive responsibilities in the young people's education, and are not the daily sufferers by the lack of due discipline.

Aunt Penelope's presents were lovely. Aunt Penelope's stories were charming. There was generally a moral wrapped up in them, like the motto in a cracker bonbon, but it was quiet on the inside, so to speak, and there was an abundance of smart paper and sugar plums.

All things considered, it was certainly most proper that the much-injured Dot should be dressed out in her best and have access to dessert, the dining room, and

Aunt Penelope whilst Sam was kept upstairs. And yet it was Dot who (her first burst of grief being over) fought stoutly for his pardon all the time she was being dressed and was afterwards detected in the act of endeavoring to push fragments of raspberry tart through the nursery keyhole.

"You good thing!" Sam emphatically exclaimed as he heard her in fierce conflict on the other side of the door with the nurse who found her—"You good thing! leave me alone, for I deserve it."

He really was very penitent. He was too fond of Dot not to regret the unexpected degree of distress he had caused her, and Dot made much of his penitence in her intercessions in the drawing room.

"Sam is so very sorry," she said, "he says he knows he deserves it. I think he ought to come down. He is so very sorry!"

Aunt Penelope, as usual, took the lenient side, joining her entreaties to Dot's, and it ended in Master Sam's being hurriedly scrubbed and brushed, shoved into his black velvet suit, and sent down-stairs, rather red about the eyelids, and looking very sheepish.

"Oh, Dot!" he exclaimed as soon as he could get her into a corner, "I am so very, very sorry! particularly about the tea things."

"Never mind," said Dot, "I don't care, and I've asked for a story, and we're going into the library." As Dot said this, she jerked her head expressively in the direction of the sofa, where Aunt Penelope was just casting on stitches preparatory to beginning a pair of her famous ribbed socks for Papa, whilst she gave to Mamma's conversation that sympathy, which (like her knitting-needles) was always at the service of her large circle of friends. Dot anxiously watched the bow on the top of her cap as it danced and nodded with the force of Mamma's observations. At last, it gave a little chorus of jerks, as one should say, "Certainly, undoubtedly." And then the story came to an end, and Dot, who had been slowly creeping nearer, fairly took Aunt Penelope by the hand and carried her off, knitting and all, to the library.

"Now, please," said Dot when she had struggled into a chair that was too tall for her.

"Stop a minute!" cried Sam, who was perched in the opposite one, "the horsehair tickles my legs."

"Put your pocket handkerchief under them, as I do," said Dot. "Now, Aunt Penelope."

"No, wait," groaned Sam; "it isn't big enough; it only covers one leg."

Dot slid down again and ran to Sam.

"Take my handkerchief for the other."

"But what will you do?" said Sam.

"Oh, I don't care," said Dot, scrambling back into her place. "Now, Aunty, please."

And Aunt Penelope began.

The Land of the Lost Toys

"I suppose people who have children transfer their childish follies and fancies to them and become properly sedated and grown-up. Perhaps it is because I am an old maid, and have none, that some of my nursery whims stick to me, and I find myself liking things and wanting things quite out of keeping with my cap and time of life. For instance. Anything in the shape of a toy shop (from a London bazaar to a village window, with Dutch dolls, leather balls, and wooden battledores) quite unnerves me, so to speak. When I see one of those boxes containing a jar, a churn, a kettle, a pan, a coffee pot, a cauldron on three legs, and sundry dishes, all of the smoothest wood, and with the immemorial red flower on one side of each vessel, I fairly long for an excuse for playing with them, and for trying (positively for the last time) if the lids do come off, and whether the kettle will (literally, as well as metaphorically) hold water. Then if by good or ill luck, there is a child flattening its little nose against the window with longing eyes, my purse is soon empty; and as it toddles off with a square parcel under one arm and a lovely being in black ringlets and white tissue paper in the other, I wish that I were worthy of being asked to join the ensuing play. Don't suppose there is any generosity in this. I have only done what we are all glad to do. I have found an excuse for indulging a pet weakness. As I said, it is not merely the new and expensive toys that attract me; I think my weakest corner is where the penny boxes lie, the wooden tea things (with the above-named flower in miniature), the soldiers on their lazy tongs, the nine-pins, and the tiny farm.

"I need hardly say that the toy booth in a village fair tries me very hard. It tried me in childhood, when I was often short of pence, and when 'the Feast' came once a year. It never tried me more than on one occasion, lately, when I was revisiting my old home.

"It was deep Midsummer and the Feast. I had children with me of course (I find children, somehow, wherever I go), and when we got into the fair, there were children of people whom I had known as children, with just the same love for a monkey going up one side of a yellow stick and coming down the other, and just as strong heads for a giddy-go-round on a hot day and a diet of peppermint lozenges, as their fathers and mothers before them. There were the very same names —and here and there, it seemed the very same faces—I knew so long ago. A few shillings were indeed well expended in brightening those familiar eyes: and then there were the children with me... Besides, there really did seem to be an unusually nice assortment of things, and the man was very intelligent (in reference to his wares:).... Well, well! It was two o'clock p. m. when we went in at one end of that glittering avenue of drums, dolls, trumpets, accordions, work-boxes and what not; but what o'clock it was when I came out at the other end, with a shilling and some coppers in my pocket, and was cheered, I can't say, though I should like to have been able to be accurate about the time, because of what followed.

"I thought the best thing I could do was to get out of the fair at once, so I went up the village and struck off across some fields into a little wood that lay near. (A favorite walk in old times.) As I turned out of the booth, my foot struck against one of the yellow sticks of the climbing monkeys. The monkey was gone, and the stick was broken. It set me thinking as I walked along.

"What an untold number of pretty and ingenious things one does (not wear out in honorable wear and tear, but) utterly lose, and wilfully destroy, in one's young days—things that would have given pleasure to so many more young eyes, if they had been kept a little longer—things that one would so value in later years if some of them had survived the dissipating and destructive days of Nurserydom. I recalled a young lady I knew whose room was adorned with knick-knacks of a kind I had often envied. They were not plaster figures, old china, wax-work flowers under glass, or ordinary ornaments of any kind. They were her old toys. Perhaps she had not had many of them and had been the more careful of those she had. She had certainly been very fond of them and had kept more of them than anyone I ever knew. A faded doll slept in its cradle at the foot of her bed. A wooden elephant stood on the dressing table, and a poodle that had lost his bark put out a red-flannel tongue with quixotic violence at a windmill on the opposite corner of the mantelpiece. Everything had a story of its own.

Indeed the whole room must have been redolent with the sweet story of childhood, of which the toys were the illustrations, or like a poem of which the toys were the verses. She used to have children to play with them sometimes, and this was a high honor. She is married now and has children of her own, who, on birthdays and holidays, will forsake the newest of their own possessions to play with 'mamma's toys.'

"I was roused from these recollections by the pleasure of getting into the wood.

"If I have a stronger predilection than my love for toys, it is my love for woods, and, like the other, it dates from childhood. It was born and bred with me, and I fancy it will stay with me till I die. The soothing scents of leaf mould, moss, and fern (not to speak of flowers) —the pale green veil in spring, the rich shade in summer, the rustle of the dry leaves in autumn, I suppose an old woman may enjoy all these, my dears, as well as you. But I think I could make 'fairy jam' of hips and haws in acorn cups now if any child would be condescending enough to play with me.

"This wood, too, had associations.

"I strolled on in leisurely enjoyment and at last, seated myself at the foot of a tree to rest. I was hot and tired, partly with the mid-day heat and the atmosphere of the fair, partly with the exertion of calculating the change in the purchase of articles ranging in price from three farthings upwards. The tree under which I sat was an old friend. There was a hole at its base that I knew well. Two roots covered with exquisite moss ran out from each side, like the arms of a chair, and between them, there accumulated year after year a rich, though tiny store of dark leafmould. We always used to say that fairies lived within, though I never saw anything go in myself but wood beetles. There was one going in at that moment.

"How little the wood was changed! I bent my head for a few seconds and, closing my eyes, drank in the delicious and suggestive scents of earth and moss about the dear old tree. I had been so long parted from the place that I could hardly believe that I was in the old familiar spot. Surely it was only one of the many dreams in which I had played again beneath those trees! But when I reopened my eyes, there was the same hole and, oddly enough, the same beetle or one just like it. I had not noticed till that moment how much larger the hole was than it used to be in my young days.

"'I suppose the rain and so forth wears them away in time,' I said vaguely.

"'Suppose it does,' said the beetle politely; 'will you walk in?'

"I don't know why I was not so overpoweringly astonished as you would imagine. I think I was a good deal absorbed in considering the size of the hole and the very foolish wish that seized me to do what I had often longed to do in childhood and creep in. I had so much regard for propriety as to see that there was no one to witness the escapade. Then I tucked my skirts round me, put my spectacles into my pocket for fear they should get broken, and in I went.

"I must say one thing. A wood is charming enough (no one appreciates it more than myself), but if you have never been there, you have no idea how much nicer it is inside than on the surface. Oh, the mosses—the gorgeous mosses! The fretted lichens! The fungi like flowers for beauty, and the flowers like nothing you have ever seen!

"Where the beetle went to, I don't know. I could stand up now quite well, and I wandered on till dusk in unwearied admiration. I was among some large beeches as it grew dark and was beginning to wonder how I should find my way (not that I had lost it, having none to lose) when suddenly lights burst from every tree, and the whole place was illuminated. The nearest approach to this scene that I ever witnessed above ground was in a wood near the Hague in Holland. There, what look like tiny glass tumblers holding floating wicks, are fastened to the trunks of the fine old trees, at intervals of sufficient distance to make the light and shade mysterious, and to give effect to the full blaze when you reach the spot where hanging chains of lamps illuminate the 'Pavilion' and the open space where the band plays, and where the townsfolk assemble by hundreds to drink coffee and enjoy the music. I was the more reminded of the Dutch 'bosch' because, after wandering some time among the lighted trees, I heard distant sounds of music and came at last upon a glade lit up in a similar manner, except that the whole effect was incomparably more brilliant.

"As I stood for a moment doubting whether I should proceed, and a good deal puzzled about the whole affair, I caught sight of a large spider crouched up in a corner with his stomach on the ground and his knees above his head, as some spiders do sit, and looking at me, as I fancied, through a pair of spectacles. (About the spectacles, I do not feel sure. It may have been two of his bent legs in apparent connection with his prominent eyes.) I thought of the beetle and said civilly, 'Can you tell me, sir, if this is Fairyland?' The spider took off his spectacles (or untucked his legs) and took a sideways run out of his corner.

"'Well,' he said, 'it's a Province. The fact is, it's the Land of Lost Toys. You haven't such a thing as a fly anywhere about you, have you?'

"'No,' I said, 'I'm sorry to say I have not.' This was not strictly true, for I was not at all sorry, but I wished to be civil to the old gentleman, for he projected his eyes at me with such an intense (I had almost said greedy) gaze that I felt quite frightened.

"'How did you pass the sentries?' he inquired.

"'I never saw any,' I answered.

"'You couldn't have seen anything if you didn't see them,' he said; 'but perhaps you don't know. They're the glow-worms. Six to each tree, so they light the road, and challenge the passers-by. Why didn't they challenge you?'

"'I don't know,' I began, 'unless the beetle——'

"'I don't like beetles,' interrupted the spider, stretching each leg in turn by sticking it up above him, 'all shell, and no flavor. You never tried walking on anything of that sort, did you?' and he pointed with one leg to a long thread that fastened a web above his head.

"'Certainly not,' said I.

"'I'm afraid it wouldn't bear you,' he observed slowly.

"'I'm quite sure it wouldn't,' I hastened to reply. 'I wouldn't try for worlds. It would spoil your pretty work in a moment. Good-evening.'

"And I hurried forward. Once I looked back, but the spider was not following me. He was in his hole again, on his stomach, with his knees above his head, and looking (apparently through his spectacles) down the road up which I came.

"I soon forgot him in sight before me. I had reached the open place with the lights and the music, but how shall I describe the spectacle that I beheld?

"I have spoken of the effect of a toy shop on my feelings. Now imagine a toy fair, brighter and gayer than the brightest bazaar ever seen, held in an open glade, where forest trees stood majestically behind the glittering stalls, and stretched their gigantic arms above our heads, brilliant with a thousand hanging lamps. At the moment of my entrance, all was silent and quiet. The toys lay in their places looking so incredibly attractive that I reflected with disgust that all my ready cash, except one shilling and some coppers, had melted away amid the tawdry fascinations of a village booth. I was counting the coppers (seven pence halfpenny), when all in a moment a dozen sixpenny fiddles leaped from their places and began to play, accordions of all sizes joined them, the drumsticks beat upon the drums, the penny trumpets sounded, and the yellow flutes took up the melody on high notes, and bore it away through the trees. It was weird fairy music but quite delightful. The nearest approach to it that I know of above ground is to hear a wild dreamy air very well whistled to a pianoforte accompaniment.

"When the music began, all the toys rose. The dolls jumped down and began to dance. The poodles barked, the pannier donkeys wagged their ears, the windmills turned, the puzzles put themselves together, the bricks built houses, the balls flew from side to side, the battle doors and shuttlecocks kept it up among themselves, and the skipping ropes went round, the hoops ran off, and the sticks went after them, the cobbler's wax at the tails of all the green frogs gave way, and they jumped at the same moment whilst an old-fashioned go-cart ran madly about with nobody inside. It was most exhilarating.

"I soon became aware that the beetle was once more at my elbow.

"'There are some beautiful toys here,' I said.

"'Well, yes,' he replied, 'and some odd-looking ones,

too. You see, whatever has been really used by any child as a plaything gets a right to come down here in the end, and there is some very queer company, I assure you. Look there.'

"I looked and said, 'It seems to be a potato.'

"'So it is,' said the beetle. 'It belonged to an Irish child in one of your great cities. But to whom the child belonged, I don't know, and I don't think he knew himself. He lived in the corner of a dirty, overcrowded room, and into this corner, one day, the potato rolled. It was the only plaything he ever had. He stuck two cinders into it for eyes, scraped a nose and mouth, and loved it. He sat upon it during the day for fear it should be taken from him, but in the dark, he took it out and played with it. He was often hungry, but he never ate that potato. When he died, it rolled out of the corner and was swept into the ashes. Then it came down here.'

"'What a sad story!' I exclaimed.

"The beetle seemed in no way affected.

"'It is a curious thing,' he rambled on, 'that potato takes quite a good place among the toys. You see, rank and precedence down here is entirely a question of age; that is, of the length of time that any plaything has been in the possession of a child; and all kinds of ugly old things hold the first rank; whereas the most costly and beautiful works of art have often been smashed or lost, by the spoilt children of rich people, in two or three days. If you care for sad stories, there is another queer thing belonging to a child who died.'

"It appeared to be a large sheet of canvas with some strange kind of needlework upon it.

"'It belonged to a little girl in a rich household,' the beetle continued; 'she was invalid and difficult to amuse. We have lots of her toys, and very pretty ones too. At last, someone taught her to make caterpillars in wool-work. A bit of work was to be done in a certain stitch and then cut with scissors, which made it look like a hairy caterpillar. The child took to this and cared for nothing else. Wool of every shade was procured for her, and she made caterpillars of all colors. Her only complaint was that they did not turn into butterflies. However, she was a sweet, gentle-tempered child, and she went on, hoping that they would do so and making new ones. One day she was heard talking and laughing in her bed for joy. She said that all the caterpillars had become butterflies of many colors, and that the room was full of them. In that happy fancy, she died.'

"'And the caterpillars came down here?'

"'Not for a long time,' said the beetle; 'her mother kept them while she lived, and then they were lost and came down. No toys come down here till they are broken or lost.'

"'What are those sticks doing here?' I asked.

"The music had ceased, and all the toys were lying quiet. Up in a corner leaned a large bundle of walking sticks. They are often sold in toy shops, but I wondered on what grounds they came here.

"'Did you ever meet with a too benevolent old gentleman wondering where on earth his sticks go to?' said the beetle. 'Why do they lend them to their grandchildren? The young rogues use them as hobby horses and lose them, and down they come, and the sentinels cannot stop them. The real hobby horses won't allow them to ride with them, however. There was a meeting on the subject. Every stick was put through an examination. 'Where is your nose? Where is your mane? Where are your wheels?' The last was a poser. Some of them had got noses, but none of them had got wheels. So they were not true hobby horses. Something of the kind occurred with the elder whistles.'

"'The what?' I asked.

"'Whistles that boys make of elder sticks with the pith scooped out,' said the beetle. 'The real instruments would not allow them to play with them. The elder whistles said they would not have joined had they been asked. They were amateurs and never played with professionals. So they have private concerts with the combs and curl papers. But, bless you, toys of this kind are endless here! Teetotums made of old cotton reels, tea sets of acorn cups, dinner sets of old shells, monkeys made of bits of sponge, all sorts of things made of breastbones and merrythoughts, old packs of cards that are always building themselves into houses and getting knocked down when the band begins to play, feathers, rabbits' tails——

"'Ah! I have heard about rabbits' tails,' I said.

"'There they are,' the beetle continued, 'and when the band plays you will see how they skip and run. I don't believe you would find out that they had no bodies, for my experience of a warren is, that when rabbits skip and run it is the tails chiefly that you do see. But of all the amateur toys the most successful are the boats. We have a lake for our craft, you know, and there's quite a fleet of boats made out of old cork floats in fishing villages. Then, you see, the old bits of cork have really been to sea and seen a good deal of service on the herring nets, and so they quite take the lead of the smart shop ships that have never been beyond a pond or a tub of water. But that's an exception. Amateur toys are mostly very dowdy. Look at that box.'

"I looked, thought I must have seen it before, and wondered why a very common-looking box without a lid should affect me so strangely and why my memory should seem struggling to bring it back out of the past. Suddenly it came to me—it was our old Toy Box.

"I had completely forgotten that nursery institution till recalled by the familiar aspect of the inside, which was papered with proof sheets of some old novel on which black stars had been stamped by way of ornament. Dim memories of how these stars, the angles of the box, and certain projecting nails interfered with the letter-press and defeated all attempts to trace the thread of the nameless narrative stole back over my brain and I seemed once more, with my head in the Toy Box, to beguile a wet afternoon by apoplectic endeavors to follow the fortunes of Sir Charles and Lady Belinda, as they took a favorable turn in the left-hand corner at the bottom of the trunk.

"'What are you staring at?' said the beetle.

"'It's my old Toy Box!' I exclaimed.

"The beetle rolled onto his back and struggled helplessly with his legs: I turned him over. (Neither the first nor the last time of my showing that attention to beetles.)

"'That's right,' he said, 'set me on my legs. What a turn you gave me! You don't mean to say you have any toys here? If you have, the sooner you make your way home, the better.'

"'Why?' I inquired.

"'Well,' he said, 'there's a very strong feeling in the place. The toys think that they are ill-treated and not taken care of by children in general. And there is some truth in it. Toys come down here by scores that have been broken the first day. And they are all quite resolved that if any of their old masters or mistresses come this way they shall be punished.'

"'How will they be punished?' I inquired.

"'Exactly as they did to their toys, their toys will do to them. All is perfectly fair and regular.'

"'I don't know that I treated mine particularly badly,' I said, 'but I think I would rather go.'

"'I think you'd better,' said the beetle. 'Good evening!' and I saw him no more.

"I turned to go, but somehow I lost the road. At last, as I thought, I found it and had gone a few steps when I came on a detachment of wooden soldiers drawn up on their lazy tongs. I thought it better to wait till they got out of the way, so I turned back and sat down in a corner in some alarm. As I did so, I heard a click, and the lid of a small box covered with mottled paper burst open, and up jumped a figure in a blue striped shirt and a rabbit-skin beard, whose eyes were intently fixed on me. He was very much like my old Jack-in-a-box. My back began to creep, and I wildly meditated escape, frantically trying at the same time to recall whether it were I or my brother who originated the idea of making a small bonfire of our own one 5th of November, and burning the old Jack-in-a-box for Guy Fawkes, till nothing was left of him but a twirling bit of red-hot wire and a strong smell of frizzled fur. At this moment, he nodded to me and spoke.

"'Oh! That's you, is it?' he said.

"'No, it is not,' I answered hastily; for I was quite demoralized by fear and the strangeness of the situation.

"'Who is it, then?' he inquired.

"'I'm sure I don't know,' I said; and really I was so confused that I hardly did.

"'Well, we know,' said the Jack-in-a-box, 'and that's

all that's needed. 'Now, my friends,' he continued, addressing the toys who had begun to crowd around us, 'whoever recognizes a mistress and remembers a grudge—the hour of our revenge has come. Can any of us forget the treatment we received at her hands? No! When we think of the ingenious fancy, the patient skill, that went to our manufacture, that fitted the delicate joints and springs, laid on the paint and varnish and gave back hair combs and ear-rings to our smallest dolls, we feel that we deserved more care than we received. When we reflect upon the kind friends who bought us with their money and gave us away in the benevolence of their hearts, we know that, for their sakes, we ought to have been long kept and better valued. And when we remember that the sole object of our own existence was to give pleasure and amusement to our possessors, we have no hesitation in believing that we deserved a handsomer return than to have had our springs broken, our paint dirtied, and our earthly careers so untimely shortened by wilful mischief or fickle neglect. My friends, the prisoner is at the bar.'

"'I am not, I said; for I was determined not to give in as long as resistance was possible. But as I said it I became aware, to my unutterable amazement, that I was inside the go-cart. How I got there is to this moment, a mystery to me—but there I was.

"There was a great deal of excitement about the Jack-in-a-box's speech. It was evident that he was considered an orator, and, indeed, I have seen counsel in a real court look wonderfully like him. Meanwhile, my old toys appeared to be getting together. I had no idea that I had had so many. I had really been very fond of most of them, and my heart beat as the sight of them recalled scenes long forgotten and took me back to childhood and home. There were my little gardening tools, and my slate, and there was the big doll's bedstead that had a real mattress, and real sheets and blankets, all marked with the letter D, and a work-basket made in the blind school, and a shilling School of Art paint box, and a wooden doll we used to call the Dowager, and innumerable other toys which I had forgotten till the sight of them recalled them to my memory, but which have again passed from my mind. Exactly opposite to me stood the Chinese mandarin, nodding as I had never seen him nod since the day when I finally stopped his performances by ill-directed efforts to discover how he did it.

"And what was that familiar figure among the rest, in a yellow silk dress and maroon velvet cloak and hood trimmed with black lace? How those clothes recalled the friends who gave them to me! And surely this was no other than my dear doll Rosa—the beloved companion of five years of my youth, whose hair I wore in a locket after I was grown up. No one could say I had ill-treated her. Indeed, she fixed her eyes on me with a most encouraging smile—but then she always smiled, her mouth was painted so.

"'All whom it may concern, take notice,' shouted the Jack-in-a-box, at this point, 'that the rule of this honorable court is tit for tat.'

"'Tit, tat, tumble two,' muttered the slate in a cracked voice. (How well I remembered the fall that cracked it and the sly games of tit-tat that varied the monotony of our long multiplication sums!)

"'What are you talking about?' said the Jack-in-a-box sharply; 'if you have grievances, state them, and you shall have satisfaction, as I told you before.'

"'——and five make nine,' added the slate promptly, 'and six are fifteen, and eight are twenty-seven—there we go again! I wonder why I never get up to the top of a line of figures right. It will never prove at this rate.'

"'His mind is lost in calculations,' said the Jack-in-a-box, 'besides—between ourselves—he has been "cracky" for some time. Let someone else speak and observe that no one is at liberty to pass sentence on the prisoner heavier than what he has suffered from her. I reserve my judgment to the last.'

"'I know what that will be,' thought I; 'oh dear! Oh, dear! that a respectable maiden lady should live to be burnt as a Guy Fawkes!"

"'Let the prisoner drink a gallon of iced water at once and then be left to die of thirst.'

"The horrible idea that the speaker might possibly have the power to enforce his sentence diverted my attention from the slate, and I looked around. In front of the Jack-in-a-box stood a tiny red flower pot and saucer, in which was a miniature cactus. My thoughts flew back to a bazaar in London where, years ago, a stand of these fairy plants had excited my warmest longings and where a benevolent old gentleman whom I had not seen before and never saw again bought this one and gave it to me. Vague memories of his directions for re-potting and tending it reproached me from the past. My mind misgave me that after all, it had died a dusty death for lack of water. True, the cactus tribe being succulent plants, do not demand much moisture, but I had reason to fear that, in this instance, the principle had been applied too far and that after copious baths of cold spring water in the first days of its popularity it had eventually perished by drought. I suppose I looked guilty, for it nodded its prickly head towards me and said, 'Ah! You know me. You remember what I was, do you? Did you ever think of what I might have been? There was a fairy rose which came down here not long ago—a common rose enough, in a broken pot patched with string and white paint. It had lived in a street where it was the only pure, beautiful thing your eyes could see. When the girl who kept it died, there were eighteen roses upon it. She was eighteen years old, and they put the roses in the coffin with her when she was buried. That was worth living for. Who knows what I might have done? And what right had you to cut short a life that might have been useful?'

"Before I could think of a reply to these to just reproaches, the flower pot enlarged, the plant shot up, putting forth new branches as it grew; then buds burst from the prickly limbs, and in a few moments, there hung about it great drooping blossoms of lovely pink, with long white tassels in their throats. I had been gazing at it some time in silent and self-reproachful admiration when I became aware that the business of this strange court was proceeding and that the other toys were pronouncing sentence against me.

"'Tie a string round her neck and take her out bathing in the brooks,' I heard an elderly voice say in severe tones. It was the Dowager Doll. She was inflexibly wooden and had been in the family for more than one generation.

"'It's not fair,' I exclaimed, 'the string was only to keep you from being carried away by the stream. The current is strong, and the bank steep by the Hollow Oak Pool, and you had no arms or legs. You were old and ugly, but you would wash, and we loved you better than many waxen beauties.'

"'Old and ugly!' shrieked the Dowager. 'Tear her wig off! Scrub the paint off her face! Flatten her nose on the pavement! Saw off her legs and gave her no crinoline! Take her out bathing, I say, and bring her home in a wheelbarrow with fern roots on the top of her.'

"I was about to protest again when the paint-box came forward and, balancing itself in an artistic, undecided kind of way on two camel's-hair brushes which seemed to serve it for feet, addressed the Jack-in-a-box.

"'Never dip your paint into the water. Never put your brush into your mouth——'

"'That's not evidence,' said the Jack-in-a-box.

"'Your notions are crude,' said the paint-box loftily; 'it's in print, and here, all of it, or words to that effect, with which he touched the lid, as a gentleman might lay his hand upon his heart.

"'It's not evidence,' repeated the Jack-in-a-box. 'Let us proceed.'

"'Take her to pieces and see what she's made of if you please,' tittered a pretty German toy that moved to a tinkling musical accompaniment. 'If her works are available after that, it will be an era in natural science.'

"The idea tickled me, and I laughed.

"'Hard-hearted wretch!' growled the Dowager Doll.

"'Dip her in water and leave her to soak on a white soup plate,' said the paint-box; 'if that doesn't soften her feelings, deprive me of my medal from the School of Art!'

"'Give her a stiff neck!' muttered the mandarin. 'Ching Fo! give her a stiff neck.'

"'Knock her teeth out,' growled the rake in a scratchy voice; and then the tools joined in the chorus.

"'Take her out when its fine and leave her out when it's wet, and lose her in——

"'The coal hole,' said the spade.

"'The hay field,' said the rake.

"'The shrubbery,' said the hoe.

"This difference of opinion produced a quarrel, which in turn seemed to affect the general behavior of the toys, for a disturbance arose which the Jack-in-a-box vainly endeavored to quell. A dozen voices shouted for a dozen different punishments, and (happily for me) each toy insisted upon its own wrongs being the first to be avenged, and no one would hear of the claims of anyone else being attended to for an instant. Terrible sentences were passed, which I either failed to hear through the clamor then or have forgotten now. I have a vague idea that several voices cried that I was to be sent to wash in somebody's pocket; that the work-basket wished to cram my mouth with unfinished needlework; and that through all the din the thick voice of my old leather ball monotonously repeated:

"'Throw her into the dust-hole.'

"Suddenly, a clear voice pierced the confusion, and Rosa tripped up.

"'My dears,' she began, 'the only chance of restoring order is to observe method. Let us follow our usual rule of precedence. I claim the first turn as the prisoner's oldest toy.'

"'That you are not, Miss,' snapped the dowager; 'I was in the family for fifty years.'

"'In the family. Yes, ma'am, but you were never her doll in particular. I was her very own, and she kept me longer than any other plaything. My judgment must be first.'

"'She is right,' said the Jack-in-a-box, 'and now let us get on. The prisoner is delivered unreservedly into the hands of our trusty and well-beloved Rosa—a doll of the first class—for punishment according to the strict law of tit for tat.'

"'I shall request the assistance of the pewter tea things,' said Rosa, with her usual smile. 'And now, my love,' she added, turning to me, 'we will come and sit down.'

"Where the go-cart vanished to, I cannot remember, nor how I got out of it; I only know that I suddenly found myself free and walking away with my hand in Rosa's. I remember vacantly feeling the rough edge of the stitches on her flat kid fingers and wondering what would come next.

"'How very oddly you hold your feet, my dear,' she said; 'you stick out your toes in such an eccentric fashion, and you lean on your legs as if they were table legs instead of supporting yourself by my hand. Turn your heels well out, and bring your toes together. You may even let them fold over each other a little; it is considered to have a pretty effect among dolls.'

"Under one of the big trees, Miss Rosa made me sit down, propping me against the trunk as if I should otherwise have fallen, and in a moment more, a square box of pewter tea things came tumbling up to our feet, where the lid burst open, and all the tea-things fell out in perfect order; the cups on the saucers, the lid on the teapot and so on.

"'Take a little tea, my love?' said Miss Rosa pressing a pewter teacup to my lips.

"I made believe to drink but was only conscious of inhaling a draught of air with a slight flavor of tin. In taking my second cup, I nearly choked with the teaspoon, which got into my throat.

"'What are you doing?' roared the Jack-in-a-box at this moment; 'you are not punishing her.'

"'I am treating her as she treated me,' answered Rosa, looking as severe as her smile would allow. 'I believe that tit for tat is the rule and that at present it is my turn.'

"'It will be mine soon,' growled the Jack-in-a-box, and I thought of the bonfire with a shudder. However, there was no knowing what might happen before his turn did come, and meanwhile, I was in friendly hands. It was not the first time my dolly and I had set together under a tree, and, truth to say, I do not think she had any injuries to avenge.

"'When your wig comes off,' murmured Rosa, as she stole a pink kid arm tenderly round my neck, 'I'll make you a cap with blue and white rosettes and pretend that you have had a fever.'

"I thanked her gratefully and was glad to reflect that I was not yet in need of an attention which I distinctly remember having shown to her in the days of her dollhood. Presently she jumped up.

"'I think you shall go to bed now, dear,' she said, and, taking my hand once more, she led me to the big doll's bedstead, which, with its pretty bedclothes and white dimity furniture, looked tempting enough to a sleeper of suitable size. It could not have supported one-quarter of my weight.

"'I have not made you a night-dress, my love,' Rosa continued; 'I am not fond of my needle you know. You were not fond of your needle, I think. I fear you must go to bed in your clothes, my dear.'

"'You are very kind,' I said, 'but I am not tired, and—it would not bear my weight.'

"'Pooh! pooh!' said Rosa. 'My love! I remember passing one Sunday in it with the rag-doll, and the Dowager, and the Punch and Judy (the amount of pillow their two noses took up I shall never forget!), and the old doll that had nothing on, because her clothes were in the dolls' wash and did not get ironed on Saturday night, and the Highlander, whose things wouldn't come off, and who slept in his kilt. Not bear you? Nonsense! You must go to bed, my dear. I've got other things to do, and I can't leave you lying about.'

"'The whole lot of you did not weigh one quarter of what I do,' I cried desperately. 'I cannot, and will not get into that bed; I should break it all to pieces, and hurt myself into the bargain.'

"'Well, if you will not go to bed, I must put you there,' said Rosa, and without more ado, she snatched me up in her kid arms, and laid me down.

"Of course, it was just as I expected. I had hardly touched the two little pillows (they had a meal-baggy smell from being stuffed with bran), when the woodwork gave way with a crash, and I fell—fell—fell—

"Though I fully believed every bone in my body to be broken, it was really a relief to get to the ground. As soon as I could, I sat up, and felt myself all over. A little stiff, but, as it seemed, unhurt. Oddly enough, I found that I was back again under the tree; and more strange still, it was not the tree where I sat with Rosa, but the old oak-tree in the little wood. Was it all a dream? The toys had vanished, the lights were out, the mosses looked dull in the growing dusk, the evening was chilly, the hole no larger than it was thirty years ago, and when I felt in my pocket for my spectacles I found that they were on my nose.

"I have returned to the spot many times since, but I never could induce a beetle to enter into conversation on the subject. The hole remains obstinately impassable, and I have not been able to repeat my visit to the Land of Lost Toys.

"When I recall my many sins against the playthings of my childhood, I am constrained humbly to acknowledge that perhaps this is just as well."

Sam Sets Up Shop

"I think you might help me, Dot," cried Sam in

dismal and rather injured tones.

It was the morning following the day of the earthquake and of Aunt Penelope's arrival. Sam had his back to Dot and his face to the fire, over which, indeed he had bent for so long that he appeared to be half-roasted.

"What do you want?" asked Dot, who was working on a doll's night dress that had for long been partly finished and now seemed in a fair way to completion.

"It's the glue-pot," Sam continued. "It does take so long to boil. And I have been stirring at the glue with a stick for ever so long to get it to melt. It is very hot work. I wish you would take it for a bit. It's as much for your good as for mine."

"Is it?" said Dot.

"Yes it is, Miss," cried Sam. "You must know I've got a splendid idea."

"Not another earthquake, I hope?" said Dot, smiling.

"Now, Dot, that's truly unkind of you. I thought it was to be forgotten."

"So it is," said Dot, getting up. "I was only joking. What is the idea?"

"I don't think I shall tell you till I have finished my shop. I want to get to it now, and I wish you would take a turn at the glue pot."

Sam was apt to want a change of occupation. Dot, on the other hand, was equally averse to leaving what she was about till it was finished, so they suited each other like Jack Sprat and his wife. It had been an effort to Dot to leave the night dress, which she had hoped to finish at a sitting, but when she was fairly set to work on the glue business, she never moved till the glue was in working order and her face as red as a ripe tomato.

By this time, Sam had set up business in the window seat and was fastening a large paper inscription over his shop. It ran thus:—

MR. SAM,

Dolls Doctor and Toymender to Her Majesty the

Queen, and all other Potentates.

"Splendid!" shouted Dot, who was serving up the glue as if it had been a kettle of soup, and who looked herself very like an overtoasted cook.

Sam took the glue and began to bustle about.

"Now, Dot, get me all the broken toys, and we'll see what we can do. And here's a second splendid idea. Do you see that box? Into that we shall put all the toys that are quite spoiled and cannot possibly be mended. It is to be called the Hospital for Incurables. I've got a placard for that. At least it's not written yet, but here's the paper, and perhaps you would write it, Dot, for I am tired of writing and I want to begin the mending."

"For the future," he presently resumed, "when I want

a doll to scalp or behead, I shall apply to the Hospital for Incurables, and the same with any other toy that I want to destroy. And you will see, my dear Dot, that I shall be quite a blessing to the nursery; for I shall attend the dolls gratis, and keep all the furniture in repair."

Sam really kept his word. He had a natural turn for mechanical work, and, backed by Dot's more methodical genius, he prolonged the days of the broken toys by skillful mending and so acquired an interest in them which was still more favorable to their preservation. When his birthday came round, which was some months after these events, Dot (assisted by Mamma and Aunt Penelope), had prepared for him a surprise that was more than equal to any of his own "splendid ideas." The whole force of the toy cupboard was assembled on the nursery table to present Sam with a fine box of joiner's tools as a reward for his services, Papa kindly acting as spokesman on occasion.

And certain gaps in the china tea set, some scars on the dolls' faces, and a good many new legs, both amongst the furniture and the animals, are now the only remaining traces of Sam's earthquake.

The Jar of Rosemary

by Maud Lindsey

There was once a little prince whose mother, the queen, was sick. All summer, she lay in bed, and everything was kept quiet in the palace; but when the autumn came, she grew better. Every day brought color to her cheeks and strength to her limbs, and by and by, the little prince was allowed to go into her room and stand beside her bed to talk to her.

He was very glad of this, for he wanted to ask her what she would like for a Christmas present, and as soon as he had kissed her and laid his cheek against hers, he whispered his question in her ear.

"What should I like for a Christmas present?" said the queen. "A smile and a kiss and a hug around the neck; these are the dearest gifts I know."

But the prince was not satisfied with this answer. "Smiles and kisses and hugs you can have every day," he said, "but think, mother, think, if you could choose the thing you wanted most in all the world what would you take?"

So the queen thought and thought, and at last, she said:

"If I might take my choice of all the world I believe a little jar of rosemary like that which bloomed in my mother's window when I was a little girl would please me better than anything else."

The little prince was delighted to hear this, and as soon as he had gone out of the queen's room, he sent a servant to his father's greenhouses to inquire for a rosemary plant.

But the servant came back with disappointing news. There were carnation pinks in the king's greenhouses, roses with golden hearts, and lovely lilies, but there was no rosemary. Rosemary was a common herb and grew mostly in country gardens, so the king's gardeners said.

"Then go into the country for it," said the little prince. "No matter where it grows, my mother must have it for a Christmas present."

So messengers went into the country here, there, and everywhere to seek the plant, but each one came back with the same story to tell; there was rosemary, enough and to spare, in the spring, but the frost had been in the country, and there was not a green sprig left to bring to the little prince for his mother's Christmas present.

Two days before Christmas, however, the news was brought that rosemary had been found, a lovely green plant growing in a jar, right in the very city where the prince himself lived.

"But where is it?" said he. "Why have you not brought it with you? Go and get it at once."

"Well, as for that," said the servant who had found the plant, "there is a little difficulty. The old woman to whom the rosemary belongs did not want to sell it even though I offered her a handful of silver for it."

"Then give her a purse of gold," said the little prince.

So a purse filled so full of gold that it could not hold another piece was taken to the old woman, but presently it was brought back. She would not sell her rosemary; no, not even for a purse of gold.

"Perhaps if your little highness would go yourself and ask her, she might change her mind," said the prince's nurse. So the royal carriage drawn by six white horses was brought, and the little prince and his servants rode away to the old woman's house, and when they got there, the first thing they spied was the little green plant in a jar standing in the old woman's window.

The old woman, herself, came to the door, and she was glad to see the little prince. She invited him in, bade him warm his hands by the fire, and gave him a cooky from her cupboard to eat.

She had a little grandson no older than the prince, but he was sick and could not run about and play like other children. He lay in a little white bed in the old woman's room, and the little prince, after he had eaten the cooky, spoke to him and took out his favorite plaything, which he always carried in his pocket, and showed it to him.

The prince's favorite plaything was a ball which was like no other ball that had ever been made. It was woven of magic stuff as bright as the sunlight, as sparkling as the starlight, and as golden as the moon at harvest time. And when the little prince threw it into the air, or bounced it on the floor or turned it in his hands, it rang like a chime of silver bells.

The sick child laughed to hear it and held out his hands for it, and the prince let him hold it, which pleased the grandmother as much as the child.

But pleased though she was, she would not sell the rosemary. She had brought it from the home where she had lived when her little grandson's father was a boy, she said, and she hoped to keep it till she died. So the prince and his servants had to go home without it.

No sooner had they gone than the sick child began to

talk of the wonderful ball.

"If I had such a ball to hold in my hand," he said, "I should be contented all the day."

"You may as well wish for the moon in the sky," said his grandmother, but she thought of what he said, and in the evening, when he was asleep, she put her shawl around her and took the jar of rosemary with her she hastened to the king's palace.

When she got there, the servants asked her errand, but she would answer nothing till they had taken her to the little prince.

"Silver and gold would not buy the rosemary," she said when she saw him, "but if you will give me your golden ball for my little grandchild you may have the plant."

"But my ball is the most wonderful ball that was ever made!" cried the little prince, "and it is my favorite plaything. I would not give it away for anything."

And so the old woman had to go home with her jar of rosemary under her shawl.

The next day was the day before Christmas, and there was a great stir and bustle in the palace. The queen's physician had said that she might sit up to see the Christmas Tree that night and have her presents with the rest of the family, and everyone was running to and fro to get things in readiness for her.

The queen had so many presents, and very fine they

were, too, that the Christmas Tree could not hold them all, so they were put on a table before the throne and wreathed around with holly and with pine. The little prince went in with his nurse to see them and to put his gift, which was a jewel, among them.

"She wanted a jar of rosemary," he said as he looked at the glittering heap.

"She will never think of it again when she sees these things. You may be sure of that," said the nurse.

But the little prince was not sure. He thought of it himself many times that day, and once, when he was playing with his ball, he said to the nurse:

"If I had a rosemary plant I'd be willing to sell it for a purse full of gold. Wouldn't you?"

"Indeed, yes," said the nurse, "and so would any one else in his right senses. You may be sure of that."

The little boy was not satisfied, though, and presently when he had put his ball up and stood at the window watching the snow which had come to whiten the earth for Christ's birthday, he said to the nurse:

"I wish it were spring. It is easy to get rosemary then, is it not?"

"Your little highness is like the king's parrot that knows but one word with your rosemary, rosemary, rosemary," said the nurse, who was a little out of patience by that time. "Her majesty, the queen, only asked for it to please you. You may be sure of that."

But the little prince was not sure, and when the nurse had gone to her supper, and he was left by chance for a moment alone, he put on his coat of fur and, taking the ball with him, he slipped away from the palace and hastened toward the old woman's house.

He had never been out at night by himself before, and he might have felt a little afraid had it not been for the friendly stars that twinkled in the sky above him.

"We will show you the way," they seemed to say; and he trudged on bravely in their light till, by and by, he came to the house and knocked at the door.

Now the sick little child had been talking of the wonderful ball all evening. "Did you see how it shone, grandmother? And did you hear how the little bells rang?" he said, and it was just then that the little prince knocked at the door.

The old woman made haste to answer the knock, and when she saw the prince, she was too astonished to speak.

"Here is the ball," he cried, putting it into her hands. "Please give me the rosemary for my mother."

And so it happened that when the queen sat down before her great table of gifts, the first thing she spied was a jar of sweet rosemary like that which had bloomed in her mother's window when she was a little girl.

"I should rather have it than all the other gifts in the

world," she said; and she took the little prince in her arms and kissed him.

The Brave and Honest Boy, Oliver Twist

by Charles Dickens

Little Oliver Twist was an orphan. He never saw his mother or his father. He was born at the workhouse, the home for paupers, where his poor heart-broken mother had been taken just a short time before baby Oliver came; and, the very night he was born, she was so sick and weak she said: "Let me see my child and then I will die." The old nurse said: "Nonsense, my dear, you must not think of dying, you have something now to live for." The good, kind doctor said she must be very brave, and she might get well. They brought her little baby boy to her, and she hugged him in her weak arms, and she kissed him on the brow many times and cuddled him up as close as her feeble arms could hold him, and then she looked at him long and steadily, and a sweet smile came over her face, and a bright light came into her eyes, and before the smile could pass from her lips, she died.

The old nurse wept as she took the little baby from its dead mother's arms, and the good doctor had to wipe the tears from his eyes. It was so very, very sad.

After wrapping the baby in a blanket and laying him in a warm place, the old nurse straightened out the limbs of the young mother and folded her hands on her breast; and, spreading a white sheet over her still form, she called the doctor to look at her—for the nurse, and the doctor was all who were there. The same sweet smile was on her face, and the doctor said as he looked upon her: "Poor, poor girl, she is so beautiful and so young! What strange fate has brought her to this poor place? Nurse, take good care of the baby, for his mother must have been, at one time, a kind and gentle woman."

The next day they took the unknown woman out to the potter's field and buried her, and, for nine months, the old nurse at the workhouse took care of the baby; though it is sad to say, this old woman, kind-hearted though she was, was at the same time so fond of gin that she often took the money, which ought to have bought milk for the baby, to buy a drink for herself.

Nobody knew what the young mother's name was, and so this baby had no name until, at last, Mr Bumble, who was one of the parish officers who looked after the paupers, came and named him Oliver Twist.

When little Oliver was nine months old, they took him away from the workhouse and carried him to the "Poor Farm," where there were twenty-five or thirty other poor children who had no parents. A woman by the name of Mrs Mann had charge of this cottage. The parish gave her an allowance of enough money to keep the children in plenty of food and clothing, but she starved the little ones to keep the money for herself so that many of them died and others came to take their places. But young Oliver was a tough little fellow, and while he looked very pale and thin, he was, otherwise, healthy and hung on to his life.

Mrs Mann was also very cruel to the children. She would scold and beat them and shut them up in the cellar, and treat them meanly in many ways when no visitors were there. But, when any of the men who had control or visitors came around, she would smile and call the children "dear," and all sorts of pet names. She told them if any of them told on her, she would beat them; and, furthermore, that they should tell visitors that she was very kind and good to them and that they loved her very much.

Mr Bumble was a very mean man, too, as we shall see. They called him the Beadle, which means he was a sort of sheriff or policeman, and he was supposed to look after the people at the workhouse and at the poor farm and to wait on the directors who had charge of these places. He had the right to punish the boys if they did not mind, and they were all afraid of him.

Oliver remained at the cottage on the poor farm until he was nine years old, though he was a pale little fellow and did not look to be over seven.

On the morning of his birthday, Mrs Mann had given Oliver and two other boys a bad whipping and put them down in a dark coal cellar. Presently she saw Mr Bumble coming, and she told her servant to take the boys out and wash them quickly, for she did not let Mr Bumble know she ever punished them and was fearful he might hear them crying in the dark, damp place. Mrs Mann talked very nicely to Mr Bumble and made him a "toddy" (a glass of strong liquor) and kept him busy with her flattering and kindness until she knew the boys were washed.

Mr Bumble told her Oliver Twist was nine years old that day, and the Board (which meant the men in charge) had decided they must take him away from the farm and carry him back to the workhouse. Mrs Mann pretended to be very sorry, and she went out and brought Oliver in, telling him on the way that he must appear very sorry to leave her. Otherwise, she would beat him. So when Oliver was asked if he wanted to go, he said he was sorry to leave there. This was not a falsehood, for, miserable as the place was, he dearly loved his little companions. They were all the people he knew, and he did feel sad and really wept with sorrow as he told them good-by and was led by Mr Bumble back to the workhouse, where he was born and where his mother died nine years ago that very day.

When he got back there, he found the old nurse who remembered his mother, and she told him she was a beautiful sweet woman and how she had kissed him and held him in her arms when she died. Night after night, little Oliver dreamed about his beautiful mother, and she sometimes seemed to stand by his bed and look down upon him with the same beautiful eyes and the same sweet smile of which the nurse told him. Every time he had the chance, he asked questions about her, but the nurse could not tell him anything more. She did not even know her name.

Oliver had been at the workhouse only a very short time when Mr Bumble came in and told him he must appear before the Board at once. Now Oliver was puzzled at this. He thought aboard was a piece of flat wood, and he could not imagine why he was to appear before that. But he was too much afraid of Mr Bumble to ask any questions. This gentleman had treated him roughly in bringing him to the workhouse, and now, when he looked a little puzzled—for his expressive face always told what was in his honest little heart—Mr. Bumble gave him a sharp crack on the head with his cane and another rap over the back and told him to wake up and not look so sleepy and to mind to be polite when he went before the Board. Oliver could not help tears coming into his eyes as he was pushed along, and Mr Bumble gave him another sharp rap, telling him to hush, and ushered him into a room where several stern-looking gentlemen sat at a long table. One of them, in a white waistcoat, was particularly hard-looking. "Bow to the Board," said Mr Bumble to Oliver. Oliver looked about for a board, and, seeing none, he bowed to the table because it looked more like a board than anything else. The men laughed, and the man in the white waistcoat said: "The boy is a fool. I thought he was." After other ugly remarks, they told Oliver he was an orphan and that they had supported him all his life. He ought to be very thankful. (And he was when he remembered how many had been starved to death.) "Now," they said, "you are nine years old, and we must put you out to learn a trade." They told him he should begin the next morning at six o'clock to pick oakum and work at that until they could get him a place.

Oliver was faithful at his work, in which several other boys assisted, but oh! so hungry they got, for they were given but one little bowl of gruel at a meal—hardly enough for a kitten. So one day, the boys said they must ask for more, and they "drew straws" to see who should venture to do so. It fell to Oliver's lot to do it, and the next meal, when they had emptied their bowls, Oliver walked up to the man who helped them and said very politely, "Please, sir, may I not have some more? I am very hungry." This made the man so angry that he hit Oliver over the head with his ladle and called for Mr Bumble. He came, and when told that Oliver had "asked for more," he grabbed him by the collar and took him before the Board and made the complaint that he had been very naughty and rebellious, telling the circumstance in an unfair and untruthful way. The Board was angry at Oliver, and the man in the white waistcoat told them again as he had said before. "This boy will be hung sometime. We must get rid of him at once." So they offered five pounds or twenty-five dollars to anyone who would take him.

The first man who came was a very mean chimney sweeper who had almost killed other boys with his vile treatment. The Board agreed to let him have Oliver, but when they took him before the magistrates, Oliver fell on his knees and begged them not to let that man have him, and they would not. So Oliver was taken back to the workhouse.

The next man who came was Mr Sowerberry, an undertaker. He was a very good man, and the magistrates let him take Oliver along. But he had a very cross, stingy wife, a mean servant girl by the name of Charlotte, and a big overbearing boy by the name of Noah Claypole, whom he had taken to raise. Oliver thought he would like Mr Sowerberry well enough, but his heart fell when "the Mrs." met him and called him "boy" and a "measly-looking little pauper" and gave him for supper the scraps she had put for the dog. But this was so much better than he got at the workhouse, he would not complain about the food, and he hoped, by faithful work, to win kind treatment.

They made him sleep by himself in the shop among the coffins, and he was very much frightened; but he would rather sleep there than with the terrible boy, Noah. The first night he dreamed of his beautiful mother and thought again he could see her sitting among those black, fearful coffins with the same sweet smile upon her face. He was awakened the next morning by Noah, who told him he had to obey him, and he'd a better look out, or he'd wear the life out of him. Noah kicked and cuffed Oliver several times, but the poor boy was too used to that to resent it, and was determined to do his work well.

Mr Sowerberry found Oliver so good, sensible, and polite that he made him his assistant and took him to all the funerals and occasionally gave him a penny. Oliver went into fine houses and saw people and sights he had never dreamed of before. Mr Sowerberry had told him he might someday be an undertaker himself, and Oliver worked hard to please his master, though Noah and Mrs Sowerberry and Charlotte grew more unkind to him all the time because "he was put forward," they said, "and Noah was kept back." This, of course, made Noah meaner than ever to Oliver—determined to endure it all rather than complain and try to win them over after a while by being kind. He could have borne any insult to himself, but Noah tried the little fellow too far when he attacked the name of Oliver's mother, and it brought serious trouble, as we shall see.

One day, Oliver and Noah had descended into the kitchen at the usual dinner hour when Charlotte was called out of the way. There came a few minutes of time which Noah Claypole, being hungry and vicious, considered he could not possibly devote to a worthier purpose than aggravating and tantalizing young Oliver Twist.

Intent upon this innocent amusement, Noah put his feet on the tablecloth; pulled Oliver's hair; twitched his ears; expressed his opinion that he was a "sneak;" and furthermore announced his intention of coming to see him hanged whenever that desirable event should take place; and entered upon various other topics of petty annoyance, like a malicious and ill-conditioned charity-boy as he was. But, none of these taunts producing the desired effect of making Oliver cry, Noah began to talk about his mother.

"Work'us," said Noah, "how's your mother?" Noah had given Oliver this name because he had come from the workhouse.

"She's dead," replied Oliver; "don't you say anything about her to me!"

Oliver's color rose as he said this; he breathed quickly, and there was a curious working of the mouth and nostrils, which Noah thought must be the immediate precursor of a violent fit of crying. Under this impression, he returned to the charge.

"What did she die of, Work'us?" said Noah.

"Of a broken-heart, some of our old nurses told me," replied Oliver: more as if he were talking to himself than answering Noah. "I think I know what it must be to die of that!"

"Tol de rol lol lol, right fol lairy, Work'us," said Noah, as a tear rolled down Oliver's cheek. "What's set you a sniveling now?"

"Not you," replied Oliver, hastily brushing the tear away. "Don't think it."

"Oh, not me, eh?" sneered Noah.

"No, not you," replied Oliver sharply.

"There, that's enough. Don't say anything more to me about her; you'd better not!"

"Better not!" exclaimed Noah. "Well! Better not! Work'us, don't be impudent. Your mother, too! She was a nice 'un, she was. Oh, Lor'!" And here Noah nodded his head expressively and curled his small red nose.

"Yer know, Work'us," continued Noah, emboldened by Oliver's silence and speaking in a jeering tone of affected pity. "Yer know, Work'us, it can't be helped now; and of course yer couldn't help it then. But yer must know, Work'us, yer mother was a regular-down bad 'un."

"What did you say?" inquired Oliver, looking up very quickly.

"A regular right-down bad'un, Work'us," replied Noah coolly. "And it's a great deal better, Work'us, that she died when she did, or else she'd have been hard laboring in the jail, or sent out of the country, or hung; which is more likely than either, isn't it?"

Crimson with fury, Oliver started up; overthrew the chair and table; seized Noah by the throat; shook him, in the violence of his rage, till his teeth chattered in his head; and, collecting his whole force into one heavy blow, felled him to the ground.

A minute ago, the boy had looked at the quiet, mild, dejected creature that harsh treatment had made him. But his spirit was roused at last; the cruel insult to his dead mother had set his blood on fire. His breast heaved; his form was erect; his eye bright and vivid; his whole person changed as he stood glaring over the cowardly tormentor who now lay crouching at his feet; and defied him with an energy he had never known before.

"He'll murder me!" blubbered Noah. "Charlotte! missis! Here's the new boy a-murdering of me! Help! help! Oliver's gone mad! Char—lotte!"

Noah's shouts were responded to by a loud scream from Charlotte and a louder one from Mrs Sowerberry, the former of whom rushed into the kitchen by a side door while the latter paused on the staircase till she was quite certain that it was safe to come farther down.

"Oh, you little wretch!" screamed Charlotte, seizing Oliver with her utmost force, which was about equal to that of a moderately strong man in particularly good training. "Oh, you little un-grate-ful, mur-de-rous, hor-rid villain!" And between every syllable, Charlotte gave Oliver a blow with all her might.

Charlotte's fist was by no means a light one, and Mrs Sowerberry plunged into the kitchen and assisted in holding him with one hand while she scratched his face with the other. In this favorable position of affairs,

Noah rose from the ground and pommeled him behind.

When they were all wearied out and could tear and beat no longer, they dragged Oliver, struggling and shouting, but nothing daunted, into the dust cellar and there locked him up. This being done, Mrs Sowerberry sunk into a chair and burst into tears.

"Oh! Charlotte," said Mrs Sowerberry. "Oh! Charlotte, what a mercy we have not all been murdered in our beds!"

"Ah! mercy indeed, ma'am," was the reply. "I only hope this'll teach master not to have any more of these dreadful creatures, that are born to be murderers and robbers from their very cradle. Poor Noah! he was all but killed, ma'am, when I come in."

"Poor fellow!" said Mrs Sowerberry, looking piteously at the charity boy.

"What's to be done!" exclaimed Mrs Sowerberry. "Your master's not at home; there's not a man in the house, and he'll kick that door down in ten minutes." Oliver's vigorous plunges against the door did seem as if he would break it.

"Dear, dear! I don't know, ma'am," said Charlotte, "unless we send for the police officers."

"Or the millingtary," suggested Noah.

"No, no," said Mrs Sowerberry: bethinking herself of Oliver's old friend. "Run to Mr. Bumble, Noah, and tell him to come here directly, and not to lose a minute;

never mind your cap! Make haste!"

Noah set off with all his might and paused not once for breath until he reached the workhouse gate.

"Why, what's the matter with the boy!" said the people as Noah rushed up.

"Mr. Bumble! Mr. Bumble!" cried Noah with a well-pretended alarm. "Oh, Mr. Bumble, sir! Oliver, sir— Oliver has—"

"What? What?" interposed M. Bumble, with a gleam of pleasure in his steel-like eyes. "Not run away; he hasn't run away, has he, Noah?"

"No, sir, no! Not run away, sir, but he's turned wicious," replied Noah. "He tried to murder me, sir; and then he tried to murder Charlotte; and then missis. Oh! what dreadful pain it is! Such agony, please, sir!" And here Noah writhed and twisted his body into an extensive variety of eel-like positions, by which the gentleman's notice was very soon attracted; for he had not walked three paces when he turned angrily round and inquired what that young cur was howling for.

"It's a poor boy from the free school, sir," replied Mr Bumble, "who has been nearly murdered—all but murdered, sir—by young Twist."

"By Jove!" exclaimed the gentleman in the white waistcoat, stopping short. "I knew it! I felt from the very first that that terrible young savage would come to be hung!"

"He has likewise attempted, sir, to murder the female servant," said Mr Bumble, with a face of ashy paleness.

"And his missis," interposed Noah.

"And his master, too. I think you said Noah?" added Mr Bumble.

"No! He's out, or he would have murdered him," replied Noah. "He said he wanted to."

"Ah! Said he wanted to, did he, my boy?" inquired the gentleman in the white waistcoat.

"Yes, sir. And please, sir," replied Noah, "missis wants to know whether Mr Bumble can spare time to step up there, directly, and flog him—'cause master's out."

"Certainly, my boy; certainly," said the gentleman in the white waistcoat, smiling benignly and patting Noah's head, which was about three inches higher than his own. "You're a good boy—a very good boy. Here's a penny for you. Bumble, just step up to Sowerberry's with your cane and see what's to be done. Don't spare him, Bumble."

"No, I will not, sir," replied the beadle as he hurried away.

Meantime, Oliver continued to kick, with undiminished vigor, at the cellar door. The accounts of his ferocity, as related by Mrs Sowerberry and Charlotte, were of so startling a nature that Mr Bumble judged it prudent to parley before opening the door.

With this view, he gave a kick at the outside by way of prelude and then, putting his mouth to the keyhole, said, in a deep and impressive tone:

"Oliver!"

"Come, you let me out!" replied Oliver from the inside.

"Do you know this here voice, Oliver?" said Mr Bumble.

"Yes," replied Oliver.

"Ain't you afraid of it, sir? Ain't you a-trembling while I speak, sir?" said Mr Bumble.

"No!" replied Oliver boldly.

An answer so different from the one he had expected to hear and was in the habit of receiving staggered Mr Bumble not a little.

"Oh, you know, Mr Bumble, he must be mad," said Mrs Sowerberry. "No boy in half his senses could venture to speak so to you."

"It's not madness, ma'am," replied Mr Bumble after a few moments of deep meditation. "It's meat."

"What?" exclaimed Mrs Sowerberry.

"Meat, ma'am, meat," replied Bumble, with stern emphasis. "You've overfed him, ma'am."

"Dear, dear!" ejaculated Mrs Sowerberry, piously

raising her eyes to the kitchen ceiling; "this comes of being liberal!"

The liberality of Mrs Sowerberry to Oliver had consisted in a bestowal upon him of all the dirty odds and ends that nobody else would eat.

"Ah!" said Mr Bumble when the lady brought her eyes down to earth again; "the only thing that can be done now, that I know of, is to leave him in the cellar for a day or so, till he's a little starved down; and then to take him out, and keep him on gruel all through his apprenticeship. He comes of a bad family. Excitable natures, Mrs. Sowerberry! Both the nurse and doctor said that that mother of his made her way here, against difficulties and pain that would have killed any well-disposed woman weeks before."

At this point of Mr Bumble's discourse, Oliver, just hearing enough to know that some new allusion was being made to his mother, recommenced kicking with a violence that rendered every other sound inaudible. Sowerberry returned at this moment. Oliver's offence having been explained to him, with such exaggerations as the ladies thought best calculated to rouse his ire, he unlocked the cellar door in a twinkling and dragged his rebellious apprentice out by the collar.

Oliver's clothes had been torn in the beating he had received; his face was bruised and scratched, and his hair scattered over his forehead. The angry flush had not disappeared, however; and when he was pulled out of his prison, he scowled boldly at Noah and looked quite undismayed.

"Now, you are a nice young fellow, ain't you?" said Sowerberry, giving Oliver a shake and a box on the ear.

"He called my mother names," replied Oliver.

"Well, and what if he did, you little ungrateful wretch?" said Mrs Sowerberry. "She deserved what he said and worse."

"She didn't," said Oliver.

"She did," said Mrs Sowerberry.

"It's a lie!" said Oliver.

Mrs Sowerberry burst into a flood of tears.

This flood of tears left Mr Sowerberry nothing else to do, so he at once gave Oliver a drubbing, which satisfied even Mrs Sowerberry herself. For the rest of the day he was shut up in the backs kitchen, in company with a pump and a slice of bread; and, at night, Mrs Sowerberry, after making various remarks outside the door, by no means kind to the memory of his mother, looked into the room, and, amidst the jeers and pointings of Noah and Charlotte, ordered him upstairs to his dismal bed.

It was not until he was left alone in the silence and stillness of the gloomy workshop of the undertaker that Oliver gave way to the feelings which the day's treatment may be supposed likely to have awakened in a mere child. He had listened to their taunts with a look of contempt; he had borne the lash without a cry; for he felt that pride swelling in his heart which would have kept down a shriek to the last, though they had roasted him alive. But now, when there was none to see or hear him, he fell upon his knees on the floor; and, hiding his face in his hands, wept bitter tears and prayed in his bleeding heart that God would help him to get away from these cruel people. There, upon his knees, Oliver determined to run away and, rising, tied up a few clothes in a handkerchief and went to bed.

With the first ray of light that struggled through the crevices in the shutters, Oliver arose and unbarred the door. One timid look around—one moment's pause of hesitation—he had closed it behind him and was in the open street.

He looked to the right and to the left, uncertain of which way to fly. He remembered to have seen the wagons as they went out, toiling up the hill. He took the same route; and, arriving at a footpath across the fields, which he knew, after some distance, led out again into the road, struck into it and walked quickly on.

Along this same footpath, Oliver well remembered he had trotted beside Mr Bumble when he first carried him to the workhouse from the farm. His heart beat quickly when he bethought himself of this, and he half resolved to turn back. He had come a long way, though and should lose a great deal of time by doing so. Besides, it was so early that there was very little fear of his being seen, so he walked on.

He reached the house. There was no appearance of the people inside stirring at that early hour. Oliver stopped and peeped into the garden. A child was weeding one of the little beds; as he stopped, he raised his pale face and disclosed the features of one of his former companions. Oliver felt glad to see him before he went; for, though younger than himself, he had been his little friend and playmate. They had been beaten, starved, and shut up together many times.

"Hush, Dick!" said Oliver as the boy ran to the gate and thrust his thin arm between the rails to greet him. "Is anyone up?"

"Nobody but me," replied the child.

"You mustn't say you saw me, Dick," said Oliver. "I am running away. They beat and ill-use me, Dick; and I am going to seek my fortune some long way off. I don't know where. How pale you are!"

"I heard the doctor tell them I was dying," replied the child with a faint smile. "I am very glad to see you, dear; but don't stop, don't stop!"

"Yes, yes, I will to say good-by to you," replied Oliver. "I shall see you again, Dick. I know I shall. You will be well and happy!"

"I hope so," replied the child. "After I am dead, but not before. I know the doctor must be right, Oliver, because I dream so much of heaven and angels, and kind faces that I never see when I am awake. Kiss me," said the child, climbing up the low gate and flinging his little arms around Oliver's neck: "Good-by, dear! God bless you!"

The blessing was from a young child's lips, but it was the first that Oliver had ever heard invoked upon his head; through the struggles and sufferings, and troubles and changes of his after-life, he never once forgot it.

Oliver soon got into the high road. It was eight o'clock now. Though he was nearly five miles away from the town, he ran and hid behind the hedges, by turns, till noon, fearing that he might be pursued and overtaken. Then he sat down to rest by the side of the milestone.

The stone by which he was seated had a sign on it which said that it was just seventy miles from that spot to London. The name awakened a new train of ideas in the boy's mind, London!—that great large place!—nobody—not even Mr Bumble—could ever find him there! He had often heard the old men in the workhouse, too, say that no lad of spirit need want in London; and that there were ways of living in that vast city which those who had been bred in the country parts had no idea of. It was the very place for a homeless boy who must die in the streets unless someone helped him. As these things passed through his thoughts, he jumped upon his feet and again walked forward.

He had made the distance between himself and London less by full four miles more before he thought how much he must undergo ere he could hope to reach the place toward which he was going. As this consideration forced itself upon him, he slackened his pace a little and meditated upon his means of getting there. He had a crust of bread, a coarse shirt, and two pairs of stockings in his bundle. He had a penny too—a gift of Sowerberry's after some funeral in which he had acquitted himself more than ordinarily well—in his pocket. "A clean shirt," thought Oliver, "is a very comfortable thing; and so are two pairs of darned stockings; and so is a penny, but they are small helps to a sixty-five miles' walk in winter-time."

Thus day after day, the weary but plucky little boy walked on, and early on the seventh morning, after he had left his native place, Oliver limped slowly into the little town of Barnet and sat down on a doorstep to rest. Some few stopped to gaze at Oliver for a moment or two or turned round to stare at him as they hurried by, but none helped him or troubled themselves to inquire how he came there. He had no heart to beg. And there he sat for some time when he was roused by observing that a boy was watching him most earnestly from the opposite side of the way. He took little heed of this at first, but the boy remained in the same attitude so long that Oliver raised his head and returned his steady look. Upon this, the boy crossed over and, walking close up to Oliver, said:

"Hullo, my covey! What's the row?"

The boy who had spoken to the young wayfarer was about his own age: but one of the queerest-looking boys that Oliver had ever seen. He was a snub-nosed, flat-browed, common-faced boy enough; and as dirty a youth as one would wish to see, but he had about him all the airs and manners of a man. He was short for his age with rather bow legs and little, sharp, ugly eyes. His hat was stuck on the top of his head so lightly that it threatened to fall off every moment. He wore a man's coat, which reached nearly to his heels.

"Hullo, my covey! What's the row?" said the stranger.

"I am very hungry and tired," replied Oliver: the tears standing in his eyes as he spoke. "I have walked a long way. I have been walking these seven days."

"Walking for sivin days!" said the young gentleman. "Oh, I see. Beak's order, eh? But," he added, noticing Oliver's look of surprise, "I suppose you don't know what a beak is, my flash com-pan-i-on."

Oliver mildly replied that he had always heard a bird's mouth described by the word beak.

"My eyes, how green!" exclaimed the young gentleman. "Why, a beak's a madgst'rate; and when you walk by a beak's order, it's not straight forerd."

"But come," said the young gentleman, "you want grub, and you shall have it. Up with you on your pins. There! Now then!"

Assisting Oliver to rise, the young gentleman took him to a nearby grocery store, where he bought a supply of ready-dressed ham and a half-quartern loaf, or, as he himself expressed it, "a fourpenny bran!" Taking the bread under his arm, the young gentleman turned into a small public house, and led the way to a tap room in the rear of the premises. Here a pot of beer was brought in by direction of the mysterious youth, and Oliver, falling to at his new friend's bidding, made a long and hearty meal, during which the strange boy eyed him from time to time with great attention.

"Going to London?" said the strange boy when Oliver had at length concluded.

"Yes."

"Got any lodgings?"

"No."

"Money?"

"No."

The strange boy whistled and put his arms into his pockets as far as the big coat sleeves would let them go.

"Do you live in London?" inquired Oliver.

"Yes, I do when I'm at home," replied the boy. "I suppose you want someplace to sleep in tonight, don't you?"

"I do, indeed," answered Oliver. "I have not slept under a roof since I left the country."

"Don't fret your eyelids on that score," said the young gentleman. "I've got to be in London to-night;

and I know a 'spectable old genelman as lives there, wot'll give you lodgings for nothink, and never ask for the change—that is, if any genelman he knows interduces you. And don't he know me? Oh, no! not in the least! By no means. Certainly not!" which was his queer way of saying he and the old gentleman were good friends.

This unexpected offer of shelter was too tempting to be resisted, especially as it was immediately followed up by the assurance that the old gentleman referred to would doubtless provide Oliver with a comfortable place without loss of time. This led to a more friendly and free talk, from which Oliver learned that his friend's name was Jack Dawkins—among his intimate friends, better known as the "Artful Dodger"—and that he was a peculiar pet of the elderly gentleman before mentioned.

As John Dawkins objected to their entering London before nightfall, it was nearly eleven o'clock when they reached the small city street, along which the Dodger scudded at a rapid pace, directing Oliver to follow close at his heels.

Although Oliver had enough to occupy his attention in keeping sight of his leader, he could not help bestowing a few hasty glances on either side of the way as he passed along. A dirtier or more wretched place he had never seen.

Oliver was just considering whether he hadn't better run away when they reached the bottom of the hill. His conductor, catching him by the arm, pushed open the door of a house and, drawing him into the passage, closed it behind them.

"Now, then!" cried a voice from below in reply to a whistle from the Dodger.

"Plummy and slam!" was the reply.

This seemed to be some watchword or signal that all was right; for the light of a feeble candle gleamed on the wall at the remote end of the passage, and a man's face peeped out from where a balustrade of the old kitchen staircase had been broken away.

"There's two of you," said the man, thrusting the candle farther out and shading his eyes with his hand. "Who's the t'other one?"

"A new pal," replied Jack Dawkins, pulling Oliver forward.

"Where did he come from?"

"Greenland. Is Fagin up-stairs?"

"Yes; he's a sortin' the wipes. Up with you!" The candle was drawn back, and the face disappeared.

Oliver, groping his way with one hand and having the other firmly grasped by his companion, ascended with much difficulty the dark and broken stairs, which his conductor mounted with an ease and expedition that showed he was well acquainted with them. He threw open the door of a backroom and drew Oliver in after him.

The walls and ceiling of the room were perfectly black with age and dirt. There was a deal table before the fire, upon which was a candle stuck in a ginger-beer bottle, two or three pewter pots, a loaf and butter, and a plate. Seated round the table were four or five boys, none older than the Dodger, smoking clay pipes and drinking spirits, with the air of middle-aged men. These all crowded about their friend as he whispered a few words to the Jewish proprietor, and then turned round and grinned at Oliver. So did the Jew himself, toasting fork in hand.

"This is him, Fagin," said Jack Dawkins; "my friend, Oliver Twist."

The Jew grinned and, making a low bow to Oliver, took him by the hand and hoped he should have the honor of a closer acquaintance. Upon this, the young gentleman with the pipes came around him and shook both his hands very hard.

"We are very glad to see you. Oliver, very," said the Jew. "Dodger, take off the sausages, and draw a tub near the fire for Oliver. Ah! you're a-staring at the pocket-handkerchiefs! eh, my dear! There are a good many of 'em, ain't there? We've just looked 'em out, ready for the wash: that's all, Oliver—that's all. Ha! ha! ha!"

The latter part of this speech was hailed by a noisy shout from all the pupils of the merry old gentleman; in the midst of which they went to supper.

Oliver ate his share, and the Jew then mixed him a glass of hot gin and water, telling him he must drink it off directly because another gentleman wanted the tumbler. Oliver did as he was desired. Immediately afterwards he felt himself gently lifted onto one of the sacks, and then he sunk into a deep sleep.

It was late the next morning when Oliver awoke from a sound, long sleep. There was no other person in the room but the old Jew, who was boiling some coffee in a saucepan for breakfast and whistling softly to himself as he stirred it round and round with an iron spoon. He would stop every now and then to listen when there was the least noise below, and when he had satisfied himself, he would go on, whistling and stirring again as before.

Although Oliver had roused himself from sleep, he was not thoroughly awake.

Oliver was precisely in this condition. He saw the Jew with his half-closed eyes, heard his low whistling, and recognized the sound of the spoon grating against the saucepan's sides.

When the coffee was done, the Jew drew the saucepan to the hob, looked at Oliver, and called him by his name. He did not answer and was to all appearance asleep.

After satisfying himself upon this head, the Jew stepped gently to the door, which he fastened. He then drew forth, as it seemed to Oliver, from some trap in the floor a small box, which he placed carefully on the table. His eyes glistened as he raised the lid and looked in. Dragging an old chair to the table, he sat down; and took from it a magnificent gold watch sparkling with jewels.

"Aha!" said the Jew, shrugging up his shoulders and distorting every feature with a hideous grin. "Clever dogs! Clever dogs! Stanch to the last! Never told the old parson where they were. Never peached upon old Fagin! And why should they? It wouldn't have loosened the knot or kept the drop up a minute longer. No, no, no! Fine fellows! Fine fellows!"

With these and other muttered remarks of the like nature, the Jew once more laid the watch in its place of safety. At least half a dozen more were severally drawn forth from the same box and looked at with equal pleasure, besides rings, bracelets, and other articles of jewelry, of such magnificent materials and costly workmanship that Oliver had no idea even of their names.

As the Jew looked up, his bright dark eyes, which had been staring at the jewelry, fell on Oliver's face; the boy's eyes were fixed on his in mute curiosity, and although the recognition was only for an instant, it was enough to show the old man that he had been observed. He closed the lid of the box with a loud crash; and, laying his hand on a bread knife which was on the table, started furiously up.

"What's that?" said the Jew. "What do you watch me

for? Why are you awake? What have you seen? Speak out boy! Quick—quick! for your life!"

"I wasn't able to sleep any longer, sir," replied Oliver meekly. "I am very sorry if I have disturbed you, sir."

"You were not awake an hour ago?" said the Jew, scowling fiercely.

"No! No, indeed!" replied Oliver.

"Are you sure?" cried the Jew, with a still fiercer look than before and a threatening attitude.

"Upon my word I was not, sir," replied Oliver earnestly.

"Tush, tush, my dear!" said the Jew, abruptly resuming his old manner and playing with the knife a little before he laid it down; to make Oliver think that he had caught it up in the mere sport. "Of course I know that, my dear. I only tried to frighten you. You're a brave boy. Ha! ha! you're a brave boy, Oliver!" The Jew rubbed his hands with a chuckle but glanced uneasily at the box, notwithstanding.

"Did you see any of these pretty things, my dear?" said the Jew, laying his hand upon it after a short pause.

"Yes, sir," replied Oliver.

"Ah!" said the Jew, turning rather pale. "They— they're mine, Oliver: my little property. All I have to live upon in my old age. The folks call me a miser, my dear. Only a miser; that's all."

Oliver thought the old gentleman must be a decided miser to live in such a dirty place, with so many watches; but, thinking that perhaps his fondness for the Dodger and the other boys cost him a good deal of money, he only looked kindly at the Jew, and asked if he might get up.

"Certainly, my dear, certainly," replied the old gentleman. "There's a pitcher of water in the corner by the door. Bring it here, and I'll give you a basin to wash in, my dear."

Oliver got up, walked across the room, and stooped for an instant to raise the pitcher. When he turned his head, the box was gone.

He had scarcely washed himself and made everything tidy by emptying the basin out of the window, agreeably to the Jew's directions, when the Dodger returned, accompanied by a very sprightly young friend, whom Oliver had seen smoking on the previous night, and who was now formally introduced to him as Charley Bates. The four sat down to breakfast on the coffee and some hot rolls and ham, which the Dodger had brought home in the crown of his hat.

"Well," said the Jew, glancing slyly at Oliver and addressing himself to the Dodger, "I hope you've been at work this morning, my dears?"

"Hard," replied the Dodger.

"As nails," added Charley Bates.

"Good boys, good boys!" said the Jew. "What have you, Dodger?"

"A couple of pocketbooks," replied that young gentleman.

"Lined?" inquired the Jew with eagerness.

"Pretty well," replied the Dodger, producing two pocketbooks.

"Not so heavy as they might be," said the Jew, after looking at the insides carefully, "but very neat and nicely made. A good workman, ain't he, Oliver?"

"Very, indeed, sir," said Oliver. At which, Mr Charles Bates laughed uproariously, very much to the amazement of Oliver, who saw nothing to laugh at in anything that had passed.

"And what have you got, my dear?" said Fagin to Charley Bates.

"Wipes," replied Master Bates at the same time producing four pocket handkerchiefs.

"Well," said the Jew, inspecting them closely, "they're very good ones, very. You haven't marked them well, though, Charley; so the marks shall be picked out with a needle, and we'll teach Oliver how to do it. Shall us, Oliver, eh? Ha! ha! ha!"

"If you please, sir," said Oliver.

"You'd like to be able to make pocket-handkerchiefs

as easy as Charley Bates, wouldn't you, my dear?" said the Jew.

"Very much, indeed, if you'll teach me, sir," replied Oliver.

Master Bates burst into another laugh.

"He is so jolly green!" said Charley when he recovered as an apology to the company for his impolite behavior.

The Dodger said nothing, but he smoothed Oliver's hair over his eyes and said he'd know better by and by.

When the breakfast was cleared away, the merry old gentleman and the two boys played at a very curious and uncommon game, which was performed in this way: The merry old gentleman, placing a snuff box in one pocket of his trousers, a note-case in the other, and a watch in his waistcoat pocket, with a guard-chain round his neck, and sticking a mock-diamond pin in his shirt, buttoned his coat tight around him, and putting his spectacle-case and handkerchief in his pockets, trotted up and down the room with a stick, in imitation of the manner in which old gentlemen walk about the streets any hour in the day.

Now during all this time, the two boys followed him closely about, getting out of his sight so nimbly every time he turned round that it was impossible to follow their motions. At last, the Dodger trod upon his toes or ran upon his boot accidentally while Charley Bates stumbled up against him behind; and in that one moment, they took from him, with the most extraordinary rapidity, snuff-box, note-case, watch-guard, chain, shirt-pin, pocket handkerchief, even the spectacle-case. If the old gentleman felt a hand in any one of his pockets, he cried out where it was, and then the game began all over again.

When this game had been played a great many times, Charley Bates expressed his opinion that it was time to pad the hoof. This, it occurred to Oliver, must be French for going out; for directly afterwards, the Dodger and Charley went away together, having been kindly furnished by the amiable old Jew with money to spend.

"There, my dear," said Fagin. "That's a pleasant life, isn't it? They have gone out for the day."

"Have they done work, sir?" inquired Oliver.

"Yes," said the Jew; "that is, unless they should unexpectedly come across any when they are out; and they won't neglect it, if they do, my dear, depend upon it. Make 'em your models, my dear. Make 'em your models," tapping the fire-shovel on the hearth to add force to his words; "do everything they bid you, and take their advice in all matters—especially the Dodger's my dear. He'll be a great man himself, and will make you one too, if you take pattern by him. Is my handkerchief hanging out of my pocket, my dear?" said the Jew, stopping short.

"Yes, sir," said Oliver.

"See if you can take it out, without my feeling it, as you saw them do when we were at play this morning."

Oliver held up the bottom of the pocket with one hand, as he had seen the Dodger hold it, and drew the handkerchief lightly out with the other.

"Is it gone?" cried the Jew.

"Here it is, sir," said Oliver, showing it in his hand.

"You're a clever boy, my dear," said the playful old gentleman, patting Oliver on the head approvingly. "I never saw a sharper lad. Here's a shilling for you. If you go on in this way, you'll be the greatest man of the time. And now come here, and I'll show you how to take the marks out of the handkerchief."

Oliver wondered what picking the old gentleman's pocket in the play had to do with his chances of being a great man. But, thinking that the Jew, being so much older, must know best, he followed him quietly to the table and was soon deeply at work in his new study.

For many days Oliver remained in the Jew's room, picking the marks out of the pocket handkerchiefs (of which a great number were brought home) and sometimes taking part in the game already described, which the two boys and the Jew played regularly every morning.

At length, one morning, Oliver obtained permission to go out with the boys. There had been no handkerchiefs to work upon for two or three days, and the dinners had been rather meager. Perhaps these were reasons for the old gentleman giving his assent, but whether they were or no, he told Oliver he might go and place him under the joint care of Charley Bates and his friend, the Dodger.

The three boys started out; the Dodger with his coat sleeves tucked up and his hat cocked, as usual; Master Bates sauntering along with his hands in his pockets; and Oliver between them, wondering where they were going and what they would teach him to make first.

They were just coming from a narrow court not far from an open square, which is yet called "The Green," when the Dodger made a sudden stop, and, laying his finger on his lip, drew his companions back again, with the greatest caution.

"What's the matter?" demanded Oliver.

"Hush!" replied the Dodger. "Do you see that old cove at the book-stall?"

"The old gentleman over the way?" said Oliver. "Yes, I see him."

"He'll do," said the Dodger.

"A prime plant," observed Master Charley Bates.

Oliver looked from one to the other with the greatest surprise, but he was not permitted to make any inquiries; for the two boys walked stealthily across the road and slunk close behind the old gentleman. Oliver walked a few paces after them and, not knowing whether to advance or retire, stood looking on in silent amazement.

The old gentleman was a very respectable-looking personage, with a powdered head and gold spectacles, as he stood reading a book; and what was Oliver's horror and alarm as he stood a few paces off, looking on with his eyelids as wide open as they would possibly go, to see the Dodger plunge his hand into the old gentleman's pocket and draw from thence a handkerchief! To see him hand the same to Charley Bates and finally to behold them both running away round the corner.

In an instant, the whole mystery of the handkerchiefs, the watches, the jewels, and the Jew, rushed upon the boy's mind. He stood, for a moment, with the blood so tingling through all his veins from the terror that he felt as if he were in a burning fire; then, confused and frightened, he took to his heels and, not knowing what he did, made off as fast as he could lay his feet to the ground.

This was all done in a minute's space. In the very instant when Oliver began to run, the old gentleman, putting his hand to his pocket, and missing his handkerchief, turned sharp round. Seeing the boy scudding away at such a rapid pace, he very naturally concluded him to be the thief; and, shouting "Stop thief!" with all his might, made off after him, book in hand.

But the old gentleman was not the only person who

raised the hue and cry. The Dodger and Master Bates, unwilling to attract public attention by running down the open street, had merely retired into the very first doorway round the corner. They no sooner heard the cry and saw Oliver running than, guessing exactly how the matter stood, they issued forth with great quickness; and shouted, "Stop thief!" too, joined in the pursuit like good citizens.

Away they ran, pell-mell, helter-skelter, slap-dash; tearing, yelling, screaming, knocking down the passengers as they turned the corners, rousing up the dogs, and astonishing the fowls; and making streets, squares, and courts re-echo with the sound.

At last, a burly fellow struck Oliver with a terrible blow, and he went down upon the pavement, and the crowd eagerly gathered around him, each newcomer jostling and struggling with the others to catch a glimpse. "Stand aside!" "Give him a little air!" "Nonsense! he don't deserve it!" "Where's the gentleman?" "Here he is, coming down the street." "Make room there for the gentleman!" "Is this the boy, sir?"

Oliver lay covered with mud and dust and bleeding from the mouth, looking wildly round upon the heap of faces that surrounded him when the old gentleman was officiously dragged and pushed into the circle by the foremost of the pursuers.

"Yes," said the gentleman, "I am afraid it is the boy."

"Afraid!" murmured the crowd. "That's a good 'un!"

"Poor fellow!" said the gentleman, "he has hurt himself."

"I did that, sir," said a great lubberly fellow, stepping forward "and preciously I cut my knuckle agin his mouth. I stopped him, sir."

The fellow touched his hat with a grin, expecting something for his pains; but the old gentleman, eyeing him with an expression of dislike, looked anxiously around as if he contemplated running away himself; which it is very possible he might have attempted to do, and thus have afforded another chase, had not a police officer (who is generally the last person to arrive in such cases) at that moment made his way through the crowd, and seized Oliver by the collar.

"Come, get up," said the man roughly.

"It wasn't me, indeed, sir. Indeed, indeed, it was two other boys," said Oliver, clasping his hands passionately and looking around "They are here somewhere."

"Oh no, they ain't," said the officer. He meant this to be ironical, but it was true besides; for the Dodger and Charley Bates had filed off down the first convenient court they came to. "Come, get up!"

"Don't hurt him," said the old gentleman compassionately.

"Oh no, I won't hurt him," replied the officer, tearing his jacket half off his back in proof thereof. "Come, I know you; it won't do. Will you stand upon your legs, you young devil?"

Oliver, who could hardly stand, made a shift to raise himself on his feet and was at once lugged along the streets by the jacket collar at a rapid pace. The gentleman walked on with them by the officer's side.

At last, they came to a place called Mutton Hill. Here he was led beneath a low archway, and up a dirty court, where they saw a stout man with a bunch of whiskers on his face and a bunch of keys in his hand.

"What's the matter now?" said the man carelessly.

"A young fogle-hunter," replied the officer who had Oliver in charge.

"Are you the party that's been robbed, sir?" inquired the man with the keys.

"Yes, I am," replied the old gentleman, "but I am not sure that this boy actually took the handkerchief. I would rather not press the case."

"Must go before the magistrate now, sir," replied the man. "His worship will be disengaged in half a minute. Now, young gallows!"

This was an invitation for Oliver to enter through a door which he unlocked as he spoke and which led into a stone cell. Here he was searched, and nothing being found upon him, locked up.

The old gentleman looked almost as unhappy as

Oliver when the key grated in the lock.

At last, this gentleman, Mr Brownlow, was summoned before the magistrate—a very mean man, whose name was Fang. Oliver was brought in, and the magistrate, after using very abusive language to Mr Brownlow, had him sworn but would not let him tell his story. He flew into a rage and told the policeman to tell him what had happened.

The policeman, with becoming humility, related how he had taken the boy, how he had searched Oliver and found nothing on his person, and how that was all he knew about it.

"Are there any witnesses?" inquired Mr Fang.

"None, your worship," replied the policeman.

Mr Fang sat silent for some minutes and then, turning round to Mr Brownlow, said in a towering passion:

"Do you mean to state what your complaint against this boy is, man, or do you not? You have been sworn. Now, if you stand there, refusing to give evidence, I'll punish you for disrespect to the bench."

With many interruptions and repeated insults, Mr Brownlow contrived to state his case, observing that, in the surprise of the moment, he had run after the boy because he saw him running away.

"He has been hurt already," said the old gentleman in conclusion. "And I fear," he added, with great energy, looking toward the bar, "I really fear that he is ill."

"Oh! yes, I dare say!" said Mr Fang, with a sneer. "Come, none of your tricks here, you young vagabond; they won't do. What's your name?"

Oliver tried to reply, but his tongue failed him. He was deadly pale, and the whole place seemed to turn round and round.

"What's your name, you hardened scoundrel?" demanded Mr Fang.

At this point of the inquiry, Oliver raised his head and, looking around with imploring eyes, asked feebly for a drink of water.

"Stuff and nonsense!" said Fang; "don't try to make a fool of me."

"I think he really is ill, your worship," said the officer.

"I know better," said Mr Fang.

"Take care of him, officer," said the old gentleman, raising his hands instinctively; "he'll fall down."

"Stand away, officer," cried Fang; "let him, if he likes."

Oliver availed himself of the kind permission and fell to the floor in a fainting fit. The men in the office looked at each other, but no one dared to stir.

"I knew he was shamming," said Fang, as if this were enough proof of the fact. "Let him lie there; he'll soon be tired of that."

"How do you propose to deal with the case, sir?" inquired the clerk in a low voice.

"Summarily," replied Mr Fang. "He stands committed for three months—hard labor, of course. Clear the office."

The door was opened for this purpose, and a couple of men were preparing to carry the insensible boy to his cell when an elderly man of decent but poor appearance, clad in an old suit of black, rushed in.

"Stop! stop! Don't take him away! For heaven's sake stop a moment!" cried the newcomer, breathless with haste.

"What is this? Who is this? Turn this man out. Clear the office," cried Mr Fang.

"I will speak," cried the man; "I will not be turned out. I saw it all. I keep the book-stall. I demand to be sworn. I will not be put down. Mr. Fang, you must hear me. You must not refuse, sir."

The man was right. His manner was determined, and the matter was growing rather too serious to be hushed up.

"Swear the man," growled Mr Fang with very ill grace. "Now, man, what have you to say?"

"This," said the man: "I saw three boys—two two others and the prisoner here—loitering on the opposite side of the way, when this gentleman was reading. The robbery was committed by another boy. I saw it done;

and I saw this boy was perfectly amazed and stupefied by it."

"Why didn't you come here before?" said Fang after a pause.

"I hadn't a soul to mind the shop," replied the man. "Everybody who could have helped me had joined in the pursuit. I could get nobody till five minutes ago; and I have run here all the way to speak the truth."

"The boy is discharged. Clear the office!" shouted the angry magistrate.

The command was obeyed, and as Oliver was taken out, he fainted away again in the yard and lay with his face a deadly white and a cold tremble convulsing his frame.

"Poor boy! poor boy!" said Mr Brownlow, bending over him. "Call a coach, somebody, pray. Directly!"

A coach was obtained, and Oliver, having been carefully laid on one seat, the old gentleman got in and sat himself on the other.

"May I go with you?" said the book-stall keeper, looking in.

"Bless me, yes, my dear sir," said Mr Brownlow quickly. "I forgot you. Dear, dear! I have this unhappy book still! Jump in. Poor fellow! No time to lose."

The book-stall keeper got into the coach, and it rattled away. It stopped at length before a neat house in a quiet shady street. Here a bed was prepared, without loss of time, in which Mr Brownlow saw his young charge carefully and comfortably laid, and here, he was tended with a kindness and solicitude that knew no bounds.

At last, the sick boy began to recover, and one day Mr Brownlow came to see him. You may imagine how happy Oliver was to see his good friend, but he was no more delighted than was Mr Brownlow. The old gentleman came to spend a short time with him every day, and when he grew stronger, Oliver went up to the learned gentleman's study and talked with him by the hour and was astonished at the books he saw and which Mr Brownlow told him to look at and read as much as he liked.

Oliver was soon well, and no thought was in Mr Brownlow's mind but that he should keep him, and raise him and educate him to be a splendid man; for no father loves his own son better than Mr Brownlow had come to love Oliver.

Now, I know you want to ask me what became of Oliver Twist. But I cannot tell you here. Let us leave him in this beautiful home of good Mr Brownlow, and if you want to read the rest of his wonderful story, get Dickens' big book called *Oliver Twist*, and read it there. There were many surprises and much trouble yet in store for Oliver, but he was always noble, honest, and brave.

The Friendly Frog

by Charles Perrault

Once upon a time, there was a king who had been at war for a long time with his neighbours. After many battles had been fought, his capital was besieged by the enemy. Fearing for the safety of the queen, the king implored her to take refuge in a stronghold to which he himself had never been but once. The queen besought him with tears to let her remain at his side and share his fate and lamented loudly when the king placed her in the carriage which was to take her away under escort.

The king promised to slip away whenever possible and pay her a visit, seeking thus to comfort her, although he knew that there was a small chance of the hope being fulfilled. For the castle was a long way off, in the midst of a dense forest, and only those with a thorough knowledge of the roads could possibly reach it.

The queen was broken-hearted at having to leave her husband exposed to the perils of war, and though she made her journey by easy stages, lest the fatigue of so much travelling should make her ill, she was downcast and miserable when at length, she reached the castle. She made excursions into the country roundabout when sufficiently recovered but found nothing to amuse or distract her. On all sides, wide barren spaces met her eye, melancholy rather than pleasant to look upon.

'How different from my old home!' she exclaimed as she gloomily surveyed the scene; 'if I stay here long, I shall die. To whom can I talk in this solitude? To whom can I unburden my grief? What have I done that the king should exile me? He must wish me, I suppose, to feel the bitterness of separation to the utmost, since he banishes me to this hateful castle.'

She grieved long and deeply, and though the king wrote every day to her with the good news of the way the siege was going, she became more and more unhappy. At last, she determined that she would go back to him, but knowing that her attendants had been forbidden to let her return, except under special orders from the king, she kept her intention to herself. On the pretext of sometimes wishing to join the hunt, she ordered a small chariot, capable of accommodating one person only, to be built for her. This she drove herself and used to keep up with the hounds so closely that she would leave the rest of the hunt behind. The chariot being in her sole control, gave her the opportunity to escape whenever she liked, and the only obstacle was her lack of familiarity with the roads through the forest. She trusted, however, to the favour of Providence to bring her safely through it.

She now gave orders for a great hunt to be held and intimated her wish that everyone should attend. She herself was to be present in her chariot, and she proposed that every follower of the chase should choose a different line and so close every avenue of escape to the quarry. The arrangements were carried out according to the queen's plan. Confident that she would soon see her husband again, she donned her most becoming attire. Her hat was trimmed with feathers of different colours, and the front of her dress with a number of precious stones. Thus adorned, she looked in her beauty (which was of no ordinary stamp) like a second Diana.

When the excitement of the chase was at its height, she gave rein to her horses, urging them on with voice and whip until their pace quickened to a gallop. But then, getting their bits between their teeth, the team sped onwards so fast that presently the chariot seemed to be borne upon the wind and to be travelling faster than the eye could follow. Too late, the poor queen repented of her rashness. 'What possessed me,' she cried, 'to think that I could manage such wild and fiery steeds? Alack! What will become of me! What would the king do if he knew of my great peril? He only sent me away because he loves me dearly, and wished me to be in greater safety—and this is the way I repay his tender care!'

Her piteous cries rang out upon the air, but though she called on Heaven and invoked the fairies to her aid, it seemed that all the unseen powers had forsaken her.

Over went the chariot. She lacked the strength to jump clear quickly enough, and her foot was caught between the wheel and the axle tree. It was only by a miracle that she was not killed, and she lay stretched on the ground at the foot of a tree, with her heart scarcely beating and her face covered with blood, unable to speak.

For a long time, she lay thus. At last, she opened her eyes and saw, standing beside her, a woman of gigantic stature. The latter wore nought but a lion's skin; her arms and legs were bare, and her hair was tied up with a dried snake's skin, the head of which dangled over her shoulder. In her hand, she carried a walking stick, a stone club, and a quiver full of arrows hung at her side.

This extraordinary apparition convinced the queen that she was dead, and indeed it seemed impossible that she could have survived so terrible a disaster. 'No wonder death needs resolution,' she murmured, 'since sights so terrible await one in the other world.'

The giantess overheard these words and laughed to find the queen thought herself dead.

'Courage,' she said, 'you are still in the land of the living, though your lot is not improved. I am the Lion-Witch. My dwelling is nearby; you must come and live with me.'

'If you will have the kindness, good Lion-Witch, to take me back to my castle, the king, who loves me dearly, will not refuse you any ransom you demand, though it were the half of his kingdom.'

'I will not do that,' replied the giantess, 'for I have wealth enough already. Moreover, I am tired of living alone, and as you have your wits about you, it is possible you may be able to amuse me.'

With these words, she assumed the shape of a lioness and, taking the queen on her back, bore her off into the depths of a cavern. There she anointed the queen's wounds with an essence which quickly healed them.

But imagine the wonder and despair of the queen to find herself in this dismal lair! The approach to it was by ten thousand steps, which led down to the centre of the earth, and the only light was that which came from a number of lofty lamps, reflected in a lake of quicksilver. This lake teemed with monsters, each of which was hideous enough to have terrified one far less timid than the queen. Ravens, screech owls, and many other birds of evil omen filled the air with harsh cries.

Far off could be espied a mountain, from the slopes of which there flowed the tears of all hapless lovers. Its sluggish stream was fed by every ill-starred love. The trees had neither leaves nor fruit, and the ground was cumbered with briars, nettles, and rank weeds. The food, too, was such as might be expected in such a horrid clime. A few dried roots, horse chestnuts, and thorn apples—this was all the fare with which the Lion-Witch appeased the hunger of those who fell into her clutches.

When the queen was well enough to be set to work, the Witch told her she might build herself a hut since she was fated to remain in her company for the rest of her life. On hearing this, the queen burst into tears. 'Alas!' she cried, 'what have I done that you should keep me here? If my death, which I feel to be nigh, will cause you any pleasure, then I implore you to kill me: I dare not hope for any other kindness from you. But do not condemn me to the sadness of a life-long separation from my husband.'

But the Lion-Witch merely laughed at her, bidding her dry her tears if she would be wise and do her part to please her. Otherwise, she declared, her lot would be the most miserable in the world.

'And what must I do to soften your heart?' replied the queen.

'I have a liking for fly pasties,' said the Lion Witch, 'and you must contrive to catch flies enough to make me a large and tasty one.'

'But there are no flies here,' rejoined the queen, 'and even if there were, there is not enough light to catch them by. Moreover, supposing I caught some, I have never in my life made pastry. You are therefore giving me orders which I cannot possibly carry out.'

'No matter,' said the pitiless Lion-Witch; 'what I want, I will have!'

The queen made no reply, but reflected that, no matter how cruel the Witch might be, she had only one life to lose, and in her present plight what terror could death hold for her? She did not attempt to look for flies, therefore, but sat down beneath a yew tree, and gave way to tears and lamentations. 'Alas, dear husband,' she cried, 'how grieved you will be when you go to fetch me from the castle and find me gone! You will suppose me to be dead or faithless; how I hope that you will mourn the loss of my life, not the loss of my love! Perhaps the remains of my chariot will be found in the wood, with all the ornaments I had put on to please you: at the sight of these, you will not doubt anymore that I am dead. But then, how do I know that you will not bestow on someone else the heartfelt love which once belonged to me? At all events, I shall be spared the sorrow of that knowledge since I am never to return to the world.'

These thoughts would have filled her mind for a long time, but she was interrupted by the dismal croaking of a raven overhead. Lifting her eyes, she saw in the dim light a large raven on the point of swallowing a frog that it held in its beak. 'Though I have no hope of help for myself,' she said, 'I will not let this unfortunate frog die if I can save it; though our lots are so different, its sufferings are quite as great as mine.' She picked up the first stick which came to hand and made the raven let go of its prey. The frog fell to the ground and lay for a time half stunned, but as soon as it could think, in its froggish way, it began to speak. 'Beautiful queen,' it said, 'you are the first friendly soul that I have seen since my curiosity brought me here.'

'By what magic are you endowed with speech, little Frog?' replied the queen, 'and what people are they whom you see here? I have seen none at all as yet.'

'All the monsters with which the lake is teeming,' replied the little Frog, 'were once upon a time in the world. Some sat on thrones. Some held high positions at Court; there are even some royal ladies here who were the cause of strife and bloodshed. It is these latter whom you see in the shape of leeches, and they are condemned to remain here for a certain time. But of those who come here none ever returns to the world better or wiser.'

'I can quite understand,' said the queen, 'that wicked people are not improved by merely being thrown together. But how is it that you are here, my friendly little Frog?'

'I came here out of curiosity,' she replied. 'I am a part fairy, and though, in certain directions, my powers are limited, in others they are far-reaching. The Lion-Witch would kill me if she knew that I was in her domain.'

'Whatever your fairy powers,' said the queen, 'I cannot understand how you could have fallen into the raven's clutches and come so near to being devoured.'

'That is easily explained,' said the Frog. 'I have nought to fear when my little cap of roses is on my head, for that is the source of my power. Unluckily I had left it in the marsh when that ugly raven pounced upon me, and but for you, Madam, I should not now be here. Since you have saved my life, you have only to command me and I will do everything in my power to lessen the misfortunes of your lot.'

'Alas, dear Frog,' said the queen, 'the wicked fairy who holds me captive desires that I should make her a fly-pasty. But there are no flies here, and if there were I could not see to catch them in the dim light. I am like, therefore, to get a beating which will kill me.'

'Leave that to me,' said the Frog, 'I will quickly get you some.'

Thereupon the Frog smeared sugar all over herself, and the same was done by more than six thousand of her froggy friends. They then made a place where the fairy had a large store of flies, which she used to torment some of her luckless victims. No sooner did the flies smell the sugar than they flew to it and found themselves sticking to the frogs. Away, then, went the latter at a gallop to bring their friendly aid to the queen. Never was there such a catching of flies before, nor a better pasty than the one the queen made for the fairy. The surprise of the Witch was great when the queen handed it to her, for she was baffled to think how the flies could have been so cleverly caught.

The queen suffered so much from want of protection against the poisonous air that she cut down some cypress branches and began to build herself a hut. The Frog kindly offered her services. She summoned around her all those who had helped in the fly hunt, and they assisted the queen in building as pretty a little place to live in as you could find anywhere in the world.

But no sooner had she lain down to rest than the monsters of the lake, envious of her repose, gathered around the hut. They set up the most hideous noise that had ever been heard and drove her so nearly mad that she got up and fled in fear and trembling from the house. This was just what the monsters were after, and a dragon, who had once upon a time ruled tyrannously over one of the greatest countries of the world, immediately took possession of it.

The poor queen tried to protest against this ill-treatment. But no one would listen to her: the monsters laughed and jeered at her, and the Lion-Witch said that if she came and dinned lamentations into her ears again, she would give her a sound thrashing.

The queen was therefore obliged to hold her tongue. She sought out the Frog, who was the most sympathetic creature in the world, and they wept together; for the moment she put on her cap of roses, the Frog became able to laugh or weep like anybody else.

'I am so fond of you,' said the Frog to the queen, 'that I will build your house again, though every monster in the lake should be filled with envy.'

Forthwith she cut some wood, and a little country mansion for the queen sprang up so quickly that she was able to sleep in it that very night. Nothing that could make for the queen's comfort was forgotten by the Frog, and there was even a bed of wild thyme.

When the wicked fairy learnt that the queen was not sleeping on the ground, she sent for her and asked:

'What power is it, human or divine, that protects you? This land drinks only a rain of burning sulphur, and has never produced so much as a sage leaf: yet they tell me fragrant herbs spring up beneath your feet.'

'I cannot explain it, madam,' said the queen, 'unless it is due to the child, I am expecting. Perhaps for her, a less unhappy fate than mine is in store.'

'I have a craving just now,' said the Witch, 'for a posy of rare flowers. See if this happiness which you expect will enable you to get them. If you do not succeed, such a thrashing as I know well how to give is surely in store for you.'

The queen began to weep, for threats like these distressed her, and she despaired as she thought of the impossibility of finding flowers. But when she returned to her little house, the friendly Frog met her.

'How unhappy you look!' she said.

'Alas, dear friend,' said the queen, 'who would not be so? The Witch has demanded a posy of the most beautiful flowers. Where am I to find them? You see what sort of flowers grow here! Yet my life is forfeit if I do not procure them.'

'Dear queen,' said the Frog tenderly, 'we must do our best to extricate you from this dilemma. Hereabouts there lives a bat of my acquaintance—a kindly soul. She moves about more quickly than I do, so I will give her my cap of roses, and with the aid of this she will be able to find you flowers.'

The queen curtseyed low, it being quite impossible to embrace the Frog, and the latter went off at once to speak to the bat. In a few hours, the bat came back with some exquisite flowers tucked under her wings. Off went the queen with them to the Witch, who was more astonished than ever, being quite unable to understand in what marvellous way the queen had been assisted.

The queen never ceased to plot some means of escape and told the Frog of her longings. 'Madam,' said the latter, 'allow me first to take counsel with my little cap, and we will make plans according to what it advises.' Having placed her cap upon some straw, she burnt in front of it a few juniper twigs, some capers, and a couple of green peas. She then croaked five times. This completed the rites and having donned her cap again. She began to speak like an oracle.

'Fate, the all-powerful, decrees that you must not leave this place. You will have a little princess more beautiful than Venus herself. Let nothing fret you; time alone can heal.'

The queen bowed her head and shed tears, but she determined to have faith in the friend she had found. 'Whatever happens,' she said, 'do not leave me here alone, and befriend me when my little one is born.' The Frog promised to remain with her and did her best to comfort her.

It is now time to return to the king. So long as the enemy kept him confined within his capital, he could not regularly send messengers to the queen. But at length, after many sorties, he forced the enemy to raise the siege. This success gave him pleasure not so much on his own account as for the sake of the queen, who could now be brought home in safety. He knew nothing of the disaster which had befallen her, for none of his retinues had dared to tell him of it. They had found in the forest the remains of the chariot, the runaway horses, and the apparel in which she had driven forth to find her husband, and being convinced that she was killed or devoured by wild beasts, their one idea was to make the king believe that she had died suddenly.

It seemed as if the king could not survive this mournful news. He tore his hair, wept bitterly, and lamented his loss with all manner of sorrowful cries and sobs and sighs. For several days he would see nobody and hide from view. Later, he returned to his capital and entered upon a long period of mourning, to the sincerity of which his heartfelt sorrow bore even plainer testimony than his sombre garb of woe. His royal neighbours all sent ambassadors with messages of condolence, and when the ceremonies proper to these occasions were at length over, he proclaimed a period of peace. He released his subjects from military service and devoted himself to giving them every assistance in the development of commerce.

Of all this, the queen knew nothing. A little princess had been born to her in the meantime, and her beauty did not belie the Frog's prediction. They gave her the name of Moufette, but the Queen had great difficulty in persuading the Witch to let her bring up the child, for her ferocity was such that she would have liked to eat it.

At the age of six months, Moufette was a marvel of beauty, and often, as she gazed upon her with mingled tenderness and pity, the queen would say:

'Could your father but see you, my poor child, how delighted he would be, and how dear you would be to him! But perhaps even now he has begun to forget me: doubtless he believes that death has robbed him of us, and it may be that another now fills the place I had in his affections.'

Many were the tears she shed over these sad thoughts, and the Frog, whose love for her was sincere, was moved one day by the sight of her grief to say to her:

'If you like, Madam, I will go and seek your royal husband. It is a long journey, and I am but a tardy

…er or later I have no doubt I shall get

suggestion could have been more warmly approved, the queen clasping her hands and bidding little Moufette do the same, in token of the gratitude she felt towards the good Frog for offering to make the expedition. Nor would the king, she declared, be less grateful. 'Of what advantage, however,' she went on, 'will it be to him to learn that I am in this dire abode, since it will be impossible for him to rescue me from it?'

'That we must leave to Providence, Madam,' said the Frog; 'we can but make those efforts of which we are capable.'

They took farewell to each other, and the queen sent a message to the king. This was written with her blood on a piece of rag, for she had neither ink nor paper. The good Frog was bringing him news of herself, she wrote, and she implored him to give heed to all that she might tell him and to believe everything she had to say.

It took the Frog a year and four days to climb the ten thousand steps which led from the gloomy realm in which she had left the queen up into the world. Another year was spent in preparing her equipage, for she was too proud to consent to appear at Court like a poor and humble frog from the marshes. A little sedan chair was made for her, large enough to hold a couple of eggs comfortably, and this was covered outside with tortoiseshell and lined with lizard skin. From the little green frogs that hop about the meadows, she selected fifty to act as maids of honour, and each of these was mounted on a snail. They had dainty saddles and rode in dashing style with the leg thrown over the saddle-bow. Numerous bodyguards of rats, dressed like pages, ran before the snails—in short, nothing so captivating had ever been seen before. To crown all, the cap of roses, which never faded but was always in full bloom, most admirably became her. Being something of a coquette, too, she could not refrain from a touch of rouge and a patch or two; indeed, some said she was painted like a great many other ladies of the land, but it has been proved by inquiry that this report had its origin with her enemies.

The journey lasted seven years, and during all that time, the poor queen endured unutterable pain and suffering. Had it not been for the solace of the beautiful Moufette, she must have died a hundred times. Every word that the dear little creature uttered filled her with delight; indeed, with the exception of the Lion-Witch, there was nobody who was not charmed by her.

There came at length a day after the queen had lived for six years in this dismal region when the Witch told her that she could go hunting with her on condition that she yielded up everything which she killed. The queen's joy when she once more saw the sun might be imagined, though at first, she thought she would be blinded, so unaccustomed to its light had she become. So quick and lively was Moufette, even at five or six years of age, that she never failed in her aim, and mother and daughter together were thus able to appease somewhat the fierce instincts of the Witch.

Meanwhile, the Frog was travelling over hills and valleys. Day or night, she never stopped, and at last, she came nigh to the capital, where the king was now in residence. To her astonishment, signs of festivity met her eye at every turn; on all sides, there was merriment, song and dancing, and the nearer she came to the city, the more festive seemed the mood of the people. All flocked with amazement to see her rustic retinue, and by the time she reached the city, the crowd had become so large that it was with difficulty she made her way to the palace.

At the palace, all was splendour, for the king, who had been deprived of his wife's society for nine years, had, at last, yielded to the petitions of his subjects and was about to wed a princess who possessed many amiable qualities, though she lacked, admittedly, the beauty of his wife.

The good Frog descended from her sedan chair and, with her attendants in her train, entered the royal presence. To request an audience was unnecessary, for the king and his intended bride and all the princes were much too curious to learn why she had come to think of interrupting her.

'Sire,' said the Frog, 'I am in doubt whether the news I bring will cause you joy or sorrow. I can only conclude, from the marriage which you are proposing to celebrate, that you are no longer faithful to your queen.'

Tears fell from the king's eyes. 'Her memory is as dear to me as ever,' he declared, 'but you must know, good Frog, that monarchs cannot always follow their own wishes. For nine years now my subjects have been urging me to take a wife, and indeed it is due to them that there should be an heir to the throne. Hence my choice of this young princess, whose charms are apparent.'

'I warn you not to marry her,' rejoined the Frog; 'the queen is not dead, and I am the bearer of a letter from her, writ in her own blood. There has been born to you a little daughter, Moufette, who is more beautiful than the very heavens.'

The king took the rag on which the short message from the queen was written. He kissed it and moistened it with his tears; and declared, holding it up for all to see, that he recognised the handwriting of his wife. Then he plied the Frog with endless questions, to all of which she replied with lively intelligence.

The princess who was to have been queen, and the envoys who were attending the marriage ceremony, were somewhat out of countenance. 'Sire,' said one of the most distinguished guests, turning to the king, 'can you contemplate the breaking of your solemn pledge upon the word of a toad like that? This scum of the marshes has the audacity to come and lie to the entire Court, just for the gratification of being listened to!'

'I would have you know, your Excellency,' replied the Frog, 'that I am no scum of the marshes. Since you force me to display my powers—hither, fairies all!'

At these words, the frogs, the rats, the snails, and the lizards all suddenly ranged themselves behind the Frog. But in place of their familiar natural forms, they appeared now as tall, majestic figures, handsome of mien, and with eyes that outshone the stars. Each wore a crown of jewels on his head, while over his shoulders hung a royal mantle of velvet, lined with ermine, the train of which was borne by dwarfs. Simultaneously the sound of trumpets, drums, and hautboys filled the air with martial melody, and all the fairies began to dance ballet, with steps so light that the least spring lifted them to the vaulted ceiling of the chamber.

The astonishment of the king and his future bride was in no way diminished when the fairy dancers suddenly changed before their eyes into flowers— jasmine, jonquils, violets, roses, and carnations—which carried on the dance just as though they were possessed of legs and feet. It was as though a flower bed had come to life, every movement of which gave pleasure alike to eye and nostril. A moment later, the flowers vanished, and in their place were fountains of leaping water that fell in a cascade and formed a lake beneath the castle walls. On the surface of the lake were little boats painted and gilt, so pretty and dainty that the princess challenged the ambassadors to a voyage. None hesitated to do so, for they thought it was all a gay pastime and a merry prelude to the marriage festivities. But no sooner had they embarked than boats, fountains, and lake vanished, and the frogs were frogs once more.

'Sire,' said the Frog when the king asked what had become of the princess, 'your wife alone is your queen. Were my affection for her less than it is, I should not interfere; but she deserves so well, and your daughter Moufette is so charming, that you ought not to lose one moment in setting out to their rescue.'

'I do assure you, Madam Frog,' replied the king, 'that if I could believe my wife to be alive, I would shrink from nothing in the world for sight of her again.'

'Surely,' said the Frog, 'after the marvels I have shown you, there ought not to be doubt in your mind of the truth of what I say. Leave your realm in the hands of those whom you can trust, and set forth without delay. Take this ring—it will provide you with the means of seeing the queen, and of speaking with the Lion-Witch, notwithstanding that she is the most formidable creature in the world.'

The king refused to let anyone accompany him, and after bestowing handsome gifts upon the Frog, he set forth. 'Do not lose heart,' she said to him; 'you will encounter terrible difficulties, but I am convinced that your desires will meet with success.' He plucked up courage at these words and started upon the quest of his dear wife, though he had only the ring to guide him.

Now Moufette's beauty became more and more perfect as she grew older, and all the monsters of the lake of quicksilver were enamoured of her. Hideous and terrifying to behold, they came and lay at her feet. Although Moufette had seen them ever since she was born, her lovely eyes could never grow accustomed to them, and she would run away and hide in her mother's arms. 'Shall we remain here long?' she would ask; 'are we never to escape from misery?'

The queen would answer hopefully so as to keep up the spirits of the child, but in her heart, hope had died. The absence of the Frog and the lack of any news from her, together with the long time that had passed since she had heard anything from the king, filled her with grief and despair.

By now, it had become a regular thing for them to go hunting with the Lion-Witch. The latter liked good things and enjoyed the game, which they killed for her. The head or the feet of the quarry was all the share they got, but there was compensation in being allowed to look again upon the daylight. The Witch would take the shape of a lioness, and the queen and her daughter would seat themselves on her back. In this fashion, they ranged the forests a-hunting.

One day, when the king was resting in a forest to which his ring had guided him, he saw them shoot by like an arrow from the bow. They did not perceive him, and when he tried to follow them, he lost sight of them completely. The queen was still as beautiful as of old, despite all that she had suffered, and she seemed to her husband more attractive than ever so that he longed to have her with him again. He felt certain that the young princess with her was his dear little Moufette, and he resolved to face death a thousand times rather than abandon his intention of rescuing her.

With the assistance of his ring, he penetrated the gloomy region in which the queen had been for so many years. His astonishment was great to find himself descending to the centre of the earth, but with every new thing that met his eyes, his amazement grew greater.

The Lion-Witch, from whom nothing was hidden, knew well the day and hour of his destined arrival. Much did she wish that the powers in league with her could have ordered things otherwise, but she resolved to pit her strength against his to the full.

She built a palace of crystal which floated in the midst of the lake of quicksilver, rising and falling on its waves. Therein she imprisoned the queen and her daughter, and assembling the monsters, who were all admirers of Moufette, she gave them this warning:

'You will lose this beautiful princess if you do not help me to keep her from a gallant who has come to bear her away.'

The monsters vowed that they would do everything in their power, and forthwith they surrounded the palace of crystal. The less heavy stationed themselves upon the roofs and walls, others mounted guards at the doors while the remainder filled the lake.

Following the dictates of his faithful ring, the king went first to the Witch's cavern. She was waiting for him in the form of a lioness, and the moment he appeared, she sprang upon him. But she was not prepared for his valiant swordsmanship, and as she put forth a paw to fell him to the ground, he cut it off at the elbow joint. She yelped loudly and fell over, whereupon he went up to her and set his foot upon her throat, swearing that he would kill her. Notwithstanding her uncontrollable rage and the fact that she had nothing to fear from wounds, she felt cowed by him.

'What do you seek to do to me?' she asked; 'what do you want of me?'

'I intend to punish you,' replied the king with dignity, 'for having carried away my wife. Deliver her up to me, or I will strangle you on the spot.'

'Turn your eyes to the lake,' she answered, 'and see if it lies in my power to do so.'

The king followed the direction she indicated and saw the queen and her daughter in the palace of crystal, where it floated like a boat without oars or rudder on the lake of quicksilver. He was like to die of mingled joy and sorrow. He shouted to them at the top of his voice, and they heard him. But how was he to reach them?

While he pondered a plan for the accomplishment of this, the Lion-Witch vanished. He ran round and round the lake, but no sooner did the palace draw near enough, at one point or another, to let him make a spring for it than it suddenly receded with menacing speed. As often as his hopes were raised, they were dashed to the ground.

Fearing that he would presently tire, the queen cried

to him that he must not lose courage, for the Lion-Witch sought to wear him down, but that true love could brave all obstacles. She stretched out imploring hands, and so did Moufette. At the sight of this, the king felt his courage renewed within him. Lifting his voice, he declared that he would rather live the rest of his life in this dismal region than go away without them.

The patience he certainly needed, for no monarch in the world ever spent such a miserable time. There was only the ground, cumbered with briars and thorns, for bed and for food. He had only wild fruit more bitter than gall. In addition, he was under the perpetual necessity of defending himself from the monsters of the lake.

Three years went by in this fashion, and the king could not pretend that he had gained the least advantage. He was almost in despair and, many a time, was tempted to cast himself into the lake. He would have done so without hesitation had there been any hope that, thereby, the sufferings of the queen and the princess could be alleviated.

One day as he was running, after his custom, from one side of the lake to the other, he was hailed by one of the ugliest of the dragons. 'Swear by your crown and sceptre, by your kingly robe, by your wife and child,' said the monster, 'to give me a certain tit-bit to eat for which I have a fancy, whenever I shall ask for it, and I will take you on my back: none of the monsters in this lake which is guarding the palace, will prevent us from carrying away the queen and Pricess Moufette.'

'Best of dragons!' cried the king; 'I swear to you, and to all of dragon blood, that you shall have your fill of whatsoever you desire, and I will be for ever your devoted servant.'

'Promise nothing which you do not mean to fulfil,' replied the dragon, 'for otherwise life-long misfortunes may overwhelm you.'

The king repeated his assurances, for he was dying of impatience to regain his beloved queen, and mounted the dragon just as though he were the most dashing of steeds. But now, the other monsters rushed to bar the way. The combat was joined, and nought was audible save the hissing of the serpents, nought visible save the brimstone, fire and sulphur, which were belched forth in every direction.

The king reached the palace at last, but their fresh efforts were required of him, for the entrances were defended by bats and owls and ravens. But even the boldest of these was torn to pieces by the dragon, who attacked them tooth and nail. The queen, too, who was a spectator of this savage fight, kicked down chunks of the wall and, armed with these, helped her dear husband in the fray. Victory at length rested with them, and as they flew to one another's arms, the enchantment was brought to an end by a thunderbolt which plunged into the lake and dried it up.

The friendly dragon vanished, along with all the other monsters, and the king found himself (by what means he had not the least idea) home again in his own city and seated, with his queen and Moufette beside him, in a splendid dining hall before a table laid with the richest fare. Never before was there such amazement and delight as theirs. The populace came running for a sight of the queen and princess, and to add to the wonder of it all, the latter was seen to be attired in apparel of such magnificence that the gaze was almost dazzled by her jewels.

You can easily imagine what festivities now took place at the palace. There were masquerades and tournaments with tilting at the ring, which attracted the highest princes from all over the world; even more, were these drawn by the bright eyes of Moufette.

Amongst the most handsome and most accomplished in skill-at-arms, there was none anywhere who could outshine Prince Moufy. He won the applause and admiration of all, and Moufette, who had hitherto known only dragons and serpents, was not backward in according him her share of praise. Prince Moufy was deeply in love with her, and not a day passed, but he showed her some fresh attention in the hope of gaining her favour. In due course, he offered himself as a suitor, informing the king and queen that his realm was of a richness and extent that might well claim their favourable consideration.

The king replied that Moufette should make her own choice of husband, for his only wish was to please her and make her happy. With this answer, the prince was well satisfied, for he was already aware that the princess was not indifferent to him. He offered her his hand, and she declared that if he were not to be her husband, then no other man should be. Prince Moufy threw himself in rapture at her feet and exacted, lover-like, a promise that she would keep her word with him.

The prince and princess were betrothed, and Prince Moufy then returned to his own realm in order to make preparations for the marriage. Moufette wept much at his going, for she was oppressed by an inexplicable presentiment of evil. The prince likewise was much downcast, and the queen, noticing this, gave him a portrait of her daughter with an injunction to curtail the splendour of his preparations rather than allow his return to be delayed. The prince was nothing loth to obey her behest and promised to adopt a course which so well consulted his own happiness.

The princess amused herself with music during his absence, for in a few months, she had learned to play exceedingly well.

One day, when she was in the queen's apartment, the king rushed in. Tears were streaming down his face as he took his daughter in his arms and cried aloud: 'Alas, my child! O wretched father! O miserable king!' Sobs choked his utterance, and he could say no more.

Greatly alarmed, the queen and princess asked him what had happened, and at last, he got out that there had just arrived an enormously tall giant who professed to be an envoy of the dragon of the lake; and that in pursuance of the promise which the king had given in exchange for assistance in fighting the monsters, the dragon demanded that he should give up the princess, as he desired to make her into a pie for dinner. The king added that he had bound himself by solemn oaths to give the dragon what he asked—and in the days of which we are telling, no one ever broke his word.

The queen received this dire news with piercing shrieks and clasped her child to her bosom. 'My life shall be forfeit,' she cried, 'ere my daughter is delivered up to this monster. Let him rather take our kingdom and all that we have. Unnatural father! Is it possible you can consent to such cruelty? What! My child to be made into a pie! The bare notion is intolerable! Send this grim envoy to me; it may be the spectacle of my anguish will soften his heart.'

The king said nothing but went in quest of the giant. He brought him to the queen, who flung herself at his feet with her daughter. She begged him to have mercy and to persuade the dragon to take all that they possessed but to spare Moufette's life. The giant replied, however, that the matter did not rest with him. The dragon, he said, was so obstinate and so addicted to the pleasures of the table that no power on earth would restrain him from eating what he had a mind to make a meal of. Furthermore, he counselled them, as a friend, to yield with good grace lest greater ills should be in store. At these words, the queen fainted, and the princess would have been in a similar case if she had not been obliged to go to the assistance of her mother.

No sooner was the dreadful news known throughout the palace than it spread all over the city. On all sides, there was weeping and wailing, for Moufette was greatly beloved.

The king could not bring himself to give her up to the giant, and the latter, after waiting several days, grew restive and began to utter terrible threats. But the king and queen, taking counsel together, agreed. 'What is there worse that could happen to us?' they said; 'if the dragon of the lake were to come and eat us all up, we could not suffer more, for if Moufette is put into a pie that will be the end of us.'

Presently the giant informed them that he had received a message from the dragon to the effect that if the princess agreed to marry one of his nephews, he would spare her life. This nephew was not only young and handsome, but a prince to boot, and there was no doubt of her being able to live very happily with him.

This proposal somewhat assuaged their grief, but when the queen mentioned it to the princess, she found her more ready to face death than entertain this marriage. 'I cannot break faith just to save my life,' said Moufette; 'you promised me to Prince Moufy, and I will marry none else. Let me perish, for my death will enable you to live in peace.' The king, in his turn, tried, with many endearments, to persuade her, but she could not be moved. Finally, therefore, it was arranged that she should be conducted to a mountain-top, there to await the dragon.

Everything was made ready for the great sacrificial rite, and nothing so mournful had ever been seen before. Black garments and pale, distraught faces were encountered at every turn. Four hundred maidens of the noblest birth, clad in long white robes and wearing crowns of cypress, accompanied the princess. The latter was borne in an open litter of black velvet, that all men might behold the wondrous miracle of her beauty. Her tresses, tied with crape, hung over her shoulders, and she wore a crown of jasmine and marigolds. The only thing that seemed to affect her was the grief of the king and queen, who walked behind her, overwhelmed with the burden of their sorrow. Beside the litter strode the giant, armed from top to toe and looking hungrily at the princess as though already he savoured his share of the dish she was to make. The air was filled with sighs and sobs, and the tears of the spectators made rivulets along the road.

'O Frog, dear Frog,' cried the queen; 'you have indeed forsaken me! Why give me help in that dismal place and refuse it to me here? Had I but died then, I should not now be mourning the end of all my hopes, and I should have been spared the agony of waiting to see my darling Moufette devoured.'

Slowly the procession made its way to the summit of the fatal mountain. On arrival there, the cries and lamentations broke out with renewed force, and a more pitiful noise was never heard before. The giant then directed that all farewells must be said and a general withdrawal made, and his order was obeyed. Folks in those days were docile and obedient and never thought of combating ill fortune.

The king and queen, with all the Court, now climbed another hilltop, from which they could obtain a view of all that happened to the princess. They had not long to wait, for they quickly espied a dragon, half a league long, sailing through the sky. He flew laboriously, for his bulk was so great that even six large wings could hardly support it. His body was covered all over with immense blue scales and tongues of poison flame. His twisted tail had fifty coils and another half coil beyond that, while his claws were each as big as a windmill. His jaws were agape, and inside could be seen three rows of teeth as long as an elephant's tusks.

Now while the dragon was slowly wending his way to the mountaintop, the good and faithful Frog, mounted on a hawk's back, was flying at full speed to Prince Moufy. She was wearing her cap of roses, and though he was locked in his privy chamber, she needed no key to enter.

'Hapless lover!' she cried; 'what are you doing here? This very moment, while you sit dreaming about her beauty, Moufette is in direst peril! See, here is a rose-leaf; I have but to blow upon it and it will become a mettlesome steed.'

As she spoke, there suddenly appeared a green horse. It had twelve hoofs and three heads, and from the latter, it could spit forth fire, bombshells, and cannonballs, respectively. The Frog then gave the prince a sword, eight yards long and no heavier than a feather, and a garment fashioned out of a single diamond. This he slipped on like a coat, and though it was hard as a rock, it was so pliant that his movements were in no way impeded.

'Now fly to the rescue of your love,' said the Frog; 'the green horse will carry you to her. Do not omit to let her know, when you have delivered her, of what my part has been.'

'Great-hearted fairy!' cried the prince, 'this is no moment to return you thanks, but from henceforth I am your faithful servant.'

Off went the horse with the three heads, galloping on its twelve hoofs three times as fast and more than the best of ordinary steeds, and in a very short time, the prince had reached the mountain, where he found his dear princess all alone.

As the dragon slowly drew near, the green horse began to throw out fire, bombshells, and cannon balls, which greatly disconcerted the monster. Twenty balls lodged in his throat, his scaly armour was dinted, and the bombshells put out one of his eyes. This enraged him, and he tried to hurl himself upon the prince. But the latter's long sword was so finely tempered that he could do what he liked with it, and now he plunged it in up to the hilt, now cut with it as though it had been a whip. The prince would have suffered, however, from the dragon's claws had it not been for his diamond coat, which was impenetrable.

Moufette had recognised her lover from afar, for the gleaming diamond which covered him was transparent, and she was like to die of terror at the risk he ran. The king and queen, however, felt hope revive within them. They had little thought to see arriving so opportunely a horse with three heads and twelve hoofs that breathed forth fire and flame, nor yet a prince, in diamond mail, and armed with so redoubtable a sword, who performed such prodigies of valour. The king put his hat on the end of his stick, the queen tied a handkerchief to hers, and with all the Court following suit, there was no lack of signals of encouragement to the prince. Not that such was necessary, for his own stout heart and the peril in which he saw Moufette were enough to keep his courage up.

Heavens, how he fought! Barbs, talons, horns, wings, and scales fell from the dragon till the ground was covered with them, and the soil was dyed blue and green with the mingled blood of dragon and horse. Five times the prince was unhorsed, but each time he picked himself up and composedly mounted his steed again. Then would follow such cannonades, bombardments, and flame-throwing as had never been seen or heard of before.

At length, its strength exhausted, the dragon fell, and the prince delivered a finishing stroke. None could believe their eyes when from the gaping wound so made, there stepped forth a handsome and elegant prince, clad in a coat of blue and gold velvet embroidered with pearls and wearing on his head a little Grecian helmet with a crest of white feathers. With outstretched hands, this newcomer ran to Prince Moufy and embraced him.

'How can I ever repay you, my gallant deliverer?' he cried. 'Never was monarch confined in a more dreadful prison than the one from which you have freed me. It is sixteen years since the Lion-Witch condemned me to it, and I have languished there ever since. Moreover, such is her power that she would have obliged me, against my will, to devour that sweet princess. I beg you to let me pay my respects to her, and explain my hapless plight!'

Astonished and delighted by the remarkable way in which his adventure had ended, Prince Moufy lavished courtesies upon the newly-discovered prince. Together they went to Moufette, who rendered thanks a thousand times to Providence for her unexpected happiness. Already the king and queen and all the Court had joined her, and everybody spoke at once, and nobody listened to anybody, while nearly as many tears were shed for joy as a little time ago had been shed for grief. And finally, to set the crown on their rejoicing, the good Frog was espied flying through the air on her hawk. The latter had little golden bells upon its feet, and when the faint tinkling of these caused everyone to look up, there was the Frog, beautiful as the dawn, with her cap of roses shining like the sun.

The queen ran to her and took her by one of her little paws. At that instant, the wise Frog was transformed into a majestic royal lady of gracious mien. 'I come,' she cried, 'to crown the faithful Moufette, who preferred to face death rather than break her word to Prince Moufy.'

With these words, she placed two myrtle wreaths upon the lovers' heads, and at a signal of three taps from her wand, the dragon's bones rose up and formed a triumphal arch to commemorate the auspicious occasion.

Back to the city went all the company, singing wedding songs as gladly as they had previously with sorrow bewailed the sacrifice of the princess. On the morrow, the marriage took place, and with what festivities it was solemnised may be left to the imagination.

Under the Sun

by Juliana Horatia Ewing

There once lived a farmer who was so avaricious and miserly and so hard and closes in all his dealings that, as folks say, he would skin a flint. A Jew and a Yorkshireman had each tried to bargain with him, and both had had the worst of it. It is needless to say that he never either gave or lent.

Now, by thus scraping, saving, and grinding for many years, he had become almost wealthy; though, indeed, he was no better fed and dressed than if he had not a penny to bless himself with. But what vexed him sorely was that his next neighbour's farm prospered in all matters better than his own, and this, although the owner was as open-handed as our farmer, was stingy.

When in spring he ploughed his own worn-out land and reached the top of the furrow where his field joined one of the richly-fed fields of his neighbour, he would cast an envious glance over the hedge and say, "So far and no farther?" for he would have liked to have had the whole under his plough. And so in the autumn, when he gathered his own scanty crop and had to stop his sickle short of the close ranks of his neighbour's corn, he would cry, "All this, and none of that?" and go home sorely discontented.

Now on the lands of the liberal farmer (whose name was Merryweather), there lived a dwarf or hillman who made a wager that he would both beg and borrow from the covetous farmer and out-bargain him to boot. So he went one day to his house and asked him if he would kindly give him half a stone of flour to make hasty pudding with, adding that if he would lend him a bag to carry it into the hill, this should be returned clean and in good condition.

The farmer saw with half an eye that this was the dwarf from his neighbour's estate, and as he had always laid the luck of the liberal farmer to his being favoured by the good people, he resolved to treat the little man with all civility.

"Look you, wife," said he, "this is no time to be

saving half a stone of flour when we may make our fortunes at one stroke. I have heard my grandfather tell of a man who lent a sack of oats to one of the fairies, and got it back filled with gold pieces. And as good measure as he gave of oats so he got of gold;" saying this, the farmer took a canvas bag to the flour bin and began to fill it. Meanwhile, the dwarf sat in the larder window and cried—"We've a big party for supper to-night; give us good measure, neighbour, and you shall have anything under the sun that you like to ask for."

When the farmer heard this, he was nearly out of his wits with delight, and his hands shook so that the flour spilled all about the larder floor.

"Thank you, dear sir," he said; "it's a bargain, and I agree to it. My wife hears us, and is witness. Wife! wife!" he cried, running into the kitchen, "I am to have anything under the sun that I choose to ask for. I think of asking for neighbour Merryweather's estate, but this is a chance never likely to happen again, and I should like to make a wise choice, and that is not easy at a moment's notice."

"You will have a week to think it over in," said the dwarf, who had come in behind him; "I must be off now, so give me my flour, and come to the hill behind your house seven days hence at midnight, and you shall have your share of the bargain."

So the farmer tied up the flour sack and helped the dwarf with it onto his back, and as he did so, he began thinking how easily the bargain had been made and casting about in his mind whether, he could not get more where he had so easily got much.

"And half a stone of flour is half a stone of flour," he muttered to himself, "and whatever it may do with thriftless people, it goes a long way in our house. And there's the bag—and a terrible lot spilled on the larder floor—and the string to tie it with, which doubtless he'll never think of returning—and my time, which must be counted, and nothing whatever for it all for a week to come." And the outlay so weighed upon his mind that he cleared his throat and began:

"Not for seven days, did you say, sir? You know, dear sir, or perhaps, indeed, you do not know, that when amongst each other we men have to wait for the settlement of an account, we expect something over and above the exact amount. Interest we call it, my dear sir."

"And you want me to give you something extra for waiting a week?" asked the dwarf. "Pray, what do you expect?"

"Oh, dear sir, I leave it to you," said the farmer. "Perhaps you may add some trifle—in the flour-bag, or not, as you think fit—but I leave it entirely to you."

"I will give you something over and above what you shall choose," said the dwarf, "but, as you say, I shall decide what it is to be." With which he shouldered the flour sack and went his way.

For the next seven days, the farmer had no peace in thinking and planning and scheming how to get the most out of his one wish. His wife made many suggestions to which he did not agree, but he was careful not to quarrel with her, "for," he said, "we will not be like the foolish couple who wasted three wishes on black-puddings. Neither will I desire useless grandeur and unreasonable elevation, like the fisherman's wife. I will have a solid and substantial benefit."

And so, after a week of sleepless nights and anxious days, he came back to his first thought and resolved to ask for his neighbour's estate.

At last, the night came. It was a full moon, and the farmer looked anxiously about, fearing the dwarf might not be true to his appointment. But at midnight, he appeared with the flour bag neatly folded in his hand.

"You hold to the agreement," said the farmer, "of course. My wife was witness. I am to have anything under the sun that I ask for; and I am to have it now."

"Ask away," said the dwarf.

"I want neighbour Merryweather's estate," said the farmer.

"What, all this land below here, that joins on to your own?"

"Every acre," said the farmer.

"Farmer Merryweather's fields are under the moon at present," said the dwarf coolly, "and thus not within the terms of the agreement. You must choose again."

But as the farmer could choose nothing that was not then under the moon, he soon saw that he had been outwitted, and his rage knew no bounds at the trick the dwarf had played him.

"Give me my bag, at any rate," he screamed, "and the string—and your own extra gift that you promised. For half a loaf is better than no bread," he muttered, "and I may yet come in for a few gold pieces."

"There's your bag," cried the dwarf, clapping it over the miser's head like an extinguisher; "it's clean enough for a nightcap. And there's your string," he added, tying it tightly around the farmer's throat till he was almost throttled. "And, for my part, I'll give you what you deserve;" saying which he gave the farmer such a hearty kick that he kicked him straight down from the top of the hill to his own back door.

"If that does not satisfy you, I'll give you as much again," shouted the dwarf, and as the farmer made no reply, he went chuckling back to his hill.

Briar Rose

by The Brothers Grimm

Aking and queen once upon a time reigned in a country a great way off, where there were in those days fairies. Now, this king and queen had plenty of money, plenty of fine clothes to wear, plenty of good things to eat and drink, and a coach to ride out in every day: but though they had been married many years, they had no children, and this grieved them very much indeed. But one day, as the queen was walking by the side of the river, at the bottom of the garden, she saw a poor little fish that had thrown itself out of the water and lay gasping and nearly dead on the bank. Then the queen took pity on the little fish and threw it back again into the river, and before it swam away, it lifted its head out of the water and said, 'I know what your wish is, and it shall be fulfilled, in return for your kindness to me—you will soon have a daughter.' What the little fish had foretold soon came to pass, and the queen had a little girl, so very beautiful that the king could not cease looking on it for joy, and said he would hold a great feast and make merry and show the child to all the land. So he asked his kinsmen, nobles, friends, and neighbours. But the queen said, 'I will have the fairies also, that they might be kind and good to our little daughter.' Now there were thirteen fairies in the kingdom, but as the king and queen had only twelve golden dishes for them to eat out of, they were forced to leave one of the fairies without asking her. So twelve fairies came, each with a high red cap on her head, and red shoes with high heels on her feet, and a long white wand in her hand: and after the feast was over, they gathered round in a ring and gave all their best gifts to the little princess. One gave her goodness, another beauty, another riches, and so on till she had all that was good in the world.

Just as eleven of them had done blessing her, a great noise was heard in the courtyard, and the word was brought that the thirteenth fairy was come, with a black cap on her head, black shoes on her feet, and a broomstick in her hand: and presently up she came into the dining hall. Now, as she had not been asked to the feast, she was very angry and scolded the king and queen very much and set to work to take her revenge. So she cried out, 'The king's daughter shall, in her fifteenth year, be wounded by a spindle, and fall down dead.' Then the twelfth of the friendly fairies, who had not yet given her gift, came forward and said that the evil wish must be fulfilled but that she could soften its mischief; so her gift was that the king's daughter, when the spindle wounded her, should not really die, but should only fall asleep for a hundred years.

However, the king hoped still to save his dear child altogether from the threatened evil, so he ordered that all the spindles in the kingdom should be bought up and burnt. But all the gifts of the first eleven fairies were in the meantime fulfilled; for the princess was so beautiful, and well behaved, and good, and wise, that everyone who knew her loved her.

It happened that, on the very day she was fifteen years old, the king and queen were not at home, and she was left alone in the palace. So she roved about by herself and looked at all the rooms and chambers till, at last, she came to an old tower, to which there was a narrow staircase ending with a little door. In the door, there was a golden key, and when she turned it, the door sprang open, and there sat an old lady spinning away very busily. 'Why, how now, good mother,' said the princess; 'what are you doing there?' 'Spinning,' said the old lady, and nodded her head, humming a tune while buzzing! went the wheel. 'How prettily that little thing turns round!' said the princess, and took the spindle and began to try and spin. But scarcely had she touched it before the fairy's prophecy was fulfilled; the spindle wounded her, and she fell lifeless on the ground.

However, she was not dead but had only fallen into a deep sleep; and the king and the queen, who had just come home, and all their court, fell asleep too; and the horses slept in the stables, and the dogs in the court, the pigeons on the house-top, and the very flies slept upon the walls. Even the fire on the hearth left off blazing and went to sleep; the jack stopped, and the spit that was turning about with a goose upon it for the king's dinner stood still; and the cook, who was at that moment pulling the kitchen-boy by the hair to give him a box on the ear for something he had done amiss, let him go, and both fell asleep; the butler, who was slyly tasting the ale, fell asleep with the jug at his lips: and thus everything stood still, and slept soundly.

A large hedge of thorns soon grew around the palace, and every year it became higher and thicker; till, at last, the old palace was surrounded and hidden so that not even the roof or the chimneys could be seen. But there went a report through all the land of the beautiful sleeping Briar Rose (for so the king's daughter was called): so that, from time to time, several kings' sons came and tried to break through the thicket into the palace. This, however, none of them could ever do; for the thorns and bushes laid hold of them, as it were with hands; and there they stuck fast and died wretchedly.

After many, many years, there came a king's son into that land: and an old man told him the story of the thicket of thorns, and how a beautiful palace stood behind it, and how a wonderful princess, called Briar Rose, lay in it asleep, with all her court. He told, too, how he had heard from his grandfather that many, many princes had come and had tried to break through the thicket but that they had all stuck fast in it and died. Then the young prince said, 'All this shall not frighten me; I will go and see this Briar Rose.' The old man tried to hinder him, but he was bent upon going.

Now that very day, the hundred years were ended; and as the prince came to the thicket, he saw nothing but beautiful flowering shrubs, through which he went with ease, and they shut in after him as thick as ever. Then he came at last to the palace, and there in the court lay the dogs asleep, and the horses were standing in the stables, and on the roof sat the pigeons fast asleep, with their heads under their wings. And when he came into the palace, the flies were sleeping on the walls; the spit was standing still; the butler had the jug of ale at his lips, going to drink a draught; the maid sat with a fowl in her lap ready to be plucked, and the cook in the kitchen was still holding up her hand as if she was going to beat the boy.

Then he went on still farther, and all was so still that he could hear every breath he drew; till at last he came to the old tower and opened the door of the little room in which Briar Rose was; and there she lay, fast asleep on a couch by the window. She looked so beautiful that he could not take his eyes off her, so he stooped down and gave her a kiss. But the moment he kissed her, she opened her eyes and awoke and smiled upon him, and they went out together, and soon the king and queen also awoke, and all the court, and gazed on each other with great wonder. And the horses shook themselves, and the dogs jumped up and barked; the pigeons took their heads from under their wings and looked about and flew into the fields; the flies on the walls buzzed again; the fire in the kitchen blazed up; round went the jack, and round went the spit, with the goose for the king's dinner upon it; the butler finished his draught of ale; the maid went on plucking the fowl, and the cook gave the boy the box on his ear.

And then the prince and Briar Rose were married, and the wedding feast was given, and they lived happily together all their lives long.

A Remarkable Watch

by Mrs Molesworth

"May we bathe this morning, Mamma?" said the children, putting their heads in at the door of the drawing room. Mamma glanced at the timepiece. "It is rather late," she said doubtfully. "You would have to be very quick. Which of the big ones are going with you?"

"None of them," answered Joan, the smallest of the small party. "They've all gone for a walk except Lilly, and she's drawing in the garden, but I'm sure she'd come if we asked her. Lilly's always so kind—if only you'd say we might."

"It is so fine and sunny, and the tide won't suit again for ever so many days," added two or three imploring voices.

"Very well, then if Lilly will go you may bathe, but you must be quick. I can't have luncheon kept waiting again," said Mamma.

In another moment, loud eager cries from the garden reached her through the open window. "Lilly, Lilly, where are you? Mamma says if you will come—" and then the voices fade away in the distance.

"Poor Lilly," thought Mamma with a smile. "I wonder if it's a shame of me to let those wild children torment her. I dare say she was counting on a quiet morning."

But whether Lilly was disappointed or not, no sign of anything but content and pleasure appeared on her pretty, bright face when the little group of bathers, all brushed up and tidied again, took their places around the luncheon table.

"That's right," said Mamma. "You really have been very expeditious this morning. Whom am I to praise?"

She knew before it came what the answer would be.

"Oh, Lilly. Lilly, of course," said Joan, always ready to be a spokeswoman. "Lilly made us promise to do exactly as she told us before we went."

"She timed us," said Bill.

"Yes," Joan went on, "wasn't it a good plan? Lilly put her watch on a rock and gave us five minutes to undress in, and a quarter of an hour to stay in the sea, and ten minutes to dress in. Bill and Humphrey were in the gentlemen's dressing-room, of course—that's what we call the other little bay—and Lilly had to roar out to them, 'one minute more only,'—'two minutes more,' just like a railway man at a station. It was such fun, and—"

"My dear Joan, you will never eat your dinner if you chatter so," said her mother, "and we can't wait for you. I am going a long drive this afternoon, and I shall only just have time," and Mamma looked at her watch. "I hope I am a little fast," she added. "What time do you make it, Lilly dear? Your watch is always to be relied on."

Lilly's hand instinctively went to her watch pocket—then she suddenly looked up with a rather startled expression.

"My watch!" she exclaimed. "I must have left it up stairs. Mamma—might I run up for a moment and see, if you don't mind?"

Mamma nodded. She knew that Lilly's watch was one of the girl's most prized treasures. It was handsome, though a rather bulky one, which had been left to her by her godmother, and Lilly cared for it both because she had loved her godmother and also for its own sake. It kept excellent time and never got out of order as the little fairy-like watches that are now the fashion are rather apt to do.

Lilly's moment extended to several minutes without her coming back, and the faces round the table grew rather concerned-looking.

"May I—" Joan was beginning, but just as she spoke, Lilly appeared. She was pale and almost seemed as if she had difficulty keeping back her tears.

"Mamma," she said, "I can't forgive myself, I am dreadfully afraid my dear watch is gone. I must have left it on the shore."

Up started Bill and Humphrey.

"You'll let us go, Mamma. We don't care about any more dinner. We know where Lilly left it—no one's likely to have been there."

"And the people about here are so honest," said Joan.

"But," said Mamma, "was the stone where you laid it, Lilly, out of reach of the tide? It was almost low tide when you bathed."

All looked startled at this, but the boys persisted.

"All the more reason to go at once," they said, and off they set.

Lilly would fain have gone too, but she gave in to her Mother, and sat quietly, trying to eat, though I fear her luncheon was flavoured by some drops of salt water.

And in a few minutes, the whole party started down the road to meet the boys and hear the news.

Alas! as soon as Bill and Humphrey appeared, even

in the distance, all hopes were gone. Both boys shook their heads sadly.

"You saw nothing of it?" asked their Mother eagerly. Poor Lilly was past speaking.

"Nothing—as well as we could make out, the tide must have covered the stones where the girls dressed, some time ago," they replied.

"Then I fear there is nothing to be done," said Mamma. "Poor Lilly, I am so sorry for you."

"And to think it was all my own carelessness," sobbed Lilly. "My dear watch and chain—there was the chain too, Mamma."

But Lilly was so seldom careless, and even if she had been so for once, it was in the service of others that no one would let her blame herself, and all the family joined to try to console her.

"There is one chance," said Bill to Humphrey when they were alone—their Mother and elder sisters having gone out for the afternoon—"the watch is heavy, and the sea is calm. It may be left there when the tide goes back. Let's see—it will be high tide by about five, and low again by eleven. Those stones should be uncovered by ten o'clock, and it is bright moonlight just now. I tell you what, Humphrey, we'll get Mamma's leave to sit up later to-night, and we'll go off to the shore and have another try for the watch and chain."

Humphrey's eyes sparkled with sympathy.

"We'll say nothing to Lilly—it would be cruel to raise her hopes again on such a chance," he said. "We'll only tell Mamma."

The plan was carried out. At ten o'clock that evening, just as poor Lilly was going to bed and thinking sadly how strange it seemed to have no watch to wind up, two small figures might have been seen in the moonlight, carefully picking their way among the stones over which the little waves were still softly lapping, for the special group of small rocks they were in search of was not yet uncovered.

It was more difficult than they had expected to find the exact spot. The moonlight and the sheen it cast on the water were rather dazzling. The boys crept along slowly and carefully.

"I say, what a beautiful night it is," said Bill. "It's a good thing the watch is a gold one; if it were silver there wouldn't be much chance of seeing it—everything looks silver, and—"

But Humphrey interrupted him.

"This is the place—I'm sure it is—look, the smooth sand just beyond is where the girls jumped in, and—"

In his turn, he was interrupted.

"You're right," cried Bill, "and—I do believe—no, there's a little wave hiding it again—now, look, Humphrey—isn't there something glittering still more than the wet stones, down there—on that smooth flat rock?"

Yes—another wave or two came gently lapping in as if to say goodbye to the treasure they had been playing with, and then the boys stepped forward over the slippery stones, and Bill stooped down and quickly stood up again, with a shout of triumph, for the rescued prize was in his hands.

"And it really doesn't seem much the worse," said he and Humphrey to each other, as they made their way home.

Lilly was not in her first sleep—she was too unhappy to fall asleep as quietly as usual—when a tap at the door made her jump up. There stood her brothers, and behind them, Mamma, smiling with pleasure, and for a minute or two, Lilly's delight almost stupefied her. She could scarcely believe it was her own dear watch that Bill held out, and when she did believe it, she could not kiss and thank him and Humphrey enough.

The watch had to go to a watch doctor, of course, and it cost several shillings to put it right, but that is now many years ago, and it still keeps time as well as ever.

The Gingerbread Rock

by Abbie Phillips Walker

Once there lived near a forest, a little boy named Hans and his sister, whose name was Lisbeth. Their parents had died when they were tiny, and their uncle had taken them because he thought they could do all the work and so save the money he would have to pay for a servant.

But this uncle was a miser and gave Hans and Lisbeth very little to eat, so very little that often they went to bed very hungry.

One night when they were more hungry than usual, for they had worked hard all day, Hans whispered from his cot in one corner of the room: "Lisbeth, let us get up and go into the woods. It is bright moonlight and we may be able to find some berries. I am so hungry I cannot go to sleep."

So out of the house, they went, making sure their uncle was sound asleep, and soon they were running along the path through the woods.

Suddenly Hans stopped and drew Lisbeth back of a tree. "Look!" he said in a whisper, "there is smoke coming from the side of that great rock."

Lisbeth looked, and sure enough, a tiny curling smoke was coming from a little opening in the rock.

Very cautiously, the children crept up to the rock, and Hans stood on tiptoe and sniffed at the smoke.

"It is a pipe," he whispered into Lisbeth's ear. "Some one is inside the rock, smoking."

"No one could live inside a rock," said Lisbeth, creeping closer and standing on a stone that she, too, might sniff at the curling smoke.

Lisbeth became curious when she discovered it was the smoke from a pipe. "You could boost me, Hans," she said, "and I could peep in and see if some one is inside."

Hans told her he did not think it was nice to peek, but Lisbeth told him it was very different from peeking into a house, and so Hans boosted her, for he was just as curious as his sister.

Lisbeth grasped the edge of the opening in the big rock with both her little hands when, to the surprise of both children, it crumbled, and Lisbeth lost her balance.

Over went both of them on the soft moss, and when they sat up Lisbeth held something in both her little hands.

"It's cake!" she said with wide-open eyes. "No; it is gingerbread!" she corrected as she tasted it.

And, sure enough, it was gingerbread; the rock, instead of stone, was all gingerbread.

Hans and Lisbeth forgot the smoke and, their curiosity in the joy of their discovery, and soon both of them were eating as fast as they could big pieces of the Gingerbread Rock.

Hans and Lisbeth were not greedy children. So when they had satisfied their hunger, they ran off home without taking even a piece of the gingerbread with them to eat the next day.

They were soon in bed and asleep, and if each had not told the other the same story the next morning, they would have been sure they had dreamed it all.

The next night they were hungry, as usual, and when the moon was well up in the sky, they crept again and ran into the woods.

But this time, there was no curling smoke to guide them, and they tried several rocks before they found the gingerbread. For, strange to say, the place they had broken away did not show at all, and there were so many rocks the children could not find it.

But at last, Hans cried out with joy, "Here it is, Lisbeth!" and held up a big piece of gingerbread he had broken off.

Lisbeth, in her hurry to get a piece, broke off much more than she intended, and, to the surprise of both children, a big opening was made, large enough for them to step through.

"Perhaps we may find out where the smoke came from," said Lisbeth, suddenly remembering the smoke they had seen the night before.

Eating as they went, both of them stepped inside the rock and walked into a big room where, by the table, sat an old man asleep.

His glasses had tumbled off his nose, and the pipe he had been smoking was on the floor beside him, where it had tumbled. His lamp had gone out, and his paper had slipped from his hand.

Lisbeth and Hans looked at him and then at the gingerbread they held. "It is his house," said Hans.

"And we are eating it up! What shall we do?" asked Lisbeth, looking very much frightened.

"Better wake him up and tell him," said Hans, "and perhaps he will let us bake some more and mend the place we have broken."

"I'll pick up his paper and pipe and brush up the ashes," said tidy little Lisbeth, "and you light his lamp, and perhaps he will forgive us when we tell him we did not know it was his house we were eating."

But instead of being cross when he awoke, the old man smiled at them and asked, "Did you eat all you wanted of the gingerbread?"

Hans told him they were very sorry and that they did not know anyone lived inside when they ate the gingerbread.

"We will bake you some more and patch the place we made," said Lisbeth.

"Right through that door you will find the kitchen," said the old man. "Run along, if you like, and bake it."

And such a kitchen as Hans and Lisbeth found for Hans went along, you may be sure, to fix the fire for his sister!

The shelves and cupboards were filled with flour and butter and eggs and milk and cream and meat and pies, cookies, and puddings, but no gingerbread.

"We will get breakfast first for the man," said Lisbeth, "for I am sure he must be hungry and it is growing light. Look out the window."

To Hans's surprise, there was a window. Then he saw a door, and when he looked out, he found they were in a pretty white house with green blinds and not a rock, as he had supposed.

Hans and Lisbeth became so interested in cooking they quite forgot their own home or the unkind uncle who almost starved them, and when the breakfast was ready, they put it on the table beside the old man.

"I thought you would like your breakfast," explained Lisbeth, "and now we will make the gingerbread and repair your house."

"After breakfast you may, if you like," said the old man, "but first both of you must eat with me."

My, how Hans and Lisbeth did eat. For a while, Lisbeth had cooked only ham and eggs, enough for the old man's breakfast. There seemed to be quite enough for them all.

And while they are eating, we will see what the miser uncle was doing, for he had called the children at break of day, and they were not to be found.

It happened that the ground was damp and the uncle saw the prints of their feet from the door to the road and along the road to the path in the woods, and then the soft leaves and moss did not show where they went.

Thinking they had run away and gone into the woods, their uncle hurried along, calling their names at the top of his voice.

As he came near the Gingerbread Rock, the children heard him and began to tremble. "It is uncle," said Hans. "He will be very angry because we have not done our work."

"Sit still," said the old man as the children started to leave the table, and, taking his pipe, the old man sat down under a little opening like a tiny window and began to smoke.

Soon the children could hear their uncle climbing up outside, and they knew he had seen the smoke just as they had the night before and was trying to look in.

Then they heard him tumble just as Lisbeth had when the Gingerbread Rock broke off in her hands, and they knew he had discovered it was good to eat, for all was still for a few minutes.

Nothing was heard again for a long time, and then the sound of someone breaking off big pieces was heard, and when Hans and Lisbeth climbed up, as the old man told them to do, and looked out of the opening, they saw their uncle with a shovel and a wheelbarrow.

He was breaking off big pieces of gingerbread and filling the barrow as fast as he could.

But when he had filled it, he could not move it, for it was no longer gingerbread but stone he had to carry.

The old man motioned to the children to keep quiet, and he opened a door they had not noticed and went out.

Just what he said, the children never knew. But they soon found out that instead of being poor, as they had thought, their miser uncle had taken all the silver and gold their parents had left and hidden it in his cellar under the stones.

The miser uncle disappeared and was never seen again, and the old man, who was really a wizard, told them where to go and what to do with their wealth. So they were happy ever after.

Of course, they never forgot the Gingerbread Rock or the kind old man. But because he was a wizard, they knew they would never see him again, for fairies and witches and wizards are all enchanted and disappear in a very strange manner.

"Our good fortune came to us because we tried to be kind to the old man, I am sure," said Hans one day when they were talking about the Gingerbread Rock.

"Yes, and because we wanted to repair the damage we had done he knew we did not mean to do any harm," said Lisbeth, "but I shall never eat gingerbread again without thinking of him."

"Nor I," said Hans.

The Light on the Hills

by Mrs W.K. Clifford

"I want to work at my picture," he said and went into the field. The little sister went too and stood by him, watching while he painted. "The trees are not quite straight," she said presently, "and oh, dear brother, the sky is not blue enough."

"It will all come right soon," he answered. "Will it be of any good?"

"Oh yes," she said, wondering that he should even ask, "it will make people happy to look at it. They will feel as if they were in the field."

"If I do it badly, will it make them unhappy?"

"Not if you do your very best," she answered, "for they will know how hard you have tried. Look up," she said suddenly, "look up at the light upon the hills," and they stood together looking at all he was trying to paint, at the trees and the field, at the deep shadows and the hills beyond, and the light that rested upon them.

"It is a beautiful world," the girl said. "It is a great honour to make things for it."

"It is a beautiful world," the boy echoed sadly. "It is a sin to disgrace it with things that are badly done."

"But you will do things well?"

"I get so tired," he said, "and long to leave off so much. What do you do when you want to do your best, —your very, very best?" he asked suddenly.

"I think that I am doing it for the people I love," she answered. "It makes you very strong if you think of them; you can bear pain, and walk far, and do all manner of things, and you don't get tired so soon."

He thought for a moment. "Then I shall paint my picture for you," he said; "I shall think of you all the time I am doing it."

Once more, they looked at the hills that seemed to rise up out of the deep shadows into the light, and then together, they went home.

Soon afterwards, a great sorrow came to the boy. While the little sister slept, she wandered into another world and journeyed on so far that she lost the clue to earth and came back no more. The boy painted many pictures before he saw the field again, but in the long hours, as he sat and worked, there came to him a strange power that answered more and more true to the longing in his heart—the longing to put into the world something of which he was not ashamed, something which should make it, if only in the person of its meanest, humblest citizen, a little happier or better.

At last, when he knew that his eye was true and his touch sure, he took up the picture he had promised to paint for the dear sister and worked at it until he was finished.

"This is better than all he has done before," the beholders said. "It is surely beautiful, for it makes one happy to look at it."

"And yet my heart ached as I did it," the boy said as he went back to the field. "I thought of her all the time I worked,—it was sorrow that gave me power." It seemed as if a soft voice that spoke only to his heart answered back—

"Not sorrow but love, and perfect love has all things in its gift, and of it are all things born save happiness, and though that may be born too——"

"How does one find happiness?" interrupted the boy.

"It is a strange chase," the answer seemed to be; "to find it for one's own self, one must seek it for others. We all throw the ball for each other."

"But it is so difficult to seize."

"Perfect love helps one to live without happiness," his own heart answered to himself, "and above all things it helps one to work and to wait."

"But if it gives one happiness too?" he asked eagerly.

"Ah, then it is called Heaven."

The Enchanted Boat

by Abbie Phillips Walker

O nce, there was a King who had a very beautiful daughter, and when the Queen died, the King married a woman who had a son named Tito because he thought this new Queen would be kind and good to the Princess.

But in this, the King was greatly mistaken, for the Queen thought only of her son and wished to make him King.

She told the King that if he would make the Princess marry Tito that he need have no fear about the future of his kingdom, for he could be sure her son would make a good king.

"And a woman should not be Queen and rule alone

such a big kingdom as you possess," said the scheming Queen.

The King, who thought more of his daughter's happiness than anything in the world, called the Princess and told her of his plan. "Marry your stepmother's son and all will be well with you and I can die happy," he told the Princess.

But the Princess did not want to marry Tito, for she did not love him, and when she found that her father would not listen to her pleadings but told her that very night she should wed Tito, the little Princess ran out of the palace and threw herself face down on the grass and wept.

When it came time for the wedding, she was nowhere to be found, and though the palace and the gardens were searched, it was all in vain. The Princess had disappeared.

What had happened was that while the Princess was crying and bemoaning her sad lot, she heard a sound, and when she looked up, there was a lake she had never seen at the foot of the garden, and on it a beautiful boat with a sail of silk the color of gold.

There was no one in the boat, and the Princess, forgetting her sorrow in her wonderment at this strange sight, ran down to the water's edge, where another surprise awaited her, for the boat came sailing straight to the place where she stood.

The Princess stepped in, and away went the boat out over the blue water, and in a few minutes, she was in a country she had never seen before.

The little Princess was not frightened, for she felt nothing worse could befall her than if she stayed at the palace and had to marry Tito, and while she was sorry to leave her father, she could not be happy with a man she did not love.

The lake led to a river, along the banks of which were high hills and beautiful woods, and the Princess was so lost in admiring the beauty of the scene she did not notice they were approaching a castle until her boat sailed under a white marble bridge, which soon brought her at the steps which led into the garden of the castle.

Here the strange boat stopped, and the Princess knew she was expected to get out.

She walked up the steps into a garden filled with pink and white roses, with a fountain of pearl and gold in the centre which threw a perfumed spray all about, which filled the air with fragrance.

There were no paths in the garden, but the grass was like green velvet, and yellow birds flittered among the small green trees and sang sweet songs.

Through the roses and trees, the Princess saw the entrance to the castle, and on the broad steps of marble and gold came a queer-looking creature followed by more servants than the Princess had ever seen in her father's palace.

The Princess did not feel at all afraid, although the strange-looking creature had the body of a beautiful leopard, while his head was that of the handsomest youth the Princess had ever beheld.

His hair was dark, and as he came nearer to her, the Princess saw that his eyes were deep blue, the kindest eyes she had ever seen.

He held out one huge paw toward her and then withdrew it and said, "I fear you will not care to take the paw of such a beast as I am, but I can assure you I will not harm you, Princess."

"I am not afraid," said the Princess, putting out her hand, "but tell me how you know that I am a princess?"

After the leopard-man had taken her hand, he led her up the steps, and as they walked along, he told her that no one but a princess could have entered the boat. "It had sailed for many a year in quest of the princess who would be willing to sail away in it," he told her, "and as only a princess can help me, no one but a princess could get into the enchanted boat."

When the Princess and the leopard man entered the castle, he told her his strange story. He was a prince who had been changed by a witch into the shape she saw, and the only thing that could save him was a gold root which grew far up on a blue mountain peak.

"But that root must be brought to me by a princess

and no one else," said the leopard-man, "so you see how impossible it is that I shall ever regain my own shape."

"If you will tell me where this blue mountain peak can be found," said the Princess, "I will undertake the task, for I do not wish to return to my father's palace, and I would like to help you."

"The enchanted boat will take you if you really wish to try," said the leopard-man, "but I fear it is a task you are far from fitted to undertake, for no one can go with you; that would break the spell."

The Princess, however, told him she would try and at once set out on the strange errand, the boat sailing along the river and then out into the open sea.

By and by, the Princess saw on the side of a high mountain, the top of which was blue, something growing which shone like gold, and she knew it must be the golden root for which she was seeking. The enchanted boat sailed close to the foot of the mountain and stopped, and the Princess knew she was to get out, but how was she to reach the golden root which grew far up on the mountain?

The Princess stepped out of the boat on the rocks and sat down to think what she could do, for a climb up the steep, smooth side of the mountain was out of the question; if only she could fly, she thought she might reach it.

Just then, she heard a swishing sound and, looking

up. She saw a big eagle coming toward her with a broken leg.

The bird fell at her feet, and, as so many strange things had already happened, the Princess did not feel afraid of the big creature, for she felt sure that in some way he would help her.

"Oh, you poor hurt bird!" she said, tearing off a piece of her dress to bind up its leg; then, from a stream falling from the mountain, she brought in the hollow of her hand water for him to drink.

At night the Princess took off her cloak and covered the eagle while she huddled close to the mountain and behind a rock to keep the cold from herself.

In the morning, she was surprised to find the eagle had flown away, but on the rocks was her cloak, and two feathers from the wings of the bird lay beside it.

The Princess put on her cloak and took up one of the feathers, and to her surprise, the hand that held the feather flew up over her head.

She picked up the other feather with the other hand, and up she was carried, her cloak spreading out like a pair of wings.

With the feathers, she guided herself until she alighted on the top of the blue-peaked mountain.

She laid the feathers down and began to dig for the root, which the Prince had said was the only thing that could save him. When she had enough of the golden root, she again took the feathers, one in each hand, and flew down to the water, where the enchanted boat, which had sailed away when she left it, now stood waiting.

She the feathers from the eagle she put carefully on the rocks, but the bird was nowhere to be seen, and, knowing that it must have been a part of the magic plan to help her, the Princess sailed away, feeling sure the eagle was safe and his broken leg quite well.

When she reached the castle of the leopard-man, he was on the steps to meet her, and without waiting to enter the castle, he took the golden root from her and tasted it.

The leopard's body disappeared, and there he stood before her, a tall, handsome youth whom any maiden, even a princess, would fall in love with.

The Princess told him her story, and the Prince told her they would go at once to her father, and he would ask for her hand, for he had already asked for her heart and found that it was his.

The enchanted boat took them back to the garden of the King, where they found that the Queen, when she knew that her son had lost the chance of becoming King when the Princess disappeared, had put the King in a dungeon under the palace and she and her son had become the rulers of the kingdom.

The Prince quickly undid all this mischief by setting the King free, and when he found out how treacherous his Queen really was, he sent her, with her son, away from the palace and told them never to return or they would both be put in prison.

He was a kind-hearted King and gave them gold to care for them the rest of their days, and it did not take them long to leave the palace, you may be sure, for already the wedding feast was being made ready for the marriage of the Princess and her Prince.

The enchanted boat now was not needed, and the lake had disappeared, but when the Princess set out with her husband to go to the castle, she found that it was within her father's kingdom that the Prince had lived.

At the end of the castle garden where the Prince and the Princess live is a long stone seat, and at one end grows a bush of golden flowers, the like of which no one ever saw before, and at the other is the figure of a big eagle made of gold and bronze, but only the Princess and her husband know what these things mean.

The Kitchen Cat

by Amy Walton

CHAPTER I

The Visitor from the Cellar

The whole house in London was dull and gloomy. Its lofty rooms and staircases were filled with a sort of misty twilight all day, and the sun very seldom looked in at its windows. Ruth Lorimer thought, however, that the very dullest room of all was the nursery, in which she had to pass so much of her time. It was so high up that the people and carts and horses in the street below looked like toys. She could not even see these properly because there were iron bars to prevent her from stretching her head out too far so that all she could do was to look straight across to the row of tall houses opposite or up at the sky between the chimney-pots how she longed for something different to look at!

The houses always looked the same, and though the sky changed sometimes, it was often of a dirty grey colour and then Ruth gave a little sigh and looked back from the window seat where she was kneeling, into the nursery, for something to amuse her. It was full of all sorts of toys—dolls, and dolls' houses elegantly furnished, pictures and books and many pretty things; but in spite of all these, she often found nothing to please her, for what she wanted more than anything else was a companion of her own age, and she had no brothers or sisters.

The dolls, however much she pretended, were never glad, or sorry, or happy, or miserable—they could not answer her when she talked to them, and their beautiful bright eyes had a hard, unfeeling look which became very tiring, for it never changed.

There was certainly Nurse Smith. She was alive and real enough; there was no necessity to "pretend" anything about her. She was always there, sitting upright and flat-backed beside her workbasket, frowning a little, not because she was cross, but because she was rather near-sighted. She had come when Ruth was quite a baby, after Mrs Lorimer's death, and Aunt Clarkson often spoke of her as "a treasure". However that might be, she was not an amusing companion, though she did her best to answer all Ruth's questions and was always careful of her comfort and particular about her being neatly dressed.

Perhaps it was not her fault that she did not understand games and was quite unable to act the part of any other character than her own. If she did make an attempt, she failed so miserably that Ruth had to tell her what to say, which made it so flat and uninteresting that she found it better to play alone. But she often became weary of this, and there were times when she was tired of her toys and tired of Nurse Smith and did not know what in the world to do with herself.

Each day passed much in the same way. Ruth's governess came to teach her for an hour every morning, and then after her early dinner, there was a walk with Nurse, generally in one direction. And after tea, it was time to go and see her father—quite a long journey, through the silent house, down the long stairs to the dining room where he sat alone at his dessert.

Ruth could not remember her mother, and she saw so little of her father that he seemed almost a stranger to her. He was so wonderfully busy, and the world he lived in was such a great way off from hers in the nursery.

In the morning, he hurried away just as she was at her breakfast, and all she knew of him was the resounding slam of the hall door, which came echoing up the staircase. Very often in the evening, he came hastily into the nursery to say goodbye on his way out to some dinner party, and at night she woke up to hear his step on the stairs as he came back late. But when he dined at home, Ruth always went downstairs for dessert. Then, as she entered the large sombre dining room, where there were great oil paintings on the walls and heavy hangings to the windows and serious-looking ponderous furniture, her father would look up from his book or from papers spread on the table and nod kindly to her:

"Ah! it's you, Ruth. Quite well, eh? There's a good child. Have an orange? That's right."

Then he would plunge into his reading again, and Ruth would climb slowly onto a great mahogany chair placed ready for her and watch him as she cut up her orange.

She wondered very much why people wrote him such long, long letters, all on blue paper and tied up with pink tape. She felt sure they were not nice letters, for his face always looked worried over them, and when he had finished, he threw them on the floor as though he were glad. This made her so curious that she once ventured to ask him what they were. They were called "briefs", he told her. But she was not much wiser; for, hearing from Nurse Smith that "brief" was another word for short, she felt sure there must be some mistake.

Exactly as the clock struck eight, Nurse's knock came at the door. Ruth got down from her chair and said goodnight.

Sometimes her father was so deeply engaged in his

reading that he stared at her with a far-away look in his eyes as if he scarcely knew who she was. After a minute, he said absently: "Bed-time, eh? Good-night. Good-night, my dear." Sometimes, when he was a little less absorbed, he put a sixpence or a shilling into her hand as he kissed her and added: "There's something to spend at the toy-shop."

Ruth received these presents without much surprise or joy. She was used to buying things and did not find them very interesting; for she could not hope for any sign of pleasure from her dolls when she brought them new clothes or furniture.

It is a little dull when all one's efforts for people are received with a perfectly unmoved face. She had once brought Nurse Smith a small china image, hoping that it would be an agreeable surprise, but that had not been successful either. "Lor', my dear, don't you go spending your money on me," she said. "Chany ornaments ain't much good for anything, to my thinking, 'cept to ketch the dust."

Thus it came to pass that Ruth never talked much about what interested her either to her father or to Nurse Smith, and as she had no brothers and sisters, she was obliged to amuse herself with fancied conversations. Sometimes these were carried on with her dolls, but her chief friend was a picture which she passed every night on the staircase. It was of a man in a flat cap and a fur robe, and he had a pointed, smooth chin and narrow eyes, which seemed to follow her slyly on her way. She did not like him, and she did not actually fear him, but she had a feeling that he listened to what she said and that she must tell him any news she had. There was never much except on "Aunt Clarkson's day", as she called it.

Aunt Clarkson was her father's sister. She lived in the country and had many little boys and girls whom Ruth had seldom seen, though she heard a great deal about them.

Once every month, this aunt came up to London for the day, had long conversations with Nurse, and looked carefully at all Ruth's clothes.

She was a sharp-eyed lady, and her visits made a stir in the house which was like a cold wind blowing so that Ruth was glad when they were over, though her aunt always spoke kindly to her and said: "Some day you must come and see your little cousins in the country."

She had said this so often without its having happened, however, that Ruth had come to look upon it as a mere form of speech—part of Aunt Clarkson's visit, like saying "How d'ye do?" or "Good-bye."

It was shortly after one of these occasions that quite by chance Ruth found a new friend, who was better than either the dolls or the man in the picture, because, though it could not answer her, it was really alive. She discovered it in this way.

One afternoon she and Nurse Smith had come in from their usual walk and were toiling slowly up from the hall to the nursery. The stairs got steeper at the last flight, and Nurse went more slowly still and panted a good deal, for she was stouter than she need have been, though Ruth would never have dreamed of saying so. Ruth was in front, and she had nearly reached the top when something came hurrying towards her, which surprised her very much. It was a long, lean, grey cat. It had a guilty look, as though it knew it had been trespassing and squeezed itself as close as it could against the wall as it passed.

"Pretty puss!" said Ruth softly and put out her hand to stop it.

The cat at once arched up its back and gave a friendly little answering mew. Ruth wondered where it came from. It was ugly, she thought, but it seemed a pleasant cat and glad to be noticed. She rubbed its head gently. It felt hard and rough like Nurse's old velvet bonnet; there was indeed no sleekness about it anywhere, and it was so thin that its sides nearly met.

"Poor puss!" said Ruth, stroking it tenderly.

The cat replied by pushing its head gently against her arm and presently began a low purring song. Delighted, Ruth bent her ear to listen.

"Whoosh! Shish! Get along! Scat!" suddenly sounded from a few steps below. Nurse's umbrella was violently flourished, the cat flew downstairs with a spit like an angry firework, and Ruth turned round indignantly.

"You shouldn't have done that," she said, stamping

her foot; "I wanted to talk to it. Whose is it?"

"It's that nasty kitchen cat," said Nurse, much excited and grasping her umbrella spitefully. "I'm not going to have it prowling about on my landing. An ugly thieving thing, as has no business above stairs at all."

Ruth pressed her face against the balusters. In the distance below, she could see the small grey form of the kitchen cat making its way swiftly and silently downstairs. It went so fast that it seemed to float rather than to run and was soon out of sight.

"I should like to have played with it up in the nursery," she said, with a sigh, as she continued her way. "I wish you hadn't frightened it away."

"Lor', Miss Ruth, my dear," answered Nurse, "what can a little lady like you want with a nasty, low, kitchen cat! Come up and play with some of your beautiful toys, there's a dear! Do."

Nevertheless, Ruth thought about the cat a great deal that afternoon, and the toys seemed even less interesting than usual. When tea was over and Nurse had taken up her sewing again, she began to make a few inquiries.

"Where does that cat live?" she asked.

"In the kitchen, to be sure," said Nurse, "and the cellar, and coal-hole, and such like. Alonger the rats and mice—and the beadles," she added, as an afterthought.

"The beadles!" repeated Ruth doubtfully. "What

beadles?"

"Why, the black beadles, to be sure," replied Nurse cheerfully.

Ruth was silent. It seemed dismal company for the kitchen cat. Then she said:

"Are there many of them?"

"Swarms!" said Nurse, breaking off her thread with a snap. "The kitchen's black with 'em at night."

What a dreadful picture!

"Who feeds the cat?" asked Ruth again.

"Oh, I don't suppose nobody feeds it," answered Nurse. "It lives on what it ketches every now and then."

No wonder it looked thin! Poor kitchen cat! How very miserable and lonely it must be with no one to take care of it, and how dreadful for it to have such nasty things to eat! And the supply even of these must be short sometimes. Ruth went on to consider. What did it do when it could find no more mice or rats? Of the beetles, she could not bear even to think. As she turned these things seriously over in her mind, she began to wish she could do something to alter them, to make the cat's life more comfortable and pleasant. If she could have it to live with her in the nursery, for instance, she could give it some of her own bread and milk and part of her own dinner; then it would get fatter and perhaps prettier too. She would tie a ribbon around its neck, and it should sleep in a basket lined with red flannel and never be scolded or chased about or hungry anymore. All these pictures were suddenly destroyed by Nurse's voice:

"But I hope you'll not encourage it up here, Miss Ruth, for I couldn't abide it, and I'm sure your Aunt Clarkson wouldn't approve of it neither. I've had a horror of cats myself from a gal. They're that stealthy and treacherous, you never know where they mayn't be hiding, or when they won't spring out at you. If ever I catch it up here I shall bannock it down again."

There was evidently no sympathy to be looked for from Nurse Smith, but Ruth was used to keeping her thoughts and plans to herself and did not miss it much. As she could not talk about it, however, she thought of her new acquaintance all the more; it was indeed seldom out of her mind, and while she seemed to be quietly amusing herself in her usual way, she was occupied with all sorts of plans and arrangements for the cat when it should come to live in the nursery. Meanwhile, it was widely separated from her; how could she let it know that she wanted to see it again? When she went up and down stairs, she peered and peeped about to see if she could catch a glimpse of its hurrying grey figure, and she never came in from a walk without expecting to meet it on her way to the nursery. But she never did. The kitchen cat kept to its own quarters and its own society. Perhaps it had been too often "bannocked" down again to venture forth. And yet Ruth felt sure that it had been glad when she had spoken kindly to it. What a pity that Nurse did not like cats!

She confided all this as usual to the man in the picture, who received it with his narrow observant glance and seemed to give it serious consideration. Perhaps it was he who at last gave her a splendid idea, which she hastened to carry out as well as she could, though remembering Nurse's strong expression of dislike, she felt obliged to do so with the greatest secrecy.

As a first step, she examined the contents of her little red purse. A whole shilling, a sixpence, and a three penny bit. That would be more than enough. Might they go to some shops that afternoon? She asked when she and Nurse were starting for their walk.

"To be sure, Miss Ruth; and what sort of shops do you want? Toy-shops, I suppose."

"N-no," said Ruth; "I think not. It must be somewhere where they sell note-paper, and a baker's, I think; but I'm not quite sure."

Arrived at the stationer's, Ruth was a long time before deciding on what she would have; but at last, after the woman had turned over a whole boxful, she came to some pink note-paper with brightly painted heads of animals upon it, and upon the envelopes also.

"Oh!" cried Ruth when she saw it, clasping her hands with delight. "That would do beautifully. Only—have you any with a cat?"

Yes, there was some with a nice fluffy cat upon it, and she left the shop quite satisfied with her first purchase.

"And now," said Nurse briskly, whose patience had been a good deal tried, "we must make haste back, it's getting late."

But Ruth still had something on her mind. She must go to one more shop, she said, though she did not know exactly which. At last, she fixed on a baker's.

"What should you think," she asked on the way, "that a cat likes to eat better than anything in the world?"

"Why, a mouse to be sure," answered Nurse promptly.

"Well, but next to mice?" persisted Ruth.

"Fish," said Nurse Smith.

"That would never do," thought Ruth to herself as she looked at a fish shop they were passing, "It's so wet and slippery I couldn't possibly carry it home. Perhaps Nurse doesn't really know what cats like best. Anyhow, I'm sure it's never tasted anything so nice as a Bath bun." A Bath bun was accordingly bought, carried home, and put carefully away in the doll's house. And now Ruth felt that she had an important piece of business before her. She spread out a sheet of the new writing paper on the window seat, knelt in front of it with a pencil in her hand, and ruled some lines. She could not write very well and was often uncertain how to spell even short words, so she bit the end of her pencil and sighed a good deal before the letter was finished. At last, it was done and put into the envelope. But now came a new difficulty: How should it be addressed? After much thought, she wrote the following:

The Kitchen Cat,

The Kitchen,

17 Gower Street.

CHAPTER II

Her Best Friend

After this letter had been dropped into the pillar box just in front of the house, Ruth began to look out still more eagerly for the kitchen cat, but days passed, and she caught no glimpse of it anywhere.

It was disappointing and troublesome, too, because she had to carry the Bath bun about with her for so long. Not only was it getting hard and dry, but it was such an awkward thing for her pocket that she had torn her frock in the effort to force it in.

"You might a' been carrying brick-bats about with you, Miss Ruth," said Nurse, "by the way you've slit your pocket open."

This went on till Ruth began to despair. "I'll try it one

more evening," she said to herself, "and if it doesn't come then I shall give it up."

Once more, therefore, when she was ready to go downstairs, she took the bun out of the dolls' house, where she kept it wrapped up in tissue paper, and squeezed it into her pocket. Rather hopelessly but still keeping a careful look-out, she proceeded slowly on her way, when behold, just as she reached the top of the last flight, a little cringing grey figure crossed the hall below.

"It's come!" she exclaimed in an excited whisper. "It's come at last!"

But though it had come, it seemed now the cat's greatest desire to go, for it was hurrying towards the kitchen stairs.

"Puss! puss!" called out Ruth in an entreating voice as she hastily ran down. "Stop a minute! Pretty puss!"

Startled at the noise and the patter of the quick little feet, the cat paused in its flight and turned its scared yellow-green eyes upon Ruth.

She had now reached the bottom step, where she stood struggling to get the Bath bun out of her small pocket, her face pink with the effort and anxiety lest the cat should go before she succeeded.

"Pretty puss!" she repeated as she tugged at the parcel. "Don't go away."

One more desperate wrench, which gashed open the

corner of the pocket, and the bun was out. The cat looked on with one paw raised, ready to fly at the first sign of danger, as with trembling fingers, Ruth managed to break a piece off the horny surface. She held it out. The cat came nearer, sniffed at it suspiciously, and then to her great joy, took the morsel, crouched down, and munched it up. "How good it must taste," she thought, "after the mice and rats."

By degrees, it was induced to make further advances and, before long to come on to the step where Ruth sat and make a hearty meal of the bun which she crumbled up for it.

"I'm afraid it's dry," she said, "but I couldn't bring any milk, you know, and you must get some water afterwards."

The cat seemed to understand and replied by pushing its head against her and purring loudly. How thin it was! Ruth wondered as she looked gravely at it whether it would soon be fatter if she fed it every day. She became so interested in talking to it and watching its behaviour, that she nearly forgot she had to go into the dining room and jumped up with a start.

"Good-night," she said. "If you'll come again I'll bring you something else another day." She looked back as she turned the handle of the heavy door. The cat was sitting primly upright on the step, washing its face after its meal. "I expect it doesn't feel so hungry now," thought Ruth as she went into the room.

The acquaintance thus fairly begun was soon followed by other meetings, and the cat was often in the hall when Ruth came downstairs, though it did not appear every evening. The uncertainty of this was most exciting, and "Will it be there to-night?" was her frequent thought during the day. As time went on, and they grew to know each other better, she began to find the kitchen cat a far superior companion to either her dolls or the man in the picture. True, it could not answer her any more than they did—in words, but it had a language of its own which she understood perfectly. She knew when it was pleased and when it said "Thank you" for some delicacy she brought for it; its yellow eyes beamed with sympathy and interest when she described the delights of that beautiful life it would enjoy in the nursery; and when she pitied it for the darkness of its present dwelling below, she knew it understood by the way it rubbed against her and arched up its back. There were many more pleasures in each day now that she had made this acquaintance. Shopping became interesting because she could look forward to the cat's surprise and enjoyment when the parcel was opened in the evening; everything that happened was treasured to tell it when they met, or, if it was not there, to write to it on the pink note-paper; the very smartest sash belonging to her best doll was taken to adorn the cat's thin neck, and the secrecy which surrounded all this made it doubly delightful. Ruth had never been a greedy child, and if Nurse Smith sometimes wondered that she now spent all her money on cakes, she concluded that they must be for a dolls' feast and troubled herself no further. Miss Ruth was always so fond of "making believe". So things went on very quietly and comfortably, and though Ruth could not discover that the kitchen cat got any fatter, it had certainly improved in some ways since her attentions. Its face had lost its scared look, and it no longer crept about as close to the ground as possible but walked with an assured tread and its tail held high. It could never be a pretty cat to the general eye, but when it came trotting noiselessly to meet Ruth, uttering its short mew of welcome, she thought it beautiful and would not have changed it for the sleekest, most handsome cat in the kingdom.

But it was the kitchen cat still. All this did not bring it one step nearer to the nursery. It must still live, Ruth often thought with sorrow, amongst the rats and mice and beetles. Nothing could ever happen which would induce Nurse Smith to allow it to come upstairs. And yet something did happen which brought this very thing to pass in a strange way which would never have entered her mind.

The spring came on with a bright sun and cold, sharp winds, and one day Ruth came in from her walk feeling shivery and tired. She could not eat her dinner, and her head had a dull ache in it, and she thought she would like to go to bed. She did not feel ill, she said, but she was at first very hot and then very cold. Nurse Smith sent for the doctor, and he came and looked kindly at her, felt her pulse and said she must stay in bed and he would send some medicine. And she went to sleep and had funny dreams in which she plainly saw the kitchen cat dressed in Aunt Clarkson's bonnet and cloak. It stood by her bed and talked in Aunt Clarkson's voice, and she saw its grey fur paws under the folds of the cloak. She wished it would go away and wondered how she could have been so fond of it. When Nurse came to give her something, she said feebly:

"Send the cat away."

"Bless you, my dear, there's no cat here," she answered. "There's nobody been here but me and Mrs. Clarkson."

At last, there came a day when she woke up from a long sleep and found that the pain in her head was gone and that the things in the room, which had been taking all manner of queer shapes, looked all right again.

"And how do you feel, Miss Ruth, my dear?" asked Nurse, who sat sewing by the bedside.

"I'm quite well, thank you," said Ruth. "Why am I in bed in the middle of the day?"

"Well, you haven't been just quite well, you know," said Nurse.

"Haven't I?" said Ruth. She considered this for some time, and when Nurse came to her with some beef tea in her hand, she asked:

"Have I been in bed more than a day?"

"You've been in bed a week," said Nurse. "But you'll get along finely now, and be up and about again in no time."

Ruth drank her beef tea and thought it over. Suddenly she dropped her spoon into the cup. The kitchen cat! How it must have missed her if she had been in bed a week. Unable to bear the idea in silence, she sat up in bed with a flushed face and asked eagerly:

"Have you seen the cat?"

The nurse instantly rose with a concerned expression and patted her soothingly on the shoulder.

"There now, my dear, we won't have any more fancies about cats and such. You drink your beef-tea up and I'll tell you something pretty."

Ruth took up her spoon again. It was of no use to talk to Nurse about it, but it was dreadful to think how disappointed the cat must have been evening after evening. Meanwhile, Nurse went on in a coaxing tone:

"If so be as you make haste and get well, you're to go alonger me and stay with your Aunt Clarkson in the country. There now!"

Ruth received the news calmly. It did not seem a very pleasant prospect or even a very real one to her.

"There'll be little boys and girls to play with," pursued Nurse, trying to heighten the picture, "and flowers—and birds and such—and medders, and a garding, and all manner."

But nothing could rouse Ruth to more than a very languid interest in these delights. Her thoughts were all with her little friend downstairs, and she felt certain that it had often been hungry and no doubt thought very badly of her for her neglect if she could only see it and explain that it had not been her fault!

The next day Aunt Clarkson herself came. She always had a great deal on her mind when she came up to town and liked to get through her shopping in time to go back in the afternoon, so she could never stay long with Ruth. She came bustling in, looking very strong, and speaking in a loud cheerful voice, and all the while she was there, she gave quick glances around her at everything in the room. Ruth was well enough to be up and was sitting in a big chair by the nursery fire, with picture books and toys near, but she was not looking at them. Her eyes were fixed thoughtfully on the fire, and her mind was full of the kitchen cat. She had tried to write to it, but the words would not come, and her fingers trembled so much that she could not hold the pencil straight. The vexation and disappointment of this had made her head ache, and altogether she presented rather a mournful little figure.

"Well, Nurse, and how are we going on?" said Aunt Clarkson, sitting down in the chair Nurse placed for her. Remembering her dream, Ruth could not help giving a glance at Aunt Clarkson's hands. They were fat, round hands, and she kept them doubled up so that they really looked rather like a cat's paws.

"Well, ma'am," replied Nurse, "Miss Ruth's better;

but she's not, so to say, as cheerful as I could wish. Still a few fancies ma'am," she added in an undertone, which Ruth heard perfectly.

"Fancies, eh?" repeated Aunt Clarkson in her most cheerful voice. "Oh, we shall get rid of them at Summerford. You'll have real things to play with there, Ruth, you know. Lucy, and Cissie, and Bobbie will be better than fancies, won't they?"

Ruth gave a faint little nod. She did not know what her aunt meant by "fancies". The cat was quite as real as Lucy, or Cissie, or Bobbie. Should she ask her about it, or did she hate cats like Nurse Smith? She gazed wistfully at Mrs Clarkson's face, who had now drawn a list from her pocket, and was running through the details half-aloud with an absorbed frown.

"I shall wait and see the doctor, Nurse," she said presently, "and if he comes soon I shall just get through my business, and catch the three o'clock express."

No, it would be of no use, Ruth concluded, as she let her head fall languidly back against the pillow—Aunt Clarkson was far too busy to think about the cat.

Fortunately for her business, the doctor did not keep her waiting long. Ruth was better, he said, and all she wanted now was cheering up a little—she looked dull and moped. "If she could have a little friend, now, to see her, or a cheerful companion," glancing at Nurse Smith, "it would have a good effect."

He withdrew with Mrs Clarkson to the door, and

they continued the conversation in low tones so that only scraps of it reached Ruth:

"—excitable—fanciful—too much alone—children of her own age—"

Aunt Clarkson's last remark came loud and clear:

"We shall cure that at Summerford, Dr. Short. We're not dull people there, and we've no time for fancies."

She smiled, the doctor smiled, they shook hands, and both soon went away. Ruth leant her head on her hand. Was there no one who would understand how much she wanted to see the kitchen cat? Would they all talk about fancies? What were Lucy and Cissie and Bobbie to her?—strangers, and the cat was a friend. She would rather stroke its rough head and listen to its purring song than have them all to play with. It was so sad to think how it must have missed her, how much she wanted to see it, and how badly her head ached that she felt obliged to shed a few tears. The nurse discovered this with much concern.

"And there was master coming up to see you to-night and all, Miss Ruth. It'll never do for him to find you crying, you know. I think you'd better go to bed."

Ruth looked up with a sudden gleam of hope and checked her tears.

"When is he coming?" she asked. "I want to see him."

"Well, I s'pose directly he comes home—about your tea-time. But if I let you sit up we mustn't have no more tears, you know, else he'll think you ain't getting well."

Ruth sank quietly back among her shawls in the big chair. An idea had darted suddenly into her mind, which comforted her very much, and she was too busy with it to cry anymore. She would ask her father! True, it was hardly likely that he would have any thoughts to spare for such a small thing as the kitchen cat; but still, there was just a faint chance that he would understand better than Nurse and Aunt Clarkson. So she waited with patience, listening anxiously for his knock and the slam of the hall door, and at last, just as Nurse was getting the tea ready, it came. Her heart beat fast. Soon there was a hurried step on the stairs, and her father entered the room. Ruth studied his face earnestly. Was he tired? Was he worried? Would he stay long enough to hear the important question?

He kissed her and sat down near her.

"How is Miss Ruth today?" he said rather wearily to Nurse.

Standing stiffly erect behind Ruth's chair, Nurse Smith repeated all that the doctor and Mrs Clarkson had said.

"And I think myself, sir," she added, "that Miss Ruth will be all the better of a cheerful change. She worrits herself with fancies."

Ruth looked earnestly up at her father's face but said nothing.

"Worries herself?" repeated Mr Lorimer with a puzzled frown. "What can she have to worry about? Is there anything you want, my dear?" he said, taking hold of Ruth's little hot hand and bending over her.

The moment had come. Ruth gathered all her courage, sat upright, and, fixing an entreating gaze upon him, said:

"I want to see my best friend."

"Your best friend, eh?" he answered, smiling as if it were a very slight affair. "One of your little cousins, I suppose? Well, you're going to Summerford, you know, and then you'll see them all. I forget their names. Tommie, Mary, Carry, which is it?"

Ruth gave a hopeless little sigh. She was so tired of these cousins.

"It's none of them," she said, shaking her head. "I don't want any of them."

"Who is it, then?"

"It's the kitchen cat."

Mr Lorimer started back with surprise at the unexpected words.

"The kitchen cat!" he repeated, looking distractedly at Nurse. "Her best friend! What does the child mean?"

"Miss Ruth has fancies, sir," she began with a superior smile. But she did not get far, for, at that word,

Ruth started to her feet in desperation.

"It isn't a fancy!" she cried; "it's a real cat. I know it very well and it knows me. And I do want to see it so. Please let it come."

The last words broke off in a sob.

Mr Lorimer lifted her gently onto his knee.

"Where is this cat?" he said, turning to Nurse with such a frown that Ruth thought he must be angry. "Why hasn't Miss Ruth had it before if she wanted it?"

"Well, I believe there is a cat somewhere below, sir," she replied in an injured tone, "but I'd no idea, I'm sure, that Miss Ruth was worritting after it. To the best of my knowledge she's only seen it once. She's so fond of making believe that it's hard to tell when she is in earnest. I thought it was a kind of a fancy she got in her head when she was ill."

"Fetch it here at once, if you please."

Nurse hesitated.

"It's hardly a fit pet for Miss Ruth, sir."

"At once, if you please," repeated Mr Lorimer. And Nurse went.

Ruth listened to this with her breath held, almost frightened at her own success. Not only was the kitchen cat to be admitted, but it was to be brought by the very hands of Nurse herself. It was wonderful—almost too wonderful to be true.

And now it seemed that her father wished to know how the kitchen cat had become her best friend. He was very much interested in it, and she thought his face looked quite different while he listened to her what it looked when he was reading his papers downstairs. Finding that he asked sensible questions and did not once say anything about "fancies", she was encouraged to tell him more and more, and at last leant her head on his shoulder and closed her eyes. It would be all right now. She had found someone at last who understood.

The entrance of the kitchen cat shortly afterwards was neither dignified nor comfortable, for it appeared dangling at the end of Nurse's outstretched arm, held by the neck as far as possible from her own person. When it was first put down, it was terrified at its new surroundings, and it was a little painful to find that it wanted to rush downstairs again at once, in spite of Ruth's fondest caresses. It was Mr Lorimer who came to her help and succeeded at last in soothing its fears and coaxing it to drink some milk, after which it settled down placidly with her in the big chair and began its usual song of contentment. She examined it carefully with a grave face and then looked apologetically at her father.

"It doesn't look its best," she said. "Its paws are white really, but I think it's been in the coal-hole."

This seemed very likely, for not only its paws but the smart ribbon Ruth had tied around its neck was grimy and black.

"It's not exactly pretty," she continued, "but it's a very nice cat. You can't think how well it knows me—generally."

Mr Lorimer studied the long, lean form of the cat curiously through his eyeglass.

"You wouldn't like a white Persian kitten better for a pet—or a nice little dog, now?" he asked doubtfully.

"Oh, please not," said Ruth with a shocked expression on her face. "I shouldn't love it half so well, and I'm sure the kitchen cat wouldn't like it."

That was a wonderful evening. Everything seemed as suddenly changed as if a fairy had touched them with her wand. Not only was the kitchen cat actually there in the nursery, drinking milk and eating toast, but there was a still stranger alteration. This father was quite different to the one she had known in the dining room downstairs, who was always reading and had no time to talk. His very face had altered, for instead of looking grave and far away, it was full of smiles and interest. And how well he understood the kitchen cat! When her bedtime came, he seemed quite sorry to go away, and his last words were:

"Remember, Nurse, Miss Ruth is to have the cat here whenever she likes and as long as she likes."

It was all so strange that Ruth woke up the next morning with a feeling that she had had a pleasant dream. The kitchen cat and the new father would both vanish with daylight; they were "fancies", as Nurse called them, and not real things at all. But as the days passed and she grew strong enough to go downstairs, as usual, it was delightful to find that this was not the case. The new father was still there. The cat was allowed to make a third in the party and soon learned to take its place with dignity and composure. But though thus honoured, it no longer received all Ruth's confidences. She had found a better friend. Her difficulties, her questions, and her news were all saved up for the evening to tell her father. It was the best bit of the whole day.

On one of these occasions they were all three sitting happily together, and Ruth had just put a new brass collar that her father had bought around the cat's neck.

"I don't want to go to Summerford," she said suddenly. "I'd much rather stay here with you."

"And the cat," added Mr Lorimer as he kissed her. "Well, you must come back soon and take care of us both, you know."

"You'll be kind to it when I'm gone, won't you?" said Ruth. "Because, you know, I don't think the servants understand cats. They're rather sharp to it."

"It shall have dinner with me every night," said Mr Lorimer.

In this way, the kitchen cat was raised from a lowly station to great honour, and its life henceforth was one of peace and freedom. It went where it would. No one questioned its right of the entrance to the nursery or dared to slight it in any way. In spite, however, of choice meals and luxury, it never grew fat and never, except in Ruth's eyes, became pretty. It also kept too many of its old habits, preferring liberty and the chimney pots at night to the softly-lined basket prepared for its repose.

But with all its faults, Ruth loved it faithfully as long as it lived, for, in her own mind, she felt that she owed it a great deal.

She remembered that evening when, a lonely little child, she had called it her "best friend". Perhaps she would not have discovered so soon that she had a better friend still without the kitchen cat.

Once Upon A Time II

And so, my dear reader, we conclude our journey through the enchanted woods of imagination. As the final page is turned, may the echoes of these timeless tales linger in your heart and mind. Let the wisdom of the old and the wonder of the new inspire your own stories. For it is in sharing these magical moments that we truly come alive.

May the bonds forged through these shared adventures grow stronger with each passing day. Let us continue to cultivate a world where storytelling is cherished, where dreams take flight, and where the human spirit is forever young.

Happy reading, and may your own stories be filled with as much joy, wonder, and magic.

kidsbooksnook.com